Born in 1946 in Clacton-on-Sea, Essex, Graham Hurley always wanted to be a writer. Before achieving his dream of getting his books published, he worked as an ice cream salesman, deckchair attendant, lifeguard, prep school teacher (scripture and cricket), Radio Victory reporter, TV promotion scriptwriter, TV researcher, award-winning TV documentary director/producer, and *Oz* TV series writer. He lived in Portsmouth for 20 years, is married to the delectable Lin, and has grown-up children and a young grandson. He now lives in Exmouth, Devon.

You can discover more about the author at www.grahamhurley.co.uk

TOUCHING DISTANCE

After the collapse of his marriage, D/S Jimmy
Suttle is plunged into a series of killings that
will test him to the limit. Michael Corrigan
has been shot through the head at the wheel
of his car on a lonely moorland road. The
only witness: his infant son, strapped into the
rear child seat. Within days, two more
killings, equally professional, and equally
motiveless. Teasing some kind of investigative
sense from this carnage is a very big ask,
but pressure for an early arrest is growing
by the day . . . Meanwhile, in the world of
journalism, Suttle's estranged wife Lizzie
finds herself within touching distance of the
story that will make her name — but that
story will lead her to the heart of Suttle's
enquiry, and into mortal danger . . .

Books by Graham Hurley
Published by Ulverscroft:

THE PERFECT SOLDIER

THE D/I JOE FARADAY SERIES:
ANGELS PASSING
DEADLIGHT
BLOOD AND HONEY
ONE UNDER
THE PRICE OF DARKNESS
HAPPY DAYS

THE D/S JIMMY SUTTLE SERIES:
WESTERN APPROACHES

GRAHAM HURLEY

TOUCHING DISTANCE

Complete and Unabridged

CHARNWOOD
Leicester

First published in Great Britain in 2013 by
Orion Books
an imprint of The Orion Publishing Group Ltd
London

First Charnwood Edition
published 2015
by arrangement with
The Orion Publishing Group Ltd
London

A catalogue record for this book is available
from the British Library.

ISBN 978–1–4448–2455–1

Published by
F. A. Thorpe (Publishing)
Anstey, Leicestershire

Set by Words & Graphics Ltd.
Anstey, Leicestershire
Printed and bound in Great Britain by
T. J. International Ltd., Padstow, Cornwall

This book is printed on acid-free paper

For Charles Wylie
Ancien Combattant

Another man's soul is darkness
Russian proverb

1

SUNDAY, 24 JUNE 2012

D/S Jimmy Suttle was watching a buzzard when he took the call. He'd paused beside the Impreza to swallow the remains of his water after the steep climb back up from the stone circle. The rain had gone, washing away to the east on a strengthening wind. The clouds had parted and it was suddenly a glorious morning, the sun still low in the east, the lone hawk circling high over the nearby tor. Among the scatter of curtained camper vans in the car park was a hippy-looking twenty-something doing t'ai chi among the puddles. Her eyes were closed and she was shaping the dawn-chilled spaces around her with a fluency that stirred Suttle's interest.

He bent to the phone.

'It's supposed to be my weekend off, boss,' he pointed out. 'I'm up on the moor.'

'I know. That's why I phoned. You've got a map?'

Suttle ducked into the Impreza. D/I Houghton was already giving him vehicle details. Black VW Golf. BG 2756 DS.

'Where, exactly?' He'd found the right page.

'Half a mile south of Teigncombe. You're looking for the road to Chagford. Someone phoned it in. Okehampton sent a couple of officers.'

Suttle had found Teigncombe. Ten minutes, he thought. Max.

'I'm on it.' He was back watching the woman doing t'ai chi. 'Anything else to tell me?'

'Nothing. Call me when you know the strength.'

★ ★ ★

He found the Golf parked untidily in the middle of a narrow lane where the bareness of the moorland surrendered to stone-walled fields and the odd cow. The Okehampton officers had closed the lane in both directions and one of them accompanied him to the driver's side of the car.

Both the driver's window and the passenger window on the other side of the car had shattered and the figure slumped behind the wheel was covered in tiny fragments of glass. As far as Suttle could judge, he'd taken a single bullet high on his temple. Blood had fountained everywhere, and grey smears of brain material, whitened with bone fragments, clung to the door surrounds behind him.

Suttle studied the driver a moment longer. His hands were folded in his lap, a hint of peace among the carnage, though a thin pinkish liquid was still trickling down his cheek from the entry wound.

'Try looking from the other side.'

Suttle glanced up at the invitation, then rounded the bonnet and bent to the remains of the passenger window. Half of this man's head had ceased to exist. The bullet had torn through his brain, shattering his skull. The exit wound was hideous, the jagged plates of bone cupping a glistening soup of grey viscera veined with tiny blood vessels. Suttle stepped back, waving the flies away.

The uniform had done a vehicle check. Michael Corrigan. DOB 26.6.1980. Paignton address.

'How long have you been up here?'

'Best part of an hour.'

'Scenes of Crime?'

'On their way.'

'Pathologist? Firearms guy?'

'They've got it in hand.'

Suttle's eyes returned to the body behind the wheel. Violent death, he knew, had a habit of diminishing people but this guy was an exception. He was still big, still fit-looking: white T-shirt, faded denim shorts, battered Nike runners, tiny curls of black hair on his well-shaped legs. The bareness of what was left of his shaved scalp was tanned a deep brown and there were laughter lines around his eyes. The eyes were open, a startling blue, and he carried a tiny star tattoo behind one ear.

The DOB sounded about right. Michael Corrigan, Suttle thought, shot to death within touching distance of his thirty-second birthday.

'So who phoned it in?'

'A woman in London.'

'*London?*'

'Yeah. Plus a couple of others. The duty Inspector's got the list. He's expecting your call.'

3

He scribbled a name and a mobile number and passed it across.

Suttle had stepped away from the Golf. The traffic car was tucked into a passing space further up the lane. The other officer was in the front passenger seat. He had something bulky in his lap.

'What's that about?'

'There was a little boy in the car.'

Suttle returned to the Golf. He'd clocked the baby seat in the back but thought nothing of it.

'Boy, you say?'

'Yeah. Maybe a year old? Dunno.' He stepped back and nodded towards the officer in the traffic car. 'Thank Christ we had a new box of tissues. The kid was howling his eyes out. There was blood and other stuff, too. All over him.'

* * *

Forty minutes later, Suttle met D/I Carole Houghton at the Major Crime complex off the A38 at Ashburton. She was sipping a coffee from the machine in the corridor, her mobile wedged against her ear as she summoned the troops from the far corners of Devon. It was still early, barely half eight. Sundays, the big open office was empty except for a single D/C wrestling with an expenses form. Within an hour or so the place would be full of MCIT detectives. MCIT was cop-speak for Major Crime Investigation Team.

'Well?' Houghton wanted to know about the multiple phone-ins.

'They must have been numbers lifted from the

4

guy's mobile, boss. Someone sent a text to the first three names on his directory. The duty Inspector made return calls. One was the shot guy's ex. The other two were mates.'

'This is Corrigan?'

'Yeah. Michael James.'

'And the mobile?'

Suttle shook his head. He was trying to find the right change for the coffee machine.

'Gone,' he said. 'I've got the number from the duty Inspector. We need to talk to Orange quick time just in case. Ping a few cell sites.'

Houghton eyeballed him a moment. Cell site analysis would reveal the whereabouts of the mobile if it was still active.

'Gut feeling?'

'A quality hit, boss. This is early morning. It's the perfect ambush, miles from anywhere, no one else around. It's quick, it's effective. A single shot through the side window, bang, then the guy's away. The way I see it, we're talking serious planning. This isn't road rage. This is an execution.'

'Motive?'

'Could be anything. Drug debts. Some other falling-out. Whatever. Either way, we're definitely talking bad guys.'

'And the phone?'

'That has to be about the kid in the back.'

'You mean our bad guy has a conscience? After taking someone out like that?'

Houghton was smiling now. She was a big woman with pale eyes behind rimless glasses and a mass of silver-blonde hair. There was a certain

5

relish in a quality job like this and they both knew it.

Suttle held her gaze for a moment, then returned to his small change.

'Early days, boss.' He poked at the coins. 'Twenty pence. That's all I need.'

* * *

It was several seconds before Lizzie brought the morning into focus. The room was bare, minimal, cold. There was a white towel draped over the wall-hung plasma TV and a hint of sunshine through the gap where the curtains didn't quite meet. She rolled over, fighting a savage headache. The other half of the big double bed was empty, the thin summer duvet thrown back. She reached out with her hand. The bottom sheet was rumpled and still warm. Shit.

Rob Merrilees, she thought. Nice man. Lovely smile. Far too much to drink. I should have known better than say yes to the taxi. And I should never have set foot in this tomb of a hotel.

She could hear a tuneless voice singing in the tiny bathroom, trying to nail one of the cheesier Queen anthems. Over the fall of water from the shower she thought it might be 'Somebody to Love'. Either way, the crooner had to be Rob.

The singing came to an end. Seconds later the door opened. Merrilees padded across to the TV and retrieved the towel. His legs, arms and face were heavily tanned, the rest of his body a milky

6

white. He was tall, well-made. He looked fit, supple, not an ounce of spare flesh, and dimly she remembered the feel of his naked body against hers.

He was beaming down at her from the foot of the bed. He'd taken a walk on the seafront earlier. It had been pouring with rain and the beach had been filthy, litter everywhere. There was a hovercraft to the Isle of Wight, he said, which had roared away from a terminal nearby. And a monster white ferry sailing in from France. Busy old place, Southsea.

'I know. I live here.'

Lizzie was still rubbing her eyes. The headache, if anything, was worse. The smile and the tone of Rob's voice suggested a physical intimacy she needed to check out. She nodded at the bed.

'Did we?'

'Did we what?'

'Fuck.'

'No. I asked nicely but you said no. Just as well, maybe.'

'Why's that?'

'I was even more wasted than you were.'

'So how come . . . ?' Lizzie tried to finish the sentence but couldn't. She wanted to know why he didn't feel the way she felt. She wanted to know why an evening on the mojitos and fuck knows what else hadn't wrecked him. Moments later she was in the bathroom, bent over the loo, throwing up. When she got back to the bedroom Rob was tugging on the jeans and tight black T-shirt she remembered from the

Old Portsmouth pub that had kicked off last night's drinking.

'You mind if I go back to bed?'

Lizzie lay flat and closed her eyes without waiting for an answer. She'd sluiced her mouth out but she could still taste the bile in the back of her throat. How come she'd got so pissed? And why didn't the Travelodge stretch to complimentary tubes of toothpaste?

She felt the mattress give with the weight of Rob's body. She opened her eyes to find him perched on the side of the bed. He seemed to respect the distance between them. She was grateful for that.

'Did I tell you I was married last night?'

'Yeah. You told me the guy's a cop. Jimmy?'

Lizzie nodded. Said nothing. It was Jimmy's birthday next week. She had a lot of ground to make up. She reached for Rob's hand, gave it a sisterly squeeze.

'Did I mention a daughter?'

'Grace. You showed me pictures.'

'Did I?'

'Yeah. Lovely little girl. Cheeky. Your mum was babysitting last night. I made you give her a ring before we went clubbing.'

'Shit. Did you?'

'Yeah.'

'And?' Lizzie was up on one elbow. This was worse than bad. She and Grace had been camping at her mum's place for nearly a year and her mother's patience was beginning to wear thin. Lately, Grace had suffered a string of colds, which only made things worse.

8

Lizzie was staring at Rob. 'So what did I say?'

'You said you were staying over with Gill.' Rob grinned. 'Gill? Have I got that right?'

'Yeah.' Lizzie collapsed again. Gill was a mate, a fellow reporter on the Pompey *News*. With luck her mum would have lost her number.

Rob was on his feet now. He opened the curtains and checked his watch. Lizzie peered up at him, shielding her eyes against the flooding sunshine. Then he was back beside her. The hovercraft left for the Isle of Wight every half-hour, he said. They could have breakfast in Ryde, take a bus somewhere, walk the cliffs, spend the day together.

Lizzie smiled at the thought, then shook her head. She had to get back. She had to sort Grace out. She had to make a peace with her mum.

'Shame.'

'You're right.'

'Give you a ring? About Hasler Company?'

'Of course. I'd like that. If you were serious.'

'Always.'

He was close now. She could smell the soap on his skin. The thing about guys like this was how wholesome they felt. They knew who they were. They were relaxed and talkative and unthreatening and eternally curious. They glowed with good health and the kind of physical fitness she could only imagine. Hence, she assumed, the man's astonishing powers of recovery.

'Tell me something . . . ' She felt for his hand again.

'Whatever.'

'That tan you've got.' She touched his face

9

and legs. 'Afghanistan, right?'

He studied her a moment, the smile dying on his lips. Then he retrieved his hand and checked his watch again.

'I'll sort us a cab,' he said. 'And drop you off.'

★   ★   ★

It took Suttle nearly an hour to organise armed back-up for his visit to Corrigan's home address. D/I Houghton had already declared the property a crime scene and insisted that Suttle took no chances with whoever might be inside. One gangland killing, she said, was quite enough.

Suttle's request was routed through the Tactical Aid Group and confirmation for the R/V arrived by email. 10.45. Torquay nick.

D/I Houghton had pitched her tent in a nearby office. Suttle looked in before descending to the car park and heading south for Torbay.

'Did you get hold of a CSM, boss?'

'Terry Bryant. He's duty. He's on his way.'

Suttle nodded. Bryant was a Crime Scene Manager from the old days, an increasingly rare breed in a force shedding experienced officers by the hundreds.

Houghton was trying to make sense of a spreadsheet on her borrowed PC. She also had Nandy on the phone from his car somewhere on the A38. The Det-Supt, having abandoned his plans for a Sunday lunchtime darts session in his favoured local, was already bidding for substantial squad overtime. The enquiry now had an operational code name: *Graduate*. Still glued to the screen, Houghton wanted to know who Suttle was taking with him.

'Luke.'

'Good. Take care, yeah?'

She spared him a look. She wasn't smiling.

★ ★ ★

Torquay police station lies off a busy intersection in the middle of the town. Suttle was there by half ten. Parking lay at the back of the building. There was no sign of the Armed Response Vehicle so he and Golding settled down to wait.

D/C Luke Golding, at twenty-five, was still the baby of the squad, but a year with Major Crime had won him the beginnings of a serious reputation. Short and slight, he was nerveless in tight situations and the chaos of his private life was frequently the talk of the office. Last night, to his surprise and delight, he'd scored a young blonde Lithuanian in an Exeter nightclub, only to be hauled out of bed an hour ago by one of Houghton's speciality wake-up calls.

He'd fetched coffees from one of the station's machines. Now he stirred in extra sugar from a sachet with the end of Suttle's pen.

'I told her I worked for the Border Agency. Turns out there's nothing these ladies won't do to stay in the country.'

'She believed you?'

'She came across. She must have done.'

'Nice?'

'Lovely. One day I might even be able to pronounce her name. Salomeyer? Salomeeya?

Christ knows. She says it means powerful. She wasn't joking.'

The Armed Response Vehicle appeared, a white BMW estate, two guys inside. One of them gave Suttle the nod. Suttle recognised the face from an operation earlier in the year. Maddened hill farmer on a smallholding up beyond Bodmin. An ancient shotgun, two boxes of shells and the cooling corpse of a bailiff in the bottom field.

Suttle gave Golding his coffee cup and reached for the ignition keys.

Ten forty-four, he thought. Deeply impressive.

★ ★ ★

Belle Vue Road was half a mile inland from the long curve of Torbay, a ten-minute drive away. Number 76, like the neighbouring houses, was a pebble-dashed semi that had seen better days. Suttle didn't know Paignton well but sensed at once that he could never live here. Too many people. Too many cars. And a hint of real poverty in the faces of some of the single men who seemed to haunt the area.

The Armed Response car double-parked outside the address. Suttle and Golding had a brief huddle with the guys inside. They were both carrying Heckler & Koch MP5 semi-automatics and wore body armour. They'd secure the premises first, then give Suttle the OK.

Suttle watched them split. One sought a rear entrance while the other waited on the

12

pavement. A poster in the curtained front bay window featured a guy kitesurfing. A fat tabby sprawled among the weeds in the tiny crescent of front garden. Suttle was thinking about the slumped figure in the VW Golf. Whatever else he'd done with his life, this individual had a limited interest in gardening.

The officer on the pavement muttered something into his radio and approached the front door. The second knock drew a response. The tanned figure shading his eyes in the blaze of sunshine was wearing a pair of denim cut-offs and not much else. He looked middle-aged, maybe older. He was tall and thin with a slight stoop. Barefoot, he studied the proffered ID before stepping aside to let the officer in.

Minutes later, Suttle and Golding joined them. The figure on the doorstep was folded onto a low sofa in the front room, fingering a loop of glass beads around his neck. Behind the still-closed curtains, the room was in half-darkness. Suttle could make out a couple of armchairs, a battered Ikea table, a bookcase stuffed with magazines, and a scatter of kid's clothes across the floor. An open laptop lay on the table and the bitter sweetness of last night's weed still hung in the air. In the corner, propped against the wall, were a couple of acoustic guitars. The room felt cave-like, fuggy. It had a warmth that had nothing to do with temperature. Suttle rather liked it.

The guy's name was Ian Goodyer. When Suttle asked for ID he got to his feet and produced a driving licence from the wallet in his pocket. Suttle gave the licence to Golding and nodded at the door. Goodyer wanted to know why two men with guns had come visiting on a Sunday morning.

'You live here?' Suttle asked.

'Yeah.'

'Then you'll know a guy called Michael Corrigan.'

'Of course.' He frowned. 'This is about him? About Mick?'

'Yes.'

Suttle explained what had happened out on the moor. The look of shock on Goodyer's face appeared to be unfeigned.

'Someone *killed* him?' He couldn't believe it.

'I'm afraid so.'

'But why? Why would they?'

'Very good question.'

Suttle wanted to know about the relationship between the two men, about how well Goodyer knew him, about the kind of stuff they got up to.

'I work for him,' Goodyer said. 'Mick's got a kitesurfing school down on the bay.' He broke off. 'What about the kid? Leo?'

'He's fine. Still in one piece.'

'So where is he?'

'I don't know. But he'll be safe, well looked after.'

'And he was there? When this thing happened?'

'Yes.'

'Shit.'

He turned away, shaking his head. First things first, Suttle thought.

14

'Mick was Leo's dad, am I right?'

'Yeah. Of course.'

'And his mum?'

'A woman called Bella.'

'She lives here too?'

'Not really. Not now.'

'They live apart?'

'Yeah, they do . . . Yeah . . . ' He nodded. 'Shit happens, you know?'

'What kind of shit?'

Goodyer had recovered his composure. He was shaking his head.

'I'm not sure I should be telling you this stuff . . . ' he said slowly. 'I'm not sure that's right.'

'This is a mate of yours?'

'Mick? Definitely.'

'And someone's shot him to death? And you're not sure how much you should be saying?'

'It's not that.'

'What is it, then?'

'It's just . . . I dunno . . . To be honest this is all a bit of a bummer.'

'Meaning?'

'Nothing.'

There was movement by the door. Golding had stepped back into the room. He gestured Suttle into the hall and closed the door. Terry Bryant and a Scenes of Crime Officer had just arrived. They were outside in the street, unloading equipment from the SOC van. They wanted to know whether Suttle wanted a flash intel walk-through first, before they began work.

Suttle nodded, said yes. There was a framed photo of Corrigan and his infant son in the hall. Corrigan was wearing some kind of sports shirt and cradling the child in his arms.

'Plymouth Albion, if you're wondering.' The shirt had caught Golding's eye too. 'He must have been into rugby.'

Suttle's eyes returned to the photo. Grace, his daughter, had been this age only a couple of years ago. Another fucked-up relationship.

'Something else, boss.' Golding hadn't finished. 'I raised a PNC enquiry on Goodyer.'

'And?'

'Multiple convictions for possession and supply. They go way back but he was definitely a player. He did three years for the last offence.'

'We're talking Class A?'

'Cocaine.'

Suttle held Golding's gaze for a moment or two, then stepped back into the room. Goodyer was standing in the window, watching the Scenes of Crime guys on the pavement. When he turned round, his face betrayed nothing beyond a mild curiosity.

Suttle asked him to get dressed while he and Golding took a quick look round. After that he wanted Goodyer to accompany them to Torquay police station.

'What for?'

'That's something we can discuss at the station.' Suttle nodded at the window. 'Unless you'd like to spare those guys the trouble.'

'What's that supposed to mean?'

'Only you can say, Mr Goodyer. People don't

16

get shot without good reason.'

'So why the nick?'

'Because we think you can help us.'

'And what if I say no?' He checked his watch. 'I've got a lesson booked for eleven down on the beach. These are people who've paid up front. I have to be there.'

'Cancel them. Give them a ring. Postpone them. This needn't take long.'

'No way.' He shook his head, angry now. 'Getting a job in this town isn't something that happens every day of the fucking week. You guys don't know the half of it.'

'You're telling me you won't come with us?'

'Yeah.' He nodded. 'And there's no way you can make me.'

'Wrong, my friend.'

'How come?'

'Easy.' Suttle was checking his watch. 'I'll arrest you.'

★ ★ ★

After a quiet ruck with her mum, Lizzie decided to spend the rest of the morning on the beach with Grace. Her mother, a schoolteacher who'd taken early retirement in search of a quieter life, had laid hands on Gill's number. Worried about Grace's cold, she'd phoned first thing to check when her daughter might be back. Gill, of course, hadn't a clue what she was talking about. Hence the confrontation.

Lizzie phoned Gill from the beach. The pebbles were still wet after the rain but it was

17

warm in the sun and she'd made base camp with an old blanket and an assortment of toys. Grace seemed happy enough planting a nest of plastic flags on the little piles of stones Lizzie had built.

On the phone Gill wanted to join them. Her new flat was minutes away. She arrived with a picnic she'd thrown together from the remains of last night's soirée. The guy's name was Edouard and unhappily he'd turned out to be a veggie.

Lizzie, realising how hungry she was, helped herself to a beef sandwich.

Gill's account of what she'd got up to with Edouard left little to the imagination. The guy was French. He was a marine archaeologist working with the *Mary Rose* lot in the Historic Dockyard and was evidently mega-gifted in all kinds of ways. Gill had always fancied herself as a cook but Edouard had had no time for foreplay. At first she'd put him down as an academic: pale, sensitive, hard to reach. Now, thank God, she knew a whole lot better.

'Total animal,' she concluded. 'How about you, you old slapper?'

Lizzie had been dreading the question. In truth, she had no appetite for keeping up with Gill's voracious sex life and resented the unspoken assumption that weekends were the shortest cut to getting laid. She was, after all, still married. She had a daughter. Jimmy came down at weekends, at least once a month if the Job let him, and lately they'd tried to repair a little of the damage that had led to the separation. Jimmy stayed over at her mum's place. On his last visit he'd taken her out for the evening and they'd

18

even got pissed enough to risk sleeping together again, much to her mum's delight. So how come she'd ended up at the Southsea Travelodge?

'It was the Marine guy, wasn't it?' Gill was trying to interest Grace in a pot of lightly curried chickpeas.

'Yeah.'

'The one I met at the office?'

'Yeah.'

'Tall? Tanned? Great eyes?'

'Yeah.'

'So where's the shame in that?'

Lizzie turned away. For all her showboating Gill could be extremely perceptive when she tried.

'We didn't get it on,' Lizzie said. 'If you were wondering.'

'Why not?'

Lizzie didn't answer. Rob Merrilees, oddly enough, had come her way because of Gill. The *Pompey News* had fielded a request for an experienced reporter to be guest interviewer on a two-day course the Navy was running on Whale Island. The intention was to sharpen young officers up about the kind of media pressure they'd meet in theatre in Afghanistan, and Gill had volunteered Lizzie. Rob had been the Royal Marine rep on the course, a young Captain fast-tracked for greatness, and they'd taken a liking to each other at first glance. She'd tried to snare him with every media trick in the book but he'd scored brilliantly, ticking every box on the assessment form she'd had to fill in afterwards. Grasp of his material? First class. Coolness and

19

charm under pressure? Second to none. Personal skills? Irresistible.

That first evening they'd had a drink in the mess and swapped phone numbers. The following day, over a buffet lunch, he'd started talking in earnest about the two tours he'd done in Afghanistan. By the time they'd said goodbye, Lizzie had known she was looking at a great story as well as the possibility of a deepening friendship. Then came last night.

'He tells it the way it is, Gill. Absolutely no bullshit.'

'Tells what?'

'Afghan. What a fuck-up it all is. How we haven't got a prayer. There's a place called Hasler Company. It's down in Plymouth somewhere. That's where they send all the amputees, all the guys you never hear about. That's our dirty little secret. You know how many of these guys end up there? Zillions. You know the odds on coming back from Afghan dead or maimed? One in six. One in *six*, Gill.'

'This sounds like a post-shag rationale. You don't need it, Lou. Just enjoy.'

Lou was Gill's nickname for Lizzie. Lizzie felt the anger rising inside her.

'Fuck off. I told you it didn't happen.'

'Says you.'

'It's true. Listen, he says he can get me in there.'

'In where?'

'Hasler Company.'

'Really?'

At last the penny dropped. Ignore the scarlet

20

nails and the tightness of the leather hot pants, Lizzie thought, and you might be looking at a decent journalist.

'This is some kind of secret, this place?'

'No. But it's bloody hard to get access. These guys are well protected. The place is state-of-the-art. The MoD only wants the right kind of publicity.'

'And this guy of yours can deliver?'

'That's what he tells me.'

'Was this to get you into bed?'

'No way. I'd have gone in any case.'

'Why?'

'Because I was pissed out of my head. And because I fancied him.'

'Excellent.' Gill had given up with the chickpeas. 'So when are you seeing him again?'

'Is that a serious question?'

'Yes. This is your feature editor speaking, as well as your social secretary. Where does he live?'

'Some village near Plymouth.'

'Married?'

'I never asked.'

'But you think he might be?'

Lizzie frowned. It was a good question. A mile away she could hear the roar of the hovercraft and seconds later it appeared from behind the low crouch of Southsea Castle, a noisy insect trailing a plume of spray. *We could have been on the Isle of Wight by now*, she thought. *We could be walking some cliff, thinking about a light lunch and whatever might follow.*

Gill put the question again. Was this guy legit?

Or was last night just a pit stop until he got home to wifey?

'I dunno.' Lizzie was reaching for a tissue to wipe Grace's nose. 'And if I'm honest, I'm not sure I care.'

2

SUNDAY, 24 JUNE 2012

The interview with Goodyer started badly. His criminal record predated the national DNA database and when Suttle asked for a hand swab at the Custody Centre to check for firearms residue, insisting it was for the purposes of elimination, Goodyer wasn't keen. Of course he was happy to help out in any way he could, but just for the record he resented being treated as a potential suspect.

Suttle had borrowed an office at the back of Torquay police station for the interview. Once they'd settled down, he reminded Goodyer that he wasn't under caution, neither was the session being recorded. All he and Golding wanted was to find out a little more about Michael Corrigan.

'We need to put together his last twenty-four hours. Who he might have met. What he was up to. Is that OK with you?'

Goodyer said nothing. Just picked at a scab on the back of his hand.

'Well?'

Goodyer rubbed his eyes, checked his watch, then finally looked up. He and Mick, he said, had spent yesterday on the beach at the kitesurfing school. They had a series of booked sessions, mainly novices looking to master the basics. They'd packed up in the late afternoon and got back home by around half five.

Suttle scribbled himself a note. Was there anyone among this clientele who might have had a grudge against Corrigan?

'No.'

'Any competitors? Rival set-ups?'

'No.'

'Anyone in his private life you know about? Someone he'd fallen out with? Over money, maybe? Or something else?'

'No.'

The pattern of answers told its own story. Despite his protestations to the contrary, Goodyer wasn't here to make life easier for a bunch of nosey cops.

Suttle changed tack. Playing Mr Nice was getting him nowhere.

'These clients of yours are young? Kids, maybe?'

'Some of them, yeah. We get all ages.'

Suttle held his gaze. Working with young people these days was heavily regulated.

'You've got previous for drugs offences. Am I right?'

'Yeah.'

'You're CRB-checked?'

'No.'

'So how come you're around kids all day?'

'I'm not. I sort out the kit for Mick. That's the way it works. I keep the paperwork together. I make the teas. I take the money. I keep the accounts. I run the errands. You don't need a CRB check for that.' A nerve was fluttering beneath his right eye. He was taking this

24

extremely personally. 'Criminal Records Bureau, right? You lot never give up, do you? You want to know the truth about why I went down? Here's why. Because I got stitched up by a bunch of evil Scousers who you tossers never even bothered to check out. And why was that? Because it was too much fucking trouble. Was I clean? Was I fuck. I was up to my ears in all kinds of shit but no way did I deserve a stretch like that. So here we are, twenty fucking years later, and nothing's changed. I was an easy mark then. And now you're into the same old game. Am I right? Or is this just my imagination?'

Suttle held his gaze.

'Where were you first thing this morning, Mr Goodyer?'

'In bed. Asleep.'

'Alone?'

'Yeah. Sad old bastard, eh? But yeah.'

'No corroboration, then? No one to vouch for you?'

'No. I just said.'

'So how do we know you're telling the truth?'

'You don't. You have to accept my word. Either that or charge me.'

'With what?'

'Make it up. Like you did before.'

Suttle let the comment go. There was real anger in this man. He could feel it.

'You heard Corrigan leave?'

'No. I just told you. I was asleep.'

'Did you know where he was going?'

'Yeah. Of course I did.'

'So where was that?'

25

'He had a friend. Up on the moor. Lady called Erika. Sweet chick.'

'Why so early?'

'Because she was going to look after Leo all day. That way Mick would be back down on the beach with me. Except that never fucking happened, did it? Because someone had other ideas.'

'So who might that someone be?'

Goodyer gazed at him for a long moment. Then he shook his head, a gesture of disbelief.

'You're talking shit, you people. You know I don't know. Is this for laughs? Or do you get some kind of kick out of it? Just give me a clue.'

Suttle's mobile rang. It was Terry Bryant, the CSM at the Paignton house. Suttle shot a look at Golding and stepped out of the room. He'd asked Bryant to do a quick trawl for meaningful quantities of gear and bell him asap. The news wasn't good. Nothing in the way of Class A drugs. No deal lists or scribbled records of outstanding debts. Nothing to suggest that Goodyer was still any kind of player on the local scene. Just a smallish lump of cannabis resin, wrapped in cellophane.

'Where did you find it, Terry?'

'Corrigan's bedroom. Ashtray on the chest of drawers.'

'Nothing else?'

'Afraid not. Early days though. We live in hope.'

Suttle returned to the office, sensing at once that something in the atmosphere had changed. Goodyer was telling Golding about the woman

26

with the place on Dartmoor.

Erika, he said, was German. She had a kind of hobby farm miles from anywhere: some sheep, a goat, chickens, a couple of horses. She also boarded out dogs, mainly for friends and friends of friends. One of these people had bought her lessons at the kitesurfing school at the back end of last summer. Kitesurfing, it turned out, wasn't really her bag, but she'd got a thing going with Mick and was happy to look after Leo from time to time.

'What kind of thing?'

'I dunno the details. He'd never say.'

'But he trusted her enough to look after the boy?'

'Yeah.'

'So they must have been close, surely?'

'Yeah. She still comes down the beach sometimes to play with Leo. She made Mick laugh, that woman, because Mick could be a gloombag sometimes.'

Golding asked for contact details. Goodyer said her number would be on Mick's phone.

'The phone's gone.' Suttle this time. 'We can't find it.'

'Really?' Goodyer was frowning. Erika's details would also be on the enrolment form she'd filled in for the kitesurfing, he said. He'd check his records when he got back home.

Suttle wanted to know more about Leo.

'You and Corrigan are out most days, working. Right?'

'Right.'

'So who looks after the boy?'

'Nicky.'

'Nicky?'

'Yeah. Black lady. Her real name's Nicinha but we call her Nicky. She's got the back bedroom. There's three of us in the house, four if you include Leo.'

Suttle nodded. He and Golding had scouted the property before driving Goodyer down to the nick.

'This is the little bedroom at the back?'

'That's right.'

'Everything neat and tidy? Big painting over the bed? All reds and yellows?'

'Yeah. Nicky's the only one who manages to keep her shit together. That woman could live in a cardboard box if she had to. Maybe she did once. Fuck knows. She never talks about it.'

'She's a lodger? A blow-in? Someone who happened by?'

'No. Not really.'

'You want to tell us more?'

'I just did. You asked who looks after Leo. She does. She's the closest that kid's got to a mother. She adores him. Like we all do.'

'She's been there a while?'

'Yeah.'

'How long?'

'About a year.'

'So where's the real mother?'

'She lives in London. Her name's Bella.'

Suttle nodded. Bella Prentiss was one of the names on the duty Inspector's list of callers who'd rung the VW in. Suttle had left her name with Houghton for further development.

Golding wanted to know more about Bella Prentiss. Wasn't it rare for a mother to abandon her son?

'Sure. But that woman's a one-off. Total headcase. She used to be big on the arts scene down here, worked for the council for a while, organising festivals and stuff. She shagged the arse off Mick for a whole summer then got pregnant. Mick was her bit of rough. Since then her life's moved on.'

'She was happy to leave the baby with Mick?'

'Yeah. She scored a big movie deal over some book or other. Most of the time she spends in the States. That's what Mick told me, anyway.'

'So what happens to him now? Leo?'

'Dunno. I expect someone'll have a form for him, won't they? You lot? Social services? Sally Army? Bunch of bent Catholic priests? Fuck knows.'

Goodyer pushed his chair back from the table and turned away, crossing his legs. There was disgust in his face as well as resentment. Suttle sensed there was much more to come.

'How well did you know Mick?' he asked after a while.

'We go back years.'

'Best mates?'

'Good mates. When I got in trouble with the gear he was there for me, helped me out, talked me through the really shit times. He was a great bloke, Mick. He had time for other people. He cared. All this is fucking sad, you know what I mean?'

29

He ducked his head and for a moment Suttle thought he was going to lose it. Golding was looking uncomfortable. He reached across the table, a steadying hand.

'You want a glass of water? Coffee?'

'No.' Goodyer looked up, his eyes moist. 'Shit happens, yeah? You have to live with it. You'd go mental otherwise, believe me.'

Believe me?

Suttle was watching him carefully. He gave Goodyer a moment or two to recover then asked him how the childcare thing worked in the house.

'Childcare?'

'Leo. There was a child's cot in the bedroom at the front. That was Corrigan's room, am I right?'

'Yeah.'

'And Leo slept there?'

'Yeah.'

'Rather than Nicky's room?'

'Nicky's room was too small. You've seen it. Tidy as you like but a box. Even smaller than mine. If Leo was a pain in the middle of the night Mick would take him through to Nicky. It worked OK.'

'So where's Nicky now?'

'She went up to London last night to see some friends. That's why Mick was taking Leo out to Erika. That's why he was on the moor.'

'So when's Nicky back?'

'This evening.'

'You got her number?'

'Sure.' He produced his mobile and scrolled

30

through the directory. Golding wrote the number down.

Suttle was thinking about Corrigan's phone. Nicky's number had to be on his directory as well. So why hadn't she been in touch? Maybe the text had gone to a handful of names at the head of the list. Like B for Bella Prentiss.

Golding wanted to know how Nicky was going to take the news of Corrigan's death.

'She'll be fucking upset. Like I am.'

'Were they close?'

'In all the ways that matter she was Leo's mum. Still is. That says close to me.'

'Did they have a sexual relationship?' Suttle this time. 'Mick and Nicky?'

'What kind of fucking question is that?'

'I'm just asking, that's all. We're trying to get a picture here, Mr Goodyer. We're trying to understand how the house worked. If Mick and Nicky were sleeping together, that might be germane.'

'*Germane*?'

'Important.'

'How?'

'I've no idea. Not yet. So why don't you just answer the question?'

'I can't.'

'Why not?'

'Because I don't know. Mick could be very private about stuff like that. Same for Nicky. She's a lovely woman. A lovely, lovely girl. If she's been shagging Mick, good luck to her. But like I say, I don't know.'

Suttle reached for his pad and scribbled

himself a note. Goodyer was lying, he knew he was. There was no way you could live in a house that small and not be aware of the way things were. So why pretend otherwise?

Suttle's head came up.

'Let's start with what we know,' he said. 'Someone shot your mate at point-blank range, Mr Goodyer. They cared enough about the baby to take a risk or two by raising the alarm. Who might that have been? And why would they have wanted Corrigan dead?'

'You're asking *me?*'

'I am. You must have thought about it.'

'No.' He shook his head. 'I haven't.'

'I don't believe you.'

'Surprise, surprise.' He was staring at Suttle, his eyes huge in the seamed gauntness of his face. 'Nothing fucking changes in this world, does it? You lot were arsewipes then and you're arsewipes now. Me? I wake up to find two guys at the door with guns. You get my licence off me. You check me out. You see I've been a bad boy zillions of years ago and you decide I'm in the fucking frame. Does that surprise me? No. Am I fucking upset that you don't have the time or the energy or the imagination to look a bit further? Yes. But you know something that pisses me off, *really* pisses me off? The fact that I have to sit here taking all this shit and there's absolute nothing I can do about it.'

'But there is, Mr Goodyer. Like I explained at the beginning, you're not under arrest. You can leave at any time. Your call. Your decision. You want to do that? You want to call this thing to a halt?'

'Yeah, I do. Except . . . '

'Except what?'

'Except it'll all go down in your little book, won't it?' He nodded at Suttle's notepad. 'Stroppy lodger. Dope fiend. Convicted badass. Just give me a break, eh? Just leave me fucking alone.'

He was on his feet now, ignoring Golding, still eyeballing Suttle, his face contorted with something close to rage. Damaged goods, Suttle thought. Someone whom life had stretched to breaking point.

He reached for his pen again and made a note of the time.

'I wouldn't bother going back home just yet.' He glanced up at Goodyer. 'The Scenes of Crime boys may take a while.'

* * *

After making a couple of phone calls, Suttle and Golding drove back to the Paignton house. En route, skirting the long curve of the bay, they passed Goodyer. He was alone on the promenade, walking fast, head down, his hands thrust in the pockets of his scabby leather jacket. Golding threw him a little wave, which he didn't see.

'Up and down, isn't he?' Suttle said. 'All over the fucking place. Sweetness and light one minute. Mr Angry the next. Nuts, d'you think? Or just bipolar?'

'Schizo. Definitely.' He glanced across at Suttle. 'That licence of his. He's qualified to drive a motorbike.'

'Is he?' Suttle came to a halt at a pedestrian crossing.

'Yeah.'

'So why didn't you raise it?'

'I would have done. It was on my list.'

'You think I let him go too soon?'

'I'm not sure you had a choice. The guy was in bits.'

'Because of Corrigan?'

'Hard to tell. Were they mates? Yeah. Close mates? Maybe. Do close mates fall out? Yeah. All the fucking time. And you're talking to someone who knows.' He laughed at some private memory.

Suttle was watching Goodyer in the rear-view mirror. He'd stopped now and was standing by the railings overlooking the beach. He had his mobile pressed to his ear and he seemed to be doing most of the talking.

'We can't nick him for getting upset,' he said. 'More's the pity.'

★ ★ ★

At the Paignton house he belled Terry Bryant. The Crime Scene Manager emerged from the house in his one-piece forensic suit, mopping his face in the sunshine. Suttle wanted to know whether they'd made a start on the bedroom at the back.

'That has to be the girlie room, right?'

He'd found documentation in a cardboard

box, correspondence from the Home Office and an asylum adjudication from a tribunal hearing back in 1997. There'd been bank statements too, and various bills, all neatly filed away. Nicinha Felicidad Pereira DOB 12.5.1975.

'What else did you find?'

'Personal stuff. Trinkets. Clothes, obviously. Shoes. Photos. Lots of books.' He frowned. 'There were a couple of posters too, for a local gig. They looked like keepsakes, something she wanted to hang onto. She seems to be some kind of singer. The photo matched with the mugshot in her passport.'

'Singer?' Suttle wanted to know more.

Bryant nodded. The group fronted by Nicinha called themselves Consolo. The poster was years old. She might have binned the singing by now.

'Nothing else?'

'Yeah.' Bryant grinned. 'Three packs of Featherlite in her bedside drawer, one of them half empty.'

'You look at the sheets?'

'Yeah. Ripe. We bagged them. Just in case.'

* * *

It was Gill who volunteered to take Grace for a walk. Deeply grateful, Lizzie stood at the front door of her mother's new house and watched them disappearing down the close towards the distant roar of the Eastern Road. Beyond the Eastern Road, at the top of Portsea Island, was a nature reserve thick with birdlife. Grace loved birds.

Anchorage Park was a relic of the 80s mania for newbuild estates, acres of little boxes, street after street of Ford Sierras and freshly painted front doors. Lizzie knew it was meant to be aspirational, a pitstop for young families on the move, but she hated it. The family house had been down the road in North End, a comfortable Victorian property with decent-sized rooms and a proper garden, and she'd somehow assumed that her mother would live there forever. That was where Lizzie had spent her youth, exploring the freedoms of the city with her sister, bike trips around Hilsea Lines when they were young, then Friday-night gigs at the Guildhall as they crept boldly into late adolescence, followed by whole weekends of mad partying in smoky Southsea basement flats. Mum and the North End house had always backstopped those giddy years, and it was only now that she was beginning to realise just how much that unfailing support had mattered.

Her mum was waiting in the lounge-diner. Her name was Angela. She was a small woman, beginning to age visibly. Years of teaching mathematics at one of the tougher inner-city comps had left its mark, and the windfall cheque that came with early retirement had bought her this cramped perch on the very edge of the island. To Lizzie's alarm, her mum appeared to love it. Another surprise. Another disappointment.

'Tea?'

Lizzie said yes. The headache and the nausea had gone now, leaving a gritty residue that still tasted of last night's mojitos. She felt flat, spiritless. She'd somehow slipped her moorings on a falling tide and neither knew nor cared where the next half-hour or so might take her. Her mother wanted a serious chat. So be it.

She curled herself into the corner of the two-seat sofa, watching her mother in the kitchen hunting for biscuits, wondering whether it might be better to conjure herself into invisibility. Lizzie Hodson, Madam Naughty, the stay-out mum who couldn't even be bothered to muster a decent alibi. Through the kitchen window she could see the tiny patch of back garden, littered with Grace's toys. In North End her mother had taken huge pride in her flower beds and her vegetable patch and her precious cherry trees, and here in her new life she'd done her best with the balding turf she'd inherited from the last owner. But nothing could resist the attentions of a hyperactive three-year-old and in the end she'd given up.

'Custard creams, I'm afraid.'

Her mother settled at the table and poured the tea. Lizzie didn't move. The silence stretched and stretched.

'I'm sorry about last night,' Lizzie said at last. 'It was my fault.'

Her mother didn't reply, not at first, then she slid the cup and saucer towards her daughter and folded her arms. The tightness of her mouth told Lizzie everything she needed to know. She felt about thirteen.

'That man loves you,' her mother began. 'You can see it.'

'Who, Mum? Who are we talking about?'

'Jimmy. He might not love what you did to him, whatever that was, whatever you both got up to last year, but deep down where it matters he's still there for you. And for Grace, which is probably more important. Kids are much brighter than we think. They can sense when things have gone wrong. That little girl reads you like a book, believe me.'

'Then she knows I'm in a good place.'

'I don't understand.'

'I mean at work. I need it, Mum. I was dying down in Devon. Now I'm me again. Am I allowed that? Am I allowed to be me?'

'Of course you are. But then you might ask me the same question.'

'You don't like being a grandmother?'

'I don't appreciate being taken for granted.'

'Is that what I do?'

'Yes, if you want the truth. One day it might occur to you that I've got a life too. Most days Grace is no problem. I'm lucky to have her. I'm lucky to have the pair of you. But if I was that desperate for company, I'd never have given up the job. I never thought I'd hear myself say this, but some days, especially lately, I can see this thing . . . this little arrangement of ours . . . going on forever. That's not what I want. And neither should you.'

'What are you telling me?'

'I'm telling you to decide on who you really want to be. We can't have it all, Lizzie. Sometimes we can't even have most of it. You have to compromise. And that way you might

38

start getting the most out of motherhood.'

'I'm a crap mum? Is that what you're saying?'

'I wouldn't know, and more to the point neither would Grace. And that's because you've never really given it a chance. When you were Grace's age, I thought I'd given up teaching for good. Why? Because children have needs. They need their mums. That happened to be you and Elaine. So why don't you surprise yourself? Why not give it a proper go?'

Lizzie stared at her. She couldn't remember her mother being so honest, so quietly forceful, so fucking *articulate*, and for a moment her determination to hang onto the job she loved wavered. But then she remembered the long winter she'd barely survived down at the cottage in the Otter Valley: the silence, the rain, the way the clouds never seem to lift. This was an existence scored for someone who'd pretty much given up on real life, someone older, someone far happier in the comfort of their own company. Not Lizzie Hodson, the go-to girl on the features desk, the bright young investigative journo with a number of impressive scalps already hanging from her belt. Would she really trade a job she loved for trips to the Fratton Lidl and afternoons in front of the telly with Grace? She thought not.

Her mother belonged to a generation who liked to resolve an argument. She was still waiting for some kind of response.

'You went back to teaching in the end,' Lizzie said defensively.

'That was after your father walked out. It was either that or the poorhouse.'

39

'But I was still at school.'

'That's true. You were also fifteen. Grace is three. There's a difference.'

'OK ... ' Lizzie was flying blind now, increasingly lost in what felt the grimmest of weather. 'So what do you suggest I do?'

'Is that a serious question?'

'Yes.'

'Number one, you stop lying to me about where you might be on a Saturday night. Number two, you start thinking about other people.'

'Meaning Grace?'

'No.' Her mother shook her head. 'Meaning Jimmy.'

★ ★ ★

Suttle and Luke Golding were back at Ashburton by early afternoon. The Major Incident Room had filled by now — civvy inputters at the computer terminals, a couple of detectives waiting for actions from the D/S in charge of the General Enquiry Team, the Statement Reader attacking the whiteboard with a scarlet Pentel — and Suttle left Golding to find himself a desk while he sought out D/I Carole Houghton.

She was in an office with Det-Supt Nandy. Nandy was wrestling with the packaging on a cheese sandwich while he barked at some functionary on his mobile. Media pressures were building by the hour. Interviews on lunchtime TV from a couple of Devon MPs about violent

40

crime getting out of control had revved Nandy up and he was in no mood to take prisoners. A post-mortem late tomorrow afternoon, he snapped, was totally unacceptable. He needed first sight of the pathologist's findings by noon.

The phone call came to an end. Houghton wanted to know about Goodyer. Suttle outlined what little progress they'd made over the course of the interview. In his view there was lots the man wasn't telling them.

'Like?'

'Like the fact that the woman who looks after the kid is obviously in a sexual relationship.'

He explained about Nicinha, and Terry Bryant's findings in her bedroom.

'Goodyer would have known about that,' Suttle said. 'There's no way he couldn't.'

'Meaning?'

'I dunno, boss. The woman's back tonight. She has to be top of the list.'

'Does she know what's happened?'

'Not to my knowledge.'

'So who's going to tell her?'

'Me, if I have to. I belled her just now. I'm meeting her off the train. My guess is she'll have made a call or two before she arrives, probably to Goodyer.'

'So she'll know already? Is that what you're saying?'

'Yeah. But we need to take a run at her, boss, while this thing's still fresh. My guess is she was sleeping with Corrigan. If anyone knows what might have happened it has to be her.'

Houghton nodded, turning her attention to an

41

email that had just arrived on her PC. Orange had confirmed that Corrigan's mobile had been switched off at 06.12. Not a peep since. Nandy was attacking the cheese sandwich. A curl of onion hung from his lower lip. The news from Orange drew no comment.

Suttle wanted to know what had happened to Leo. The last time he'd seen the child was in the arms of a uniformed traffic officer out on the edge of Dartmoor. Where was he now?

'Torbay General,' Nandy said. 'I sent him for a full check-up. We've heard nothing so far.'

'Is there anyone with him?'

'Carole tasked a FLO. Wendy Atkins. She's been in touch with the natural mother. Bella someone?'

'Prentiss. Goodyer thinks she's a fruitcake. She must be minted though. She hit the jackpot with some book or other and managed to sell the film rights. She spends most of her time in the States.'

'Not today, son. Wendy got her on the phone, had a chat. She's just moved into a place in Salisbury. She's down tomorrow to pick the boy up.' He wiped his mouth with a tissue. 'Someone else we need to take a look at.'

Suttle nodded. Wendy Atkins was a Family Liaison Officer, a big-hearted ex-Wren, mad about allotments, one of the best.

Houghton was back in the loop. She wanted to know what else Suttle had prised out of Goodyer.

'He's qualified to ride a motorbike, boss. It's not something he told us. Luke spotted it on the licence.'

42

'You're telling me he's got a bike?'

'We don't know. I asked Terry whether there was a garage or parking or some kind of storage out the back but he said not. There's an old shed full of cardboard boxes and all kinds of other shit, but that's pretty much it.'

'Rear access?'

'No. But he could always keep a bike in the road.'

'So where does that take us?'

Suttle did his best to lay it out. We knew the guy could drive a bike. We knew he was in a bit of a state. We knew there was stuff, probably loads of stuff, he wasn't telling us. What if something had kicked off between him and Corrigan? What if he'd borrowed a bike and followed Corrigan out to the moor, chosen his time and place, and settled a personal quarrel at gunpoint? Or what if he'd set up some kind of ambush?

Goodyer had admitted in interview he'd been out to the German woman's farm a couple of times with Corrigan and Leo. He knew it was remote. He knew what time Corrigan would be leaving. He'd make sure he got there well in advance. Piece of piss if you had the right motivation.

'Sure. Plus access to a firearm.' Houghton wasn't convinced.

Nandy ignored her. He reached for his coffee. In the opening stages of any major crime enquiry MCIT's Det-Supt was famously impatient. He liked to pile all his assets on the board, rattle the dice and pray for a double six. Nothing would please him more than an early arrest.

'You really think that might be a runner?'

'I've no idea, sir, but we might be talking gunshot residues. I asked Terry to bag all his clothing, everything he could find. We also need to raise an action on the neighbours. Check out whether there was a bike there last night.'

'Leave it to me.' Houghton was already reaching for the phone. 'We'll have officers round there this afternoon. Not just the bike but anything else they might have noticed. Regular callers, strange faces, whatever. People don't get shot at random. Not with this kind of MO. There has to be a story.' She paused, looking up at Suttle. 'So what's your gut feeling?'

'About Goodyer?'

'Yes.'

Suttle took his time. He'd been asking himself exactly the same question since they'd left Torquay police station.

'I think we need to keep tabs on him, boss.'

'You mean surveillance?'

'Yeah.'

Surveillance cost an arm and a leg. An incident like this had first claim on all kinds of resources, even when money was tight, but Nandy wanted Suttle to make the case.

'From where I'm sitting, boss, he's definitely in the frame. All kinds of stuff might have been happening in that house. So far he's told us very little. If he had the motive and the means to do Corrigan, out there on the moor, then that would explain the mobile thing. He knows Leo. He probably loves the boy. No

44

way would he just abandon him.'

'And surveillance?'

'I'd say yes. As soon as. There's no way I can get to the woman Nicky before this evening. If Goodyer does something silly in the meantime, makes some kind of mistake, we'd never know about it.'

Nandy nodded. Houghton was already talking to the D/S in charge of the General Enquiry Team about raising actions on Corrigan's neighbours.

'Done.' She put the phone down. 'So where do we go with Goodyer?'

'We plot him up.' Nandy swallowed the rest of his coffee. 'I'll make the call.'

'And me, sir?' Suttle was checking his watch.

'The surveillance guys will need briefing. What's the mugshot on PNC like?'

'It's old. He's got a bit thinner since those days. But it'll do.'

'OK, son. Off you go. Quick as you like.'

★ ★ ★

Suttle was in the Major Incident Room, trying to get Luke Golding off the phone, when he heard the voice. He recognised the song at once, an aria from one of the Puccini operas. Puccini was a big favourite of a guy called Lenahan. Lenahan had been his lodger for the best part of a year. On the wetter days out at Chantry Cottage he played this aria over and over again, a slanting shaft of the purest sunshine against the enveloping grey.

45

At first Suttle had laughed at this affectation. Then something in the music began to grow on him. Weeks later Lenahan had laid hands on two tickets for a live broadcast of the entire opera at the Exeter Picturehouse. With some reluctance Suttle had gone along with this mad adventure, only to find himself unexpectedly moved by the experience.

The MIR had come to a halt. Everyone seemed to be looking at him. The civvy inputter at the nearest terminal knew a bit about Puccini.

''O mio babbino caro',' she said. 'Anna Netrebko.'

Suttle was carrying two phones. One was the Job mobile, exclusively for MCIT calls. The other, a smartphone, had been an early birthday present from Lenahan.

Suttle pulled out the new Samsung. Wee Eamonn, he thought. With his special birthday download. Typically, the daft bugger had got the wrong Sunday. He put the phone to his ear, recognising the soft Irish vowels.

'I'm making lunch in case you'd forgotten. The scallops are queuing for the fucking wok. Care to join me?' Suttle was right. It was his precious lodger.

'I'm on a job, mate. Came out of nowhere. Can't talk now. Bell you later.'

Suttle pocketed the phone, ignoring the applause that rippled round the MIR. Suttle's previous ringtone had been the opening bars of an Adele song. Now this.

Golding had at last finished his conversation. Suttle gave him a list of calls to make. He was off to brief the surveillance guys. Back in half an hour. Golding asked him to hang on. He fired up his PC and entered a couple of keystrokes. Moments later, Suttle was looking at a YouTube clip. A black woman was singing. She had an amazing voice. She wasn't Anna Netrebko but she was close: the same fullness of tone, the same reach, the same presence. The song was mournful, full of an aching sadness. Her eyes were closed and the tide of lyrics seemed close to sweeping her away.

'What language is that?'

'Portuguese. They call it *fado*.'

Suttle was still watching the screen. The camerawork was rubbish and the tiny stage was underlit, but there was no mistaking the tall acoustic guitarist half a step behind her. Ian Goodyer.

'I googled Consolo.' Golding was grinning. 'And this is what I got.'

★ ★ ★

Lizzie phoned Rob Merrilees from the privacy of her bedroom. The sound insulation in these newbuilds was famously crap. She could hear Grace downstairs, howling her eyes out. The visit to the nature reserve hadn't been a success.

Merrilees answered after the third ring. Lizzie could hear voices in the background, and then laughter. Was he tucked up in some pub? Or was this a late lunch with a bunch of mates?

'It's me,' she said. 'Your favourite scribe.'

She wanted him to know that she'd talked to

47

her editor on the paper and that an in-depth piece on Hasler Company was a definite runner. Now she needed to be sure that access wouldn't be a problem.

'It won't.' Merrilees must have stepped out of the room. The background noise had gone. 'I'll sort it tomorrow, as soon as I get back to Plymouth. The guys there owe me a favour.' He paused. 'What are you doing this evening? Only I thought we might . . . you know . . . '

'What?'

'Get together. Have a drink. Pick up where we left off.'

Lizzie closed her eyes. She could hear her mother trying to placate Grace. Within minutes they'd all be round the telly, watching the CBeebies DVD.

'Lizzie? Are you still with me?'

Good question. This, she knew, was an important bend in the road. Her mother's patience was fast running out. Pissing her off for the second time in twenty-four hours would definitely have consequences. She paused for a moment, trying to think it through, then she bent to the phone.

'Wonderful idea,' she said. 'That would be great.'

3

Suttle was at Torquay railway station by half past six. The London connection was on time and he had ten minutes to kill before it arrived. He was tallying the calls he had to make when he caught sight of a familiar figure brushing the rain from his thinning hair, the gauntness of his face uplifted to the Arrivals monitor. Ian Goodyer.

Suttle ducked behind a news-stand, checking the entrance and the gleaming wet spaces of the car park beyond. The obs guys would have Goodyer plotted up. They'd be out there somewhere, mob-handed, covering all the angles, monitoring his every move.

Goodyer was checking his watch. He looked nervous, ill-at-ease, and he was still worrying at the scab on the back of his hand. Suttle thought again about the YouTube clip he'd seen earlier. Goodyer's guitar work had been deft and confident, every note perfect, as if he'd been born to this strange music, shadowing the voice as it swooped and soared. It had to be Nicinha — Nicky — out front, and the longer Suttle had watched, the more obvious it became that the music had soldered this pair together. There seemed to be an intimacy between them that went further than the haunting chords, and when the song came to an end and the pub

49

crowd roared its approval, Suttle caught the tiny nod of approval that told him everything he needed to know. Goodyer had once owned this woman. She'd been his.

The train arrived a minute or so early. Goodyer was at the barrier, up on his toes, oblivious of the stream of passengers pushing past. There was an impatience about him now. The nervousness seemed to have gone.

Nicinha was one of the last off the platform. She'd lost weight since the YouTube video but she was still a big woman. She wore a light black cagoule against the rain and she was carrying a cheap scarlet holdall. The sight of Goodyer at the barrier brought her to a halt. She wasn't pleased to see him.

Suttle was in the coffee shop now, watching the scene develop through the big plate-glass door. He was too far away to catch any conversation, but Nicinha's body language told him she wanted nothing to do with the man who'd come to meet her. When he gestured towards the car park, she shook her head. When he reached for the holdall, she snatched it away. Finally, he grabbed her by the upper arm and began to head for the exit. He was stronger than he looked. Nicinha fought back. An older woman heading for the ticket office stopped and asked what was going on. Other passers-by were visibly nervous. Goodyer had come to a halt. Judging by the expression on the older woman's face, he'd just told her to fuck off. Nicinha, released from his grip, was rubbing her arm.

Suttle stepped out of the coffee shop and

crossed the concourse. Goodyer had his back to him. He'd taken Nicinha by the hand and was trying to drag her towards the car park again. Suttle tapped him on the shoulder, told him to let go. Goodyer spun round, fist raised, then paused.

'Shit,' he muttered. 'You again.'

The incident was over. Goodyer slunk away without a backward glance. Nicinha was staring at Suttle's warrant card.

'Thank you,' she said.

★ ★ ★

Suttle drove her to Torquay police station. By the first set of traffic lights she'd recovered enough to ask Suttle what was going on.

'It's about Michael Corrigan. I understand he's a friend of yours.'

'He is. That's right. What about him?'

'You haven't heard?'

'Heard what?'

She was looking alarmed again and Suttle found himself wondering whether it was possible that she still didn't know what had happened. Goodyer would have phoned her, surely, and told her the news.

'The guy back there, Goodyer, has he been in touch at all?'

'You know him? Ian?' Her eyes were even wider.

'Yes. I asked you whether he'd been in touch. Just answer the question.'

'Of course. He phones me non-stop, all the time, today, yesterday, all the time, on the train

51

even, half an hour ago.'

'And what did he say? What did he tell you?'

'About Michael?'

'Yes.'

She was frowning now, trying to work out the thrust of these questions, where they led, what they meant.

'Why?' she said at last. 'Why do you ask?'

'Because it's important.'

'You're telling me something's happened? To Michael?'

'Yes. What did Ian say?'

'He said he'd gone away. With Leo. He said we had to go too.'

'When?'

'Tonight. He's bought a van. A camper van. Tonight. We had to leave tonight.'

'So where were you going?'

'Dover. France. I don't know. Wherever Michael is. And Leo.'

Suttle shot her a look. The traffic was on the move again. There was no way he could avoid the next thirty seconds. Should he go into details? Should he tell her about young Leo? Covered in his father's blood and brain tissue? He thought not.

'I'm afraid Michael's dead,' he said softly. 'Someone killed him this morning. That's what all this is about.'

★ ★ ★

Inside the police station Golding was waiting with news from the surveillance team. Goodyer

52

had made two visits to a backstreet garage in Brixham. On the second occasion, barely an hour ago, he'd emerged at the wheel of a Toyota camper van. Squad officers were on their way to interview the garage owner.

Suttle nodded. He still had his arm round Nicinha. She turned into him, her face buried in the jacket of his suit, her shoulders heaving.

'So where's Goodyer now?' Suttle asked Golding.

'Dunno. Maybe you should talk to Houghton.'

Suttle nodded. The civvy behind the front desk wanted to know whether he wanted any tissues. Suttle said yes then turned back to Golding.

'We've got the same office?'

'Yeah.'

The office was at the back of the building. Suttle followed Golding, his arm still round Nicinha. When they got to a vending machine he stopped, but when he suggested something to drink she shook her head. She just wanted to sit down. She just needed to hold someone.

Suttle phoned Houghton from the office. He wanted to know about Goodyer.

'He's back at the house. The camper van's out front. You met the woman off the train?'

'Yes.'

'So what's happened? What's the story?'

'I'll bell you later. The surveillance boys are sitting on Goodyer, right?'

'Right.'

'And they're there for the duration, right?'

'Right.'

Suttle ended the call with a grunt. Nicinha was in the chair beside him, staring at the blankness of the wall, her face a mask, her hand still in his. Suttle asked about coffee again. This time she said yes.

Golding left the office. For a long moment there was silence. Then came the distant wail of an ambulance and Nicinha gave a little shudder before closing her eyes.

'Where's Leo?'

'At the hospital.'

'He's hurt?' The eyes were open again.

'No. They're just looking after him.'

'I need to go there. To be with him.'

'Later.'

'Now. Please.'

'Later. As soon as we've finished.'

She nodded, seemed to accept it.

'You really didn't know?' Suttle asked. 'About Michael?'

'No.'

'Goodyer didn't tell you?'

'No.'

'Why might that be?'

'I don't know. He can be a strange man sometimes.'

'You've known him long?'

'Half my life.' She turned her head to face him. 'This is crazy. You want me to tell you about it? You want me to tell you how it happened? All those years ago? Would that help?'

She'd grown up in Angola, she said, in a city called Huambo. There was a war going on, rebel fighters everywhere, Savimbi's men, bad men.

54

They'd kidnapped her father and tortured him to death and she'd fled to Luanda on the coast. After a while she'd managed to get a flight to England. She was seventeen years old. She'd applied for asylum at Heathrow and spent months at a detention centre before her case came up. In the end she'd been granted leave to stay and had ended up in Plymouth. From Plymouth, a couple of years later, she'd moved to Torquay, which is where she'd met Ian.

Her account was deadpan, flat, a story she'd probably told a thousand strangers. Suttle had been in situations like this before in Pompey. Kosovans. Somalis. Dead-eyed youngsters from Mali and Chad. The same tone of voice. The same weary acceptance of violence and exile. Except this woman had made a life here.

'What was Ian like?'

'Crazy. Like me. Crazy and wild. He did drugs. He'd been in prison. We talked the same language. He was the first white man I met who understood me.'

Golding was back by now, making notes. Suttle sipped his coffee. He wanted to know what happened next.

'I had an aunt in Huambo. She taught me to be a fortune-teller. Ian loved that. He said there was money in fortune-telling and he was right. People came to me. I read their hands, looked in their eyes, looked inside them. If you have the gift, it's easy. You talk to the spirits. And the spirits talk back.'

Ian, she said, had taught himself the guitar in prison and he was good. She'd sung all her life.

55

She'd sung in a choir as a girl in Huambo, and she'd sung later, by herself, living alone in the hugeness of Luanda, to keep herself sane. She sang *fado* because *fado* was the shortest cut into her own past. It was the music of loss and regret.

'You sang with Ian? He played for you?'

'Yes. He was good. I was surprised. He played like the Portuguese play, like the Angolans play. He had music, that man. We were good together. It made me happy.'

Suttle nodded, noting the past tense. Had.

'Was this Consolo?'

His knowledge of the name took her by surprise. For the first time she smiled, a sudden spark of warmth that turned her into someone else. This was a woman, he thought, who could fill a whole evening with her spontaneity and her presence. No wonder she was so great with Leo.

'You know about Consolo?' she asked.

'Yes.'

'You heard us play, maybe?'

'Yes.' Suttle didn't go into details. 'Tell me more.'

'More about what?'

'More about how you started.'

'Sure.' She seemed to take it as a compliment. 'We started playing properly, in front of audiences, big audiences ... ' She nodded, animated by this happy passage in her life. 'Ian had met somebody. She was an organiser, this woman. She booked us for a festival. She liked us. She liked what she heard.'

'What was her name?'

'Bella. Bella Prentiss. She came to me for a

reading. She wanted to know whether she'd ever have children. I told her yes. A boy.'

'And?'

'I was right. That was Leo.'

Her head tipped back and she reached for a tissue. Ian, she said after a moment or two, was living in Michael's house. This was a couple of years ago, maybe more. The two men were friends. Which was how Bella and Michael got to meet. They were good with each other. Close. It was nice to see. Then Leo came along.

Suttle wanted to know more about her and Ian.

'You had a relationship? You were living together?'

'Yes. I had a room near Ian's place. Some nights I stayed with him. Some nights he was with me.'

'It worked?'

'Yes.'

'So what changed?'

She gave the question some thought. She had lovely hands, long unvarnished nails with interesting rings on both index fingers.

'The baby came. Leo. Bella wanted to be a writer. She made a big success. We were all happy for her. Especially Michael. Then she went.'

'Left?'

'Yes.'

'Suddenly? Just like that?'

'Yes.'

'Any reason?'

'I think she met someone.' She shook her

57

head. 'Michael was so hurt. He loved her. He really loved her. Maybe he still does.' She turned her head again, those huge eyes. 'You tell me he's dead, but nothing ends, not if you're like me, not if you're a believer.'

Suttle nodded. He was thinking about Goodyer's take on Bella Prentiss. *Mick was her bit of rough*, he'd said. *Since then her life's moved on.* Had Corrigan ever sussed this? Or had he carried his disappointment to the grave?

Golding looked up from his notebook. He asked what happened after Bella left.

'I looked after Leo,' she said. 'Instead of Bella.'

'Did that surprise you? A mother leaving her child?'

'Of course.'

'And what about Leo? Did he miss his mother?'

'A little. To begin with.'

'And now?'

'No. I don't think he knows who she is.' Her voice had hardened. Suttle picked it up at once. Golding hadn't finished

'So you were there all the time after Bella left?'

'Yes.'

'Living with Ian?'

'Yes.'

'And Michael?'

'I don't understand.'

'He was happy with what had happened? It all worked for him? You looking after Leo? You still with Ian?'

'Yes . . . ' She hesitated. 'At first, yes.'

'And then?'

58

'And then everything changed.'

'Why? How?'

She looked at each of them in turn, trying to gauge how far to go. Suttle reminded her about the hospital. The quicker they got through this interview, the sooner she'd see Leo again.

'It was to do with Bella,' she said at last. 'She and her man, they wanted Leo.'

'This is the man she left for?'

'Yes. He was older. He came down to the house from London to meet Bella. He played with Leo.'

This had to be the agent, Suttle thought. Maybe he was looking for a ready-made family of his own. And maybe, in the shape of his hot new writer and her lovely son, he'd found just that.

'So what happened?'

'Michael got letters. Lawyer's letters. Then things happened. Horrible things. A man from the council came about the rats.'

'Rats?'

'He said we had rats. He said a neighbour had phoned. Big rats in our garden.'

'Was it true?'

'No.'

'Then someone else came. Someone from the gas company about our boiler. It hadn't been checked. He said it was dangerous. Then more letters from the lawyer. He said our whole house was dangerous. He said Leo shouldn't be living there. It wasn't true but we couldn't do anything about it. We had no money. We couldn't fight. Then something else happened.'

'What?'

'A woman from the social services. She said she'd heard rumours that I was doing bad things.'

'What bad things?'

'That I was a *puta*.'

'A what?'

'A whore.' This from Golding.

'Really?' Suttle was still looking at Nicinha 'So where did that come from?'

She wouldn't answer. Suttle put the question again. She turned away, visibly uncomfortable. At length she took another tissue and blew her nose.

'Can we go now?' she said. 'Can we go to the hospital?'

'I'm afraid not. Not yet.'

Suttle sat back and let the silence do the work. Golding was gazing at his notebook.

Finally Nicinha admitted that life in her little ménage had got complicated. Michael couldn't cope with the thought of losing his child. She felt sorry for him — really, really sorry for him. He needed help. He needed a woman. She was looking down at the table. She wouldn't lift her head.

'So you went with him?'

'Yes.'

'Instead of Ian?'

'Yes.'

'And what did Ian think?'

'He hated it. He wanted me back. He wanted everything the way it was. I said it was impossible. I was with Michael now. And Leo.

60

That's where I was. Because everything had changed.' At last her head came up. Her eyes were swimming again. 'Do you know what it is to lose a child?'

Suttle held her gaze. Then he got to his feet.

'D/C Golding will take you to the hospital,' he said. 'Thank you for your time.'

★ ★ ★

Lizzie was late for the restaurant. She'd agreed half seven on the phone and it was nearly eight by the time she pushed in through the door and shook the rain from her mum's umbrella. Rob Merrilees was at a table at the back. His glass was nearly empty. Lizzie kissed him on the lips. Getting Grace to go to sleep had been a pain, she said. Never have children if you can possibly avoid it.

'How about your mum?'

'Don't ask.'

'That bad?'

'Worse. I got a beasting this afternoon. I'm a shit daughter, little Ms Selfish, and my mothering skills are zilch. Think probation from now on.'

'So what are you doing here?'

'I told her it was business. Another chance to further my fabulous career.'

'And is it?'

'Yeah. Partly. The rest you don't want to know about.'

Rob eyed her for a moment, then signalled to the waiter. Lizzie settled for a pint of Cobra.

61

When she nodded at his near-empty glass, Rob shook his head.

'Tell me about your husband,' he said.

The question stopped Lizzie in her tracks. This wasn't a guy who had ever needed a media course, she thought. Cut to the chase. Go for the jugular. Never fails.

'Why do you ask?'

'Because it interests me. Because I want to know.'

'But why?'

He smiled at her and shook his head. Another great move. Say nothing.

'He's a cop,' Lizzie said. 'I think I told you that.'

'What kind of cop?'

'A detective. CID. He used to be based here in Pompey. That's where we met.'

'So what was he like?'

'He was lovely. I fancied him like mad. We got it on like that.' The snap of her fingers caught the waiter's eye. He stepped across again but Rob waved him away.

'Good cop?' he asked.

'The best. I got to know his mates, like you do. They all thought he was something pretty special and so did I. He had the knack of getting into people's heads, into their hearts. Journalists do it too.'

'Takes one to know one?'

'Exactly. Except he was probably better at it than me.'

'Was?'

'Is. We fucked up big-time. And if you want

the truth, most of that was down to me.'

'You want to talk about it?'

'Not really. Not here. Not tonight.'

The steadiness of Rob's gaze was beginning to unsettle Lizzie. She was normally the one asking the questions, shaping the conversation, dictating the pace. How come she was so suddenly on the receiving end?

'Listen . . . ' she began. 'We made a daft decision. Jimmy got a job offer down in the West Country. I think he'd had enough of Pompey. He was always a country boy at heart and he thought a bit of peace and quiet would do us all good.'

'And you?'

'I was silly enough to believe him. Grace was still a baby. You start thinking cows and buttercups and decent food and head space and all the rest of it, and seconds later you're looking at a pile of cardboard boxes and a Transit at the door.'

'You're telling me you had no say in any of that?'

'Not really. Jimmy was down there first. He had to make some quick decisions. Grace and I trailed along later.'

'So what happened?'

'It rained. And then it rained some more. Jimmy had found this cottage in the back of nowhere. He was a detective for Christ's sake. He should have sussed the holes in the roof and the knackered boiler and the doors that never closed. We were living with an army of wildlife. The place was a zoo — dormice, spiders, you

63

name it. No kidding. And you know what? He loved it. Which was great if you happened to have an interesting job and you were out of the door most days. Me? I became the resident depressive. And that was just week one.'

Lizzie ducked her head and reached for her fork, something to play with, something to finger, anything to hide her embarrassment. How come she'd let it all spill out? How come this glorious man had known exactly which buttons to press?

'So what happened?'

Lizzie spared him a glance. Then she shrugged, a small gesture of surrender, and told him the rest of the story. How autumn and the wettest of winters had marched down the valley and banged her up. How life had shrunk to the view from the kitchen window, and the *drip-drip* of countless leaks, and the endless attempts to pacify a squalling daughter who somehow sensed that things had gone catastrophically wrong. In another life, she said, she'd been the go-to journalist with the brightest of futures. She'd laid the foundations for a decent career and faced every new day with a smile on her face. Now, for reasons that became ever more bewildering, she'd become the village recluse, the mum down the lane who was beginning to lose track of who she really was.

'I was going mad,' she said. 'I was losing it.'

'Losing what?'

'Everything. I had no one to talk to, nothing to get me going. All I could count on was the rain. You can't believe what rain can do to a girl. It was driving me nuts.'

'Friends? Mates?'

'Never happened. You go into yourself. You lose your confidence. Even a conversation in the street becomes a massive ask. You shrink. You become someone else. I had all the toys. I had a PC and a laptop, but there was no broadband and the mobile signal was a joke. Most days you had to take the phone outside to have a chance of making the thing work. And like I say, it was always fucking raining.'

Rob nodded. Lizzie took a long swallow of Cobra. In for a penny, she thought.

'You're going to ask how I coped,' she said.

'You're right.'

'So what's the answer?'

'You had an affair,' he suggested.

'You're right. I did. Sort of. But that didn't work either. The guy involved turned out to be an obsessive. He was also the prime suspect in a murder enquiry. And guess who was the cop trying to nail him?'

'Your husband.'

'Right.'

'Fuck.'

'Exactly.' Lizzie offered him a thin smile. 'Never get between a man and his work, eh?'

'You're bitter?'

'No. If you want the truth I'm relieved.'

'About Jimmy? About the marriage?'

'About moving back. It never rains in Pompey. And that, believe me, is a blessing.' She reached for the glass again, holding Rob's gaze. 'So here we are, Captain Merrilees. Your turn now.'

'What do you want to know?'
'Everything. Starting with Afghanistan.'

★ ★ ★

Nandy and Houghton were still at the MIR when Jimmy Suttle got back from Torquay. Nandy was pacing the office Houghton had commandeered, his mobile pressed to his ear, while the D/I added yet another name to the whiteboard with her blue Pentel.

'Who's Sy Rosen?' Suttle was looking at the whiteboard.

'The guy who might be coming down tomorrow with Bella Prentiss.'

'This is her agent?'

'Yeah, and everything else.' She glanced round. 'Half eleven at the hospital. They'll be collecting the boy, Leo, but we need to talk to them. You're good with that?'

Suttle nodded. Houghton looked exhausted. Early start, Suttle thought. And probably worse to come.

Nandy was off the phone. He wanted to know about the black girl Suttle had met off the train. What did she have to say for herself? What was the strength?

Suttle gave them the bones of the interview. Nicky had been with Goodyer for a while. They'd performed together and pretty much lived together. Then Bella Prentiss had turned her back on life in Torquay and Nicky had found herself acting as a kind of surrogate mother.

'Still kipping with Goodyer?'

'At first, yes.'

'And then?'

'Then she got it on with Corrigan. She says she felt sorry for him.' Suttle shrugged. 'Whatever that means.'

'And Goodyer?' This from Houghton.

'Extremely pissed off.'

'And they're all still living under one roof?'

'Yes.'

'Awkward.'

'Very.'

Suttle wanted to know whether Corrigan's neighbours had been actioned.

'Yeah. We did it this afternoon.'

'And?'

'Nothing. No bike. No car except for the Golf.'

'Did anyone see Goodyer leave first thing this morning?'

'No.'

'Or come back?'

'No.' Houghton paused. 'There's access at the back of the property, though. You could leave and get back in without being spotted.'

'You're still thinking Goodyer?' Nandy was looking at Suttle.

'I'm thinking the guy has a motive, sir. First off, it might have been some kind of drugs thing but we'll never stand that up. The way I'm seeing it, the woman Nicky changes everything. Situations like that can get out of hand. They'd been together a while. Goodyer's unstable. You can see it in his face, in the way he tries to handle us. Having Corrigan off the plot would

67

have suited him nicely.'

'But you're telling us they were mates, Goodyer and Corrigan.'

'They were. Until he started shagging Nicky.' Suttle's eyes strayed to the whiteboard. Another name he didn't recognise.

'So who's Trevor West?'

Nandy seemed to have difficulty remembering. Houghton came to his rescue.

'He's the guy who sold Goodyer the van this afternoon. He's got premises over in Brixham.'

'How much are we talking?'

'Four and a half grand. In cash.'

'*Cash?*' Suttle was astonished. 'So where does Goodyer get that kind of money? This is a guy who might pull fifty quid for a pub gig. The kitesurfing business must be struggling, given the weather. So how come he can suddenly lay hands on four and a half grand?'

'Good question, son.' Nandy was back in the loop. 'Maybe you were a bit hasty with the laughing powder.'

'You think he's still dealing?'

'Has to be. How else do you explain it?'

Suttle said he didn't know. He told them about the legal problems Corrigan and Nicky had been facing over the recent months. Letters from high-powered London lawyers representing Bella Prentiss. Demands that Leo be returned to his natural mother and her new beau. Plus problems of a different sort. He described the call from the environmental health people hunting for rats. Then came concerns about a dodgy boiler. Finally, he said, Nicky found

68

herself in front of a Child Protection Officer, denying that she was on the game.

'You're telling me there was some kind of conspiracy going on?' Nandy seemed unimpressed.

'I'm telling you some of this stuff needs inside knowledge.'

'You mean Goodyer again? The cuckoo in the nest?'

'Yeah.'

'To what end?'

'Settling a personal debt. Goodyer's pissed off with Corrigan. Plus he wants his woman back.'

'So he grasses Corrigan up? To the environmental health people? To social services?'

'Exactly.'

'And gets paid for his efforts?'

'Yes.'

'And you really think that might be worth four and a half grand?'

'To the right person, yes.'

'So who might that be?'

'Good question, sir.' Suttle was looking at the board again. Bella Prentiss, he thought. The absentee mum desperate to lay hands on her precious son.

★   ★   ★

It was mid-evening when Rob Merrilees called for the bill. The food had been indifferent, but Lizzie had scarcely bothered with the under-spiced chicken jalfrezi and yesterday's bowl of thin dahl. What mattered was the man across the table and the way he'd seemed so ready to share his take on the realities of Afghanistan. Like most guys his age he'd done two tours in Helmand province, the perfect opportunity — in his phrase — to watch the conflict mutate from war fighting to something altogether different.

In the early days, he said, the guys had gone out for a decent ruck with the Taliban and had rarely been disappointed. This was the kind of war they'd trained for, but the Talib had wised up pretty fast. There was no way they could match ISAF's technology and so they'd melted away into the towns and villages, baiting the infidels with IEDs and long-distance sniper fire.

Nowadays, he said, you were fighting ghosts. In a way it was like Northern Ireland in the 70s. The enemy declined to wear uniforms. You had no idea who were the bad guys. All you knew was the weight of body armour on your back and the fact that your next footfall could be your last. On summer rotations the temperature could top fifty degrees, and if you were trying to dodge the IEDs by getting off the usual paths and pushing through a head-high field of crops it could be even hotter. Afghan, he said, knackers you in every conceivable way. You get very old very quickly. Until one morning you wake up and realise you shouldn't be there.

'You're serious?'

'Yeah. Absolutely. These people don't want us, don't need us. All they know is that we attract trouble. They want peace. We give them war. Better to live under the Taliban. That way, at the very least, they can get on with their lives.'

70

'But that's losing, isn't it?'

'Sure, if you're a politician. But bootnecks, my guys, we don't think that way. We're there, in the end, for each other. That's the way it works. And if you get to survive a couple of tours you're wise enough to know that your luck can run out. Every day you're cheating the odds. The Talib are gutsy and they're smart. They're good at this stuff, at blowing people up. They're also fighting a war they believe in, and that matters.'

A lot of the experienced guys, he said, were jacking it in. A month working for one of the maritime protection companies off the Horn of Africa could earn them £10K. Knocking lumps off a bunch of Somali pirates was child's play compared to Afghan, and they got decent leave allocations on top: flights, transit hotels, free car hire, the lot. Just now, he said, serving bootnecks were virtual strangers to their wives and kids. The divorce rate had gone beyond 50 per cent and the MoD had started hiring whole floors of hotel rooms next to the UK commando camps because all the mess accommodation was full.

'With who?'

'With single guys thrown out by their wives. That's the way it is now. You go to Afghan. You do your six months. You see some truly horrible things. You watch your best mate blown apart and you help tidy up afterwards. Then you're home for a couple of weeks before the training kicks off for the next rotation and you start all over again. Like I say, it's a marriage killer. Is Afghan family-friendly? Alas, no.'

Lizzie was still trying to imagine the carnage

left by an IED. What did images like that do to a man?

Rob acknowledged the question with a weary nod.

'If your mate's dead he's one of the lucky ones. The rest end up minus a limb or three, trying to figure out what went wrong. Hasler Company's full of them. We're talking serious rage here. The pencil heads in the MoD try to spin it, try to make us believe all these guys are warrior heroes, guys who've taken it on the chin and half-died for a noble cause. They're certainly right about the hero bit, about the way they crack on and try to hack it. But that's not the whole story, not when you're looking at the rest of your life on meds in a wheelchair. These people are angry, seriously pissed off. And there are more of them than you'd ever believe for every bootneck who comes back in a box.'

Lizzie nodded. This, she knew, would make brilliant copy when it came to a feature piece.

'And how about you?' she said softly. 'Where are you in all this?'

'I'm nowhere. I'm sitting in an average curry house in the best possible company and I'm telling you far more than I should.'

'Because you trust me?'

'Yes. Like the way you trusted me.'

'My story is pathetic. It's a whine. You're talking life and death. I don't recall too many IEDs in Colaton Raleigh.'

'Was that where you lived?'

'Yeah. So maybe I was lucky with the rain. Afghan sounds horrible.'

'It was. It is. But we do what we do.'

'And live with the consequences?'

'Yeah. If we're lucky.' He reached for her hand, looking away across the gloom of the restaurant.

Lizzie fought the urge to wreck this rare moment of neediness but knew there was no alternative.

'So do I still get to see Hasler Company?'

'Of course.' Rob permitted himself a tiny smile. 'But only on one condition.'

'What's that?'

'I have to be there with you. Otherwise it won't happen. You think you could handle that?'

'Of course. When?'

'It has to be in the next couple of weeks. I'm away again after that.'

'Where?'

'Cyprus. We have a facility for troops rotating out of theatre. We call it decompression. We're talking twenty-four hours on the beach in the sunshine with a couple of tinnies before we fly the guys back to Brize. I'm there for six months behind a desk. It's a sensitive posting. That's why they put me through the media course. I gather the idea is to shoot you lot with your own bullets. Lucky me, eh?'

Lizzie leaned forward and kissed him. She couldn't remember when she'd last wanted to fuck someone so badly. This man had a story to tell but he had more than that. He had a centre, a core. He seemed to believe in something, and believe in it enough for it to really matter. What that something might be was still unclear but she relished the opportunity to find out. How many other service people had she met who'd ever be this candid? This brave? This reflective? This fucking *aware*? And how many had the looks to go with it?

She was tallying the ways she could make it unforgettable for him, ways that could make him remember her for a very long time, when he glanced at his watch, pushed back his chair, and said he had to go.

'Why?'

'I have to be home by eleven.'

'Where's home?'

'Bere Ferrers. It's in the Tamar Valley. I thought I mentioned it.'

'But it's still only eight.'

'Sure. And it's a three-hour ride.'

'*Ride?*'

'I'm on a motorbike. I thought I mentioned that too.'

'But why the deadline? Am I allowed to ask?'

'No.' He bent and kissed her. 'Come and stay when we go to Hasler. Then I might tell you.'

★ ★ ★

Suttle was home by nine o'clock. Chantry Cottage lay beside a narrow country lane about a mile from the village of Colaton Raleigh. In the thickening dusk Suttle could see the throw of light from Lenahan's bedroom. He hauled the Impreza onto the gravel parking area and killed the engine. Through the open window he could smell fresh dung from the cows a local farmer

74

drove back to his cattle shed every night. From the wetness of the meadow beside the stream, already cloaked in darkness, came the soft burble of a curlew. Closer, from the cottage, an aria he recognised from *Die Fledermaus*. Nice, he thought, reaching for the keys.

Lenahan was in the kitchen, perched on a stool beside the stove. He was a tiny guy, a year or two older than Suttle. His taste in clothes was as colourful and exotic as more or less everything else in his life. As a locum registrar at Exeter's A&E unit, he was obliged to wear something at least resembling a suit, but every evening he made a point of shedding his work skin and becoming — in his own phrase — somebody fucking human again. This evening he'd favoured a faded white dishdasha embroidered in whorls of delicate purple, a souvenir — Suttle assumed — from last year's posting as a front-line medic in South Sudan.

Barefoot on the cracked tiles, Lenahan hopped off the stool and seized a bottle of white wine from the fridge. Suttle had twice warned him that he'd got the date of his birthday wrong but in certain moods Lenahan appeared to be deaf. Tonight was to be a celebration with his Irish pixie. So be it.

'You'll be wanting this, my friend. Here's to death and eternity.'

Suttle found himself holding a glass of ice-cold Chablis. The kitchen smelled of garlic and fresh ginger. A dozen scallops glistened in a bowl beside the wok. Rice was coming nicely to the boil and the candles on the tiny table threw a soft light on a mountain of salad. For the first time Suttle realised how hungry he was.

'Thanks for the ringtone,' he said. 'I've never been the squad gay before.'

'Sure, and why not?' Lenahan was grinning over the rim of his glass. 'Those guys don't know what they're missing.'

'Thanks.'

'My pleasure. As always.'

Lenahan took a swallow of Chablis and went back to the stove. Suttle sank into one of the two chairs at the kitchen table and watched him slicing spring onions for the wok.

He'd met this man during a job last year. Lenahan had been cox in a seagoing racing quad belonging to a rowing club down in nearby Exmouth. The boat had been gifted by a businessman who'd died under circumstances that only Suttle had regarded as suspicious. In the end, at the cost of his marriage, he'd worked the case to a more or less successful conclusion.

Operation *Constantine* had done wonders for his reputation among the Major Crime guys, which was nice, but Suttle was honest enough to acknowledge that Lenahan's input had been critical. He'd been a key witness throughout the investigation, as well as a rich source of gossip and encouragement, and when the lease on his Lympstone rental came to an end, Suttle was only too happy to offer him a room at Chantry Cottage. He liked his company. Lenahan made him laugh. They were easy together. And the fact that he'd turned out to be gay hadn't made the slightest difference. On the contrary, Suttle had begun to depend on this man's intelligence, on his wit, on the way he could so quickly transform a mood or head off a quarrel.

After the darkness and silence of his first and only winter in the cottage with Lizzie, sharing the place with Lenahan had been a lifesaver. The man cooked like an angel. He was an unending source of stories, all of them framed to capture the madness of the world around him. Lenahan, on his own admission, had a cheerful pessimism about the human condition that had been coloured by postings to the far corners of the planet, but nothing, it seemed, could shake his faith that the journey — wherever it led — was still worthwhile. You had a duty to tease laughter out of chaos, to salve life's wounds as best you could, and to recognise that certain battles were best left unfought. In this respect, Suttle had often thought, he'd led a cop's life. He'd seen the worst. Yet he soldiered on.

Just now Lenahan was telling him about a drunk from one of Exeter's heavier areas. The guy was huge, he said, way over six foot, and was a regular visitor to A&E. He drank every penny that came his way and when the money ran out he'd make do with whatever he could lay his hands on. One night he'd broken into a funeral parlour and got wasted on embalming fluid. On that occasion a stomach pump had probably saved his life but this morning had been different. The guy had been found at the bottom of a trench dug by one of the utility companies in the backstreets of Heavitree. He'd been badly beaten and injuries to his face alone had taken more than forty stitches. Briefly sober, he'd done his best to answer questions from the attending police officers, but his memory was as wrecked as the rest of him. All he needed, he'd muttered through his swollen lips, was something to fucking drink.

Suttle half-followed the story, wondering where it might lead. Listening to Lenahan in these moods was like tuning into a foreign radio station. He spoke at a thousand miles an hour, hopscotching from one detail to the next as he tried to lay his hands on another bottle of fish sauce, leaving a zigzag of pithy home truths in his boiling wake. The world was an arsewipe. The guy in the trench doubtless had it coming to him. Thank fuck for scallops and yer lovely man's birthday and a decent bottle of white.

The meal lived up to Suttle's best expectations. They devoured the scallops, kicked a difficult day to death and agreed that birthdays were better celebrated in advance. Only an hour or two later, when Lenahan produced a particularly fine bottle of Armagnac, did a shadow fall over the evening.

'I got an offer this morning.'

'Lucky old you.'

'Listen to me, eejit. This one came in an envelope. Guy from MSF I once shagged in Senegal.'

'And?'

'There's a job going in Somalia. A lot of the guys are shipping out.'

'I'm not surprised. Don't they kill people there?'

'They do, my friend, they do. Plus we're talking famine, shit water, and all the atrocities you could possibly imagine. A fella needs a bit of that from time to time. Just to keep him earthed.'

Suttle smiled. He'd heard enough about Lenahan's days in South Sudan to know he wasn't kidding. No one signed up with Médecins Sans Frontières for an easy life.

'You think we're spoiling you here? Decent wages? Flushing toilets?' Suttle nodded at the pile of plates in the kitchen sink. 'Scallops?'

'Yeah. I was never one for guilt trips, but there comes a time . . . You know what I mean?'

Suttle shook his head. It had begun to occur to him that Lenahan was serious.

'You've got a date?'

'August.'

'That's next month. Nearly.'

'Sure.' Lenahan reached for Suttle's hand over the table. 'So what do you think, Hawkeye?'

Hawkeye was a recent nickname. Lenahan had picked it up from one of the comics that apparently littered the staff lounge at A&E. Suttle didn't know what to say.

'I'll miss you,' he managed at last.

'Is that right?'

'Yeah.'

'Why?'

'I dunno . . . ' He shrugged. 'Because . . . I dunno . . . '

It was true. Not once over the last seven months had it occurred to Suttle that Lenahan, this precious bird of passage, might move on. The thought of an autumn alone again was infinitely depressing.

'Is it the silence that would get to you? Or the shit television?' Lenahan could read him like a book.

'Both. Either. Fuck knows.'

'Look on the bright side then. I'll leave you my Puccini CDs. And a couple of decent recipes.'

'Yeah?' Inexplicably Suttle felt close to tears. 'You'd do that?'

'I would. Cross my heart and hope to die. You know what a bent priest of my acquaintance said to me? Once he'd got his hand out of my trousers?'

'Tell me.'

'Never invest in a relationship. Gold's safer. Or maybe the horses.'

'Thanks.'

'It's a joke, Hawkeye, you eejit. And you know something else?'

'No.'

'I haven't made my mind up yet.' He put Suttle's hand to his lips and kissed it. 'So here's hoping, eh?'

4

Det-Supt Nandy called a full squad meet for half
eight next morning. Suttle, fighting both the
early rush-hour traffic and a raging hangover,
made it with minutes to spare. The Major
Incident Room was packed. Nandy had used last
night's media coverage of the Corrigan killing to
leverage yet more D/Cs onto the *Graduate*
squad. The BBC's crime reporter on the local
TV news had talked of 'an execution' on the
fringes of Dartmoor, while a breathless DJ on
one of the commercial radio stations, inviting
listeners to call in, had come close to suggesting
that violent crime in sleepy Devon was slipping
out of control. No one is safe, went the message.
Lobby your MP *now*.

Suttle counted thirty-three bodies in the
Det-Supt's expanded squad. There were even
faces he'd never seen before. Corrigan's killer
had sucked Major Crime detectives from every
corner of the South West.

At Nandy's invitation, Houghton opened with
a brisk summary of lines of enquiry actioned to
date. Scenes of Crime had finished with
Corrigan's car. Neither the vehicle itself, nor the
road and surrounds where the incident had
taken place had so far yielded anything
evidentially helpful. The single bullet which had

killed Corrigan hadn't been recovered. The probable line of flight would put it somewhere in the vastness of the moorland landscape beyond the single-track road, and though a team of uniformed officers had made a start on a fingertip search, it was a huge ask to expect them to find it. Neither had there been any sign of an expended shell case in the vicinity of the car.

Nandy interrupted. He'd been talking to 3 Commando Brigade HQ down in Plymouth and expected a team of Royal Marine Ammunition Technical Officers to help out with the moorland search first thing tomorrow. These ATOs worked in the field of bomb disposal, bringing high-tech gear and years of experience to one of *Graduate*'s toughest challenges. More bodies on the ground would enable Scenes of Crime to expand the search parameters. With luck, in the end, they'd find the magic bullet.

The phrase drew a wan smile from Houghton. Officers had been checking the handful of properties in the area, she said, but the house calls had simply confirmed that no one had heard or seen anything unusual. The nearest CCTV coverage began seven miles away. Recordings had been seized for analysis and detectives were still tracing the handful of vehicles in the area between 01.00 and 08.00 — two hours after the incident had been rung in. While these enquiries might turn up a useful lead or two, there was every indication that *Graduate* was looking at a professional killing planned in every detail. Unlikely, therefore, that the person or persons responsible would be silly enough to drive past a CCTV camera.

An audible murmur of interest rippled around the room. These men and women were all too familiar with homicide enquiries. Most killings in the force area involved petty drug debts, or random violence, or a domestic that had got out of hand, plus — in most cases — vast quantities of booze. To be faced with something a great deal subtler and more challenging was, to be frank, a bit of a windfall. Lately, faced with savage cuts in the operational budget, headquarters was cutting overtime to the bone. *Graduate*, to everyone's immense relief, promised to be a serious earner.

'So what do we know about Corrigan?' Houghton asked.

Suttle realised the question was directed his way. He stepped forward and offered a compressed account of what he knew. This was a guy, he said, with no previous. He ran a kitesurfing school on the Bay. He was thirty-one years old and had a little boy called Leo, who'd been in the back of the car when the attack took place. He shared a rented house in Paignton with a mate called Ian Goodyer and a black lady called Nicinha. This couple had been an item for several years but recently Nicinha, known as Nicky, had transferred her affections to Corrigan.

Suttle paused. He could see the disappointment on face after face. Just another domestic. Arrest by lunchtime. The guy charged by half five. Back to real life and the ever-mounting pile of unpaid bills on the kitchen table.

83

Suttle shook his head. Goodyer, he said, was an obvious suspect. He had the motivation for sure, and he may have had the opportunity, but he and Luke Golding had talked to the guy at length and his gut feeling told him that there was something more complicated going on.

Corrigan and his new girlfriend had been looking after young Leo. His natural mother, a woman called Bella Prentiss, wanted the child back. She appeared to have made a whack of money on selling the film rights to a book she'd written and lately she'd been looking for all kinds of ways to get a custody order. One of them, an organised campaign to rubbish Corrigan's parenting skills, might well have involved Goodyer. Hence — maybe — the four and a half grand the man had just exchanged for a camper van. None of this stuff, said Suttle, did Goodyer any favours, but it didn't necessarily make him the kind of super-organised killer who'd taken Corrigan's life.

'So where's Goodyer now?' This from Frank Miller, one of the older D/Cs on the squad.

Houghton stepped back in. Surveillance teams had kept Corrigan's house under obs all night, she said, back and front. The camper van was still parked outside and there was no way he could have done a runner.

'But he's a flight risk, yeah?'

'Definitely.'

'So what's the plan?'

Houghton glanced at Suttle and then at Nandy. Before they'd all left last night they'd agreed another session with Goodyer this

84

morning. This time, she said, he'd be under caution with legal representation. The interviewing team would go hard on the four and a half grand. Only if he was very thick would he miss the inference *Graduate* would be making: that he had the motive and maybe the means to have killed Corrigan and get his lovely Nicky back.

'And is he thick?' Frank Miller again.

'Not at all,' Suttle said. 'We did him for possession and supply yonks ago. The guy pulled three years. He thinks he knows the way we work. And he hates us.'

'So he *is* in the frame.'

'Of course he is. But did he actually do it?' Suttle shook his head. 'I doubt it.'

This was fighting talk, and Suttle knew it. Raising a serious query against a promising line of enquiry so soon was, at the very least, professionally reckless, but when he glanced at Nandy there was just a hint of a smile on the Det-Supt's face. Nandy had always been a man to back his own judgement. Maybe he recognised something similar in Suttle.

Houghton had moved on to today's game plan. The woman Nicky was to be re-interviewed at length. Mr Nandy wanted every last particle of her life with Goodyer and Corrigan teased out. Nicky's account would doubtless raise a number of actions — stuff she'd done with Goodyer and latterly with Corrigan, contacts they'd made, people they might have upset.

Later in the morning young Leo's natural mother and maybe her partner were due down at the hospital to pick him up. They too would be

85

interviewed at length. Mr Nandy, meanwhile, was still battling to have the post-mortem on Corrigan advanced, and with luck the first results should be available by lunchtime. A bullet in the head was enough to kill anyone but there remained an outside chance that the pathologist would come up with something else.

'Any questions?'

Suttle was watching the faces around the room. These people were canny. He'd tried to spice his briefing on the set-up at Corrigan's house as best he could and he sensed that *Graduate*'s finest suspected the investigative road ahead might be longer and a good deal trickier than Goodyer's obvious involvement suggested. This was a guy who ticked an awful lot of boxes, but there remained a deeply satisfying gap between his raging jealousy over Nicky and the corpse on a remote moorland lane. Nandy, it turned out, was thinking exactly the same.

He turned to face Suttle as the MIR began to empty. He rarely smiled.

'Nice one, son.' He gave Suttle a pat on the arm. 'Always take the racing line, eh?'

★ ★ ★

Lizzie Hodson was in the editor's office by close to ten. The morning editorial meet was over but she knew Gill Reynolds would already have laid the bait. This morning, checking her emails before leaving for work, she'd come across a message Gill must have left the previous evening:

86

'Your mum says you're out again, you old slapper. Trust you did the biz this time. FCN counts for nothing these days. I'm expecting something deeply inventive. Debrief over coffee? G. xx'. Reading the email, Lizzie had risked a tight smile. 'FCN' stood for full carnal knowledge. 'FFC', she typed back. Fat fucking chance.

The editor's name was Mark Boulton. A recent regime of early-morning runs and twice-weekly visits to the squash court had shed a lot of weight, giving his face a gauntness that Gill, no stranger to the gym, found physically off-putting. The guy looks like an Aids victim, she'd recently told Lizzie. Just who is he trying to shag?

Lizzie settled into the chair in front of the editorial desk. Gill, she knew, would have prepared the ground during the morning conference. It wasn't every day that the Pompey *News* found itself looking at a story as potentially controversial as this.

Boulton came off the phone. Gill might be right, Lizzie thought. The man looked ill.

'OK . . . ' Boulton checked his watch. 'You've got ten minutes, max.'

'Fine.'

Lizzie sketched the conversations she'd had with Rob Merrilees. The real focus, she said, was a rehab outfit down in Plymouth. Anchor it there, in Hasler Company, and the rest of the story would tell itself.

'I'm not with you.'

'What we're really up to in Afghanistan. How

we're getting it wrong. How we've pissed off the locals. How the guys come back in bits, often literally. How we're losing a war we should never have started. The politicians and the MoD are in a bad place. They know we're stuffed but they can never admit it. So maybe we should be doing it for them.'

'Who says?' Boulton was reading an email on his PC screen. 'Little you?'

'Excuse me?' Lizzie felt her pulse quickening. Debate was one thing, casual insults quite another.

Boulton's eyes at last left the screen.

'I'm sorry,' he said at once. 'But we need to source all this stuff.'

'Of course.'

'So who's saying it?'

'Rob Merrilees. He was part of the course I was guesting on. The Whale Island thing. He's a Captain in the Marines. Destined for glory.'

'And he said all that? In public?'

'Of course not.'

'So how come . . . ?'

'We talked afterwards.'

'At length?'

'Yes.'

'In what circumstances?'

'That's a question you shouldn't be asking.'

'But he's prepared to go on the record? Tell it the way it is?'

For the first time Lizzie faltered.

'He may be,' she said. 'I imagine that's up to him.'

Boulton nodded. He was far too shrewd a

88

journalist not to recognise the potential of a story like this, especially in a town as martial as Pompey. SERVING MARINE OFFICER SLAMS AFGHAN WAR EFFORT. Irresistible.

'So what would it take?' he said. 'Money?'

'No way.'

'What else?'

Lizzie said nothing, just held his gaze. Finally he smiled, then checked his watch again.

'Time's up,' he said. 'Whatever it needs, eh?'

★   ★   ★

Jimmy Suttle was at Torbay Hospital by quarter to eleven. Luke Golding had already negotiated another interview room at Torquay nick and was sorting a coffee from a machine down the corridor from the children's ward to smother the remains of Suttle's hangover. Young Leo was still under the hospital's care until his natural mother came to pick him up.

Nicky, according to the sister on the ward, had been at his bedside for nearly an hour last night before staff had encouraged her to leave. She'd tried to take Leo with her but Wendy Atkins, *Graduate*'s Family Liaison Officer, had left instructions that Leo was to await the arrival of Ms Prentiss. According to D/I Houghton, who'd sent a car to pick Nicky up for the second interview, she'd spent a doubtless tearful night at a friend's house in Brixham.

Suttle was reading Leo a story when a woman appeared at the door of the single-bedded room.

She looked late thirties, maybe a year or two younger. She was tall and striking with neatly bobbed hair and a thin coat of scarlet lipgloss. She wore a simple linen suit, no jewellery, and the paleness of her face was accentuated by sunglasses. She radiated money and good taste. Her sole concession to what must have been an important occasion was a small teddy bear tucked beneath one arm. The bear, like everything else about her, looked box-fresh.

Golding stepped round her with a coffee. They must have met in the corridor.

'Bella Prentiss,' he said. 'D/S Suttle.'

Suttle abandoned the book and got to his feet. Her token handshake was icy, the eyes invisible behind the sunglasses. Leo, trying to retrieve the book, didn't appear to recognise her.

'Is your partner with you?' Suttle asked.

Prentiss shook her head.

'I'm parked outside,' she said. 'I've got fifteen minutes before the rates get silly.'

Suttle was reaching for his jacket, wondering about the light American accent. Was this an affectation? A boast? Or would a couple of months in the States really change the way you talked?

'I'm afraid you'll be coming with us first, Ms Prentiss. We'll drive you back when we're through.'

'Come where?'

'Torquay police station.'

'Why on earth would I want to do that?'

Suttle studied her for a moment. It was hard to be certain but he thought he detected a flicker of irritation in the tightness of her mouth.

'I'm not sure that's a question I can answer,' he said. 'Until we've had a chance to talk.'

* * *

At Torquay nick Suttle left Golding to take Prentiss through to the interview room while he made a call to Carole Houghton. Ian Goodyer had been at Paignton police station for a couple of hours now and Suttle wanted an update. He listened to the D/I's account and then returned the mobile to his pocket. The civvy behind the enquiry desk had recognised Prentiss when she'd walked through.

'I went to school with that woman,' she said. 'And she was a real pain.'

The interview began badly. Suttle had made it clear that Prentiss wasn't under caution, that he simply wanted to clarify certain issues arising from her former partner's death, and that a degree of cooperation would make life easier all round.

'For whom, exactly?'

'For us, Ms Prentiss. And maybe for you as well. One way or another we have to bottom this thing out. People don't get shot without good reason. It's our job to find out why.'

'I see. Should I have said yes to a lawyer? Do you think I was being hasty?'

'That's your decision. You're welcome to legal representation. It might take a while to sort out. You want me to make a call?'

She frowned and then checked her watch. She

91

was still wearing the sunglasses. At length she shook her head.

'Let's just do it,' she said. 'What do you want to know?'

Suttle asked her about meeting Corrigan. How long had she known him? How quickly had the relationship become important to them both? These questions appeared to take her by surprise. She'd come to pick up her son. Not open her heart to a couple of strangers.

'We first met three or four years ago. I was doing some work with a couple of local musicians. Michael shared a house with one of them.'

'This would be Ian Goodyer?'

'Yes.' She frowned. 'You know Ian?'

'We've talked to him.'

'I see.' Her head went down for a moment or two, then she looked up again. 'Ian's a flaky guy. You should take that into account.'

'In what way?'

'He's a fantasist. He lives in a world of his own. Sometimes he and the truth can be strangers.'

'You're telling me he lies?'

'I'm telling you he kids himself so I guess you're right. Sure.' The curtest of nods. 'He lies.'

Suttle wanted to get back to Corrigan. Where, exactly, had they met?

'I just told you. At the house.'

'And the relationship took off from there?'

'Yeah, it did. Like relationships do.'

'You moved in?'

'Not right away. But yeah, sure, it happened.'

92

She was frowning again. 'What's any of this got to do with Michael getting killed?'

Suttle ignored the question. He badly wanted this woman to take her shades off but knew he had no right to insist. He needed to see her eyes. He needed to get past the irritation and the icy self-control. He needed a way in.

'Ian gave us the impression you and Michael were pretty full-on.'

'Did he?'

'Yes. So when did the baby come along?'

'Ten months after we met.' For the first time, the hint of a smile. 'So I guess Ian's right. Full-on pretty much nails it. Michael was a good-looking guy. We enjoyed each other. It was fun.'

'So what happened?'

'Leo. You know that already.'

'I meant afterwards.'

'I became a mother.'

'You did. And then I understand you left.'

Prentiss nodded, said nothing. Then she switched her attention to Golding, bending towards him the way you might share a confidence with an old friend.

'Is this what this is about? Are you charging me with desertion? Maybe a lawyer might be a neater idea than I thought.'

'D/S Suttle simply wants to know the way things were,' Golding said. 'It would help if you just answered the question.'

'There wasn't a question. You seem to have this thing taped already. The wanton lover. The callous mother. Do I get a say in any of this?'

'Go ahead.' Suttle again. 'Just tell us what happened.'

'I took charge of my life. That's what happened.'

'How?'

'By writing a book, if you really want to know. Why did I do that? Because everything else was driving me insane. Was it hard? It was the most difficult thing I ever did in my life. Was it any *good?* No, not really, not good enough to find a publisher, but yeah, it worked the way it needed to because it got me an agent, and that led to places I'd only ever dreamed about.'

'This agent has a name?'

'Of course he has a name. Everyone has a name. His name is Sy Rosen, but I guess you'd know that already because Ian would have told you.'

'This is the guy who became your new partner?'

'My husband. As of last week.'

'But he's the man you left Michael for?'

'Michael and I were history. We had a great time while it lasted but you should never confuse real life with great sex.'

'And Leo?'

'Leo was a casualty. Sy loved my first book. He loved the writing. He knew I could do it. He knew he could sell me. All I needed was a proper story, and he was generous enough to put one my way.'

'About what?'

She was revved up now, Suttle could feel it. The real story was what had happened to her, what she'd done with her life, and here was yet another opportunity to share a boast or two. How many times had she been in this situation? Pitching herself across a table?

Sy, she said, had come across a guy in a bar in Los Angeles who'd told him a story about wetbacks smuggled across the Rio Grande into the remote hill country in western Texas. These were young guys from Mexico who'd do literally anything in exchange for an American passport. A wealthy businessman who owned a ranch gave them board and lodging. Every other Saturday, before a small invited audience of like-minded buddies, they'd fight each other, *mano a mano*, one on one. The winner got the passport. The loser died.

Sy, she said, had no idea whether this story about illegals fighting each other to the death was true or not, but he'd known at once that it would make the basis for a great feature film. First, though, he had to get it out there in book form. It had to be sharp. It had to be compelling. And above all it had to be credible.

'And he asked you to write it?'

'He did. And you know who came up with the killer twist? Me.'

One of the young wetbacks, she said, would turn out to be a woman. Not just a woman, but the once-lover of the guy she had to fight. Hollywood producers just loved big splashy moral dilemmas. And here was one of the splashiest.

'I'm not with you.' Suttle was lost.

'The guy had really loved her. Really, *really*

loved her. But how far would he take that passion? Would he let her kill him? Would he *die* for her?'

Suttle let the question hang in the air between them. There was something deeply disturbing about this woman, about the way this bizarre fantasy had made her come alive. Were there any limits to what she'd do for fame and fortune? What else might she have done if real life got in her way?

'So what happened?' he said at last.

'In the story, you mean?'

'Yes.'

'No chance.' The smile this time was broader. 'Either you read the book or wait for the movie.'

'You wrote the movie too?'

'It's in development. Sy negotiated a co-writer deal. That's unusual, believe me, but then my husband's an unusual guy.'

One of the reasons, she said, for not seeing enough of Leo recently was all the research she'd had to do. A month and a half in Texas and Mexico had given her a feel for the people and the locations, and then she'd camped in LA for another five months while the script came together. Draft thirteen, she said, was looking promising, but she'd had no idea what a pain in the arse Hollywood could be. The producers had raised seventeen million dollars to fund the movie, and for that kind of money you had to live with trillions of fingers in the editorial pie. Endless script conferences. Endless rewrites. Lots of stressing about this line or that. In the end her co-writer had quit, which was nice because it left her with a solo credit, but the fact was you had to be tough to survive out there.

'And you were tough?'

'I *am* tough. You bet. This is ongoing.'

'So where does Leo fit in?'

'Leo is my son. Sy's stepson. And therefore *our* son.'

'But you're in the States.'

'Only sometimes. The heavy lifting is over. And we have help. Lots of help. A dream of a girl. Jelena. Slovenian. Leo's going to love her.'

She was relaxed now, almost radiant, and Suttle glimpsed the kind of woman Mick Corrigan must have fallen in love with: eager, ambitious, driven, and to a certain kind of man deeply fanciable.

'So when did you decide to get Leo back?'

'When he had a home to come to. When I had proper time for him. When Sy and I had sorted ourselves out.'

'And when would that be?'

'Around Christmas I got in touch with Michael, told him what I wanted, what I thought was best for Leo.'

'And what did he say?'

'You want the truth?'

'Yes, please.'

'He told me to fuck off. He said I'd never been there for Leo. He said I'd never properly figured in his life.'

'And was he right?'

'Yeah, I guess he was. He also told me I was a selfish bitch and I'd no right even making the call. Leo was happy where he was. They'd got everything sorted. He even had a proper mum at last. But you'd know all this already. Ian would have told you.'

'You're right. He did. This was after Nicky had started a relationship with Michael, yes?'

'Sure. Interesting dynamic in that little house. Ian's a control freak, classic example, older guy, clever, manipulative, bit of an obsessive. Nicky had always done his bidding until Leo came along. Then I left and Michael was on his own with the baby, and I guess that changed everything.'

'So how did Ian feel? About Nicky?'

'Bitter as hell. Nicky belonged to him. He had sole rights. He felt he'd been robbed.'

'He told you that?'

'No. He didn't have to. This is a story that tells itself.'

This is a story that tells itself.

Suttle scribbled himself a note, wondering whether this woman ever had a problem working out exactly where fiction took over from real life. Keeping your bearings in a world you'd half-created must sometimes be a challenge.

'Ian says you gave him five thousand pounds for certain information. Is that true?'

'I beg your pardon?' The shades at last came off. Green eyes. Ice-cold.

Suttle repeated the allegation. Maybe she was right about Ian. Maybe this was a guy who'd do anything that might bring Nicky back to him. And if that meant grassing up his old mate, then so be it.

'He *said* that?'

'Yes. A couple of hours ago. In interview. Under caution.'

'So what might he be offering for five thousand pounds?'

Suttle tallied the mounting pressures that Corrigan and Nicky had been under: rats in the property, a dodgy gas boiler, and finally the suspicion that Leo's new mum might have been on the game.

'And I gave him five thousand pounds? For having some hand in *that?*'

'That's the allegation. He says he was your ears and eyes inside the house. Do you deny it?'

'Of course I do. Where's the proof? Did I send him a cheque?'

'He says cash. He says you came down specially. He says you met at the station, gave him the money, and then took the train back to London.'

'But why? Why would I do something like that?'

'Because you wanted the baby back. Are you denying that was the case?'

'Of course not. Leo is my child. A mother has rights. It was a shame that Sy and I had to hire lawyers, but Michael wasn't even up for a conversation. In a situation like that you have no choice.'

'And what was your lawyer's advice?'

'He said we'd have to take it to a tribunal. We had a strong case. In the end he was sure we'd get custody.'

'Because you're the natural mother?'

'Of course.'

Suttle bent to his pad again. Prentiss watched

him note the lawyer's contact details.

'You don't believe me?'

'We check everything, Ms Prentiss. That's our job.' He paused. 'Ian says he contacted you by phone on a number of occasions.'

'That's right. He did. He was always on about Michael.'

'Why would he have done that?'

'God knows. Maybe it was cheaper than therapy.'

'He says he was giving you the information you'd paid for. Keeping you up to date.'

'Then he's lying again. This is a guy who lives in his head. He's in a bad place, Ian. I think I mentioned it.'

'He also said you'd promised him some kind of a bonus if he could come up with information your lawyer could use in the tribunal.'

'That's crap. Fairy tales. Make-believe. I never gave him a penny. That man's a lost cause and I don't do lost causes.'

Suttle nodded, taking his time. Then he leaned forward over the table.

'Ian paid four and a half thousand pounds to a car dealer yesterday afternoon. Where do you suggest that money came from?'

'I haven't a clue. Maybe Michael might have known.'

'Sure.' Suttle nodded. 'Shame we can't ask him, eh?'

There was a long silence. Prentiss was toying with her glasses, avoiding Suttle's gaze. Golding asked her whether she wanted a drink of water. She shook her head but said nothing.

At length Suttle asked her exactly where she'd been last night.

'In Salisbury,' she said. 'With Sy.'

'Did you go out at all?'

'No.'

'Did you take any calls?'

'A few.'

'We'll need to check them all. How many phones have you got?'

'Me, you mean? Personally?'

'Between you.'

She frowned, doing the sums.

'Seven,' she said. 'Three landlines and four mobiles.'

'I'll need the numbers. We'll access the billing records and see what we come up with.'

'Is that some kind of warning?'

'Not at all. If you're telling us the truth, the conversation ends here. If you're not . . . ' Suttle shrugged and pushed his chair away from the table.

Prentiss didn't move. At length she attempted a smile.

'I need to know what you're suggesting,' she said. 'I need to know the story here. Do you think I had something to do with what happened to Michael? Is that it?'

'I don't know. Not yet.'

'But you think it's a possibility?'

'Of course. Everything's a possibility until we can rule it out.'

'I see.' She glanced at Golding and then got to her feet. 'So can I have my baby now? Is that OK?'

5

Lizzie was at her desk when the email arrived. She could see Gill Reynolds sitting back in her chair on the other side of the big open-plan newsroom, looking across at Lizzie, a broad smile on her face. 'Guess who's just been asked to suss out supporting copy for an Afghan special? Stiffietime or what? xxx'.

Stiffietime was journo-speak for a state of high excitement. When a particular occasion justified the punt, the *News* would invest time and money in special supplements. These glossy publications were sold alongside the paper and normally marked a big public event: a fleet review out in Spithead, a D-Day anniversary or — when Pompey were still a proper football team — an FA Cup final. To make that kind of splash with a regular news story would be a real departure, but already Lizzie could see the editorial logic behind the decision.

Portsmouth had always been a city with war in its DNA. Generation after generation had been bred and schooled in the export of serious violence, and there were hundreds of local families who carried the scars to prove it. It would be child's play for Gill to lay her hands on Pompey mums who'd lost a cherished son to a Taliban IED. Another couple of phone calls

102

would establish the huge sums that had sustained the military campaign over the last decade. Gill could source a guy from one of the big logistics companies who'd tally the endless supply convoys that bumped through the mountains to Camp Bastion. And she'd doubtless be talking to the medics, often reservists, who dispatched the worst of the wounded back to the UK. Not just blood, Lizzie thought, but treasure too.

She bent to her keyboard, trying to work out how to reply. She'd no idea whether Rob Merrilees would agree to share his disgust at what was happening with the rest of the nation but equally she had absolutely no doubt about the impact an interview like this would have. Mark Boulton had recognised it from the start. As had Gill. The story would be very big indeed. It would play locally. It would be picked up by the nationals. It would make it onto TV and the Internet. And the byline, with everything that implied, would be hers.

Gill, across the newsroom, was waiting for a reply.

'Early days,' Lizzie wrote. 'But watch this space.'

★ ★ ★

Nandy had disappeared for a private phone conference with the Chief Constable when Suttle got back to the MIR. Carole Houghton was in her office with two of her star D/Cs, Simon Maffett and Rosie Tremayne.

103

Tremayne was a quietly spoken woman in her late thirties. Married to a vicar in one of Exeter's tougher parishes, she had the knack of allowing interviewees to seriously underestimate her, a mistake they rarely made twice.

Maffett was nearly a decade older, a big cheerful Cornishman with grown-up kids and a lifelong passion for rugby. He had a gift for getting alongside the bad guys, for winning their trust and their confidence, and even after he'd talked them into confessing, they still seemed to think he'd done them a favour. In this respect he reminded Suttle of Paul Winter, the renegade Pompey detective to whom he owed a very special apprenticeship: same MO, same matey charm, same reputation for stitching up the opposition with a smile on his face.

At Houghton's invitation, Suttle sank into the spare chair. Tremayne, it turned out, had been lead on the interview with Nicky, while Maffett had been in with Ian Goodyer.

'How was he?' Suttle asked.

'Bloody upset.' Maffett smiled. 'I was just telling Carole. Once he'd sussed he was seriously in the frame for Corrigan, he pretty much lost it.'

Goodyer, he said, had denied point-blank any involvement in the moor killing. Yes, he'd been pissed off that Corrigan had nicked his woman. And yes, he'd bought the van to try and spirit Nicky out of the country. But no way would he have killed someone who — until recently — had been his best mate. For one thing, he hated loud bangs. And for another, he was a veggie.

'He *said* that?'

'Yeah.' Maffett was laughing now. 'He seemed to think that was the clincher.'

'Only meat-eaters kill people?'

'Exactly. Carnivores was the word he used. Sweet, eh?'

As agreed pre-interview, Maffett had pressed him on the money he'd somehow acquired to pay for the van. Alarmed by the realisation that he might get stitched up yet again, this time for murder, Goodyer had blamed young Leo's natural mum. Prentiss, he'd said, had bunged him five grand to come up with ways to smooth the path to a successful custody hearing. Hence the sequence of visits from various inspectorates.

'That was his doing?'

'Yeah.'

'Including all the stuff about Nicky?'

'Absolutely. He said she had it coming to her. He said she deserved it. One night she was in his bed, the next she's kipping with Corrigan. According to his own account, that's when he lost it. He said he went potty for a while, wasn't really responsible for his actions.'

'You believed him?'

'I believe he was crazy about her. And the way I see it, he probably still is. The guy's missing a fuse or two. You can see it in his eyes. Mad.'

'But he didn't kill Corrigan?'

'No way. Not in my book.'

'Or find someone else to do it for him?'

Maffett shrugged. If Suttle meant hiring a hit man to exact Goodyer's own revenge, he'd say no. If, on the other hand, he'd been acting as an agent for someone else — like Prentiss — then it might be a different outcome.

'But it's the same, isn't it? Either way, his best mate gets a bullet through his head.'

'Ex-best mate.'

'Sure. But it still boils down to murder.'

Maffett nodded, said nothing. Houghton was looking at Suttle.

'Prentiss?' she enquired.

Suttle summarised the interview. Bella Prentiss, he said, was one of the oddest interviewees he'd ever encountered. Success and serious money appeared to have spared her the treadmill of real life, a process that writing a best-seller could only have accelerated. She seemed curiously weightless, as if the rules of gravity no longer applied. The only thing that interested her was getting Leo back. Asked whether she'd paid Goodyer to make life tough for Corrigan, she'd flatly denied it. Invited to comment on whether or not she might have had some hand in her ex-partner's death, she'd dismissed the possibility out of hand. She seemed to float above the chore of detailed rebuttal. In short, she'd become a character in one of her own stories.

'So what do you think?'

'I think we do the usual. Phone billing. Production orders on all their accounts.'

'Their?'

'She's just got married to her agent, to the guy who made her rich. There'll be business accounts. It won't be easy. These are people who are used to getting their own way.'

'So what do you think?' Houghton asked again.

'I think she definitely has the means and definitely has the motive. Money buys everything in her world, and getting rid of Corrigan, if it had to happen, would be a minor detail.'

'Tidying up?' This from Tremayne.

'Exactly.' Suttle nodded. 'The way I see it, this woman's almost autistic. What matters in her world is getting to where she wants to be. Everything else is conversation.'

'That's what Nicky said. Not in those words, but pretty close.'

Tremayne described the interview with Nicky. The prospect of losing Leo had concentrated her mind wonderfully, and once she'd got over the tears, she'd been a dream interviewee.

'She first met Prentiss years back. She was working part-time as a fortune-teller and she did a reading for Prentiss as a favour. Even then she was struck by how determined she was, and how impatient. She needed to *know*, to be certain, to rule out chance or fate as any kind of factors in her life. Nicky had tried to point out that fate was everything, that it was the spirits who were really in charge, who mapped out where you were going, but apparently Prentiss just laughed. What she'd put in was what she'd get out. Fate, in other words, was in her own hands.'

'So why go to a fortune-teller?' Houghton asked.

'Because she wanted confirmation. And a timetable.'

'And Nicky gave her that?'

'Nicky told her she'd have a baby. Soon. And

107

that it would be a boy. On both counts she was right.'

'Impressive.'

'Not really.' Tremayne permitted herself a smile. 'She and Goodyer were sharing the house by then. And Prentiss and Corrigan were forever at it. Prentiss had no time for contraception so a baby had to be odds-on.'

'A son?'

'Fifty-fifty.' Tremayne glanced across at Suttle. 'Nicky's an honest woman. I've no idea whether she communes with the spirits, but her take on Prentiss is exactly yours. She never used the word autistic but that's pretty much what she meant. This was a woman in a very big hurry. Success was more important than her own son. Until the day arrived when he might deserve a place in her life.'

'Fucking sad.'

'It is. Especially for Nicky.'

'And Leo?'

'Who knows? I'm sure he'll get the best of everything. Whether that amounts to mother-hood . . . ' Tremayne shrugged.

Houghton stirred. D/Cs kept appearing outside her door. Time was short.

'So where are we?' She was looking at Suttle. 'Aside from phones and bank accounts?'

'We need to develop Prentiss,' he said. 'In my view she's pissed off with the time it's taking to get Leo back. She's spent a fortune on lawyers and probably blown another five grand on Goodyer, but there's no absolute guarantee that a tribunal will see it her way. Impatience is the key. This is a woman who takes the shortest of short cuts. She wants to shag the arse off Corrigan? No problem, job done. Writing a best-seller that might take her to where she wants to be? She gets her head down and does it. A year later she's rich and successful and sitting in some Hollywood pad writing the film script of her dreams. Doing all this stuff tells her that it's often smart to be creative when it comes to a problem. Corrigan is a problem. On the page, the way she writes it, the guy would be history by chapter Two.'

'This is real life, Jimmy.' Houghton was trying to be gentle.

'I know, boss. But London's where we should be putting in some effort. That's where she lives during the week. Ten grand would buy a quality hit, especially these days.'

Houghton scribbled herself a note. The Met kept an index of contract killers. Maybe Suttle was right. Maybe that's where *Graduate* should be turning next.

'You want me to handle that, boss?'

'No.' Houghton shook her head. 'We've been trying to raise Erika all morning but no joy.'

'Erika?'

'Corrigan's lady friend out on the moor. Erika Maier. We left a message on her phone. She called back about an hour ago. She's back home.' She got to her feet and stifled a yawn. 'Yours, I think, Jimmy. Luke's got the details.'

★ ★ ★

Suttle and Golding were out on the eastern edges of the moor within striking distance of Erika Maier's place within the hour. The drive had taken them down the lane Suttle recognised from yesterday's shooting. Driving past a line of vans tucked into the verge, he spotted a glint of sunshine from tiny shards of glass at the edge of the road. He stopped to explain to Golding exactly the way it had been: Corrigan slumped behind the wheel, his eyes still open, splats of blood and brain tissue smearing the window surrounds behind him.

Golding was gazing out at the moor. Half a dozen of Nandy's promised Marine ATOs were thigh-deep in the heather about 150 metres away, still hunting for the bullet that had killed Corrigan. Then he looked down at the road again and noticed a tiny smear of what looked like white paint on the tarmac.

'Scenes of Crime,' Suttle said. 'Just in case they have to come back.'

Golding nodded. He was leaning forward now, checking out the view on the other side. The lane was unhedged. A field beyond a line of barbed wire sloped gently upwards. Beyond the stone wall at the top were half a dozen sheep.

'Seat belt?' Golding asked.

'Still secured.'

'No attempt to get out, then?'

'Not that I could see.'

'So maybe he knew the guy.'

'Sure. Or maybe the guy knew his business.' Suttle drew a bead on Golding's head with two fingers. 'Bam. End of.'

Minutes later, they rounded a bend in the single-track lane and stopped. A Devon long-house lay beneath them, accessed by a hairpin drive knobbly with shards of rock. A modern extension, unlovely but functional, had been added relatively recently, and the extensive paddock at the back of the property was dotted with sheep.

Golding lowered the passenger window. Above the sigh of the wind Suttle could hear the barking of dogs.

They bumped down to the farmhouse and got out. Suttle pocketed the keys, tilting his nose to the wind. He could smell woodsmoke and the sweetness of horse dung. Chickens were pecking for scraps in the L formed by the extension, and a couple of cats lazed — untroubled — in the hot sun. Suttle threw Golding a look and grinned. There were definitely worse places in the world than this if you fancied a quiet life. No wonder Corrigan had been so keen.

A tug on the bell pull brought a woman to the door. She was very tanned, very lean. She wore a pair of patched jeans and a T-shirt. The Hendrix face on the T-shirt had been bleached to a ghost by years of moorland weather. She had a serpent tattoo which coiled around her wrist and snaked along her middle finger, the forked tongue darting towards her knuckle. She stood barefoot on the flagstones, a single toenail painted black. Her age Suttle put at mid-forties, maybe a year or two older. She looked, to borrow Golding's favourite word, fit.

'Erika Maier? D/S Suttle. Major Crime. My colleague phoned earlier.'

Suttle nodded at Golding. Golding couldn't take his eyes off the Great Dane lurking in the semi-darkness of the hall.

'You don't like dogs?' The German accent was lighter than Suttle had expected. She seemed amused.

'Hate them,' he muttered. 'Got bitten as a nipper.'

'Nipper?' She laughed, turning to give the dog a pat. 'She's harmless. Be nice to her and she'll lick you to death.'

They talked in the kitchen. The room occupied one end of the longhouse and reflected exactly the degree of domestic chaos that Suttle had come to love. Piles of unwashed plates in the kitchen sink. A corkboard jigsawed with fading snaps. A scatter of magazines and sundry post on the kitchen table. Stubs of candles on chipped white saucers. Yet another cat.

Suttle, perched on a stool, wanted to know about Corrigan. How long had Erika known him? How close had they become?

'Close?' The assumption appeared to take her by surprise.

'Yes.'

'You think we were . . . ' She was pouring boiling water into a cafetière ' . . . together?'

'Yes.'

'No.' She shook her head. 'I have a partner of my own. Michael knew that.'

'But you looked after his son? Leo?'

'Of course. We were friends. I liked him a lot. I helped with Leo when I could. Sometimes we'd go for a drink together when I was down in Paignton. But that's all we were. Just friends.' She paused, looking up from the cafetière. 'What's happened is horrible. Why would someone do something like that? To Michael?'

'Very good question.'

Suttle asked about the life she led out here on the moor. He wanted to get a feel for the kind of woman that Corrigan might have found attractive, the kind of company in which he might have opened his heart. She had amazing eyes, porcelain-blue, and a frankness that would unsettle most men.

Erika passed the coffee round. Golding found himself nursing an Exeter City mug, badged with the club's colours.

'I've been here nearly ten years,' she said. 'I came from Zimbabwe. You could call me a refugee.'

'From the regime?'

'From a bad marriage. I was lucky. I got out early. Never marry a German tobacco farmer. Divorce makes you wiser. And if you're lucky, a little bit rich.'

'This place is yours?'

'Yes. Absolutely. It's mine and no one else's. I do what I like. It's what Zim should have been.'

'Without the sunshine.'

'*Ja*.' She smiled. 'And without my husband.'

Golding and the Great Dane were still eyeing each other. Long threads of saliva hung from an immense maw. If Erika was serious about the licking, Golding was in for a treat. He dragged his attention back to Erika.

'You mentioned a partner,' he said.

'I did. He's with me sometimes. He's a photographer. He works for magazines. He makes videos too. For television. He travels everywhere. When he's back it's nice. But when he's not — ' she shrugged ' — it's nice also.'

'Did Corrigan know him?'

'Of course. Why do you ask?'

Golding didn't answer. The Great Dane was edging closer to his stool. Suttle could hear the scrape of its claws on the slate floor. *Give me a pat. Tell me you love me.*

Suttle turned his attention back to Erika, sparing Golding the effort of more questions.

'How much did you know about the set-up in Michael's house?' he asked.

'You mean with the child? Leo?'

'Yeah. And with everything else.'

'Like?'

'Nicky. And the other man, Ian Goodyer.'

'I know Nicky. She's lovely, that woman. She was the one person who kept Michael sane. There were lots of Nickys in Zim. African women have something special. I always said it.'

'And Michael knew that?'

'Michael adored her. He really loved her. It was nice to see.'

Nice to see. Nicky had said exactly the same about Corrigan and Bella Prentiss in the early days.

'What about the child? Leo?'

'Leo was what brought them together. Without

114

Leo maybe nothing would have happened. It was Leo who made Michael a better person, by bringing Nicky to his bed.'

'But what about Bella? Leo's natural mother?'

'She left.'

'I know that. But did Michael miss her?'

'Of course he did. I never knew this woman, never met her, but I know what she did to Michael. After she left he was hopeless, broken, not a man at all. Nicky changed all that.'

'And you?'

'Me?'

'Michael would have talked to you, told you things.'

'Sure.'

'So what did he say?'

Erika hesitated, seeming to weigh the question, seeming to decide quite how far to go. Finally she eased off her stool, dragged the Great Dane out of the kitchen and shut the door.

'You want the truth? The truth about Michael? Why maybe this terrible thing happened to him?'

Suttle nodded, said nothing. Golding had slumped on his stool, his face flooded with relief.

Erika retrieved her coffee, leaning back on the Aga.

'The last time I saw Michael was last week,' she said. 'He was very upset. He came out here to the house. He stayed for a meal. We had a lot to drink. I tried to make things better for him.'

'How?'

'By listening. By talking. By telling him he was crazy to say the things he said.'

'What did he say?'

'He said that it was becoming impossible with Leo. He said that woman had too much money. He said it wasn't a fair fight, that she was bound to win, that she was bound to get Leo back. He'd had lots of letters from lawyers in London. He didn't think he had a chance.'

'So what did he do?'

'He said he'd take Leo abroad. Either that or something worse, something terrible, something you'd never imagine.'

'Like what?'

Erika was frowning now. Her head was down and she was gazing at her hands. With her cropped blonde hair she looked about twelve. Finally, she looked up.

'He said he'd kill them both. He said he'd end it all.'

'You mean him and Leo?'

'Yes.'

'You think he meant it?'

'Yes. I think he was depressed. And a little bit crazy.'

'So what did you say?'

'I told him he was mad. And I told him something else too.'

'What?'

'I told him that maybe he should be honest.'

'With who?'

'With Bella. She needed to know how much Leo mattered to him. To Nicky too. To both of them.'

'You mean he should tell her what he told you? About ending it all?'

'Yes.'

'And do you think he did that? Do you think he took your advice?'

'I know he did. He called her.'

'From here?' Suttle raised an eyebrow.

'Yes. He was very drunk.'

'And what did Bella say?'

'She said nothing. Except that she didn't believe him.'

'And then?'

'She put the phone down.'

★　★　★

Suttle rang D/I Houghton from the car as soon as the interview was over. Golding was still in the farmhouse, admiring more of the photos that Erika had selected from her partner's portfolio. She'd framed them and hung them in the hall that led to the front door. A single glance on the way out had told Suttle the guy was attracted to combat situations: black kids toting AK-47s in some African civil war, the shell-blasted remains of an apartment block in what could have been Chechnya, Brit squaddies crouching in an Afghan rotor storm from a departing Chinook. And one of the same guys, stripped to the waist, making a big fuss of some local dog. What seemed to link these images was a fascination with — almost a celebration of — the bittersweet madness of war. Strange way to earn a living, Suttle thought.

Houghton finally answered.

'I'm in conference,' she said. 'Can this wait?'

Suttle told her briefly about Erika Maier.

Corrigan, she said, had been threatening to do a runner. Either that, or kill himself and the child.

'Did Prentiss know?'

'Yeah. He phoned her up and told her.'

'Like some kind of threat?'

'I guess so.'

'Jesus.'

'Exactly.'

Houghton told him to hang on. Suttle could hear another voice in the background. Nandy, he thought. Readying himself for the evening squad meet.

'There's something else you ought to know.' Houghton again. 'We just got word from the pathologist. Cause of death was the bullet but he's puzzled by the absence of residues on Corrigan's face. Point-blank range, you'd expect to find them. They weren't there.'

'Meaning?'

'We're not sure. I talked to Scenes of Crime just now. They collected most of the glass from both the vehicle windows and they'll be doing tests. If they draw a blank on the residues, we might have a problem. Either way, Mr Nandy's expecting you back by six.'

She rang off, leaving Suttle gazing at the phone. Losing the battle for an earlier PM would have seriously pissed off the Det-Supt, and now *Graduate* was faced with a piece of forensic evidence that questioned every assumption they'd made to date. Shooting someone at close range always left a tell-tale dusting of powder from the discharge. If that hadn't happened, then how else might someone have put a bullet

118

through Corrigan's pretty head?

Suttle thought himself back to the moment he'd arrived beside the VW yesterday morning. The sight of the body slumped behind the wheel had pretty much stopped him in his tracks but even then something had snagged at the back of his mind. Something was missing and only now did he realise what it was. Modern smokeless gunpowder left a smell you could never mistake for anything else. It was bitter, acrid, a harsh chemical irritant that left a greasiness at the back of your throat, and hours later it would still be there. Yet standing beside the VW, staring down at Corrigan's shattered skull, he'd smelled nothing.

Suttle glanced at his watch, then reached for his mobile again. As Crime Scene Manager, Terry Bryant had a desk in the MIR. He answered on the second ring.

Suttle explained he was out on the moor.

'And?' Bryant wanted to move the conversation on.

'Tell me something. Did you put some kind of marker on the road after Corrigan's Golf was collected?'

'I'm not with you.'

'White paint? Chalk? Whatever?'

'Why would we do that?'

'In case you had to come back?'

There was a brief pause in the conversation. Bryant was talking to someone else. Then he was back on the phone, more impatient than ever.

'We have a photographer,' he said. 'You may

have met him. Harry Baines. Nice man. Great snaps. So why would we need white paint?'

* * *

Suttle and Golding were a couple of minutes late for the evening squad meet. Nandy was addressing the troops. *Graduate*, he said, had made significant progress over the last twenty-four hours. Ian Goodyer had been released on police bail, his passport confiscated until further notice. Nicky had made a full statement about the time she'd spent in the Paignton house, and had corroborated much of Goodyer's account. Prime suspect in the case was Bella Prentiss, young Leo's natural mother, and most of *Graduate*'s resources would now be concentrated on unpicking her denial of any involvement in her ex-partner's death. In the light of Corrigan's threat to end it all, she had a powerful motivation for pre-empting that possibility, and she had more than enough money to buy a hit. Tying her and her partner to a conspiracy charge would now be *Graduate*'s top priority.

There were very few questions. Suttle joined Houghton and Nandy in the D/I's office afterwards. Neither had yet to hear Suttle's latest thinking.

He explained about the marker in the road. Nandy was studying his watch.

'How do you know it's a marker?'

'I don't, sir. But it was plumb beside what was left of the glass. That's exactly where the hit happened.'

120

'Seagull shit?'

'Definitely paint. We stopped on the way back, checked it out.'

'So what are you saying?'

'I'm not saying anything, sir. I'm just suggesting we need to revisit our thinking about the way this thing might have happened.'

Nandy nodded. In the wake of the findings from the PM, he and Houghton had clearly come to the same conclusion.

'And?'

'I think we're talking a long-distance hit. Someone with a rifle. If that's the case, then you want to minimise the odds. A moving target could be dodgy. Much better if the car stops.'

'Or is stopped?' This from Houghton.

'Exactly, boss. I'm thinking two guys, not one. One stops the car. The other does the business.'

'Hence the marker?'

'Yeah.'

Nandy was at last looking interested.

'So where's the advantage?' he said.

Suttle had anticipated this question. He and Golding had talked it through on the way back.

'These are guys who know what they're doing,' he began. 'That's an assumption we can comfortably make. The issue is evidence. They don't want to make it easy for us. They don't want to leave a single clue.'

'Agreed.'

'So think about the bullet, sir. Use a handgun, and it could go anywhere. It might lodge in the car somewhere. It might even stay inside the guy's head. Then we have a definite lead. Use something heftier, like a high-powered rifle, and you're home free. Especially if you've been canny about the spot you've chosen to make the hit.'

Suttle described the shape of the moorland in the vicinity of the VW. The road, he said, was slightly elevated on a kind of embankment. He explained the way the field to the right sloped gently upwards, a tumble of rough heather falling abruptly away on the other side of the road.

'Choose the right spot and the guy with the rifle can see nothing but thin air beyond the target. This can still be short range, maybe fifty metres. Use the right kind of bullet and it's going to do you a very big favour. Number one it nearly takes the guy's head off. And number two it probably ends up half a mile away.'

'And afterwards?'

'You make your excuses and leave. Job done.'

Nandy nodded.

'So what are you suggesting?' he said.

'I'm suggesting we might revisit the field above the road just in case there's anything we missed first time round. I'm also suggesting we've got a useful set of parameters when it comes to the Met index. How many contract hitmen specialise in long-range jobs? There can't be that many.'

'Good.' Nandy nodded. 'And the woman, Prentiss?'

'Still in the frame. She's obviously someone who shops around, gives every purchase a bit of thought. One way or another I get the feeling she's only interested in the best. Fuck knows how much these guys must have cost her.'

Nandy glanced at Houghton, who was already on the point of phoning Scenes of Crime. Suttle lifted his hand to stop her.

'Something else, Jimmy?'

'No, boss. Except I ought to come clean. I agree it's a neat piece of deduction. But it's Luke you should be thanking, not me.'

★　★　★

Lizzie got the text as she was walking home. The offices of the Portsmouth *News* were on the northern edge of the island, as was Anchorage Park, out on the eastern shore. Lizzie's path took her along the low swell of nineteenth-century fortifications known as Hilsea Lines. If you ever wanted proof that Pompey had grown up on a diet of blood and treasure, then here it was. These days the thin belt of woodland was the haunt of joggers and trysting gays, but remnants of the brick-built defences were still visible through the summer foliage, and it didn't take much to people these battlements with generations of uniformed young scrappers pledged to defend the city against all-comers.

Lizzie stepped into the shade of a nearby beech tree and opened the text. It was brief. 'Hasler Company sorted,' it read. 'Can you make it at the weekend? Bed and breakfast on me. Lucky you. xxx'. Lizzie read the text again, her spirits lifting. By close of play, fending off yet another email from Gill, she'd half-convinced herself that Rob Merrilees had been a figment of her imagination, a fantasy she'd conjured from

God knows where, a small but precious moment of release from the treadmill of motherhood and a faltering career. She loved her job. The best part of a year in the numbing silence of East Devon had taught her how precious it was. She was good at it too, yet she knew, like everyone else in the newsroom, that the days of the provincial press were probably numbered and she'd be mad to think otherwise. Only something really special would lift her into the super-league of investigative reporters who could command feature space in the national press. And here, just maybe, was that chance.

She wandered on, out in the sunshine again, watching a raft of brent geese on the muddy brown trickle of Portsea Creek, trying to imagine what she'd find at Hasler Company. Like everyone else on the planet, she'd seen endless news coverage of the guys who hadn't made it returning to the UK. The footage was always the same. A carefully posed shot of the warrior who'd died, probably lifted from someone's mantelpiece. A tearful on-screen farewell from a mother or occasionally a wife. A fulsome tribute from the unit's commanding officer. And then video pix from the homecoming as the slow dip of Union Jacks rippled the length of Wootton Bassett's main street.

These scenes had become part of the nation's collective soul, as had all the applause that awaited the maimed and the legless as they gamely tried to repair their shattered lives. She had nothing but admiration for these men, but something colder in her heart told her that pictures like these served a political purpose, that a thousand fund-raising stunts for Help the Heroes simply postponed the moment when people might start asking whether any of the pain and loss was really worth it.

The doubters were out there in their thousands, of course they were, but the voices that were never raised were the voices of the guys who really *knew*. And Rob Merrilees was very definitely one of those. Not only that, but he was still serving, still in uniform, still at the very heart of the fighting machine that had made the war possible. Was it really her job to bring this man's anger, this man's disgust, to a wider public? Wouldn't it be easier for both of them to stay mute and sustain the fantasy that a bunch of murdering Taliban might one day turn up on the streets of the UK? This would probably be the shortest cut to the fuck of her dreams and maybe something more long-term to follow, but the moment she voiced the question she knew she had no choice. Meeting Rob had offered her the opportunity of achieving something incredibly rare. What she must do now was make it happen.

Her daughter was playing in the tiny patch of front garden when she finally got back to the trim little house in Anchorage Park. Grace looked up at her mum, shading her eyes against the low slant of sunshine. She and Nana had been out shopping. She wanted to show Lizzie what they'd bought.

Lizzie followed her into the house. Grace tugged her into the lounge-diner. The stuffed panda bear was nearly as big as she was. It was wearing Pompey strip and had a football tucked beneath one arm. Grace had already given it a name.

'His name's David,' Grace said. 'David James.'

'David James was a goalkeeper.'

'I know. Panda says it doesn't matter. He says it's OK.'

'You asked him?'

'Yeah. Of course. He's really nice, really friendly.'

There was a stir of movement in the doorway. Lizzie turned to find herself looking at her mother.

'She bought it for Jimmy,' she murmured. 'It's his birthday on Sunday, in case you'd forgotten.'

★ ★ ★

Suttle was on his second pint. He'd taken Luke Golding to a discreet pub in the backstreets of Ashburton when they'd left work, partly because it had been a bloody long day, but mainly because the lad had earned it. The first time they'd paused at the scene of crime en route to Erika's place, he seemed to have sussed that there might be more to this killing than a guy at the roadside with a big fat automatic, and when Suttle had shared the news from the post-mortem, he'd insisted on a second look. He'd left the car and paced up and down while Suttle caught up on some phone calls, and by the time he got back he'd rewritten the entire script.

'Two guys.' He'd pointed beyond the thin line of wire, up towards the sheep. 'One there. And one down here on the road. The guy on the road stops the car. The other bloke pulls the trigger. No trace of the bullet. No prints. No shell case. Neat as you like.'

Suttle had made him go through it again, testing this radical new thesis to death, but before they got back to the MIR he had to admit it was a perfect fit with the pathologist's finding. There'd been no trace of residues on what was left of Corrigan's face because he'd been killed from a distance. Neat indeed.

Now, in the pub, Golding was telling Suttle about his trophy Lithuanian. The eager Salomeyer, it seemed, had a friend called Laima. Golding had met her. She was tall, great legs, great arse, and couldn't wait to do the Salomeyer thing.

'What's that?'

'Fuck an English cop. I kid you not. These women are deeply fit.'

'And you're looking at me?' Suttle laughed. 'I'm flattered.'

'You need it, boss. Do you good.'

'Are you serious?'

'Of course I'm serious. This lady is a phone call away. You can use my place if you don't want to take her home. I'll drag Salomeyer off for a drink. Sorted or what?'

For a moment or two Suttle was tempted. Apart from a recent visit to Portsmouth, he hadn't had sex for months. An on-off affair with a D/I called Gina Hamilton had come to an end when she'd fallen in love with a fellow D/I on the Fraud Squad, an older man who'd recently lost his wife to breast cancer. Gina had cast herself in the role of therapist and ended up in the marital bed. Suttle still kept in touch with her and was amused to learn that she'd got men all wrong. This one was both kind and decent. It couldn't, she said, possibly last.

Golding had his mobile out. He was scrolling through the directory, hunting for S, but Suttle shook his head. One more pint might be acceptable. But no way was he off to screw some strange lady he'd never had the pleasure of meeting. Nice thought. But no thanks.

Golding said he was mad. The worst that could happen might be a dose of something nasty, but ladies from the Baltic states came highly recommended. According to the word in clubland, they were clean as well as hot.

'It's not that. I mean it. I'm grateful.'

'What is it, then? Only from where I'm sitting you could do yourself a favour.'

'How?'

'By loosening up. And fucking yourself witless always does it.'

'For you.'

'Sure, boss. And for you too, unless you've lost the urge.'

'What's that supposed to mean?'

'Nothing.' He reached for his drink. 'How was Pompey the other weekend?'

'OK.'

'Did you get it on? D'you mind me asking?'

'With my wife, you mean?'

'Yeah.'

Suttle gave the question some thought. Was he

128

really obliged to share the mysteries of a failing marriage with a pushy twenty-five-year-old? He gazed at Golding for a moment or two, then shrugged. What the fuck.

'Yeah.' He nodded. 'We did.'

'And was it OK?'

'Yeah. More or less.'

'What does that mean?'

'It means it felt strange.'

'Had you both been out on the piss?'

'Of course. But it still felt odd. It was like being with a stranger. Unreal. Have you ever felt that?'

'All the time, boss. That's why I end up with slappers like Salomeyer.'

Golding grinned, still toying with his mobile. He'd met Lizzie a couple of times when she was still living with Suttle and had been deeply impressed. Nice lady, bright, and a bit of a looker too. Later, when Suttle had told him what it was like to live with a manic depressive, he'd found it hard to believe. Avoid marriage at all costs, he'd concluded. Keep playing the field.

Suttle got to his feet and nodded at Golding's glass.

'Another? My shout.'

'No thanks.' He nodded at the mobile. 'You're sure about this? I can make the call now. Piece of piss.'

Suttle shook his head and gave Golding's shoulder a squeeze before heading for the door.

'Be happy,' he said. 'You deserve it.'

⋆　⋆　⋆

It was nearly dark by the time Suttle was driving back through Colaton Raleigh. He'd stopped at a pub he liked in a nearby village, tempted to put a call in to Lizzie. He made a point of phoning a couple of times a week to keep in touch with Grace. He knew the conversations were no substitute for parenthood, but he'd developed the knack of being silly on the phone and he knew how to make his daughter laugh.

Just now, though, he was curious to know whether Lizzie might have any plans to meet up for his birthday. He wasn't due weekend leave for a fortnight, and the direction *Graduate* was heading even those precious days off might be up for negotiation, but there might be ways that he and Lizzie could meet halfway, have supper in a pub, maybe stay over. Twice he reached for his phone, and once he was even on the point of making the call, but in the end he decided against it. Lizzie would know at once that he'd been drinking. And that wouldn't help at all.

Lenahan's ancient Fiat was parked outside the cottage when Suttle finally made it back. He'd stopped for a bottle of Rioja from the local store and he took it into the kitchen, expecting to find his lodger at the stove. The light was on but the kitchen was empty. Lenahan's laptop lay open on the table beside a can of Stella. Suttle glanced at the open email. It came from Médecins Sans Frontières. The job in Somalia was still unfilled but the guys in Geneva needed a decision. Was he up for it or not? Good question, Suttle thought. As far as he could see, Lenahan had yet to make a decision.

He wandered through to the living room and shouted from the foot of the stairs. No response. Returning to the kitchen, he checked the time. Nearly ten. There was a pile of vegetables and a loaf of bread on the table, and a recipe book lay open, propped against the big jar of Patna rice Lenahan never bothered to put away. Suttle glanced at the recipe. Eggplant and potato curry. Nice.

Sometimes Lenahan went down the lane to a neighbour he'd befriended. She was a trusty source of the spices he regularly forgot to replenish. Maybe he'd popped out. Maybe that was it. Suttle opened the wine and poured himself a glass. Twenty minutes later, the glass empty, he went out into the garden.

It was dark by now and he could hear the stir of wind in the stand of trees beside the stream. He called Lenahan's name again — Eamonn — and waited for an answer. When nothing happened, he picked his way past the lean-to where he kept his gardening tools, realising for the first time that the lights were on in Lenahan's pride and joy. The garden extended nearly a hundred metres, a long narrow strip of untended land that paralleled the road. At the far end Lenahan had erected a makeshift polytunnel, a bespoke marriage of scavenged metal ribs and heavy-duty polythene. He'd run power and water supplies from the cottage and spent most of his spring weekends planting a variety of crops for the summer. It was, he agreed, very Third World. As you might expect.

Suttle could hear music on the night wind. It

had to come from the polytunnel. The long grass was already wet with early dew and as he made his way closer he felt a growing sense of alarm. Through the walls of the polytunnel he could normally make out the busy smudge of Lenahan. Once again, nothing.

A flap secured with a wire coat hanger served as a door. Suttle paused, then opened the flap and stepped in. The hot embrace of the polytunnel always took him by surprise. The moistness of the air smelled of the garlic Lenahan had been growing. The music was suddenly louder, Hector Berlioz, *Symphonie Fantastique*. Suttle spotted the radio. It was lying on the beaten earth between rows of courgettes. He bent low, turned down the volume.

'Eamonn? You here?'

The groan was barely audible. Suttle looked round, knowing now that something was badly wrong.

'Eamonn?'

Another groan, louder this time. It came from the far end of the polytunnel, down beyond the rows of lettuce and spring onions they'd been consuming for weeks.

'Eamonn? You there? Speak to me.'

Suttle found him curled behind a line of runner beans. He was lying on his side, his knees drawn up. His face was chalk-white and he seemed to be having trouble breathing. The pair of metal steps lay beside him, collapsed across a strip of freshly turned earth.

Suttle knelt quickly, cradled his head, asked

him what had happened, asked him where it hurt.

Lenahan's eyes opened. When he saw Suttle, he tried to smile through the pain. The fucking sprinkler, he muttered. I tried to mend it. He gestured limply up at the pipework he'd installed overhead. The ladder had collapsed, dumping him on top of a metal bucket full of new potatoes. The rim of the bucket had caught him in the ribs. He must have lost consciousness for a bit but he was back with the living now though his ribs hurt like fuck and breathing was no longer a pleasure.

His voice was a whisper. When Suttle tried to get him to his feet, he yelped in pain.

'You need a hospital,' Suttle said. 'I'll call an ambulance.'

'No.' He shook his head. 'Don't.'

'Why not?'

'I know what's wrong. Hospitals are a waste of time. You're talking to an expert.'

He shut his eyes and asked for something to drink. Suttle rinsed a jam jar with water from the standpipe beside the entrance and brought it back. As gently as he could, he tipped the jar to Lenahan's lips. Lenahan took a sip or two, then lay back again. He looked more peaceful now and the smile was less troubled.

'You're fucking good at this,' he managed. 'The wee man's impressed.'

'Don't be.'

'No?' Lenahan's hand found his. Suttle gave it a squeeze.

'Relax,' he said. 'It'll all be fine. We need to get

133

you back to the cottage.'

'You'll look after me?'

'Of course I will.'

'Properly?'

Suttle gazed down at him. He hadn't the least idea what the question meant but he knew it didn't matter.

'Of course,' he said. 'My pleasure, you eejit.'

Suttle put the jam jar to one side and eased Lenahan up to a sitting position. He could see the pain on his face every time he moved. Suttle hoisted him to his feet and knew at once that walking was out of the question. He put his arms round him. Despite the heat of the polytunnel, Suttle could feel the shivers running through his thin frame.

'Just relax,' he said again. 'I'm going to carry you.'

He knelt quickly and folded Lenahan over his shoulder. The movement took him by surprise, and he yelped with pain.

Suttle made it to the door. Lenahan weighed nothing. Outside in the sudden chill of the garden, Suttle picked his way back through the knee-high grass, praying that he didn't trip or fall. Every time he missed his footing, Lenahan gasped. Finally, they were back inside the cottage.

Suttle carried him through the kitchen and into the sitting room. The sofa was just big enough for Lenahan to lie flat, his legs dangling over the end. Suttle was eyeing the stairs. No way was he carrying Lenahan up to the bedroom. Better to make him comfortable down here on the floor.

Upstairs, in Lenahan's room, Suttle stripped the duvet and sheets off the bed and hauled the mattress to the head of the stairs. He could see Lenahan on the sofa. His eyes were closed and he was back in the foetal position, his knees drawn up. His colour, if anything, was worse, grey with a hint of purple.

Suttle manhandled the mattress downstairs, returned for the sheets and duvet, and then transferred Lenahan from the sofa. It was an awkward manoeuvre, further complicated by Lenahan's attempts to help. At length he said he was comfortable.

Suttle was still worried about his colour.

'I'll phone for an ambulance,' he said again.

Lenahan fumbled for his hand. He didn't want an ambulance. No way. He knew exactly what had happened. Self-diagnosis, he whispered, was a neglected art. He'd bust a rib or two. The pain was vicious. Upstairs, in his top drawer, Suttle would find some brown tablets. Two now. Two later. He wouldn't shit for a week but that would be the least of it.

'Hospital,' Suttle repeated.

'No. There's nothing they can do. Believe me, I know about hospitals. World class on hospitals, me.'

Suttle didn't know whether to believe him. He fetched the tablets and came back downstairs.

'You want some water with these?'

'Water?' He was trying to smile.

Suttle took the hint. He stepped into the kitchen and poured a couple of glasses of wine. As an afterthought, he tore a chunk of bread

135

from the loaf. Back beside Lenahan, he knelt on the floor.

'Hungry?'

Lenahan had spotted the bread. It was a real smile this time.

'A miracle,' he said. 'Welcome to the fucking priesthood.'

Suttle fed him the bread. Lenahan's eyes went to the brimming glass. Suttle lifted it to his mouth, tipping it gently until Lenahan could take a sip or two. When Lenahan started to dribble Rioja onto the duvet, he wiped his lips with the flat of his thumb. Lenahan caught it, licked it.

'A man has to take his chances,' he whispered. 'You ever find that in life?'

Suttle grinned. This was better, a glimpse of the old Lenahan, the Irish imp who — over a difficult winter — had rescued him from the miseries of solitude.

'Tablets,' he said.

'More wine?'

'No problem, Father.'

Lenahan swallowed both the tablets. The wine appeared to calm him. There was even a hint of pinkness back in his face.

'One more favour?' he was looking up at Suttle.

'Anything. Name it.'

'Later, my friend. Music first.'

He wanted *La Bohème*. Anna Netrebko. Rolando Villazon. Abbado conducting. Suttle found the CD, slipped it into the player. Lenahan's glass was empty. He appeared to be asleep. Suttle waited for the music to start, turned down the volume, then refilled the glass before putting his mouth to Lenahan's ear.

'More?'

Another smile, softer this time.

'Give me a kiss.'

'What?'

'A kiss, you eejit. Just do it.' He tried to smother a cough with his hand, wincing with the pain. Then his eyes opened. 'No one's watching,' he whispered. 'It needn't hurt.'

Suttle looked at him a moment, then kissed him softly on the temple.

Lenahan's flesh was cold. Sweat beaded his forehead. 'You're a good man,' he managed. 'I love you.'

Suttle didn't know what to say. He asked again about the ambulance, the hospital. Lenahan lifted a hand, waved him away.

'Go to bed,' he said. 'Please.'

Suttle got to his feet, glanced round, wondering whether the spill of light through the open kitchen door might be a help if Lenahan wanted to move during the night. When he suggested it, Lenahan lifted a thumb. Great idea. Now fuck off to bed.

Upstairs, Suttle undressed and slipped under the duvet. Downstairs, barely audible, Anna Netrebko was revving up for her first aria. To his own surprise, he was asleep within minutes. When he awoke, the music had gone. He could hear the drumming of rain on the slate tiles overhead, and the first of the usual drips from somewhere along the upstairs landing.

He rolled over, fumbling for his watch. Twenty to two. He turned on the light, got out of bed, wound a towel around his waist. From the top of the stairs, in the half-light from the kitchen, he could see Lenahan on the mattress on the floor. His head was turned away towards the nearest speaker. Otherwise, he didn't appear to have moved since last night, his knees still tucked into his belly, his knotted hands hugging his crotch. Suttle was about to go back to bed but had second thoughts. Maybe there was something Lenahan needed. Maybe he should go down.

He took the stairs one at a time, moving slowly, not wanting to wake the sleeping figure. His mouth was dry and he could use a drink. As far as he could remember, there was juice in the fridge.

At the foot of the stairs, he tripped over his towel and fell heavily. The crash would have woken anyone. Lenahan didn't move. Suttle retrieved the towel, the first premonitions beginning to ice his veins. *No*, he thought. *Fuck, no*.

He knelt beside Lenahan, touched his face. His skin was cold. His eyes were open. And when Suttle fumbled for a pulse, he found nothing. For a long moment he didn't know what to do. Then the room began to blur as he got to his feet and reached for the phone.

6

THURSDAY, 28 JUNE 2012

Three days later, an overweight man in his late forties emerged from the living room of a mobile home on the edge of a holiday camp in East Devon. He was wearing grubby black tracksuit bottoms and his T-shirt barely covered his belly. He lowered himself into the lounger on the balcony and opened a copy of the *Daily Star* before shouting to someone inside. Seconds later a woman's face appeared in the gap in the sliding door. Then she disappeared again.

The fat guy struggled up from the lounger and dragged it round until it was pointing at the sun, already high in the blueness of the sky. The usual onshore breeze would get up later but this early there wasn't a breath of wind. The sea was mirror-flat. The beach was near-empty. A cloud of seagulls wheeled over a distant fishing boat. Everything appeared to suggest the perfect start to a perfect day.

The woman brought a mug of coffee out within minutes. The man in the lounger didn't spare her a glance. He was deep in the *Daily Star* and he'd yet to touch the coffee when it happened.

A handful of witnesses in nearby mobile homes heard nothing. One man, interviewed much later in the day, was walking his dog along the coastal path on the cliffs above the holiday camp. He said he remembered a soft *phutt*, the kind of noise a cork makes, popped from a bottle of sparkling wine. The noise, he said, raised a couple of pigeons from the trees ahead. Walking on, he thought nothing of it.

The man in the lounger fell to his right. As he sprawled across the warm decking, blood fountained from a gaping wound on his temple. He moved just once, a tiny involuntary twitch, as the blood began to drip between the boards. It was nearly a quarter of an hour before the woman appeared. Her screams brought first the neighbours. And then the police.

★ ★ ★

D/S Jimmy Suttle was at his desk at the MCIT complex in Exeter when he took the call. D/I Carole Houghton was still over in Ashburton, deputy SIO to Nandy on *Graduate*. Suttle had been on compassionate leave these last two days while he dealt with the death of his lodger. Mid-morning, he was looking at a long list of calls he still had to make and thinking about a third coffee.

'We've got another killing, Jimmy. It's looking horribly like the hit on Corrigan. Nandy's spitting nails.'

Houghton gave him the bare details. Guy called Tommy McGrath. Shot to death on the balcony of a mobile home in a holiday camp east of Exmouth. No witnesses. No warning. No leads. Nothing.

Suttle was already reaching for his coat. Houghton was still on the phone. The mobile home had been secured and neighbouring units evacuated pending a Scenes of Crime search. She gave Suttle the name and contact details for the senior officer on site and told him to report back as soon as he'd made an assessment.

'How's *Graduate?*' he asked.

'Don't ask.'

★ ★ ★

The holiday camp was forty minutes by car from police HQ in Middlemoor. Suttle did it in half an hour. In truth, he was glad of the sudden rush of adrenalin that went with a call-out like this. The last couple of days had been the blackest he could remember, blacker even than the moment his wife and child turned their backs on Devon and got on a train for Portsmouth. Thank Christ for crime, he thought, pulling out to overtake and narrowly missing an oncoming bus.

The holiday camp was huge, field after field of caravans and mobile homes rolling up from the clifftop. A uniform at the main gate bent to his open window, checked his warrant card and directed him down through the camp to the mobile home where the killing had taken place. Overhead, a helicopter dipped and circled. TV, he thought. Ever eager for pictures of the freshest kill.

The crime scene was on the seaward edge of the camp, where the sprawl of mobile homes gave way to a farmer's field. Uniformed officers

141

were out in force, patrolling the lines of blue and white NO ENTRY tape. Suttle spotted a Scenes of Crime van parked among a couple of traffic cars. There was a Transit too, with a guy in a black jumpsuit standing guard, and Suttle recognised the mountain of gear inside. The force Firearms Unit was only deployed on an Assistant Chief Constable's say-so. Another hint that Carole Houghton's fears about serial killings might be right.

Suttle brought his Impreza to a halt. The mobile home at the centre of this shit storm was at the end of the clifftop row and a couple of the Scenes of Crime guys were already at work. The inner cordon was policed by a single PC. He gave Suttle the nod and let him through. The door to the mobile home was open. Suttle peered inside and found himself looking at a big plasma screen tuned to one of the daytime talk shows. The volume was low but a couple of women seemed to be trading insults about the virtues of an open marriage.

Suttle edged a little closer, taking care not to contaminate the scene. The mobile home was generously kitted out. An unwashed plate in the sink was smeared with brown sauce and there was a smell of bacon in the air. On the floor beside the banquette was a plastic bottle of lemon juice. It looked empty.

The sliding French door at the end of the lounge area was also open. Two SOC guys were working slowly out from the body, a fingertip search that didn't seem to be yielding much. So far, the scatter of polythene evidence bags appeared to be empty.

Suttle stepped back and tracked around the mobile home, enjoying the warmth of the sun on his face. One of the SOC guys was Terry Bryant. Busy man.

'So . . . ?' Suttle nodded at the body still sprawled on the decking. From this angle Suttle had a perfect view of what must have been the exit wound and he sensed at once that this was a carbon copy of the hit on Corrigan. The way the man's skull had exploded outwards. The glistening mush of brain matter inside, so delicately veined. A great deal of the blood on the decking had already dried in the sun, a violent pattern of dark ochre splats that chronicled the last milliseconds of this man's life.

Bryant got to his feet.

'Sorry about your mate,' he said at once.

'What?'

'Your lodger. The guy who died. I understand you two were close.'

Suttle nodded, said nothing, wondering how the word had got round. He wanted to know who else might have been sharing the mobile home.

'The guy had a partner. Or girlfriend. Or whatever. She calls herself Birdy.'

'And McGrath?' Suttle nodded at the body.

'We talked to the management earlier. He took the rental on the unit for a month.'

'When?'

'Last week. That's all we know.'

'Shame.'

'You're not kidding.'

'I meant the rental. Do you get a refund in situations like this? Can you claim on insurance?'

Bryant shot him a look but Suttle didn't care. There was a deadness inside him he'd never felt before. Guy gets slotted. Big deal.

He was looking around now, trying to map the angles, trying to place the living Tommy McGrath in the middle of this happy landscape, trying to plot where the killer shot might have come from. The pathologist had yet to arrive but in the meantime it did no harm to speculate.

'He was in the lounger when it happened?'

'That's what the woman says.'

'You mean Birdy?'

'Yeah. She's in one of the area cars waiting to be interviewed.'

Suttle nodded, returning his attention to the lounger.

'So matey was sitting right there?'

'Presumably.'

'And the force of the hit knocks him off his perch . . . leaving him here?' Suttle nodded down at the body.

'Yeah.'

'Right.' Suttle shaded his eyes against the glare of the sun. Beyond the fence that marked the camp's perimeter, the cliffs soared up towards a wooded hill. Suttle had been here before, with Lizzie and Grace. The walk along the cliff path zigzagged up the hill. On the top, beyond the trees, was a golf course. Further on lay the seaside town of Budleigh Salterton. Plenty of cover, he thought. Plenty of opportunity.

He turned back to Bryant, gesturing towards the hill.

'What do you think? A mile?'

'Max.'

'Line of sight?'

'Sure. If you knew what you were doing.'

'So what's your feeling?'

'They knew what they were doing.'

Suttle nodded, agreed. Then he was struck by another thought. On the seaward side of the camp, on the tongue of land that nosed into the blueness of the sea, was a firing range used by Royal Marines from the training centre upriver at Lympstone. Was the range active this morning? Might the killer have hidden his own shot behind the snap and crackle of live gunfire?

'No chance.' Bryant was still looking at Suttle. 'The place was empty this morning. We checked.'

Bryant told him again where to find Birdy. Suttle stepped away from the mobile home and side-stepped through the litter of parked cars. A word with a uniform directed him to an unbadged Mondeo. A female PC was leaning against the bonnet, a mobile to her ear. When she'd finished her conversation she checked Suttle's ID and unlocked the car.

The woman was in her mid-thirties. She was blonde, slightly built, wearing denim shorts and a thin cotton shirt several sizes too big. Curled in the corner of the back seat, she was wolfing a tube of Pringles and watching television on her smartphone. Same show. Same women. Same whoops from the audience when a particular insult hit the mark. Her bloke gets shot to death, Suttle thought, and here she is watching shit TV. Weird.

He slipped into the front seat and turned to face her. When he told her to turn the phone off, she just stared at him. For the first time he saw the bruises on her face. Some of them looked recent. Others, less so.

'Who the fuck are you?'

Suttle offered his warrant card. She barely spared it a glance. Suttle shifted his weight on the seat.

'I need your real name,' he said.

'Layla Bird.'

'How well did you know the guy who got shot?'

'Very well. Too fucking well.'

'You want to talk about it?'

She studied him a moment. Something in Suttle's manner had alarmed her. Suttle could see it in her face. Maybe I should be this way more often, he thought. Maybe putting the fear of God up fuckwit daytime TV junkies is the way to go.

'Well?'

She yawned then rubbed her arm.

'When do I get out of this fucking car?' she said. 'Only it's doing my head in.'

★　★　★

Lizzie had somehow expected the editorial conference to be bigger. In the event it was only her and Gill in Boulton's office.

At the editor's invitation, Gill kicked off. The MoD, she said, had been sticky about sharing details of recently bereaved next of kin, but through a variety of other sources she'd managed to identify half a dozen families in the city who'd lost sons or husbands to either the Taliban or Afghani policemen with a serious grudge against the coalition. She'd yet to make contact with any of these families, but her sweet-talking skills were second to none and she had absolutely no doubt that most of them would, if asked nicely, come across.

She'd also laid hands on a guy from the Royal Logistics Corps who'd recently binned the army and was now working for a local haulage company. In theatre he'd taken part in fuck knows how many supply convoys and he'd seen first-hand just how much it cost to keep the war going. On top of that, Gill could offer a choice of Army Reserve medics only too eager to talk about their front-line life-saving skills. These were interviews, she said, that would leave no reader in any doubt as to the war's other cost.

'Meaning?'

'Arms. Legs. Whatever else you lose. This guy told me about one squaddie who had half his todger blown away. He said that reconstructive surgery's really good these days but there's no way the guy won't be pissing in six directions for the rest of his life.'

'Shit.' Boulton was impressed. 'You think you can find him?'

'No problem.'

'Excellent.' He made a note then looked up

147

again. 'How about some kind of overview?'

'Sorted.' Gill was beaming now. 'Guy from Chatham House. Writes like an angel. Lovely voice too. Says he'll do us a thousand words on where the war came from and why it's probably going nowhere.'

'How much?'

'It's for free.'

'*Free?*'

'Zilch.'

'How come?'

'I asked nicely. And I promised to take him out for lunch.'

'Where?'

'Down here. He can't wait.'

Boulton turned to Lizzie. He wanted to know whether she was getting the picture.

'Of course,' she said. 'Do I progress this or does Gill?'

'I'm not sure yet. It all depends on your tame Marine.'

'Of course.'

'So what's the word?'

'There isn't one. I'm seeing him at the weekend. He's taking me round the Hasler place.'

'I know that. I'm asking about the rest of it. What he thinks. The way he'll put it. Whether or not . . . ' he frowned ' . . . he might have second thoughts. This is your call, Lizzie. You're the only one who knows him. Without the interview on the record, we're stuffed.'

'Of course.'

'So what's your feeling?'

Lizzie shrugged.

'I've no idea,' she said. 'A girl can only do her best.'

★ ★ ★

Suttle and Birdy were still in the Mondeo. Birdy had finished the Pringles.

'So how come?' Suttle wanted to know about the bruises.

Birdy shook her head. She said she didn't want to talk about it. All this stuff was a pain in the arse. They were supposed to be having a holiday, for fuck's sake. Now this.

Pain in the arse? Suttle was beginning to wonder about this woman's mental state. Having someone you knew, and maybe even loved, shot to death just metres away would be a major trauma. Neighbours, according to Houghton on the phone, had heard the woman screaming. Yet barely an hour later she appeared oblivious to what had happened.

'I need to know more about Tommy.' Suttle had his notebook out.

'Like what?'

'Like where he lives. Lived. Like what he did jobwise. Like who might have done something like this.'

'Put a bullet through his head? You want a list?'

'Yes, please. That's exactly what I want.'

'No way.' She shook her head. 'When did the Filth ever do me any favours? Or Tommy for that matter? Jesus, you guys . . . ' She started

149

scratching herself again, both forearms this time. It was hot in the car, uncomfortably so, but the way she hugged herself, rocking back and forth on the back seat, suggested she was feeling chilly.

Junkie, thought Suttle, remembering the bottle of lemon juice in the mobile home. She'd probably been using the stuff to cook up another fix. Once Terry Bryant got round to boshing it properly, he'd doubtless find crumpled sheets of foil wrap and a flame-scarred spoon. No wonder this woman looked so wrecked.

'When's your birthday?' he said.

'Fourteenth of June. Week before last.'

'How old are you?'

'Twenty-nine.' She frowned. 'What's that got to do with anything?'

Suttle didn't answer. His mobile was ringing. Luke Golding.

Out in the fresh air Suttle put the phone to his ear. Golding was at his desk in the *Graduate* MIR at Ashburton. It was the first time they'd been in touch since Monday night.

'Been meaning to bell you, boss, but it's mad here. What the fuck happened with that lodger of yours?'

Suttle didn't want to talk about it. He wanted PNC checks on two names. Layla Bird. Tommy McGrath. Golding offered to ring back but Suttle said he'd hang on. Down on the beach half a dozen horses were splashing through the shallows, their riders urging them on until they were at full gallop. Suttle watched them as they headed for the distant jut of Orcombe Point, his mind suddenly blank. He loved the colour of the cliffs here, a deep ochre seamed with plates of rock. Jurassic didn't do them justice. They belonged on Mars or somewhere in even deeper space. Along with the rest of the human race.

'Result, boss.' Golding was back on the phone. 'Bird's got previous for possession, shoplifting and benefit fraud. She also stabbed a guy with a pair of scissors over some drug debt.'

'Possession?'

'Yeah. Smack.'

'And McGrath?'

'Three counts of ABH and one of GBH. He copped eighteen months for the GBH and only came out last year. These people obviously deserve each other. Mr and Mrs Happy, eh?'

Suttle was still looking at the horses. They appeared to have stopped.

'Anything else?'

'Not that I can see. Except I checked for an address and found a last known in Heavitree.'

Suttle wrote it down. Heavitree was in Exeter, a drab patchwork of red-brick terraces much favoured by students, druggies and sundry lowlife. You only lived here if you'd pretty much run out of all the other options.

Golding was asking about a meet and a catch-up. Maybe a pint or two when Suttle could find the time?

'Yeah. Whatever.'

Suttle ended the call without saying goodbye. The horses were on the move again, black dots in the distance. He turned to head back to the Mondeo but found himself looking at D/I Carole Houghton. She took one glance at Suttle's face and nodded back down the hill towards the complex overlooking the beach that served as a restaurant and a bar.

'Coffee?'

★   ★   ★

She updated him first on what was happening around the McGrath hit. Nandy, she said, was organising a squad to work out of the Major Incident Room at police headquarters at Middlemoor. He was drafting in D/Cs from the far corners of Devon and Cornwall, while the Chief Officer Group defended the stockade against the media and a small army of marauding hysterics. The McGrath killing, it seemed, was already creating a modest storm on Twitter, and a bunch of students at Plymouth Uni were running a book on where the mystery sniper would strike next.

'Sniper?'

'That has to be the assumption. Some of my guys on *Graduate* are running down recent sales of high-powered rifles. We've already boshed the Firearms Register.'

'And?'

'We're still looking at one hundred-plus actions.'

Suttle nodded. Each name on the register would get a personal visit. These would either be target shooters, using their weapons on a range, or maybe hunters out in the field looking for game. Every single one of them would require an alibi for early Sunday. And now this morning.

Houghton was peering up at the line of mobile homes that commanded the best sea views. McGrath's, at the very limit of the camp, was out of sight.

'He's done it again, hasn't he?'

'What, boss?'

'Denied us the bullet.'

Suttle frowned, re-imagining McGrath's bulk sprawled on the lounger. Houghton was right. The angle of fire would have sent the bullet clear through his head and out towards the sea. Suttle never discounted luck in any investigation but finding the spent round on acres of beach or even underwater would be little short of a miracle.

'Neat,' he said. 'Same MO.'

Houghton hadn't finished. Once the guys from the Firearms Unit had cleared the likely areas, Scenes of Crime and maybe the Royal Marine ATOs would be combing the fields and high ground to the north in the hope of finding some trace of the shooter. The attending pathologist might be able to give them a steer on the probable angle of fire, which would narrow the search parameters, but even so Houghton wasn't holding her breath.

'These people are meticulous,' she said. 'They don't make silly mistakes.'

Suttle wanted to check who'd be SIO on this latest job. Already it had an operational code name: *Scorpion*.

'Nandy,' Houghton said. 'He's starting to take this thing personally.'

'And you?'

'Deputy.'

Suttle nodded. He knew exactly what was coming next. Intel would be the key to putting a name to these killings. It always was. And as Nandy's second-in-command, Houghton would know exactly where to turn.

'We need to develop McGrath,' she was saying. 'There has to be a pattern here. People don't get killed without good reason. Find the reason, the link, and we're home safe.'

Suttle reached for his coffee. *Easy*, he thought. First an absentee mother with money to burn and now a fat ugly bastard, undoubtedly violent, who couldn't get enough of the *Daily Star*. What could these people possibly have in common? Apart from the swiftest of deaths?

'You want me to handle that?'

'I do. If you think you can. We'll be detaching Luke from *Graduate*. You won't be on your own.'

Suttle shrugged. Just now, he thought, being on his own was exactly where he was. No wife. No daughter. No Lenahan. Just the crushing knowledge that he should have made the call, should have summoned the ambulance, should have got the guy to hospital. Having any death on your conscience was bad enough. Losing someone who, for whatever reason, really mattered to you was careless in the extreme.

Houghton had pushed her coffee aside. In these situations, for someone so busy, so driven, so exposed to the manic drumbeat of serious crime, she could be remarkably sensitive. When he'd thought about it last time, he'd put it down to the fact that she too was gay. Her partner was a lawyer called Jules, a tall handsome woman, equally able. They rode horses together and laughed a lot. Nice.

'So where are we with your Mr Lenahan?'

'The post-mortem's this afternoon.'

'Still no idea why he died?'

'No. They were thinking little me at first. You probably heard.'

'I did. And . . . ?'

'They binned it after twenty-four hours. NFA.'

Suttle ducked his head. The morning after Lenahan died, he said, he'd taken a call at the cottage. He was still picking his way through the little man's mobile directory, trying to get some kind of fix on his family life, marvelling that he'd been so close to the guy and yet known so little. In the end, he'd started phoning the stored numbers in alphabetical order, breaking the news, offering his sympathies, having no idea who he was talking to. Then came the phone call.

'Who was it?'

Suttle named a D/C who worked out of Exmouth nick, an older guy, a bit of a plodder with a reputation for steadiness under fire. He'd once been a decent surfer and still worked for the Beach Rescue people as a volunteer in his spare time.

'Nigel Benning? It could have been worse.'

'Nigel was fine,' Suttle said. 'Apart from the damage to his ribs there wasn't a mark on Lenahan, but I could see it Nigel's way. We might have had a disagreement. We might have been pissed. It might have got out of hand. These

155

were questions he had to ask. He did a good job. I'm not complaining.'

Suttle had told Benning exactly the way it had been. His account included the visits to both pubs and the subsequent call at the village store for a bottle of Rioja. Benning had raised an eyebrow about drink-driving but Suttle knew how important it was to evidence this story of his.

When Benning seized Lenahan's mobile and checked the last outgoing call, it transpired he'd been talking to a mate from the hospital who was a bit of a gardener himself. This guy had been giving Lenahan advice about the sprinkler system. Lenahan, he said, had been standing on top of a ladder in his polytunnel looking at a dodgy joint. The guy explained what to do and called half an hour later to see whether it had worked. No reply.

'What time was that?' Houghton asked.

'Half nine. I was in a pub in Newton Poppleford. By then my wee man was in a bad way.' He pushed the coffee away and shook his head. 'NFA. No further action.'

'A relief, I imagine.'

'That I wasn't done for homicide? Sure.'

'But it still hurts.'

'Of course it does. I loved that little man. I didn't realise it at the time but that's what it boiled down to. He was so fucking optimistic. He didn't have an ounce of malice in him. He didn't know the meaning of the word moody. And what did I do? I let him down. He didn't want to go to hospital. He just wouldn't have it. I should have

156

insisted. I should have put him in the car and bloody driven him there myself. And do you know what I did instead? I went to fucking bed. The next thing I know, the guy's died. That was me, boss. My fault. My doing. Hurt doesn't do it justice. I killed that man. And that's something he never deserved.'

'I thought he was a medic?'

'He was.'

'Then how come he didn't know?'

'Know what?'

'How badly injured he was?'

'Fuck knows. That's a question I can't answer. I think about it all the time. It won't go away. Why was I so stupid? So lazy? Why did I *believe* him? Me of all people? Mr fucking Detective?'

'Because you'd had a drink or two?'

'That didn't help, sure, but there's something else, something I can't put my finger on.' He stopped, aware that his voice was rising. Steady, he told himself. Wind your neck in. Take your time. *Think*.

Finally he looked Houghton in the eye. He was deeply grateful for this moment of clarity before the darkness swamped him again but he knew her time was limited. Not just one killing, for God's sake. But now two.

'I didn't want to part with him,' he said softly. 'I didn't want to lose him. When he told me he could sort himself out, I believed him. And I believed him because I wanted to believe him. That little man wasn't for sharing. Not with anyone. Not with the paramedics, not with the hospital, not with anyone. He got me into *opera*, for God's sake. Puccini. Verdi. He was turning me into someone nicer, softer, less fucked up. He knew how to laugh. He'd sussed how crazy the whole thing is. He'd sussed what mattered and what didn't. He'd spent loads of time abroad, Third World mainly, more than half his working life. This is someone who'd seen stuff, *lived* stuff you wouldn't believe. And that made him the kind of person I got to know. He was precious. He was a one-off. And I was fucking lucky to have known him. Does any of that make sense? Or should you be looking for a new D/S?'

Houghton covered his hand with hers. Suttle could sense how badly she wanted to check her watch.

'I understand it completely,' she said. 'And just for the record, lucky is what you are. Hang onto that thought. Why? Because otherwise you'll go potty. I've been there. Believe me. Thank God for Jules.'

She gave his hand a squeeze then she was on her feet. She had a million calls to make. So did Suttle. She wanted him all over McGrath's life. She wanted to know how he'd got by, who he'd pissed off, and why some distant stranger had blown half his head away.

Suttle was gazing up at her. Grateful was too small a word.

'No problem, boss. Consider it done.' He paused, staring out of the window at the long arm of Straight Point. 'One thought about our man with the gun. Assuming we're dealing with the same guy.'

158

Houghton said nothing, just raised an enquiring eyebrow.

'There has to be some kind of link to the military, doesn't there? Those kind of skills? Single bullet? Bang on target?' Suttle turned back to her. 'Or have I got that wrong?'

Houghton shook her head and got to her feet.

'That's our thinking too,' she said. 'Mr Nandy's got it in hand.'

* * *

Lizzie texted her estranged husband just before lunch. Gill was in the car outside. The guy from Chatham House had decided to take the train down sooner rather than later, and in a moment of uncharacteristic generosity Gill had offered to share the occasion. The entire supplement, after all, depended on Lizzie producing the goods. Gill was realistic enough to know how difficult that might be and had decided that any additional motivation would be more than welcome.

This was a young academic who was making his name in some of the weightier journals. A piece on the disaster in Iraq had just run in the *London Review of Books*, attracting considerable attention. He'd appeared on *Channel Four News* on no less than three occasions. He was telegenic, witty, and according to his own website, sitting on a big fat book contract with a leading publisher. Whichever way you cut it, this guy was very definitely hot.

Lizzie paused at the top of the stairs that led

to the car park. 'What is Birthday Boy up 2 this w/end?' she keyed. 'Only I might be down yr way. Lx'. She reread the message, wondering whether she wasn't offering a hostage to fortune. She knew Jimmy's shift pattern didn't give him a spare weekend until next Saturday. Given the staffing levels on the Major Crime team, it was highly unlikely he'd be able to find the time for a meet. But what would happen if something had changed at the office? If he came back and said fine, yeah, let's have a meal, let's push the boat out, let's see whether we can end up in bed again and sort something out?

She hesitated, knowing in her heart of hearts that this pathetic little message was nothing more than a sop to her conscience, an opportunity to reassure her mum that she and Jimmy were still in touch, still talking, and that the last thing she'd ever do would be to ignore his fucking birthday. Her mum had bought a card. It had roses on the front. She shook her head in disgust, pressed the Save button so she could think about it later, and headed on down the stairs.

★　★　★

The address for McGrath that Golding had unearthed from force records turned out to be accurate. Suttle drove Birdy into Exeter. The flat she'd shared with McGrath was on the ground floor of a scruffy Victorian terraced house five minutes from the city's Central Station. Moss was growing out of the window frames and the

160

front garden was littered with empty cans of Special Brew. When Terry Bryant was through with the mobile home, he'd be starting on the flat. In the meantime Suttle wanted a sneak preview.

Birdy had a key. The moment she let them both into the darkness of the hall, she was heading for the stairs. When Suttle called her back, she threw him the keys.

'Help yourself,' she said, taking the stairs two at a time.

Suttle didn't bother to stop her. It had been obvious since he met her that she badly needed to score. Maybe her dealer lived upstairs. Maybe he could coax some sense from her once she'd had a lie-down.

He unlocked the door and stepped inside. The overpowering stench of dog shit took him by surprise. He fumbled for a light switch. Already the dog was going ape. It was in one of the rooms down the narrow corridor. He could hear it pawing at the door.

Suttle made his way to the tiny lounge. The TV was on — *The Weakest Link* this time — and the curtains were pulled tight against the blaze of sunshine outside. More empty tinnies lay abandoned in the fireplace, along with the remains of a Chinese takeaway, and there was a scatter of newspapers and magazines on the floor. Suttle found a light switch, wondering what kind of people left the telly on when they went away on holiday, and then stooped to take a look at the stuff on the carpet. Quite why McGrath or Birdy had any interest in catalogues from a garden centre was beyond him, but some of the other material made more sense. Lots of porn from the harder end of the market. And a month's backcopies of the *Daily Star*.

Birdy had come downstairs again. He could hear her footsteps along the hall. When she appeared at the door her eyes appeared to have lost focus. She even managed a dreamy smile.

Suttle asked about the dog. Who fed it? Who took it out for a walk and a shit?

Birdy pointed at the ceiling. Upstairs, she seemed to be saying.

'Big dog?'

Birdy held her arms wide, the full spread. A grin this time.

'Ralphie,' she managed. 'After my dad.'

Suttle nodded, knowing that any attempt at conversation was pointless. Birdy badly needed somewhere to crash and Suttle was only too happy to oblige. He'd bell Bryant and warn him about the dog. The CSM could pick up the key from Heavitree nick and help himself to whatever he could find in this shit hole.

Birdy was eyeing the sofa. The dog must have had a tussle with the stuffed leopard because half its head was missing. Suttle took her by the arm and led her towards the door.

'Where are we going?' She was looking alarmed again.

Suttle went through the motions of arresting her. Suspicion of being in possession of Class A drugs. Anything you say may be taken down as evidence and used against you. She wouldn't remember a word and he couldn't care a fuck if she did.

'I'm taking you into custody,' he said. 'We'll talk later.'

★ ★ ★

Gill Reynolds chose a fish restaurant in Gunwharf for the lunch with the guy from Chatham House. His name was Duncan Wingrave. He was in his mid-thirties: tall and rangy with thinning blond hair and pale blue eyes behind black horn-rimmed glasses. He wore a light linen jacket over designer jeans and toted a shoulder-slung leather briefcase he deposited beside his chair. Every few minutes Lizzie watched his eyes flick down to the bag, the way you might check on a pet spaniel, just to make sure it was still there.

Gill had obviously done most of the heavy lifting on the phone. Without naming names, she'd made it clear that they had access to a highly placed source whose credibility would be hard to challenge. This guy had a great deal to say about the realities of the front-line situation in Afghanistan and deserved the biggest possible audience because he was still out there doing it. Wingrave's job, over sea bass on a bed of mash spiked with scallions, was to fill in the background bits.

The news that he was to be interviewed, rather than simply pen an authored article, appeared to take him by surprise.

'You prefer that?'

'We thought it might save you the trouble of writing the thing.'

'Fine. As you see it.'

He was filleting his fish with immense panache. This, thought Lizzie, was a man who was no stranger to expensive lunches on someone else's tab.

Gill, as ever, was after a headline. She'd propped a small recorder beside the ice bucket.

'It's a fuck-up, isn't? We should never have been there in the first place.'

He looked up, amused by her bluntness, then nodded.

'You're right. It's not quite as simple as that because nothing ever is, but in my trade it's hard not to arrive at certain conclusions.'

'Like?'

'Like politicians should read more books. Ignore the past, and history will screw you.'

The Afghans, he said, had always held the keys to India. The Brits, wary of Russian intentions, had spent most of the nineteenth century trying to impose themselves on this barearsed rugged landscape, but the expenditure of much blood and treasure had secured little in return. The Afghans were tough, quarrelsome and unforgiving. Nearly a century later it was the Russians' turn. Eager to protect the Soviet Union's southern border from an imminent civil war, they'd poured men, armour and helicopter gunships into the towering landscapes of the Hindu Kush and got an equally bloody nose. Ten years on, the Russian generals had taken Gorbachev aside and told him the war was unwinnable. Within months the tanks and the gun-ships had gone.

'That should have told us something.' Wingrave speared a flake of sea bass. 'It didn't.'

'But this is down to 9/11, surely?'

'You're right — 9/11 changed everything. Politically Bush was out of options. He had to react. The intel was telling him the bad guys were still in Afghanistan, and he had to find them, Osama Bin Laden especially. Think cancer. You identify the tumour and root it out. Special Forces? Obviously. B-52s? Probably useful. You chase these guys over the mountains and precision-bomb the spots where you think they might be hiding, and after a while, to no one's surprise, they bail out and head for Pakistan. At that point your interest in Afghanistan should cease. Sadly that didn't happen.'

The Americans' key mistake, he said, had been to conflate al-Qaeda with the Taliban. The two elements were chalk and cheese. The Taliban had little time for a bunch of well financed Arabs bent on world jihad and absolutely no interest in bringing America to its knees. They simply wanted to impose a certain way of life on their own country. And they didn't welcome interference from a coalition army determined to stop them.

'But we stayed.' This from Lizzie.

'We did. A lot of our guys went off to Iraq for a while, but that didn't work out either so back they came.'

'To take on the Taliban?'

'Sure. And the corruption. And all the tribal unhappiness. And the poppy. And the infrastructure — which mostly didn't exist. You're talking about a country that had been at war for forty years. Things were just going backwards. And in many respects I'm afraid they still are.'

'And that's something that should matter to us?'

'Not at all. If you want a personal view, we don't have a dog in this fight. Not any more. Not since al-Qaeda fled and the Americans nailed Bin Laden in Pakistan. Politicians in this country are still banging on about terrorist cells in Afghanistan, about keeping the streets of Birmingham safe by killing the Taliban in Helmand, but I'm afraid it's nonsense. Those bombs in London were made in Leeds, by UK nationals. They had nothing to do with the Taliban.'

'So what about al-Qaeda?'

'Al-Qaeda is a franchise. It's a cast of mind. It'll spring up everywhere. Sub-Saharan Africa. Asia. Everywhere. You need a very clever and very expensive strategy to control it, but essentially you're talking police actions. You don't need boots on the ground. You need to view these people as criminals. Not some foreign army.'

Lizzie reached for her notebook. She rather liked this man. Behind the languid Oxbridge delivery, he was extremely sharp.

'So what do we do?' she said.

'We get out. Which is what is sort of happening.'

166

'Sort of?'

'We're playing the pretend game. We're talking about passing the baton to the Afghans. We're offering them the blessings of democracy. We're dressing up defeat as victory and then we'll be on our way.'

'Like the Russians?'

'Sure. Except the Russians didn't hang around. Once Gorbachev got the message from the generals, the thing was over. Saving face only matters to Western politicians. Why? Because success is where votes come from.'

Lizzie nodded. Already, she knew Gill had enough to make a decent piece to frame the supplement — history thickly larded with academic regret — and this would give everything else a degree of authority. Wingrave had returned to the remains of his fish. Lizzie watched him for a moment, aware that the implications of what he'd just said were deeply shocking. Politicians, for whatever reason, make the wrong call. And thousands die as a direct result.

She leaned forward over the table. She needed to check her bearings.

'You're Chatham House, right?'

'Right.'

'You have the ear of the top military guys, the guys who make the decisions, the guys in the loop, the guys who *know*.'

'Yes.'

'So do you think we're doing the right thing? By publishing something like this?'

Wingrave at last looked up. He reached for his

napkin and nodded.

'I do, yes,' he said. 'But that isn't the issue.'

'No?'

'No.' He shook his head. 'The issue is whether or not your man comes across. I've no idea what he's saying, what he told you, but you need to be very sure about his motivation. The minute he goes into print he's going to have some serious players on his case. If they find the slightest weakness, the slightest hint that he's there for the taking, they'll tear him apart. Gill tells me he's a high-flyer. To be frank, I'll be amazed if he decides to go public.'

Lizzie nodded. She didn't know what to say. Gill was reaching for the recorder, a smile on her face.

'I think we've taken care of that,' she said. 'Eh, Lizzie?'

* * *

Jimmy Suttle was back at the Heavitree address within the hour. The Desk Sergeant had booked Birdy into the custody suite and she was now in one of the cells, under the watchful eye of the presiding turnkey, fast asleep. A police doctor would check her over on waking and certify that she was fit for interview. Until then Suttle had other business in mind.

Luke Golding had turned up from Ashburton with the news that *Graduate* was stumbling.

'We're all over that woman,' he said. 'Bella Prentiss. We're after everything — bank statements, phone records, laptops, PCs, you name it.

168

And you know what happened? She volunteered the lot, just handed the data over.'

'And?'

'Sod all. To make this thing work, she has to have had some contact with whoever took Corrigan out. The only admission she's prepared to make is spending squillions on a London brief to get her son back. We can't do her for that and she knows it.'

'Goodyer?'

'He's off the radar.'

'Nicky?'

'Fuck knows. She thinks Goodyer was insane enough to take the woman's money and grass them all up, but that's just an opinion. She can't prove it.'

Suttle tried the doorbell again. When there was still no answer, he found the Yale on Birdy's key ring and let himself in. It was even darker in the shared hall than the first time he'd been here, just hours ago. He could feel weeks of flyers and uncollected mail under his feet.

'Upstairs,' he said. 'First door on the left.'

He'd coaxed the information from Birdy in the cell before she'd drifted off. Guy by the name of Alain Seydou. Black dude. Great dreads and a collection of brilliant music.

He opened the door to Suttle's knock, a towering figure in cargo pants and a white vest that stopped well short of his waist. Expecting the usual variation on Heavitree low life — thin, pale, bitten nails, three days of stubble, lots of nervy attitude — Suttle found himself looking at someone who obviously worked out. The guy also smiled. Perfect teeth, as white as his vest.

'Mr Seydou?'

'Yeah.' He was inspecting Suttle's warrant card.

'You didn't hear the doorbell?'

'Sure I heard the doorbell. Round here, Mr Policeman, the doorbell's what you never answer. You want to come in? *Mon plaisir.*'

A mock bow and a big stagey sweep of the arm invited them into the flat. Again, Suttle had got it all wrong. This wasn't the doss he'd told Golding to expect. On the contrary, the place was immaculate: maple-wood flooring, huge wall-hung plasma screen, two low sofas, plants everywhere. The scent of joss hung in the air, pleasantly sweet, and from somewhere else in the flat came music that Suttle recognised from one of Lenahan's nightly sessions with world music on BBC radio. Easy African rhythms stiffened with a rolling drumbeat.

'You guys want anything to drink? Coffee maybe?'

Suttle shook his head. He wanted to talk about the flat downstairs. Specifically he wanted to know about a woman called Layla Bird.

'Birdy? You know her?'

'We've met.'

'Cool chick. The best. Crazy, you know?' He touched his forehead. 'But the best.'

'You know her well?'

'Sure. I take care of her some nights. Babysit her stuff.'

'Stuff?'

'Stuff she leaves with me.'

170

'Like what?'

The smile again, and a slow wag of the head.

'Yours to find out, man.'

Suttle held his gaze.

'We could take this place apart. You want that to happen? One phone call and I can have the guys here within the hour. Believe me, they're not gentle.'

'Help yourself, man. Sugar? Milk?'

He left the room without waiting for an answer. From down the corridor came the splash of water into a kettle. Then he was back. He was happy to talk about Birdy, he said. But he could do without the threats.

'*Pas nécessaire.*' He gestured at the sofa again. 'Please.'

'*Vous êtes français?*' This was Golding.

'*Côte d'Ivoire.*'

'*Comme Drogba?*'

'*Exactement.*' The smile was genuine this time. '*Mon pote, quoi?*'

Suttle was staring at Golding. Since when did his infant D/C speak French?

Golding ignored him. He was back in English now, wanting to know how come Seydou had ended up in Heavitree. He'd folded his lean frame onto the other sofa. Seydou told Golding he'd done a philosophy degree at the university and now taught part time to meet his bills. He'd been renting the flat for years. He liked Exeter. He sang with a reggae band most weekends and played striker with a decent Sunday league side. When Golding asked about the area, he said he had no problem with it.

He'd grown up in the suburbs of north-east Paris and he knew a great deal about what happened when poverty collided with racism. Burned cars. Kids out of control. The odd riot at the weekends to bring the cops within range of *un cocktail*. Heavitree, by contrast, was *tranquil*.

'A cocktail?' Suttle was looking at Golding.

'A petrol bomb,' he said. 'I think.'

Suttle nodded. At this rate he'd be the one making coffee.

'About Birdy . . . ' Suttle turned to Seydou. 'You saw the bruises on her face this afternoon?'

'Yeah.'

'How come?'

Seydou got to his feet and left the room again. When he returned he was carrying a cafetiére and three mugs. He gestured for Golding to do the pouring and resumed his seat on the sofa.

'You know Tommy?' he said at length.

Suttle nodded, said nothing. Seydou leaned forward, then pumped a fist into his open palm.

'Tommy did that? He smacks her around?'

'*Oui.*'

'Regularly?'

'Yeah. We talk about it, Birdy and me. I say . . . you know . . . I offer . . . but she doesn't want help. She says he can't help himself. She says he has a problem. She's right. He does. *Putain.*'

'What does he do for a living? Tommy?'

'Lots of stuff. He buys and sells. He's got a van. He does house clearances. But he's shit, man. He's shit with everything. Everything he

172

touches turns to shit. First he drinks. Then he drinks some more. Then Birdy comes home and . . . ' The fist again, harder this time.

Suttle wanted to know whether the violence extended beyond Birdy. Was there anyone else who got on the wrong side of Tommy McGrath?

'Sure.'

'Like who?'

'Like most people he meets. Maybe the guy's really unhappy. Or maybe Birdy's right. Maybe he just has this big, big problem. But violence is what he does. Talk to the guy, and you're wasting your time. One day he's going to have a real problem, Because one day somebody's going to — ' he shot a look at Golding ' — *renvoyer l'ascenseur?*'

'Return the favour,' Golding said.

Suttle nodded, picturing McGrath's shattered scalp leaking blood and brain fluid onto the warm decking beside the upturned sunlounger. A man with this many enemies had the makings of an investigative nightmare.

He was still looking at Seydou.

'You've got names?'

'No. Talk to Birdy.'

'I will.'

'*Bonne chance.*'

'You're telling me that might be a problem?'

'Sure. She's terrified of the guy. That's why she's so wasted.' He paused, catching the exchange of glances between the two detectives. 'You're here because of Birdy, right? Because of what that guy's done to her?'

'No.' Suttle reached at last for his coffee. 'That

favour you mentioned? Someone repaid it. In spades.'

Seydou looked briefly confused. Then he understood.

'Someone hurt him?'

'Yeah.'

'Is he bad?'

'He's dead.'

'You're kidding me.'

'I'm not.'

There was a moment of silence while Seydou looked from one face to the other. Then he was off the sofa, hauling Golding to his feet, high-fiving him before punching the air.

'Tommy McGrath dead?' He began to dance. '*Putain, quoi?*'

★ ★ ★

Birdy had surfaced when Suttle and Golding made it back to Heavitree nick. The turnkey, a stout woman of uncertain age, was kindlier than she looked. Birdy was sitting on the edge of the concrete plinth that served as a bed, her head down, her thin hands wrapped around a cup of coffee from the machine down the corridor.

Suttle introduced Golding. Birdy didn't spare him a glance.

'He's really gone?' she whispered.

Suttle nodded. For some unfathomable reason, Birdy appeared to miss McGrath.

'Why?' she said. 'Why would anyone do that?'

'That's what we need to find out. That's why we're here.'

She nodded, numbed by everything that had happened. Then she started to shiver. Coffee slopped onto the floor.

'Help me out?' she said at last. 'Please?'

'You'll see the doctor soon. It's sorted.'

'I don't need the doctor.'

'You do, my love. He'll be here.' Suttle pulled the chair a little closer. 'Tommy ran a business, am I right?'

Birdy's head came up again. Her eyes were swimming, tears pouring down her face.

'Business?'

'A van. Removals. Carting stuff around.'

'Yeah.' She sniffed, then accepted a tissue from Golding and blew her nose. 'But it wasn't his fault. He couldn't help himself, Tommy.'

'I don't understand. Fault, how? What couldn't he help?'

'He'd nick stuff, the good stuff, the stuff he could resell. Then he'd pretend he'd lost it or it got smashed or whatever. No one ever believed him. But no one ever took him on.'

'These are removal jobs?'

'Yeah. Of course. Once a guy tried to get heavy but Tommy just laughed in his face.'

'And then what?'

'He gave him a kicking. Half killed the guy. A&E.'

'This was recently?'

'Dunno.' She smothered a yawn. 'Last week? Last month? Whatever. It happened round the corner. The bloke was in the gutter for hours before anyone stopped.'

'And what was that about?'

'A toaster. And some Coldplay CDs.'

'He nearly killed him for that?'

'No. It was for answering back. You never got lippy with Tommy. Not if you had a brain in your head.'

She was scratching her arms now, exactly the way she'd been in the unmarked Mondeo. Suttle shot a glance at Golding. Even with an OK from the police doctor, a formal interview would be a joke, open to instant challenge if it ever came to using the evidence in court. Better to do the business now, just the three of them, in the privacy of the cell.

Golding wanted to know more about the money McGrath was earning. Was he into cut-price removals? Was that the way he kept the jobs coming?

'Yeah. Of course. Two hundred quid the lot. And that would take you fifty miles. Any further and you paid extra for the diesel.'

'Who helped him?'

'No one. That was the deal. The punter helped. No one would work with Tommy, and you know why? Because no one fucking understood the man. Because no one would give him the time of day.'

She began to choke up again at some half-forgotten memory. Another tissue.

Suttle was doing the sums. Subtract the van costs from two hundred quid and you were looking at a pittance.

'So how many of these jobs would Tommy do a week? Typically?'

She didn't seem to have heard the question.

Suttle repeated it. She balled the tissue and let it fall to the floor. Then she wiped her nose on the back of her hand and looked up.

'One, two maybe. You had to be fucking desperate to go to Tommy McGrath.'

'So what else did he live on?'

She gazed at Suttle, then shook her head.

'He was so good to me, that man.' Her voice was a whisper again.

'He paid for your gear?'

'Always. Always. He'd give me the money. He never complained once. He was so good. So . . . ' she frowned ' . . . *reliable* — you know what I mean?'

'And in return?'

'Nothing. Not that way.'

'*Nothing?*'

'No. Tommy couldn't get it up. That's terrible, isn't it? Me telling you? He'd kill me, he really would.'

'Maybe that's why he kept giving you the money.'

'Yeah?' She was staring at him now, as if the thought had never occurred to her. 'You really think that? Buying my . . . whatever?'

'Silence?'

'Yeah? Buying that? Keeping me quiet?'

Her head went down, buried in a swamp of memories, and she began to ramble. How Tommy had loved his dogs. He'd had two of them, then one got run over when he was walking it late one night, some kid in a racer, pissed out of his head, and Tommy had torn into him, given him a real battering, another body left

177

in the gutter, the car still there in the middle of the road while Tommy carried the dead dog home. He'd buried it somewhere out the back, carried it in through the hall, still bleeding, poor fucking thing, and when he was pissed sometimes he'd go nicking flowers from gardens and make them into little bunches and then go out in the garden and put them where he'd buried the dog and talk to him.

'He'd be out there for hours,' she said. 'Hours and hours in the freezing cold. He really loved that dog. Sometimes he'd say that's all you had in the world. He thought human beings were a waste of fucking space. Only dogs did it for Tommy.'

Suttle glanced up. Golding was making notes. So far they had two possibles who might have had an interest in seeing McGrath punished. One was a punter who'd traded his toaster and a couple of CDs for a savage beating. And the other was the boy racer who'd killed his favourite dog. Both would need further development, and there were doubtless more victims to scoop up from the wreckage of Birdy's memory, but Suttle was aware that their time with this woman was limited.

The shivering and the compulsive scratching had got worse. Any minute now the police doctor would arrived. At that point *Scorpion* would have to re-emerge into the sunlit uplands of PACE protocols: access to a lawyer, strict controls on the kind of pressures you could exert, and time limits on pretty much everything.

Suttle bent to her ear again, put his arm round her.

'Someone must have been in touch,' he murmured. 'He must have had a phone call, a knock at the door. He might have met someone. Someone might have threatened him. He'd have talked about it. He might even have mentioned a name. Think, my love. *Think*.'

Birdy looked up at him, grabbed his hand, squeezed very hard. She wanted to help. She really, *really*, wanted to help. But it was beyond her. Everything had gone. Her memory. Tommy. The cash she'd relied on for so long to stay half-normal. Everything. She was in a place she'd never been in her life. And it terrified her.

It was Golding who broke the silence.

'The holiday,' he said. 'The mobile home.'

'Yeah?' She was searching for his face, a vagueness in her eyes.

'So who paid for it?'

'Tommy.'

'How?'

She stared at him for a long moment, then something occurred to her and she started laughing, a dry, cracked, retching sound that had nothing to do with amusement.

'You know what?' she said. 'He was so fucking *lucky*, that man.'

7

Lizzie was in the newsroom when the email arrived from Rob Merrilees. She abandoned the copy she was rewriting for a feature in tomorrow's paper and turned her attention to the PC.

The email had a slightly military feel. A set of instructions directed her west on the A303 and thence to Plymouth, where she was to turn right and head north. Merrilees lived in the Tamar Valley. An attached Google map threaded her through a maze of country lanes to a village called Bere Ferrers. The address came with a second attachment, a helpful shot of 5 Aspen Road which she guessed Rob had taken himself, back in the spring. The neat little terraced house featured a red front door. A window box was brimming with dwarf daffs and a serious-looking motorbike was parked at the kerb.

Lizzie's gaze returned to the text, wondering whether Rob had added a GPS reference and compass bearings. To her relief, he'd settled for a cheerful heads-up on the catering arrangements. He knew she wasn't a veggie. He hoped she could cope with his homecooking. And if a leg of local lamb was any kind of a problem, maybe she could get in touch. Hasler Company was on standby for Saturday afternoon. Which meant that they had plenty of time for a lie-in.

She grinned at the thought, and quickly fired off a reply. 'Can't think of anything nicer,' she typed. 'And the lamb sounds great, too. xxx'.

She hit Send and sat back, recognising the flutter of excitement Rob's message had stirred. For years she'd been strict with herself whenever her job threatened a collision with her personal life. With the exception of her husband, she'd always resisted invitations for a drink or a meal with guys she'd just interviewed. And, by the same token, she'd generally turned a deaf ear to mates trying to enlist her help in riding some private hobby horse into print.

But Rob Merrilees, for reasons she still couldn't quite grasp, had blown a gaping hole in all that. She couldn't wait to see him again. She wanted to touch him, to catch his scent. She wanted to get close to him, to open him up, to understand the real source of his doubts and his disgust. Above all she wanted them to be together, to be a pair, to become comrades in arms — as she saw it — in the battle to expose the Afghan war for what it really was: a needless spilling of blood in the service of a shabby political decision that should never have been taken in the first place.

Still staring at the screen, she found herself nodding. Of course there were dangers. You couldn't tackle this kind of journalism without them. Rob would be putting his career on the line, and she too would be exposed to all kinds of pressure. But in the end she had no doubts that what they were doing was right. And that, as

181

ever, was what really mattered.

She checked her watch. This time tomorrow she'd be on the road west. By Saturday night, having spent the afternoon with God knows how many amputees, she'd know the real weight of the story. But what of Sunday? Not once, since they'd met, had she been away from Jimmy on his birthday. Before Grace happened along they'd always celebrated alone: champagne in bed in the early evening, a meal in a favourite restaurant to follow, a walk by the sea on the way home, then bed again.

She'd cherished these moments because they'd seemed to catch the essence of their relationship: warm, intimate, richly physical. Jimmy would light the candles around the bed and put on one of his Neil Young CDs and they'd make love like they'd only just met. Having a baby, she knew, had changed all that, but the need and the yearning and the laughter were still there. But then Devon had happened, and the laughter had gone, and most nights they'd slept back to back, strangers in a marriage that had emptied them both.

She opened her mobile and checked the text she'd saved. 'What is Birthday Boy up 2 this w/end?' she'd written. 'Only I might be down yr way. Lx'.

She gazed at it for a long moment, knowing that her memories of bygone birthdays still mattered to her and that this was the very least she owed a man who'd once made her very happy. All that might be history but she still felt for him, still respected him, still valued what they'd had together. *What the fuck*, she thought. *He'll be busy anyway.*

Her gaze straying back to the copy she'd been revising, she pressed Send.

★   ★   ★

Suttle had gone back to the MCIT offices in Middlemoor, the sprawling force headquarters complex on the eastern edge of Exeter that housed the Chief Officer Group and a number of other specialist departments. Houghton's Major Crime squad occupied a converted police house in the middle of the site. From Suttle's desk, on the ground floor, he had ready access to the squad biscuit tin, squatter's rights on the biggest of the photocopying machines, plus a view of the car park.

Expecting Carole Houghton at any moment, Suttle was reviewing *Scorpion*'s options when his personal mobile began to ring. 'O mio babbino caro', Lenahan's birthday present. The wee man's last toehold in a world he'd left behind.

Suttle froze for a moment, fighting the waves of despair that had been threatening to engulf him all week. Then he opened the text. Lizzie, he thought. He read the message again, recognising at once the bright-eyed jauntiness that had never been part of their relationship. Lizzie could do passionate. She could do worried. She could do funny. She could, over an entire winter, do depressed. But this voice wasn't hers.

She's covering her arse, he thought. She's

183

looked at the diary and decided to do her duty. Would she ever make it back to Chantry Cottage? Even for a birthday cup of tea? He doubted it. Did he even want her to make the effort? If she was coming up with this kind of drivel? No.

He eyed the message a final time, then deleted it. Moments later Golding appeared at the door. He'd laid hands on the late-afternoon edition of the local paper. The front page of the *Express and Echo* was largely occupied by an aerial photo of a section of the beachside holiday camp. McGrath's body lay sprawled on the decking of the clifftop mobile home. From a thousand feet it had an insect-like quality. A woodlouse, maybe, a little curl of tissue drying in the sun. Also visible, tiny dots inside the white circle helpfully supplied by the paper's graphics department, were two other guys, one stooped, one badged by his shadow. Terry Bryant and the attending SOCO, thought Suttle. Had to be.

His eye strayed to the fleet of cars parked untidily beyond the inner cordon. He remembered the *whump-whump* of the press helicopter overhead. Was the snapper up there, alongside the video crew? And was he — the peerless D/S Suttle — in one of those cars, trying to tease some sense out of a strung-out smackhead?

'Nice, eh?' Golding was pointing to the headline.

Suttle blinked. It read DEATH STALKS THE DEVON CLIFFS. He turned the page and found himself looking at a mugshot of East Devon's MP. The guy was currently Minister of State for

184

Northern Ireland. He knew a thing or two about terrorism and he'd left the paper's reporter in no doubt about the gravity of what was happening down on his patch of the South West. First a guy shot to death on the edges of Dartmoor. Now a man murdered in cold blood elsewhere in the county for no apparent reason. No clues. No leads. Not the slightest suggestion from the investigating team that they had matters in hand. He'd be raising these appalling events in Parliament at the first possible opportunity. A civilised society deserved better protection than this.

Suttle permitted himself a smile, remembering Birdy in the custody cell barely hours ago. McGrath was no stranger to violence. A word or two about a toaster and a couple of CDs would spark a savage beating. Just how civilised was that?

Golding had news from Carole Houghton. Nandy had been summoned to a crisis meeting with the Chief Officer Group. They were busy framing a response to the growing public clamour for action. One line, according to a D/C who'd overheard a phone conversation, was to blame the cuts imposed by the Home Office. Slashing £52million from the operational budget wasn't risk-free. There were bound to be consequences, moments when the constabulary lowered its guard, and maybe this was one of them. A defence like this would be deeply controversial, provoking the government's wrath, but just now Suttle wasn't sure that he cared. Buried among the squillions of punters who

McGrath had pissed off would be the man who held the key to his death. And it was only a matter of time before *Scorpion* found him.

'When's the squad meet?'

'It's postponed. Houghton's waiting for Nandy to come back. She'll text everyone.'

Golding slipped a phone number onto Suttle's desk. Suttle spared it a glance, then studied it properly. Nigel Benning. The D/C working out of Exmouth. The guy charged with taking a look at Lenahan's death.

'Where did this come from?'

'Juliette. The guy left a message. He wants you to bell him.'

Juliette was the Major Crime Management Assistant, a workaholic single mum who'd somehow managed to keep her job as the cuts swept away layer after layer of secretarial support.

Suttle was looking pointedly at the door. Golding took the hint and left. Benning answered at the first ring. Suttle wanted to know what he was after.

'We need to talk,' he said. 'I can't do this on the phone.'

'Why not?'

'It's to do with the post-mortem. On your mate.'

'And?'

'Like I said, we need to talk.'

★ ★ ★

Suttle met him at a pub on Exmouth seafront, Benning's suggestion. Suttle had driven straight

186

from the *Scorpion* squad meet. Houghton, with Nandy still banged up with the Chief Officer Group, had outlined the latest lines of enquiry common to both *Graduate* and *Scorpion*. The breakthrough, if she dared use the word, lay in the killer's MO. Long-range skills like these were highly specialised. Nandy had opened the channels to the military and had a team of officers actively exploring possible leads. Beyond this she wasn't prepared to comment.

The revelation had met with little surprise. Suttle and Golding had already been discussing the possibility of a rogue sniper, either active or retired, but knew this was little more than speculation. How these two men had been killed was increasingly clear. The real key to both enquiries, as Golding had pointed out at the squad meet, was why.

Suttle parked his car, pausing on the promenade to glance down at the long crescent of beach. The last time he'd been here was last year during an enquiry tagged Operation *Constantine*. A wealthy entrepreneur had been found dead on the boardwalk beneath his trophy penthouse apartment in the town's new marina. There'd been no evidence of foul play but Suttle had pieced together a story that had led to members of the local rowing club. In the end he'd been proved right, securing a result of sorts, but his tenacity and persistence — while winning applause from the likes of Houghton and even Nandy — had cost him his marriage.

The aftertaste of *Constantine* had kept him

away from Exmouth ever since, but this evening he had to admit its attractions. Families gathered round barbecues. Young kids still splashing in the shallows. Dancing water, splintered with sunshine, as wind met tide off the marina dock. He lingered a moment longer, then turned to cross the road to the pub. Maybe he should come down here more often, he thought. Just pretend that *Constantine*, and everything that followed, had never happened.

Benning had found them a table in the garden at the front of the pub. The afternoon breeze off the sea had died and the sun was still hot. Benning insisted it was his shout, and while he was fetching a drink Suttle watched the kids racing round the play area at the back. Maybe he should bring Grace down here when she was a year or two older. Maybe she'd make friends, put down roots, move in with her dad, become what he'd always wanted: Jimmy's girl from the sticks.

Benning was back with a pint. He settled on the bench across the table. He had a big sun-brown face which creased easily into a smile and Suttle knew from a mutual friend that he was praying for a redundancy deal. Living down here by the sea, he couldn't wait to take full advantage.

When Benning enquired about progress on the holiday-camp hit, Suttle shrugged the question aside. Early days, he said. Impossible to say.

'Tell me about the post-mortem. What did they find?'

Benning looked briefly troubled. Then he

leaned forward across the table, a man with a confidence to impart, and Suttle suddenly realised that the meet was some kind of favour.

'Are you ready for this?' Benning asked.

'Yeah.'

'Your mate was gay.'

'I know.'

'And he was carrying the Aids virus.'

Suttle was staring at him. For some reason, HIV was the last thing he expected.

'How do they know?' he heard himself ask.

'The pathologist did a risk assessment. Stints in Africa? Workplace rumours? The fact the guy wasn't married or partnered? Then the mortuary assistant cut himself. That sealed it.'

'They tested Lenahan?'

'Yes. Like I say, HIV positive.' He paused. 'I take it you didn't know.'

'No.' Suttle reached for his drink. 'I didn't.'

'Should you get . . . you know . . . tested?'

'Why?'

Benning didn't answer. The implications were all too clear.

'You think we were at it? You think we were screwing?'

'It doesn't have to be that. Toothbrushes. Shared food. I'm here to pass the word, bud. Just in case.'

'Sure.' Suttle looked away, his mind racing. Maybe that's why Lenahan refused to go to A&E, he thought. Maybe he dreaded the possibility they might do a blood test. A positive result would probably land him in all kinds of shit. Better to stick with Chantry Cottage. Better

189

to take his chances with the mattress on the floor.

'So what did he die of?'

'One of his ribs was badly fractured. The way it works is this.' He patted the side of his chest. 'The sharp end lifts a flap of tissue in one of the lungs. Every time you breathe, air gets into the pleural cavity. The lungs compress. Then other vessels. Then the heart. You can be dead within minutes or within hours. The pathologist says it's a bit of a lottery — but either way, without intervention, you're a goner.'

'And he would have known that? Lenahan?'

'I've no idea. My guess is you busk it, hope to God it's not happening.'

'But he would have known, I know he would. He knew everything, that guy.'

'You're telling me this was a brave thing to do? Refusing the offer of treatment?'

'I'm telling you he was reckless. He loved cheating the odds. He'd do it everywhere, all the time. On the road when he was driving, out in Africa in some war zone or other, wherever the odds looked tasty. He couldn't stop, couldn't help himself. He said it made him feel alive.'

'Shame.'

'Yeah, fucking sad if you want the truth.' Suttle was thinking about the HIV diagnosis again, trying to imagine Lenahan out in the bush. 'He'd have gone bareback, I know he would. Loads of guys probably, hundreds of them. He just had such an *appetite*. It's all down to the odds again. Guys like Eamonn, they always think they're immortal.' He brooded for a

190

moment, then looked up again. 'You know what he once told me about death? About dead kids? Dead babies? He'd be dealing with this stuff day and night, 24/7. A family arrives at the township. The baby hasn't eaten for weeks. The mother unwraps it from the blanket and it's already long gone. In the end, Eamonn said, you turn off the light, lock the clinic door, sit in the darkness and have another cigarette. That's what death boiled down to. A quiet fag and the wind in the trees and the biggest fucking display of stars you've ever seen in your life. That was his phrase not mine. Believe me, life with that lovely man was never dull.'

He took another long pull at the beer, watching a little Asian girl trying to get the swing going. Lenahan would have been over there in seconds, he thought, taking charge, untangling the ropes, giving her a push, ignoring her shrieks, making her test the limits. He'd lived his life at full throttle and Suttle would never look at a night sky again without imagining the mischief of his grin among the glittering stars.

Then something else hit him.

'You remember the account I gave you? Finding him in the polytunnel?'

'Yeah.'

'I carried him back to the cottage. I had no choice. He couldn't walk, couldn't crawl, couldn't do anything.'

'So?'

'I had to put him over my shoulder.' He mimed a fireman's lift. 'He weighed fuck all but I know it hurt him.'

'Sure. You did what you could. So what are you telling me?'

'It's obvious.'

'Not from where I'm sitting.'

'I'm telling you it was down to me. I'm telling you you were right to ask all those questions. The guy's got a splinter of bone in his lung. Me carrying him like that probably killed him.'

'You could never prove it.'

Suttle stared at him a moment, before getting up and extending a hand.

'I don't have to,' he said. 'Just the fucking thought's enough.'

* * *

Lizzie knew at once that her mum had sussed her. Again.

They were having a late supper together. Grace had taken ages to settle, insisting that Lizzie rewrap the David James bear in paper she liked, and once the job was done, she produced a pad and made Lizzie spell out a birthday greeting for her dad. Her spider-writing fell off the ruled lines of the pad and dropped headfirst towards the foot of the page but the essence of the message somehow survived. *'For my lovely Daddy. Kiss Kiss Kiss. I miss you. Kiss kiss kiss (from David). PS Happy Birthday. Xxxxx'.*

Now, over the remains of last night's lasagne, Lizzie poured herself a glass of wine. Her mother wanted to know where she was staying over the next couple of days.

'Bere Ferrers,' she mumbled.

'Is that some kind of hotel?'

'It's a village, Mum. In the Tamar Valley.'

'But you have a hotel? A B&B? Somewhere you and Jimmy can meet?'

Lizzie wondered whether it was worth hiding behind a straight lie, but if she came up with some kind of fictitious hotel she knew her mum would want the details. Better to stick with the truth.

'I've got a friend down there.'

'What's her name?'

'Patsy.'

'Patsy who?'

'I'm sorry?'

Lizzie's hesitation was enough for her mother. She crossed her knife and fork over the remains of the lasagne and pushed the plate to one side.

'You're doing it again,' she said softly.

'What, Mum?'

'Lying. Taking me for a fool. Taking us all for fools. Don't you care any more? Or is it worse than that?'

'I'm not with you.'

'You're off down to the West Country. It's Jimmy's birthday on Sunday. You told me on the phone you'd sent him a text, said it would be nice to meet.'

'That's true. I did.'

'So how come he phoned up just now? When you were upstairs?'

'That was Jimmy?'

'It was.'

'What did he say?'

'He wanted to talk to Grace. He sounded

193

terrible. I think he'd been drinking.'

'But what did he *say*, Mum?'

'He didn't say anything. That's the whole point. When I asked him what plans he'd made for Sunday, whether he was looking forward to you two getting together, he just laughed. When I asked him whether he'd got that text you sent he said he'd muddled you up with someone else.'

'He said that? He thought I was someone else?'

'Yes.'

'What did he mean?'

'I've no idea. Except he might be right.'

'I'm not with you.'

'You're not?'

'No.'

'Then let me be frank. You're not who you were, Elizabeth. You're not my daughter. You're not his wife. I'm not sure you're even Grace's mother any more. And you know why? Because you don't deserve to be.'

She got up very slowly, her eyes never leaving Lizzie's face, then she collected her plate and disappeared into the kitchen. Upstairs, Lizzie could hear Grace beginning to howl.

★　★　★

Suttle had stopped twice on the way home from Exmouth. Once at a pub in a village called Knowle he'd never been to before. And again at the Otter in Colaton Raleigh. Solitary drinkers were rare in these parts. Locals turned their backs while families dining from the Special

194

Discount menu eyed him with a mixture of wariness and what he took for pity.

He didn't want pity. What he wanted was some kind of explanation, some kind of lead. Not the kind of breakthrough that would offer the key to *Graduate* or *Scorpion*. Not the kind of clue that let him nail some deranged long-distance killer. But just a hint of how he was supposed to cope with the knowledge that Benning, bless him, had so casually shared just hours ago.

All week he'd been blaming himself for Lenahan's death, but here was the proof that he'd killed him. He should have taken him to A&E. He should have insisted. Instead he'd taken the easy way out. The excuse he'd been making to himself since Monday, that Lenahan of all people should have known how bad he was, no longer washed. Lenahan, it turned out, had probably known exactly what was happening inside his broken ribcage. And by simply trusting to luck, he'd effectively condemned himself to death. Had he been alone in the cottage, that would have qualified as suicide. Because someone was with him, someone who should have been bigger, braver, smarter, it amounted to something infinitely uglier and impossible to hide from. Death by negligence. Death by not thinking straight. Death by making the easy assumptions. End of.

Back home, in the silence of the cottage, he'd wanted to talk to Grace but ended up with his mother-in-law on the line. She had Lizzie's knack of sensing when he was pissed, and Suttle had known at once that the conversation was going nowhere. Grace, she said, was nearly asleep. Lizzie was up in the bedroom watching over her. All she really wanted to say was Happy Birthday for the weekend. Her tone of voice, regretful, almost apologetic, told its own story. She'd probably read the fucking text as well. She probably knew her bright-eyed little daughter was rapidly turning into someone else. He'd ended the conversation without saying goodbye. He still wanted to talk to Grace and it broke his heart that he couldn't. Karma, he thought. You let the man die. You fucking deserve it.

Now he prowled the cottage, trying to remember where he'd put the Scotch, hating the silence, wanting Lenahan back again. He missed the tuneless whistle from the kitchen, the nightly concert from the audio stack, the mad stories from A&E, the richness of their conversations. He yearned for the tangy scents of garlic and ginger, the sizzle as the sambal oelek hit the bottom of the wok, the explosion of saltiness as Lenahan shook yet more fish sauce into the stir-fry. This was a guy who knew how to live, knew how to keep the silence at bay, knew what mattered.

The pair of them, Suttle was realising all too late, had cracked it. That had been Lenahan's diagnosis, the verb that his game little medic favoured above all others, and it turned out he'd been right. They'd cracked it because they fitted so easily together, because they knew how to laugh, because they never pulled a moody with each other. That had been a revelation to Suttle

196

— you could share a leaky old sieve of a cottage with another human being without descending into near-terminal depression — and he'd been deeply thankful. Lenahan was the living proof that Chantry Cottage had been a good move, that people should always be bigger than their surroundings, that salvation came from within.

Should he have slept with him? Should he have succumbed to the thousand cheeky hints, increasingly overt? Possibly. Would that have stopped the wee man scaling a ladder and falling off? Probably not. Would a proper life together, the whole nine yards, have kept him in the UK? Would that, in the end, have been enough? Suttle was honest enough, even in the depths of this kind of darkness, to admit he didn't know. But that, somehow, wasn't the issue. The issue, in the plainest possible terms, was that he missed the guy, and that he was nursing a deep deep wound, all the more painful for being self-inflicted. If only he'd phoned. If only he'd acted. If only he could have his little man back again, discharged from hospital, restored to the rudest of health.

Suttle was on his fourth malt when his mobile rang. He didn't answer it, savouring the hot bath of Netrebko's voice, convinced it would be Lenahan's voice leaving a message. Just popped out for some resupplies. Côtes-du-Rhône or that fucking evil Rioja again? Your choice, Hawkeye.

Instead it was Golding. He sounded revved up. He wanted Suttle to call back. Asap.

Suttle at last reached for the phone, catching Golding before he rang off.

197

'Yeah?'

'Boss? Is that you?'

'Yeah.'

'What's the matter? What's up?'

'Nothing.' Suttle knew he was slurring. Couldn't be helped. 'What is it?'

There was a moment of silence. Then Golding was back on the line.

'Are you at home, boss? A yes or no will be fine.'

'Yes.'

'Stay there. I'm on my way.'

★   ★   ★

He arrived half an hour later. It was gone midnight. He let himself in through the kitchen door and found Suttle slumped on the sofa in the sitting room. He stepped across to the audio stack, wound down the volume and gave Suttle a shake. Italian opera was for old people.

'Wake up, boss. We have to talk.'

'Yeah?' Suttle rubbed his eyes. He'd been dreaming of Faraday, his former boss. He'd been a drinker too, and a bit of a solitary. How would he have coped with something like this?

Golding was in the kitchen. Suttle heard the splash of water into a glass. Then Golding was back.

'Drink this,' he said. 'Where do you keep the aspirin?'

'Upstairs,' Suttle mumbled. 'Ibuprofen. Bathroom cupboard.'

Golding returned with the tablets and stood

over Suttle, making sure he took them.

'You want to talk about it?' Golding's gesture seemed to take in Suttle's entire life. 'You want to tell me what's going on?'

Suttle struggled upright on the sofa and swallowed a third tablet. No D/C had ever talked to him like this. He cocked his head to one side, studied Golding for a moment, then decided to take this gruff concern as a compliment. The guy seemed to care. Which came as a bit of a surprise.

'How come you speak French?' he said.

'My mum. She comes from Bordeaux. And she's got zillions of sisters.'

'She taught you?'

'Insisted. She spoke French to me all the time when I was a kid. Drove my old man nuts.' He paused, then nodded back towards the empty bottle of malt on the kitchen table. 'So what happened?'

Suttle was still coping with the news that Golding was half-French. Why had it taken him more than a year to find out?

Golding asked him for the third time what was wrong.

'I had some bad news,' Suttle said.

'About your mate? The guy who died?'

'Yeah.'

'Like what?'

Suttle toyed with sharing the pathologist's findings, then decided against it. One way or another he'd have to make a peace with what had happened but now wasn't the time.

'It's complicated,' he said. 'Maybe later.'

'No problem.'

'So what's happened?'

Golding at last sat down. There was a brightness in his eyes that Suttle had never seen before.

'I ran into Terry Bryant,' he said. 'After you left the squad meet.'

'And?'

'He'd made a start on McGrath's flat. The SOCO was still down there. They'd done a quick trawl first and found some receipts from a betting shop round the corner. We're talking pay-outs.'

'Big pay-outs?'

'Three figures. Not huge, but useful.'

Suttle nodded. Among the litter of *Daily Stars* on McGrath's lounge carpet, he remembered a copy of the *Racing Post*.

'We're talking horses?'

'Yeah. But the important thing about the receipts were the dates. The pay-outs stopped about nine months ago. Until then the guy had been a regular punter. After October last year, nothing.'

'So maybe he stopped betting. Knocked it on the head.'

'Sure, boss. And maybe he didn't.'

'I'm not with you.'

'I'm not fucking surprised.'

Golding pulled his chair closer. He wanted to spell this thing out. He needed Suttle to understand.

'We're in the Custody Centre, right? In the cells. We're talking to the woman Birdy.

Remember what she said at the end? When I asked her where the money came from for the holiday?'

'No.' Suttle shook his head.

'She said *that man was so fucking lucky.*'

'That's right. She did.'

'Meaning he was still in the game. Still gambling. Still at it.'

'But not on the horses, right?'

'Right.'

'So what did you do?'

'I went to the betting shop. Terry gave me the receipts. There's a woman who works there most days. She's on from twelve to midnight. She's been there for more than a year. I described McGrath. I showed her the betting slips. At first she didn't want to know, gave me loads of flannel, said she has a million punters, can't tell one from another, then another guy stepped in. He was checking the form cards for tomorrow's meetings. He knew everything about McGrath. And about the woman as well.'

'She was lying?'

'Definitely.'

'But McGrath gave it all up.'

'No, boss.' Golding's patience was wearing thin. 'He gave the *horses* up. In October last year the shop put in fixed-odds betting. We're talking machines. Basically you bet on casino games. The guy called them evil. He said they take your life over. They pay out, you get the taste for it, you keep feeding the money back, and in the end you've got fuck all left. They suck you dry, these machines. Unless you know when to quit, they

201

leave you skint. Which is what happened with McGrath. The guy called him an animal. He tried to smash one of them, physically attacked it. Then he started on the woman.'

'She admitted it?'

'No, boss. But she will.'

'And this takes us forward?'

'Yeah. Why? Because the woman had an admirer. Maybe more than that. And thanks to matey I think I know where he lives.'

'You're telling me this guy did McGrath?'

'No, boss. But he might have made it happen.'

8

Ever since she'd returned to work after fleeing East Devon, Lizzie had made a vow never to join the smokers in the car park. She'd kicked the habit years ago but still found something repugnant about the bunch of colleagues, mainly women, who clustered in sad little groups around the rear entrance.

This morning she spotted Gill at once. It was hot again, not a cloud in the sky, and the scoop-necked halter left absolutely nothing to the imagination.

'Given in at last?' Gill was already digging in her bag for cigarettes.

'Actually I wanted a chat.'

'Ah, I see.'

Gill stepped away from the group. A nearby wooden bench offered a little privacy. Gill arranged herself to catch the sunshine. Her legs were bare below the loose cotton frock. Lizzie couldn't take her eyes off the scarlet stilettos.

'Like them?' Gill was watching one of the guys from the print room, a fellow smoker who was rumoured to be an artist in the sack.

'I think they're amazing.'

'Sixty quid on the Internet. You get your money back if you don't pull within the hour.' Gill gave the printer a little wave and then turned back to Lizzie. 'So what's the problem?'

'Did I say there was a problem?'

'You didn't have to. You look terrible, Lou. What's going down?'

Lizzie knew that Gill would cut to the chase. It was part of her MO, an artful bluntness that certain men found irresistible.

'It's my mum. We've fallen out again — big time, I'm afraid.'

'And?'

'I'm going to have to move.'

'I?'

'We. We're going to have to get out of there. It's hopeless, Gill. She wants to run my life for me. I'm not having it. Not any longer. I'm nearly thirty, for fuck's sake. She treats me like a child.'

'Is it Jimmy?'

'Yes. But then it's always Jimmy. She wasn't married to him. She didn't have to live in that bloody cottage of his.'

'She wants you all together again?'

'Of course she does. It's in the *Manual of Married Life*, chapter one, line one. Be together. Live together. Stick together. No matter what. I try and explain that it doesn't work that way anymore, that women have lives of their own, but it's water off a duck's back. She doesn't listen. She never listens. She wants me to be her. She wants Jimmy to be my dad. Happy fucking families. How sweet is that?'

Gill's attention had strayed again. One of the senior execs this time, the car rather than the driver. She watched him hooking his jacket from the newly parked BMW.

'Series seven,' she said wistfully. 'Top of the range.'

'Did you hear what I said?'

'Of course I heard what you said.' She was back with Lizzie. 'You don't think she's got a point?'

'*What?*'

'About kids? About family? I'm no expert, Lou, but maybe Grace would like a daddy in her life.'

Lizzie looked away. She knew exactly which way this conversation was going. They both did.

'You're telling me you don't have room for us?'

'That's not the issue. What would you do with Grace? Assuming you don't chuck the job in?'

'I'd find a nursery. It would do her good. She gets too much attention at the moment.'

'And the job?'

'I'd work flexitime. Everyone's doing it.'

'Nurseries cost a fortune, Lou. I've got a girlfriend in Camden Town. You know how much she pays? For *one* three-year-old? Sixty-seven pounds a *day*. Over thirteen hundred quid a month. That's two mortgages.'

'This isn't Camden Town. Pompey rates are way lower than that.'

'How low?'

'I dunno. Not exactly. But I could manage it. I know I could.'

'As long as you had somewhere to live?'

'Yeah.'

'Which wasn't costing you a fortune?'

'Yeah.' Lizzie reached for her arm, a gesture of

reassurance. 'I'll pay the rate. Of course I will. Whatever you think is reasonable. Plus something on the top to cover everything else.'

'Like what?'

'Council tax, electricity.' She forced a smile. 'Not having a ruck every night.'

Gill sucked at her cigarette, then expelled a long blue plume of smoke.

'You mind me asking you a personal question, Lou?'

'Not at all.'

'You've started biting your nails.' She nodded down at Lizzie's hand. 'Why would that be?'

★ ★ ★

Suttle and Golding had an early meet with D/I Houghton. Golding had stayed over at Chantry Cottage, using Lenahan's bedroom and waking early to the sound of the running water from the bathroom next door. Suttle spent longer than usual under the shower, surprised that he didn't feel a great deal worse. The remains of a headache, maybe. And a whisper of queasiness while he watched Golding tucking into a monster bacon sandwich. But no trace of the hangover he deserved.

At the MIR Houghton was already at her desk. Golding briefed her on the enquiry he'd made at the Heavitree betting shop, and for a fraction of a second Suttle thought he detected the ghost of a smile on Houghton's face. Trying to straddle two high-profile investigations, coupled with intense pressure from a variety of force honchos, was taking a visible toll. Exhaustion showed in the hollows of her face, and when Golding began to speculate about what might have happened to McGrath after his outbursts over the fixed-odds betting, she cut him short.

'I'm interested in evidence, Luke. The rest is speculation. Find this guy who fancies the manageress. Press him hard. Talk to her as well. See where it takes us, yeah?' She turned to her PC, fielding yet another email, the conversation over.

★   ★   ★

Golding had a steer on the punter who'd so suddenly appeared on *Scorpion*'s radar. His name was Johnny and he was said to live beside the main entrance to Exeter Golf and Country Club. The club lay to the south of the city, off the main road that followed the river down to a village called Topsham. Suttle and Golding were there within the half-hour. The houses were detached, cared-for, well tended. This was a world of double garages and the kind of garden furniture that didn't come from Homebase. Not one of these properties, thought Suttle, would go for less than three quarters of a million.

He and Golding parked up and crossed the busy road. Faced with a house on either side of the entrance to the golf club, Suttle went for the one on the left. The woman who came to the door turned out to be the cleaner. Asked if she worked for a man called Johnny she shook her head. Her employer was an Indian surgeon.

'Lovely man.' She was still staring at Suttle's warrant card. 'Lovely family.'

The other house, if anything, was bigger. A lone sparrow was drinking from a water feature in the front garden, and there was a cheerful notice beside the front door warning visitors about the dog. Suttle rang the bell. Golding was admiring a Range Rover TDI, parked on the gravel drive. It looked brand new.

Finally the door opened. When Suttle introduced himself and asked whether a man called Johnny lived here, the answer was yes.

'It's me, pal. The name's Hamilton. How can I help you?' Scots accent, a voice thickened by cigarettes.

Golding had just clocked the warning about the dog. Hamilton laughed. The dog was long dead, he said. He'd left the notice there for any burglar who could read.

'Nae chance, eh?' Scot's accent.

He invited them in. He was a broad thickset man in his early sixties. He had a drinker's face, heavily veined, and wore a thin gold chain around his neck. In his cord slacks and open-neck check shirt he looked like a refugee from the thirteenth fairway.

The house, like the garden, was immaculate and deeply comfortable. Most of the framed photographs in the hall showed a much younger Hamilton with a woman who must have been his wife. In her wedding dress she looked a stunner beside the man who had yet to acquire a drinker's girth. Other shots were more recent. In

208

one of them the woman was beaming up from a wheelchair.

'My Ellen,' Hamilton explained. 'She passed away a couple of years ago. MS. You youngsters wouldn't know about losing someone you've lived with half your life. It's an experience I wouldn't recommend.'

He stumped on through to the huge lounge. The French windows were already open, sucking in the light, and Suttle fancied he caught the smack of a golf club as someone dispatched a shot from a nearby tee.

'Inside or out?'

Suttle was still looking round. He guessed that everything in the room remained exactly the way it had been when this man's marriage came to an end: the long fall of gold velvet curtains, the thick pile of the carpet, the carefully chosen furniture, the baby grand in the corner, the original oils on the wall. This was a world away from the backstreets of Heavitree.

Suttle said he was happy to stay indoors. Hopefully the interview wouldn't take long. He was grateful for Hamilton's cooperation.

'You haven't got it yet, laddie.' He slapped his thigh and roared with laughter. 'What am I supposed to have done?'

Suttle shot a glance at Golding, who asked Hamilton whether he used a betting shop in Heavitree.

'I do, aye.'

'Often?'

'Aye.'

'May I ask why?'

209

'Because it's well run. And because I can use my bus pass to get there. The 57, laddie. Every half-hour from the stop across the road. Don't smile. It'll happen to you one day.'

Golding scribbled himself a note. Suttle wanted to know how often he laid bets.

'I just told you. Often. I don't go there to watch. I was never a spectator.'

'Is it always the horses?'

'Aye.'

'Never the machines?'

'Wouldn't touch them.'

'Why not?'

'Because you never beat the odds. Nae bloody chance. The house wins, not every time, of course not, but the way these machines are set up you haven't got a prayer. One big pay-out and you're hooked. And you know something else? They prey on the ignorant, on the guys who can't count, on the guys who can't see beyond that first big fat pay-out.'

'The gamblers, you mean?'

'Sure. But there's gambling and gambling. Me? I always bet on the horses, and I always win more than I lose. Why? Because I take the trouble to learn how they calculate the odds, to find out about form, to know which horses, which trainers, which jockeys to avoid. It's a science, laddie, and if you want the truth it's kept me sane.'

Suttle pressed him further. How come he'd ever gambled in the first place? Hamilton seemed to welcome the question. His gambling days, he said, began on the oil platforms in the

North Sea. He was an engineer with an American corporation, highly paid, working twelve-hour shifts day after day for weeks on end. The money was fantastic and the food was even better, but he was no reader, and most of the television you wouldn't waste your time on, and so he started teaching himself about horse racing. Professionally, he lived in a world of figures, of calculations, of decisions based on the careful study of probabilities. Gambling on the horses, in essence, was very similar.

'I had an account when I was offshore. You could access live feeds from the racing during the day and I started winning. Not only that, but I enjoyed it. Most men from my neck of the woods end up there — ' he nodded towards the French windows ' — on the golf course. Me? I'm a racing junkie. And all the richer for it.'

He looked from one face to the other. He apologised for not offering them something to drink. It was a wee bit early for a dram but he could do coffee or tea if they fancied it.

Suttle said yes to coffee. When Hamilton headed for the door, Suttle caught Golding's eye and gestured for him to follow.

'You mind if I use your bathroom?' Suttle called.

Hamilton, with Golding in pursuit, was already in the kitchen.

'Use the one upstairs,' Hamilton shouted. 'The other one's out of action.'

Suttle climbed the stairs. There were six doors off the landing at the top. He tried them one after the other. With the third he struck lucky.

The big windows in the master bedroom offered a breath-taking view out over the golf course. He lingered for a moment or two, watching an ancient figure in a baseball cap trying to hook his ball from the rough, then turned back to the room.

The big double bed was unmade, the duvet thrown back. Suttle lifted both pillows, sniffed them. On one he caught the scent of perfume. Quickly he went through the drawers in the dressing table. In the top one, a collection of expensive underwear, every garment black. Silk, he thought, feeling a pair of camiknickers.

He went back to the bed. The scented pillow lay on the right. On the other side, where Hamilton probably slept, he pulled open the drawer in the bedside table. A wallet lay on top of a collection of blister packs, most of them ibuprofen. Inside the wallet was a thick wad of fifty-pound notes, a return rail ticket to Doncaster and a couple of credit cards. He gazed at them a moment before unzipping another compartment. Getting his fingers in was a squeeze, but he could feel something small and flat wedged inside. From downstairs came the murmur of voices. Thank Christ for Golding, he thought. The boy was playing a blinder.

Finally, with some care, he managed to ease the contents out. The prints had come from a photo booth. There were four of them in all. Three featured an attractive woman Suttle judged to be in her mid-forties. Her hair was cut in a blonde bob, and in every shot she was smiling at the camera, her mouth open. In the

212

other shot she had company. The cheek pressed to hers belonged to Johnny Hamilton. The smile was even broader.

Suttle replaced the photos in the wallet, returned it to the drawer and left the room. When he found the lavatory, he flushed the bowl and closed the door. The bathroom was adjacent. He washed his hands and looked around for a towel. On the back of the door was yet another photo, bigger this time and nicely framed. Johnny and Ellen, years back, arm in arm on some racecourse or other. Bookies' stands in the background and a mass of punters jostling at the rail. Suttle eyed his image in the mirror, wondering whether the neatly bobbed face in the wallet could ever fill the yawning gap in this man's life. If the someone who'd stolen your heart had gone, what else was left to discover?

Downstairs he met Hamilton emerging from the kitchen. There was a plate of biscuits on the tray as well as cups and a cafetière of coffee.

Hamilton settled himself on the sofa again and poured the coffee. When he looked up, Suttle asked him about a man called Tommy McGrath.

'Tommy who?'

For the first time Suttle detected a note of caution in his voice.

'McGrath. You may have seen a mention in the papers or on telly.'

Hamilton went through the motions of searching his memory. He was a poor actor.

'The guy who was killed yesterday?' he said at last. 'Out on that holiday camp?'

'That's him. He's alleged to have used the

213

same betting shop as you. The one in Heavitree. I'm just wondering whether you ever bumped into him.'

'What does he look like?'

'Biggish guy. Your kind of age.' Suttle was trying to picture the bit of McGrath's face that had survived the bullet. 'Shaved head. On the fat side.'

Hamilton nodded. He wanted to help. He really did.

'Could be anyone,' he said. 'A million punters go through that shop. The name rings no bells. Sorry.'

Suttle nodded. If Golding had this thing right, he knew now that the man was lying. The question was why.

'Can I ask you another question, Mr Hamilton? Do you mind?'

'Of course not.' He waved a hand at the tray. 'Biscuit?'

Suttle ignored the invitation. He wanted to know if there was anyone else in Hamilton's life. Now that he was a widower.

'Am I lonely, laddie? Is that what you're asking?'

'Not exactly.'

'Then the answer's no. Do I miss my wife? Of course I do. Is life the same as it was with Ellen? No. Could I ever get anything like that back again? Never in a million years. So why would I even try?' He paused, passing the plate of biscuits to Golding. Then he looked at Suttle again, the bonhomie gone. 'Does that answer your question?'

Against her better judgement Lizzie ignored Rob Merrilees' directions for Plymouth and instead took the road that hugged the coast. The holiday traffic thickened once she got into Devon and it was later than she'd anticipated by the time she picked her way to Colaton Raleigh. She slowed for the turn into the lane that led to Chantry Cottage, amazed at how lush everything was. Another mile took her to the cottage itself. She parked outside, relieved there was no sign of her husband. Lizzie knew he had a lodger but he didn't seem to be at home either. Perfect, she thought, opening the car door.

The heat and the warm dungy smells of the fold of the valley hit her at once. She could hear the cawing of rooks from the stand of trees away to the west, the slow trickle of water from the stream at the foot of the garden, the lowing of cattle from the farm at the top of the lane. She stood beside the car for a moment, gazing across at the cottage, letting it all sink in. It was like she'd never been away. All she needed now was a decent downpour and a bucket or twelve to catch all the leaks.

She reached into the back of the Toyota, meaning to haul out Grace's present and leave it propped against the cottage door, but then she changed her mind. First, she thought, a little wander.

She slipped in through the garden gate, noting that someone had at last reattached it to its hinges. Beyond the pile of logs in the shelter

215

of the outhouse lay the long stretch of garden neither she nor Jimmy had ever bothered to cultivate. At the bottom, though, there was something new. She made her way through the knee-high grass, recognising the humpy swell of a polytunnel. The flap that served as a door lay open and she stepped inside. The heat inside was overpowering. An old wooden table was cluttered with plastic growing pots and unopened packets of seeds. A scatter of gardening tools lay on the bare earth. The polytunnel had the same makeshift air as the cottage itself but someone had expended a lot of time and effort on the stuff growing inside.

She walked slowly between the lines of tomato plants, of cucumbers, of spring onions. She counted four kinds of lettuce. She knelt to grub up a bulb of garlic. Beyond she could see rows of runner beans and a tangle of rich green leaves hiding the fattest of marrows. Then she caught sight of something metallic. It turned out to be a step ladder, lying on its side. A metre away a galvanised metal bucket had spilled new potatoes in every direction. This little tableau brought her to a halt, and she wondered whether to gather a bagful of the potatoes as a present for Rob. This kind of size, you could wish for nothing sweeter.

She found a plastic bag in an old tea chest by the door. She took a couple of dozen potatoes, and added tomatoes, runner beans, a lettuce and some courgettes for luck. These were in the nature of reparations, she told herself. She'd lost the war to survive in this sleepy little corner of God's England, but the least it owed her was a decent meal or two. Roast lamb with new potatoes and a lightly dressed salad? Perfect.

She took the bag back to the car, swapping it for Grace's panda bear. She carried the present round to the front door, pausing to peer in through the kitchen window. Once again this was a scene that had survived all the months she'd been away. The unwashed dishes in the sink. The doors on the kitchen units that never closed properly. The flaking plaster on the far wall. The empty bottle of Scotch abandoned on the kitchen table. She shuddered, remembering the soundtrack to images like these: Grace squalling from her playpen next door, the death trap of daytime TV, the scuttle of the dormice that had nested in the chimney, the creaks and groans the cottage made in any kind of wind. These, she knew, were the months which had robbed her of who she really was. Back in Pompey, for better or worse, she was Lizzie Hodson again.

She propped the present beside the front door, wondering whether it was safe to assume it wouldn't rain. She knew where Jimmy used to keep a spare key and was certain it would still be there. She could, if she chose, let herself in and have a proper look around, but she knew that there were limits to her curiosity. Then she remembered the card she'd bought at the motorway services near Southampton.

She fetched it from the car and sat in the sunshine, her back against the warm brick, wondering what to write. The card featured a photo of St Mary's Stadium, home to the Saints,

217

the Southampton team that had just made it back into the Premiership. She knew nothing about football but fancied it might touch a nerve or two in her estranged husband. As a kid, growing up in a council house on the edges of a New Forest village, she knew Jimmy had been taken to the football by his dad. Later he'd played to a decent standard himself in a number of pub sides. She sucked her pen for a while, enjoying the sunshine on her face, then opened the card.

'*It takes one to know one,*' she wrote, '*and you're definitely a winner.*'

She signed it '*L*', added a single kiss and slipped the card into the envelope. Grace's card was already taped to the parcel. She stayed in the sunshine for another minute or so, wondering how long it would take to drive down to the Tamar Valley. Then she got to her feet and, without a backward glance, she was gone.

★ ★ ★

The moment Suttle walked into the betting shop, he knew Golding was on the money. The fixed-odds machines were at the front of the shop, impossible to miss as you went in. At first glance they looked like any other gambling machine, decked out in gaudy try-me colours, a little slice of Las Vegas among the balled-up betting slips that littered the floor.

Suttle edged past a youngish guy who was trying his luck at roulette. Even from this angle, there was no mistaking the woman behind the

218

counter. He'd seen her face only an hour ago. She'd restyled her hair, but the tilt of her head and the air of slight defiance in the eyes was exactly the same. Definitely Hamilton's lady friend.

She recognised Golding at once and turned away as if she might somehow remain invisible. Suttle offered her his warrant card. She spared it the briefest glance.

'I'm really busy,' she said at once. 'Some other time, eh?'

Suttle gazed slowly around. Three punters, including the young guy, who was blowing another ten quid on roulette. He turned back to the counter.

'I need to know your name.'

'It's Ceri.'

'Ceri what?'

'Ceri Bishop.'

'OK, Ceri.' Suttle lowered his voice. 'Here's what happens. My friend and I need to talk to you. You have half an hour to sort out some kind of cover. Either that or you close the place down for the afternoon. Do you understand what I'm saying?'

'You can't,' she said. 'You can't do that.'

'We can, Ceri. In fact we can do far more than that. We're going to be waiting here, OK? And then we're going to be taking you down to Heavitree police station.' He nodded at the phone beneath the counter. 'I'd get someone in if I were you. Sharpish.'

The relief manager arrived ten minutes later in a state of some excitement. Shedding his jacket, he asked her what the fuck was going on.

'Those gentlemen.' She nodded at Suttle and Golding. 'That's what's going on.'

They drove her to Heavitree nick. Golding had sorted a spare office for the interview. Suttle made it clear that she hadn't been arrested and she wasn't under caution.

'I haven't a clue what you're talking about,' she said. 'I just need to be through with this.'

Suttle had been on the phone to Houghton while they'd been waiting. It was clear from her manner that time was running out for *Scorpion*. To keep the Chief Officer Group at bay she needed a solid line of enquiry. Fast. Even Nandy, she said, was beginning to have doubts.

'About what?'

'About the way we're handling this.'

The office was disconcertingly bare. It had been emptied by its last occupant and was awaiting reassignment to someone else. A table. Three chairs. A filing cabinet. This was a room that wouldn't seem out of place in a Third World movie. In some deeply unsubtle way it promised nothing but pain.

Suttle eyed the woman across the table. There were interview protocols in these situations, tactics carefully developed to snare even the most seasoned criminal. Given the pressure on time and the expression on this woman's face, Suttle didn't see the point. She was terrified already. He could see it in her eyes.

'I want to give you a name,' he said. 'And I don't want you to fuck us about.'

She nodded, said nothing.

'It's a guy called Johnny Hamilton. Do you know him?'

'Yes.'

'Well?'

'Yes.'

'How well?'

She stared at him for a moment and then looked at her hands.

It was Golding who broke the silence. 'This is a murder enquiry, Mrs Bishop, in case you were wondering.'

She nodded again, then she put her face in her hands. Her shoulders were heaving. Neither Suttle nor Golding moved. Finally her face came up, shiny with tears.

'This is about McGrath, isn't it? The guy who got shot?'

Suttle was staring her out.

'Go on,' he said.

'He was horrible, that man. I can't tell you how evil he was.'

'Why do you say that?'

'Because of what he did. Because of what he was. That man . . . ' She shook her head and began to cry again.

Golding fetched her a glass of water. She was trying to mop her eyes with the back of her hand.

'So what happened?' Suttle asked. 'What did McGrath *do?*'

'It was the machines,' she said. 'He went onto the machines. When they didn't pay out, when he couldn't get what he wanted, he went mad — just lashed out, kicked them, spat on them,

221

terrible. I tried everything. I tried to get him back on the horses, but he wouldn't hear of it. It was the machines, the machines all the time. How they owed him, how they'd robbed him, how we'd fixed them so he'd never win.'

'You were there by yourself?'

'Yes. These places are run on a shoestring. You've no idea. No one does. We even supply our own tea bags, our own electric kettle.'

'And were you sometimes there alone with McGrath?'

'Yes.'

'So let me ask you again. What happened?'

She looked uncertain. Then she sniffed and tried to clear her throat before asking for a tissue. Golding didn't move.

'What happened?' Suttle said again.

'He threatened me.'

'How?'

'He said he'd do me. He said he'd slice my face. He said he'd done it before. Then he said he'd rape me. I was worthless. I was a cheating slag. I deserved it.'

'Did you tell the management?'

'Of course.'

'And what did they say?'

'They said it was something I had to live with. They said it happened at other places. These guys were all mouth. I just had to ignore him.'

'But what did they *do?*'

'Nothing.'

'Couldn't you leave? Hand in your notice?'

She gazed at Suttle a moment, then shook her head in wonderment.

'Have you any idea how hard it is to get a job? Have you any notion how much it costs to keep a daughter at university?'

'You're married?'

'Divorced.'

'Maintenance?'

'You have to be joking.'

'So what did you do?'

'Nothing. Not to begin with. I just assumed the management knew what they were talking about. But the guy never stopped. In fact it got worse. Then one night he was waiting for me when I locked up. He'd lost a shitload of money that morning. He was steaming, blind drunk.'

'Did he hurt you?'

'I ran. He couldn't. He couldn't keep up. Fat bastard.'

'Why didn't you come to us?' This from Golding.

'Because the management wouldn't have it.'

'Did they tell you that? Spell it out?'

'They didn't have to. My job is to keep the money coming in through the door. The moment something happens to stop all that, I'm out on my ear. My fault. No one else's.'

'What about the other punters? Did they help?'

'No. McGrath was clever that way, always picked his moment. I just . . . you just . . . I can't describe what it felt like, a situation like that. You're just trapped. It's unreal. You know something terrible is going to happen and you know there's absolutely nothing you can do about it.' Her head went down and she started to sob again.

Suttle told Golding to sort some tissues. He knew they were nearly there now. Just one more push.

'But there was, wasn't there?' he said softly. 'There was something you could do about it?'

She nodded, her face still hidden in her hands. Suttle could hear Golding down the corridor, going from office to office, asking for tissues.

Finally she looked up. Her face was chalk-white. For the first time Suttle noticed the ring. She wore it on the second finger of her left hand. It looked new.

'So what did you do, Ceri? Just tell me.'

'I can't.'

'You can. I'm afraid you have to.'

She nodded. The fight had gone out of her. She looked exhausted.

'Why can't you just leave me alone?' she said at last. 'That man was evil.'

Suttle held her gaze. Her fingers had found the ring, twisting it and twisting it.

'Well?' he said.

She closed her eyes, swallowed hard.

'I talked to Johnny,' she whispered. 'And told him everything.'

'This is Johnny Hamilton?'

'Yes.'

'When did you tell him?'

'Two or three months ago.'

'What did you say?'

'I told him about the threats. I told him McGrath was going to hurt me, attack me, maybe rape me. I told him how frightened I was.'

'And what happened?'

'McGrath stopped coming into the shop.'

'Just like that?'

'Yes. More or less.'

'What does that mean?'

'It started again last weekend. I don't know why. But there he was, in my face, worse than ever.'

'Worse?'

'This time he said he was going to kill me.'

'Right.' Suttle nodded. 'And Johnny? You told him about that too?'

'Of course I did.'

'And since then . . . ?'

She blinked a couple of times and managed what might have been a smile.

'I never saw him again,' she said. 'Thank God.'

The door opened. Golding had found a box of Kleenex. He put them on the table in front of Bishop and then glanced down at Suttle.

'All right, boss?'

Suttle nodded, got to his feet, checked his watch.

'Done,' he said.

9

Lizzie found the address in Bere Ferrers without difficulty. She spotted the blaze of red on the front door the moment she rounded the corner. Parking across the road, she reached for her holdall and the bag of vegetables she'd stolen from the polytunnel, and crossed the road. It was another flawless day, hot sunshine untroubled by a single cloud.

She knocked on the front door. When nothing happened, she knocked again. The tabby in the front window seemed to be asleep. Across the road was a matching terrace of houses. Most of the curtains had been pulled against the sunshine and there appeared to be no one about.

She fumbled for her mobile, aware of a tiny flicker of alarm. Had she got the right day? The right address? The right village?

'You've arrived?' It was Rob on the phone.

'I have.'

'What do you think?'

'It's bloody hot. And you're not answering the door.'

Rob laughed, said he was sorry. Something unexpected had cropped up and he'd be back as soon as he could. The ride from Devonport, on a good day, would take him forty minutes. In the meantime she might fancy a stroll down to the

226

church. Go round the back and take a look at the river. For an even better view, follow the path up the hill. Plymouth, he said, is due south. Devonport is the bit with all the cranes. Enjoy.

He rang off, leaving Lizzie studying the cat. For the first time she realised it wasn't real. Then a door opened in the house next door and an elderly face appeared, blinking in the sunshine. The Captain was out, he said. Was there anything he could do to help?

Lizzie nodded.

'I need to find the church,' she said. 'Any clues?

The church turned out to be locked. There were glimpses of water beyond the graveyard wall and she quickly found the path that Rob had mentioned on the phone. The path climbed through stands of heather which snagged on her jeans. More breathless than she'd like to admit, she finally got to the top. Miles away to the south, beyond the gleaming blue spaces of the river, she could see the dark smudge of Plymouth. She shaded her eyes against the brightness of the sun, trying to pin down the details. Huge gantry cranes, presumably in the naval dockyard. Towering blocks of flats. A couple of bridges sluicing trucks and trains into Cornwall. And, a little closer, the sleek silver-grey shapes of warships moored out in the tideway.

She made herself comfortable on the short springy turf, delighted by what she'd found. On the way down, as soon as she'd left the torrent of traffic on the main road, she'd been astonished at how quickly the sprawl of Plymouth disappeared. Within minutes she'd been driving into an England that might have belonged to a different century: lush green fields, drystone walls yellowed with moss and lichen, even a glimpse of a stag briefly silhouetted on a nearby hill. This, of course, was deepest Devon, a landscape she was supposed to loathe, but there was something very different about the feel of this place. It was something to do with the light, or maybe — if she was honest — her mood. Where East Devon had always sucked the life out of her, these wooded valleys had precisely the opposite effect. They lifted her spirits. They let her taste freedom. They put a smile on her face.

She sat on the hill for nearly an hour, letting her thoughts race. The longer she stared at Plymouth across the water, the more it reminded her of Pompey. The same refusal to pose as somewhere picturesque. The same rough truculence. The same promise of violence and mischief. There'd be a decent daily paper here. They might have room for a journalist on the features desk. The place would be thick with stories. She could find a perch for herself and Grace, maybe out here in the Tamar Valley, and commute. She could put Grace in a nursery and, when she was older, take her to school every day, bake cakes for special days, gather blackberries for the harvest festival. There'd be oodles of retired folk to offer cover if things got sticky or if her job took her away. And best of all there was Rob Merrilees.

She lay full-length in the sunshine and closed her eyes. No more rucks with her mum, she thought, plus the chance for Jimmy to catch up with his daughter without the chore of a three-hour drive. The perfect result for all four of them.

★   ★   ★

D/I Carole Houghton had come over to Heavitree nick from the MIR at Middlemoor. Suttle had briefed her about Ceri Bishop and was awaiting instructions. The essence, as she'd agreed on the phone, was speed.

Houghton wanted to know about Golding. Where was he?

'I've left him with Bishop. He's taking down a formal statement. I've told him to spin it out. The last thing we need is her getting in touch with lover boy.'

Houghton nodded. Suttle had given her Hamilton's address. She'd already gathered an arrest team and put Scenes of Crime on standby. Within the hour she could have Hamilton downstairs in the custody suite with a couple of D/Cs ready to go in. She needed Suttle's thoughts on an interviewing strategy.

'He'll deny everything,' he said at once. 'He's that kind of guy. He's been around a bit. Did time on the oil rigs. He's not bent but he's solid. He can handle himself. He's made his way in the world. He's got a bit of money. He had a decent marriage. My take on the guy is this. He did whatever he did for the best of

229

reasons. He's far too long in the tooth not to understand the consequences of all that, and the last thing he's going to do is make it easy for us. His conscience is clear. One way or another he got rid of McGrath, but no way is he going to get himself banged up for it. Not if he can avoid it.'

'He'll go No Comment?'

'Highly likely.'

'So what do we do?'

Suttle assumed the question was rhetorical. Either that or Houghton was knackered out of her brain. We do what we always do, he said. We press the passive data. Laptop. Phone records. Facebook. The other social networks. CCTV. In these situations, especially when they're in a hurry, people always make mistakes.

'You think he was in that much of a hurry?'

'Yeah. I've no idea what kind of relationship they've got. They're obviously together, but I don't know when that started. Either way it doesn't matter. Last weekend she told him McGrath had threatened to kill her. A couple of days later the guy's dead. Hamilton's got money. He may be potty about the woman. Motive? Means? Am I missing something here?'

Houghton's phone was ringing. She glanced at Caller ID and put it to one side.

'So where would you go to buy a hit? Assuming that's what he did? Yellow Pages?'

Suttle said he didn't know. Bella Prentiss would have faced the same challenge: you've got oodles of money but no real idea how to buy what you so suddenly need.

Houghton nodded. She'd started negotiations with the Ministry of Defence but military records were notoriously hard to access. What she wanted was a peek at the database listing all military personnel with some kind of sniper qualification, either still serving or recently retired. Troops with the biggest presence locally were the Royal Marines. They belonged to the Navy. Her immediate point of contact was a Lieutenant in the Special Investigation Branch, based in the huge naval complex at HMS *Drake* down in Devonport. She'd said she'd love to be more helpful but Houghton sensed she was hamstrung by layers of authority way above her pretty head.

'Everything has to go through the Service Police Crime Bureau,' she said. 'They're over near Pompey somewhere. They normally talk a seven-day turnaround. Mr Nandy's on the case. We live in hope.'

Suttle had another idea. Ceri Bishop had first told Hamilton about McGrath's attentions a couple of months back, after which he appeared to have left her alone.

'That tells me someone had a word.'

'Hamilton himself?'

'Possibly. Though on balance I'd say not. He's a biggish guy, sure, but he's old and I'm not sure he'd frighten the likes of McGrath.'

'So he bunged someone? Paid someone?'

'Yeah.' Suttle remembered the feel of Hamilton's wallet between his fingers, the thick wad of fifties tucked inside. 'The guy's a regular winner on the horses. No one knows that better than

231

Bishop. She's the one in the shop that has to pay out.'

'You think she deliberately got close to him? Knowing that?'

'I doubt it. There had to be a reason for him to go there in the first place. It's way off his patch. It's probably not his kind of place. He may have wandered in off the street, just for a look. Maybe she caught his eye, the way it happens sometimes, and he became a regular. She's much younger than him, attractive too, but he's a nice bloke, very cheerful, and if he's the one who's going to get McGrath off her back, then she's not going to say no.'

'To what?'

'To a relationship.'

'You *know* they're together?'

'Yes.'

'How?'

'She admitted it for one thing but there are photos too.'

'You've seen them?'

'Yeah.'

'How? Where?'

'Don't ask, boss.' Suttle checked his watch. 'Maybe I should go in with the arrest team. I can save Scenes of Crime a lot of time.'

'Good idea.' She held his gaze. 'There's something else, isn't there? We haven't quite bottomed this thing out yet.'

'You're right, boss. Let's assume Hamilton paid for a bit of pressure, maybe a lot of pressure, a couple of months ago. That's something Birdy might know about. Or even the guy in the flat above. Maybe McGrath got a visit. Maybe he took a beating. Maybe it was just a phone call. Whatever happened, his behaviour would have changed. Not forever but for a bit. And people would have noticed.'

'Where's Birdy?'

'Still in the cells, last time I looked.' He stifled a yawn. 'Luke's the one to have the chat. She really likes him.'

★   ★   ★

A biggish motorbike was parked outside Rob's house when Lizzie finally made it back. The bike was the same colour as the door, a splashy red. The engine was still warm and Lizzie was trying to imagine riding on the back when she felt the presence of someone behind her. Rob Merrilees.

'Six grand on the road,' he said. 'Exactly the bounty they pay us for Afghan.'

She spun round. He was still in full leathers, totally irresistible. She dropped the holdall and the vegetables and kissed him. A scatter of new potatoes rolled towards the kerb.

'How cool am I?' She disengaged herself while Rob retrieved the spuds.

They went into the house. It was dark and almost chilly after the brightness of the street and Rob put the kettle on. Lizzie dumped her bag, left the vegetables on the side, and took a look around. To her relief, you could tell at first glance that no woman had laid hands on the place. Everything was neat, sorted, deeply male. The downstairs had been knocked through, creating a slightly tunnel-like effect. The mats on the stone floor looked serviceable enough and in principle there was nothing wrong with using angle-poise lights for reading, but nowhere could she detect the slightest surrender to fashion or frilliness.

Once she'd taken in the sagging armchairs and the stack of windsurfing mags, she half expected to find a couple of Airfix models, lovingly hand-painted. Battleships, maybe. Or one of those old V-bombers. This was where you'd make camp if you were a busy guy without much interest in fresh flowers or fancy dinner parties, she thought. This was exactly the way she'd wanted Rob Merrilees to live.

They talked in the kitchen after Rob had taken a shower. He came down from the bathroom in a pair of shorts and a faded blue sweater with what looked like salt stains round the cuffs. There was a quality about this man that Lizzie could only interpret as innocence. He seemed wholly at peace with himself, not a flicker of irritation or complaint. He seemed to have a child's pleasure in the simplest things — the taste of a grape from the fruit bowl by the fridge, the prospect of a beer or two when they wandered down to the pub after supper — and his smile had an openness, and a warmth, that any woman would find deeply arousing. Life in the Marines, Lizzie decided, must plug you into a very special source of energy. If the MoD was in the market for the perfect recruiting poster, here he was.

Perched on a stool, he talked her through tomorrow's tour of Hasler Company. The visit had been brought forward to 10.00a.m., and getting into the place, he said, would be a pain. The unit lay within the walls of HMS *Drake*. MoD plod would photograph her to death and insist on a health and safety course. With luck, it shouldn't take more than an hour.

'I'll love it.' Lizzie was pouring herself another mug of tea. 'It's all attention.'

'Excellent. You also get me for the duration, like I said before. If you try to do a runner, they'll shoot you.'

'Is that some kind of promise?'

She turned to face him again. They were knee to knee. She badly wanted to touch the pinkness of his face, to feel his lips against hers.

'What next?' she said.

'You'll get the standard bullshit tour. There's a bunch of hand-picked stars they wheel out, mainly triple amputees. There'll be lots of chat about 'recovery pathways' and 'getting back in the zone', and one of these guys will take you around. Every journalist has been pre-vetted, and that pretty much goes for the guys inside as well. At some point you'll get a chance to pin the bloke down without a minder around. You won't have long so make the most of it.'

'You're telling me these people are human beings as well?'

'Absolutely. Most of them, excuse my French, are fucking nails.'

'Nails?'

'Tough as old boots. To survive what they've survived, what they're *surviving*, you have to be. You'll get lots of shiny answers, lots of chat about building funding relationships with the commercial world, all that stuff, but remember: what these guys are having to cope with won't ever stop. It's a life sentence.' He nodded, leaning forward to emphasise the point. For once he wasn't smiling. 'You think you can cope?' he said. 'You think you can do it justice?'

She wasn't quite sure what the question meant. Was he expecting some kind of breakdown? The whole girlie thing? Didn't he think she could hack it?

'I'll try,' she said. 'I'll do my best.'

'I'm sure you will.' He sat back against the work surface, his legs spread. 'I've been thinking,' he said.

'About what?'

'About Afghan. You need to know about this stuff. The first time you go there is the strangest experience.' He paused. 'You want me to go on?'

She gazed at him. Strange question.

'Yes, please,' she said.

'OK then. This is the way it works. First, they ship you off to Salisbury Plain or a place up in Norfolk. Hats off to the military — they do their best. They've built pretend compounds and stuffed them full of Afghan expats. These guys are the real thing, all robed up. They're going to be running around like lunatics and gobbing off in Pashto. They're going to be in your face all day. They're going to be making life extremely hard for you. The people designing the exercise are going to be setting you all kinds of little traps, and in its way it's really clever, but you know there's a beer waiting at the end of it all,

236

and an evening of Sky Sports or whatever floats your boat, so in the end it's not real.'

'And that's a problem?'

'Yeah. Big time.'

'Why?'

'Because what's real is getting off that C-130 at Camp Bastion after the transit. What's real is the heat and the smell and the language and the culture. What's real is the moment when you realise you've stepped onto another planet, into another world, and no one's given you a map. I can't tell you how different it feels. The place closes around you. And it never lets go.'

Out in the field, he said, you probably end up at an FOB, a Forward Operating Base. You're talking about maybe a hundred guys cooped up behind mud walls stiffened with sandbags. It's fifty degrees in the shade most days. You live on garbage rations, you piss and shit in a chopped-down oil drum, and the guys take turns to burn the solids when the thing starts overflowing. There's a little concealed door somewhere in the compound, and most days you man up, put all your gear on and step into the fields outside. You haven't the faintest idea what the enemy looks like because he doesn't wear a uniform. You're carrying half your bodyweight in Kevlar armour. You're sweating like a pig. And you're horribly aware that every footstep could be your last.

'You know what the guys say? The guys at the end of their second tour? The guys who *know?*' His face was very close now. 'Knock too often on hell's door and one day it's gonna open.'

237

Lizzie was spellbound. She wasn't sure whether to applaud or take notes. But Rob hadn't finished.

'Something else you ought to know,' he said. 'As an officer recruit, it takes you thirteen months to get through training. The course is tough, tougher than the one the guys do, but it's meant to be. You stagger through the final tests, yomp yourself silly from one end of Dartmoor to the other, then — bang — you've got a beret on your head and you're drafted. It happened to me like that. Exactly like that. I found myself in Helmand, in all that strangeness. You're at the mercy of your Troop Sergeant, and everyone knows it. Then you get tested. In my case it was a heads-up about a truck that had just driven into the local town. A crowd was gathering and the atmospherics didn't look too bright. We were over there quick time and it was down to me to sort the situation.' He paused for a moment and took Lizzie's hand. 'There was a tarpaulin over the back of that pick-up. You know what was underneath?'

'No. Tell me.'

'Women. Children. More than a dozen of them. All dead. Some of them in a state you'd never want to see. Limbs missing. Heads missing. Insides hanging out.'

'How come?'

'We'd had an AC-130 up the previous night. That's a big fat American gunship. They got the target coordinates right, but the intelligence was dodgy and they took out this entire family by mistake. It would have taken about thirty seconds, maybe less, but now I'm looking at a man who probably wants to kill me. And that's if I'm lucky.'

'So what did you do?'

'I listened to the Troop Sergeant. The guy wants money, boss, he said. Buy him off. Hard currency. Dollars are best.'

'And did it work?'

'I'm still here. But you ask a good question. Did it *work?* And to that I have to say I haven't got an answer. Will a couple of hundred dollars ever bring that guy's family back to him? No. Is he ever going to see things our way? No. Will his extended family and his mates and the rest of them around that pick-up ever feel warmly disposed towards us? No. Did we ever have the right to play God with these people's lives in the first place? Again, sadly not. Not the way I see it. Not then and not now.'

Lizzie let the silence stretch and stretch. Several gardens away someone was mowing their lawn.

'So how did we ever get into this mess?' she asked softly.

'Very good question. The best. You know what we guys really do? We get the politicians out of the shit when everything else has gone pear-shaped. They pretend they care. They pretend it matters to them. They make pretty speeches when they fly into Bastion for their hour with the squaddies. They turn up at Brize for the colour parties when they ship the coffins off. They tug on the nation's heart strings. But you know what happens when the chips are

239

really down? When the bean counters at the Treasury take them aside and tell them they're running out of money?'

'No.'

'They make us plead for our very survival. Every few years we have something called a Strategic Defence Review. It's like one of those video games. The boat's sinking and someone has to get tossed overboard. Last time round it was us or the Harrier jets. The Harrier jets lost.'

'And next time?'

'Next time it could be us. Easily. We may not be around in a couple of years.' He nodded. 'Believe me, in our game that gives you a whole different perspective.'

He stared at her, something new in his face, an unvoiced question he couldn't quite manage to get out.

'So what are you asking me, Rob?' She squeezed his hand.

'I'm asking you what it takes to get into your little world.'

'You want contacts?'

'No.' He shook his head. 'I want a steer. Everything's changing. Your world, my world, everything. I guess I'm asking you whether what you do feels worthwhile. And I guess I'm asking you whether you still enjoy it.'

'The job, you mean?'

'Of course.'

'I love it.'

'Why? Tell me.'

'Because I'm nosey. Because I like finding out stuff. Because I like hanging it all together, teasing out the story, seeing it there on the page.'

'You sound like a detective.'

'That's what Jimmy used to say.'

'And is it true?'

'Yes, in a way it is.'

'So what about me? Us? This?'

'I don't know. But I rather think that's your decision.'

He looked at her for a long moment, then slipped off the stool.

'Upstairs, I think.' He smiled and then kissed her. 'Tough call, eh?'

★   ★   ★

Johnny Hamilton was arrested at 18.17 at his house in Exeter on suspicion of conspiracy to murder. Something in his manner told Suttle that he'd been expecting the knock on the door. He enquired at once about legal representation, and the arresting officer assured him that he could call his lawyer from the Heavitree custody suite. Asked to empty his pockets, he willingly complied. Both the wad of fifty-pound notes and the snaps from the photo booth were missing. As the arresting officer went through the wallet for a second time, Hamilton's rheumy eyes never left Suttle's face. Suttle thought he detected a smile but couldn't be sure.

A Scenes of Crime team under Terry Bryant began work on the house as soon as Hamilton had gone. Priority went to his PC and a laptop, both seized from the upstairs bedroom he appeared to be using as an office. Bryant did a preliminary trawl through recent emails and Google searches but found nothing that might set the enquiry on fire. Both machines, together with Hamilton's smartphone, were driven to the High-Tech Crime Unit for stripping down. Given the intensity of the media onslaught, *Scorpion* was pushing at an open door when it came to jumping the queue for hard-disk analysis. Work would begin at once and continue through the night. With luck, if a deletions trail existed, preliminary results might be available by tomorrow morning. Even Nandy was impressed.

At the Custody Centre, once he'd been booked in, Hamilton was allowed to phone his lawyer. At the mention of Ross Wedick, Suttle's heart fell. Wedick was a pushy London brief who specialised in making life as tough as possible for detectives battling the clock. Suttle had come across him on a couple of Pompey jobs. The guy would doubtless take his time sorting himself a train from Paddington, and there was absolutely no chance of getting the first interview underway until tomorrow morning. Wedick was an artist when it came to protecting his client from undue pressure, and a late-night start would be out of the question.

Suttle conferenced briefly with Carole Houghton. She knew Wedick by reputation and agreed that Hamilton would in all probability go No Comment. By now Hamilton was occupying one of the holding cells downstairs. It was Suttle's suggestion to use Ceri Bishop.

'Remind me.'

'Hamilton's lady friend, boss, the woman from

the betting shop. She's still downstairs with Luke. Christ knows how he's strung it out so long.'

'So what do we do?'

'We take her past Hamilton's cell. Slowly. And we make sure the door's open.'

'Right.' Houghton nodded. 'Do it.'

Ceri already had her coat on when Suttle went down to the interview room. Golding confirmed that her statement was complete. In the absence of an available typist, he'd written it out longhand, a process that had taken far longer than it should.

Whether Ceri had sussed the real purpose of this pantomime wasn't clear. She looked exhausted, a woman who'd strayed into a nightmare of someone else's making and expected worse to come. When Suttle said he'd escort her to the front desk and call her a taxi, she shook her head. She lived ten minutes away. Taxis were for rich people.

Houghton had alerted the turnkey to open Hamilton's cell door. Suttle was holding Ceri lightly by the arm. She was on the cell side of the corridor and Suttle slowed briefly as the open door approached. Ceri, to his relief, appeared oblivious to her surroundings. She didn't spare the cell a second glance but that wasn't the point. Hamilton was lying on his back on the concrete plinth, his head turned towards the door. There was no way he couldn't have seen the woman, no way he couldn't have sussed the reason for his arrest, yet he remained totally impassive, not a flicker of interest or alarm.

Suttle led her out of the Custody Centre. When she asked whether this was the end of it, whether Suttle or Golding would come knocking on her door again, Suttle said it was highly likely. Murder investigations ran at full pressure. The big picture was changing by the hour. Lines of enquiry might require another interview. She looked at him a moment, shook her head and turned away. After days of glorious weather, it had started to rain.

★   ★   ★

The first distant rumbles of thunder came to the Tamar Valley in mid-evening. Lizzie lay in bed, waiting for Merrilees to return from the kitchen. They'd made love twice, the first time with an urgency she could only remember from the early days with Jimmy. Later, they'd taken their time, exploring each other with a frankness and a delight that made her feel she'd known this man forever. He seemed to sense exactly what she wanted, exactly how to please her, exactly how to salt the low murmur of shared intimacies with the soft lapping of his tongue. She folded her thighs around his head, loving his deftness, the ease with which he unlocked her secret pleasures, his smile in the semi-darkness when she came with a shudder and a long expiring sigh.

'You should do safe-breaking for real,' she told him afterwards. 'You'd make a fortune.'

He was back from the kitchen. She could smell the sweetness of the lamb he'd put in the oven a couple of hours ago. Later she'd help him with the veg, prowl the little garden for sprigs of mint, uncork another bottle of Sancerre, but for now she could think of no better place in the world than here, curled around him, listening, wondering, probing, savouring.

The first fat drops of rain splashed on the roof overhead as the storm marched up the valley. Then came more thunder, closer this time.

'Cobblestones,' she whispered, feeling for his hand.

'*Cobblestones?* Is that what you call it?'

'Yeah. I did as a kid. My mum used to tell us to imagine a storm as a big old wooden cart, getting closer and closer, bumping over the cobblestones. She could never stop doing the teacher thing. It was sweet in a way.'

'But you're serious? You really want to move out of your mum's place?'

'I have to. I've got no option.'

'I don't understand.'

'Yes, you do.'

'How come?'

She was straddling him now, looking down at the brownness of his chest, at the openness of his face. How come men looked like little boys after making love? Was life really that simple for them?

'This matters, am I right?' She licked her forefinger and scrolled it across his cheek.

He nodded, said nothing.

'So I need my freedom. I need to be able to make a decision or two without having to answer to my mum. No big deal, I promise.'

'I'm not with you.'

'Yes, you are. You want me to spell it out? Mum wants me to get it on with Jimmy again. She's practically his fucking agent. She can see no further than that. She wants happy families. She wants us back together. She wants next Christmas, and the Christmas after that, and all the Christmases to come to be just us. OK, maybe another child. Maybe a little brother for Grace. Matching set. Like I said, sweet.'

'Is it Jimmy, then?'

'Is what Jimmy?'

'Is it over between you? Has it really gone belly up?'

'The marriage? Yes. Why? Because it's not just Jimmy. Jimmy's fine. He's a nice man. And if you want the truth he's way more than that. But staying married to Jimmy means living in the country, in that nightmare of a cottage I've told you about, and that will never happen.'

'For you?'

'For both of us. There's no way I can ever go back to that. Jimmy's a country boy. He loves it all. I can never take that out of him. It took me a while to realise it, but that's who he is. There's no room for me in a set-up like that, and he knows it. So yeah, you're right: it's over.'

'And you? What do you want?'

'I want this. Why? Because it's real. And it's honest. And I love it.'

'It?'

'You. This. The whole thing.'

For a moment she thought she'd blown it. Too pushy. Too eager. Too Gill. But then he was reaching up for her again, and she felt him stiffening beneath her, and she reached down, guiding him deep inside, moving slowly, waiting for the thunder, knowing with a rich certainty that this thing of theirs was going to work.

Afterwards, once the thunder had gone, and the storm had rolled away up the valley, he asked her about the job. They were very close, arms around each other, nose to nose.

'There are newspapers everywhere,' she whispered. 'Even down here.'

★   ★   ★

By half eight Birdy had seen both the police doctor and a specialist social worker Luke Golding had managed to lay his hands on. Both of these steps had to happen before Birdy could be formally interviewed. The social worker confirmed that there were a number of rehab pathways available to the likes of Birdy, but the immediate priority was a formal assessment. In the meantime the doctor had prescribed methadone, a heroin substitute that would ease her cravings.

Birdy, who'd tried the bright orange liquid before, wasn't impressed. She wanted the real thing and she wanted Golding to score it for her.

By this time Golding had realised that Birdy was falling in love with him. After Ceri Bishop's departure, he'd returned to her cell. They sat side by side on the concrete plinth, with Birdy holding his hand. Golding, who could look like a teenager in certain lights, initially regarded this sudden passion as nothing more than a short cut to a spoonful of warm smack, but slowly it began to dawn on him that a combination of neediness and blind panic had made her deeply vulnerable. For whatever reason, she'd decided that D/C Luke Golding had earned her trust and perhaps a great deal more. Even so, the offer of a blow job took him by surprise.

'Why would you want to do that?'

'Because I like you. Because you're not like the rest of them.'

'Rest of who?'

'Men. Don't laugh. I mean it.'

Golding could see she was upset. He put his arm round her. She was shivering again, bone-thin, and the gauntness of her upturned face made her eyes look huge.

The methadone was still on offer. The Custody Sergeant had stored it in a drawer, complete with a plastic spoon. Golding told her to take it. Otherwise she was in for a difficult night.

'You're not letting me go?'

'No. Not yet.'

'Not just for a little bit? I'll come back. I promise.'

'Where would you go?'

'Places.'

'To score?'

'Yeah. Of course. Then I'll be back.' She paused, struck by another thought. 'You can come with me if you want. Just to make sure.'

'But what will you do for money?'

'Tommy gives me money.'

'I know, love. But Tommy's gone.'

'Yeah?' She rolled her eyes, her head on Golding's shoulder. 'Fucking bummer, eh?'

She started crying again. Golding found some tissues, dabbed at the tears pouring down her cheeks. Her hand was crabbing softly up his thigh. He trapped it and gave it a little squeeze.

'You're better than this, Birdy. You don't need to be out there gobbling some arsehole for smack. We'll make things better for you. I'll get the methadone.'

'Wait. Don't go. Don't leave me.'

Golding sank back onto the plinth. For someone so thin, so strung-out, she was remarkably strong.

'I want to say thank you,' she said. 'Is that OK?'

'Thank you for what?'

'For being kind. For listening. The blowjob's not a problem. Maybe some other time.'

Golding was staring at her now. She was going to tell him something; she was going to come across. Why hadn't he sussed this before?

'What is it, Birdy? What have you remembered?' He cupped her face in his hands. 'Just tell me.'

Her hands found his. She kissed him on the lips and then made a little tiny noise the way a baby might, a tiny grunt that seemed to signal a deep contentment.

'Round Easter,' she said. 'He was a big bloke, tall, fit-looking. I'd come in from somewhere, fuck knows, and I was standing in the hall, and the door was open at the end, and I could see him in the living room. He had Tommy on his knees, and he was squeezing his face like this, his whole hand, squeezing and squeezing, and Tommy was squealing, a horrible noise, like a noise I'd never heard before.'

She'd tried to copy the action on Golding's face but her hands were too small. Instead, she told Golding to do it to her.

Golding opened his hand wide, squeezing gently on the hollows beneath her cheekbones, trying to imagine which nerves this stranger had been trying to find.

'Harder. Do it harder.'

'No.'

'Please, for me, for Birdy.'

'No.'

'Why not?' She tried to kiss him again but Golding fought her off.

'You owe us this story,' he said. 'Right?'

'You. I owe you.'

'Sure. So what happened next?'

She gazed at him for a long moment, then nodded.

'He was like an animal, Tommy. It was an animal noise. Pain. *Real* pain. Horrible.'

'So what did you do?'

'I didn't do nothing. I left, got out of there. You want the truth? I was shitting myself. The guy was so big, not big, *tall*. He hadn't seen me. Tommy hadn't seen me. So I went upstairs. Alain's place.'

'And?'

'Al looked after me. He always looks after me. He said the guy would be gone soon. And he was right too. We heard the door go. Al went to the window. I was still shit-scared but I knew I had to go down for Tommy. Anything could have happened. He could have been dead, yeah?'

'But he wasn't.'

'No, he wasn't. And it was weird too. It was like nothing had happened. No marks on his face, nothing. When I asked whether anything had gone down he just shook his head. When I told him he was lying, he said I was out of it again. We started having a ruck about my habit, which was something that never normally bothered him, and it was then I knew something evil was kicking off.'

'Did he say what?'

'No, he said nothing, wouldn't talk about it no more. He had a few drinks then we went to bed. But this guy had hurt him. I could tell. No one makes noises like that in their dreams.'

Golding sat back. The timeline was a perfect fit. According to Ceri Bishop, the threats from McGrath had stopped two or three months ago. That would be April, around Easter. The tall stranger with the big hands had to have been Hamilton's present to the woman he was so desperate to protect.

Golding was on his feet now. Suttle was upstairs with Carole Houghton and Det-Supt Nandy. Time to share the good news.

At the cell door he paused, glancing back. Birdy was still on the plinth, her back against the wall, hugging her knees. She looked, if anything, disappointed.

'I meant it,' she said.

251

'Meant what?'

'About the blowjob.'

* * *

It was Nandy who voiced the obvious. After a series of blind alleys, here at last was a line of enquiry that might lead somewhere. He wanted Suttle and Golding round to the French guy's place sharpish. And he wanted bodies round the back in case the bloke tried to do a runner. While Golding sorted the back-up, Houghton reached for an email she'd just printed off. It came from the Service Police Crime Bureau, based at Southwick Park, north of Portsmouth. Suttle had had dealings with them on a number of Pompey enquiries. They had a reputation for treading extremely carefully when it came to sharing details from their huge database.

Houghton slipped the email across the desk. For once they appeared to have pulled their finger out on a civvy request. The Ops Room at Southwick Park was in the process of compiling an exhaustive list of snipers, current and recently active. Some of them, mainly Royal Marines, were based in the West Country. So far, they were looking at nearly one hundred and eighty names. The full list would be with *Graduate* within twelve hours.

Impressed, Suttle looked up.

'Who swung this?'

'Me, son.' Nandy was looking pleased with himself. 'Plus a couple of our sainted MPs. Nice to see them earning their corn at last.'

★ ★ ★

Lizzie and Rob Merrilees had a late supper. The lamb, if a little overcooked, was still delicious. Lizzie took charge of the trophy veg she'd scored from the polytunnel at Chantry Cottage and sorted another bottle of white wine from the chiller. They ate on stools at the breakfast bar, Lizzie naked under a borrowed dressing gown.

She wanted to know more about Afghan: the scars it would leave, the memories Rob would never forget.

'You never give up, do you?' He shot her a look. 'We fuck like angels and here we are back again.'

'Do you mind?'

'Not at all. The scar thing's interesting. How much do you know about the Falklands War?'

Lizzie carved herself another slice of lamb. She'd been exactly three weeks old when the task force set sail from Portsmouth, a fact that seemed to offer a decent excuse.

'Not a lot,' she said. 'An away victory against the odds? Lots of grief about some Argie battleship? And that's about it.'

'Right. So here's something interesting. That war killed well over five hundred of our blokes. And you know how many died in combat?'

'Tell me.'

'Two hundred and fifty five.'

'So what happened to the rest? They died later? Is that what you're telling me? From wounds?'

'Yeah. Sort of.'

'I'm not with you.'

'They committed suicide, all of them, some very recently. I guess that's what we mean by scars.'

Lizzie abandoned the lamb. She knew a great deal about the kind of killer stats that would give a feature paragraph a real edge. The Falklands War was history. It was also very brief. Yet here was a serving officer telling her that men and their families — way past middle age — were still paying the price. So what kind of long-term shadow might ten years of war in Afghan cast?

'No one knows. We're supposed to be good at handling battlefield trauma now. It's certainly way better than the guys in the Falklands ever had. But that's not the point.'

'It's not?'

'No. The point is that time moves on. The young guys we're sending out there these days come from a completely different generation. If I flew you to Afghan now, you'd be amazed. You're banged up in some FOB, shit and flies and incoming and all the rest, and yet the blokes are still wired into their Facebook pages and their Twitter feeds and their video games. It's truly weird. Afghan is a bubble, no question about it. But within the bubble there are all kinds of other bubbles. Some days, the bad days, you start to lose it. What's reality? Is it out on patrol? In what feels like the Middle Ages? Or is it on the laptops? Some hoofing war game the blokes have just got hold of? Then — bang — some guy gets blown up for real and you know what we have to do? We have to beat Facebook. We have to get to the next of kin before the message goes viral and half the world's sobbing their bloody hearts out.'

'So how do you do that?'

'We close down all comms out of Afghan. We call it Operation *Minimise*. It's not perfect but it gives us a couple of hours to get the job sorted. We need to deliver the death message, so if you get knocked up at three in the morning and see a padre and a bloke like me in uniform on your front doorstep you know you're in the shit. Terrible job, by the way. The worst.'

'You've done it?'

'Twice. The first time it was like a scene out of *Eastenders*. Major grief. The second time the wife was amazing. Her mum happened to be staying and was in floods of tears the moment we passed on the bad news, and you know what her daughter said? She told her mum to go upstairs and get a grip. There were kids involved too, a couple of nippers up in their little bunk beds, wondering what on earth was going on. That guy's missus was amazing, so strong. Brilliant.'

Lizzie tried to imagine the scene, failed completely. She reached for Rob's hand.

'You like strength, don't you?'

'I admire it. It's what we need. And these days it's too often what we've lost.'

'You're telling me this stuff never gets to you?'

'Stuff?'

'Afghan? Guys dying? Guys coming back in bits?'

Rob shook his head. Lizzie sensed she'd come to the end of the line, that the rest of the evening would benefit from a change of subject, but there was something inside her that needed an answer.

'There's nothing wrong with being human,' she said softly. 'Just tell me.'

'You don't want to know.'

'I do. You might not want to tell me, but I do.'

'Why?'

'Because it matters. Because otherwise I might start thinking it all goes over that pretty head of yours. And I'd be wrong, wouldn't I?'

'Yes.' He nodded. 'You would.'

'Fine. So tell me.'

Rob reached for his wine, then had second thoughts.

'It was a while back,' he said. 'Back when casualties went to Selly Oak in Birmingham. It was Christmas Eve and I'd gone up to see a guy from my troop who'd come back a triple amputee. He'd been in an induced coma for a couple of weeks and he definitely wasn't a well boy. I met his wife outside the ward. She was one of the stronger ones. She said he was in Intensive Care. To get to IC you had to go through a ward called SI.' He broke off. 'You're sure about this? You really want me to go on?'

'Yes, please.'

'OK.' He shrugged. 'There were forty-eight beds in that ward. I counted them. And you know what? They were all full. These are young guys, army, regular troops, fresh back from Afghan, and every single one of them was wrecked. I just stood there. I couldn't move. I couldn't do anything. I'd totally lost it. It was Christmas, like I say, and the staff had made an effort, they really had, but all the tinsel and cards and stuff around the ward didn't help. I just saw all those grey faces, just kids really, and I remember thinking what the fuck have we done? What are we doing? When will all this stuff end? I never made it to IC. I couldn't. I left the ward and just walked out of the hospital. It was raining. I knew there was a chippy down the road so I went and bought a bit of fish and sat on the wall outside in the rain and tried to get a grip, tried to figure out just what the fuck we were up to. No one knew about this stuff. And that was wrong. Everyone should know about those guys. Everyone should know what the war had done to them.' He ducked his head at the memory. 'Fucking nightmare . . . '

There was a long silence. Then his head came up again and Lizzie saw something new in his face, something close to disgust.

'Is that OK?' he said. 'Is that what you want?'

★   ★   ★

It was nearly ten by the time Suttle and Golding got back to McGrath's address. The lights were on in his neighbour's flat upstairs. Suttle rang the bell twice and then stepped back into the light of a street lamp, awaiting Seydou's cautionary check from the window. When he appeared, Golding gave him a little wave. Moments later the front door opened.

Upstairs, Seydou had company, a white girl, very attractive, leggy, who turned out to be French. She was curled in a corner of the big leather sofa, the remains of a joint dangling from her hand.

'*Flics.*' Seydou nodded towards the door. '*Vas-y.*'

With some reluctance the girl got to her feet and left the room. Suttle heard a door open and close, then came music, far too loud, the girl resenting the sudden intrusion.

Suttle asked Seydou to sit down. He shook his head. He wanted to know what this was about. Suttle explained about the incident that had brought Birdy up to the flat. Eastertime. Some stranger downstairs paying his respects to Tommy McGrath. And Birdy terrified that he might start on her.

Seydou went through the motions of trying to remember. Then he shook his head.

'No,' he said.

'You do, my friend. It's there. Just try harder.'

Something in Suttle's voice caught his attention. An evening on the weed seemed to have fogged him.

'This is important?'

'Very.'

'And this is about Birdy again?'

'McGrath. Tommy McGrath. Someone killed him. You probably remember.'

'*Oui. Bien sûr.* But this comes from Birdy? She told you?'

'Yes.'

He looked at them both for a moment, then beckoned them across to the window.

'I saw this guy leave. That's all I know.'

'What was he like?'

258

'Tall.'

'Did you see his face?'

'No. He was wearing . . . ' He mimed a hoodie.

'What else had he got on?'

'Jeans maybe. I don't know.'

'Did he have a vehicle?'

'*Oui.*'

'What kind of vehicle?'

He frowned and for a moment Suttle thought he couldn't remember, but Golding realised he couldn't find the words.

'*Une voiture?*'

'*Non.*'

'*Une camionette?*'

'*Oui. C'était blanche. Avec un drapeau au-dessus.*'

'*Un drapeau peint? Sur la toit?*'

'*Oui. Exacte.*'

'*Quel drapeau?*'

'*Un Union Jack . . .* ' Seydou drew the flag with his hands ' . . . *n'est-ce pas?*'

Suttle had followed most of it but needed to be sure. Golding confirmed that the tall guy had got into a white van parked on the street below.

'And the Union Jack?'

'Painted on the roof.'

★ ★ ★

Suttle phoned Houghton from his car. He could see Seydou across the street, watching him from his window.

'Boss? We've got a lead. The guy who paid

259

McGrath a visit was driving a white van.'

'Great.'

'Wait, boss. It had a Union Jack painted on the roof.'

'*A Union Jack?* Why?'

'No idea. Maybe the guy's military.'

'Or was.'

'Sure. Queen and country. All that shit. DVLA?'

'No point, Jimmy. They wouldn't carry that kind of detail. We need the chopper up first thing. This is a big flag? Covers the whole roof?'

'So it seems.'

'Excellent. We'll task the chopper to start with Exeter and then work outwards. The crews may have clocked it before. Fingers crossed, eh?'

Suttle could hear a ripple of excitement in her voice. He threw a grin at Golding and reached for the ignition key.

'Where next, boss?' Suttle glanced across the street again. Seydou had gone.

'Bed, Jimmy. Half seven tomorrow in my office, yeah? And well done.'

★ ★ ★

Suttle was back at Chantry Cottage by eleven. It was pitch-dark by now. The rain had gone, and he stood by the car enjoying the freshness of the wind on his face. There comes a moment in every investigation when a door yields to an exploratory push, offering a glimpse of a way forward, and he knew that they'd arrived at just such an opportunity. *Graduate* and *Scorpion*, the way he saw it, were obviously linked. Same MO. Same scrupulous attention to detail. The involvement of someone with a military background, probably a specialist in one of the darker arts, had always been a possibility, and now, in the shape of Seydou's sighting of a van badged with the Union Jack, they had the first confirmation that this might be the case.

Within twenty-four hours, with luck, Houghton would be looking at a list of names. She'd draw up a matrix to sieve out the rubbish, and among the survivors they'd find the guy or guys who'd killed both Corrigan and McGrath. That's the way the investigative machine worked. Suttle had tested it on countless occasions and rarely found it wanting. All that remained were the chores of TIE: trace, implicate, eliminate.

He made his way across the gravel towards the front door, aware of a vague sense of disappointment. For an entire working day he'd thought of nothing but the double killings. Trying to kick down that key investigative door had emptied his mind of everything else. No stressing about the wreckage of his private life. Not a single thought about his dead Irishman. Just the challenge of nailing a talented psycho or two, bent on serial mayhem.

Hunting for his house keys, Suttle didn't see the parcel beside the front door. Only when he had the door open and the light on did he spot the wildly patterned paper, the tell-tale splodges of yellow and red. *Grace*, he thought at once. A little prezzie for her absentee dad.

He took the parcel inside and cleared a space

on the kitchen table. He cracked a Stella from the fridge and thought briefly about something to eat. But already, within the space of a minute or so, the silence of the cottage had got to him. Where was Lenahan? What had happened to the music? How on earth was he supposed to cope with this abrupt return to the darkness of last year? Lizzie gone? Grace gone? Nothing left but the scuffle of dormice?

He tore the paper from the parcel. Grace's present, as ever, was over the top. He read her card twice, trying to get inside her head, trying to figure out how an overstuffed panda bear had become David James. Then he opened the other envelope. This, he'd guessed already, had come from Lizzie. She must have dropped it off, he thought. She must have risked the drive down the lane and the path from the car. She'd probably have taken a good look around, confirming all the things she'd known already: that this shitheap very definitely wasn't for her, that she was far better off tucked up with her mum and her daughter and a proper job in a proper life.

He slipped the card from the envelope. The image on the front — St Mary's Stadium, home of his beloved Saints — took him by surprise. Lizzie had put some thought into this. She'd remembered his passion for football, and the stories he'd told her about going to the footie with his dad.

Smiling at the memories, he opened the card. Lizzie's handwriting had been an early clue to the woman he'd fallen in love with: attractive, easy to read, with just a hint of something wilder in the way she sometimes strayed off the line. '*It takes one to know one,*' she'd written, '*and you're definitely a winner. L x*'.

The smile had gone. He held the card at arm's length, the way you might inspect something strange that has crept into your life. What the fuck was she on about? *Winner?*

He shook his head, wondering as well what she meant by the single kiss. After the welcome surprise of the choice of card, was this a duty peck on the cheek? A passing nod to his thirty-first birthday? Or did it signify something warmer? In truth he didn't know. What he suddenly wanted, very badly, was a drink.

★   ★   ★

Lizzie lay awake in the darkness of Rob Merrilees' bedroom, plotting the way she'd tackle the feature interview that would anchor the Afghan special supplement. She'd always been blessed with a near-perfect memory, especially for those moments when an interviewee happened across an image or a phrase that would light up a paragraph. Her conversations with Rob had been full of them, a treasure trove of direct quotes that she'd use as stepping stones to structure the piece.

By thinking herself back into the places they'd talked — the pub that first night, the restaurant a couple of days later and now here in his cottage — Lizzie could listen to his voice again. Already she'd taken the precaution of putting the best of this stuff on paper: how the nature of the conflict had changed, how 15 per cent of the guys who shipped out would return either dead or seriously wounded, how every sharp-end soldier had become a plaything of the politicians, and most importantly the life sentence that awaited those bootnecks unlucky enough to survive an IED. This latter element would flower naturally from her separate report on Hasler Company, the remedial facility to get these guys back on their metaphorical feet, and she'd already been prowling the Internet for material that might signpost the reader to Rob's feature interview.

One link on the Net had taken her to a stage play, *The Two Worlds of Charlie F.* She'd managed to acquire a copy of a BBC documentary called *Theatre of War* on the making of the play. The play's script had been based on exhaustive interviews with discharged soldiers, all of them in bits, and she'd been struck by the way that reliance on meds — diazepam, tramadol, morphine — so often slipped into the best painkiller of all: booze. One quote she'd carefully copied into her notebook, and the more she looked beyond her conversations with Rob, the more sense it seemed to make. The veteran, still in his twenties, was reflecting on what happens once you've put the war behind you. 'It's the darkest place . . . ' he said, ' . . . the dying place, the wishing-you-were-dead place. It's beyond belief but it's real as fuck.'

She felt for Rob's hand under the duvet, wondering whether to wake him up. He'd been right about her curiosity. In situations like these she couldn't help herself. She had to squeeze and squeeze until every last drop of the orange was hers. That's the way she'd always operated as a journalist. The road to stardom required a limitless appetite for finding out stuff, then having the stamina and the nerve to dig out more, knowing that every next step made you a little bit wiser. She'd done it instinctively at first, following her nose, worrying too much about upsetting people, but as her reputation and her confidence grew she'd realised that knowledge conferred power. And that power mattered.

In the early days she'd sometimes discussed this with Jimmy, discovering that detectives did it too. That's where success lies, he'd told her. That's how you'd crack the bad guys. By being cleverer than them. By getting inside their evil little heads. By figuring out why they'd done stuff to begin with and what they were liable to get up to next. Do it right, and you get to play God. Fuck it up, and you're looking at a new career in traffic-cone management or the lost property store.

She'd treasured this quote ever since and even now it put a smile on her face. She kissed Rob softly, careful not to wake him, wondering what Jimmy had made of Grace's little present.

* * *

Suttle had been back home for the best part of an hour before he saw the light winking on his answering machine. The single message had been left by a voice he didn't recognise. A strong Irish accent. Guy by the name of Padraig. Suttle settled beside the machine with his third can of Stella.

Padraig, it turned out, was Lenahan's adoptive dad. He'd brought the wee fella up in a village in West Cork. He himself had been the local doctor. He'd loved young Eamonn just the way he and his wife had always loved their other kids, but — to be frank now — he'd never thought the boy would make old bones. Too lively for his own good. Too bright. Too *interested*.

The voice was old, amused, and Suttle pictured him in some whitewashed stone cottage on the edge of the Atlantic, a pile of freshly dug peat drying outside in the thin sunshine, a glass or two of stout at his elbow.

Padraig had a favour to ask. He'd no idea how the wee lad had come a cropper, but before he came over for the funeral, he wanted Suttle to gather some flowers on his behalf, the wilder the better, and leave them somewhere significant.

At this point the message cut off because the answering machine was full.

Significant? Suttle stared at the machine, wondering what the word could mean.

Lenahan had never mentioned the fact that he'd been adopted. Indeed, his entire family had remained a mystery until Suttle had made contact with the names in his mobile directory, breaking the news that Eamonn had passed away. There'd been a couple of brothers who'd sounded shocked, and a sister — Mairead — who'd burst into tears. Eamonn had been her favourite person *ever* and she wasn't at all sure she could cope with this news. All the accents had been Irish, and Suttle realised that these must be Padraig's children, who presumably had grown up with Eamonn. The fact that Padraig was a doctor explained Lenahan's own calling, and the fact that Eamonn had largely practised abroad, in the most rugged surroundings, fitted nicely with Padraig's shrewd assessment of his adopted son. Lively. Bright. Interested. Yes, yes, yes. And even more so as he got older.

Suttle drained the can of Stella and headed for the garden. Significant, he'd decided, was a magnificent word, largely because it could mean anything. Should he leave the flowers in the polytunnel, where Lenahan had spent so many happy hours and where he'd suffered the fall that was to kill him? Should he put them in a vase in the living room, where he'd listened to so much opera and where he'd finally died? Or might there be some other solution, some other farewell, more fitting to the Eamonn Lenahan Suttle had been so lucky to get to know?

At the bottom of the garden, beneath the spread of a willow tree, was a drift of flowers Suttle knew Lenahan had loved. He'd said they were scabious. The little man would eye them from the kitchen when he was preparing the evening meal, voicing his admiration for their resilience, for their manners, for their cheerful good humour. He prized them as the most civilised of blooms, real diplomats on their soggy

267

little corner of God's England, and the drunker he got, the more extravagant his tributes became. Once, after finishing a bottle of decent Portuguese white, he'd expressed the desire to become a scabious in the afterlife. Then, the daftness of this proposition had made Suttle laugh. Now, he began to wonder whether Lenahan might have been some kind of clairvoyant. The gift of tongues had always been his. Maybe he'd heard the voices too.

In the throw of light from the house Suttle knelt among the scabious and gathered a generous handful. They were cornflower-blue. He fumbled for binder twine in the darkness of the shed and managed to find a pair of rusty scissors. Across the bottom of the garden ran a stream fed from springs further up the valley. Lenahan had always drunk from the stream, ignoring Suttle's qualms about nitrate run-off and cattle shit. It had never seemed to do him any harm, and now — standing in the half-darkness — Suttle knew that this was the one spot on the property that captured the essence of his dead friend.

The flowers, bunched by the binder twine, were still wet from the evening dew. Suttle muttered a prayer of farewell, put the flowers to his lips, then laid them carefully on the blackness of the water. Within seconds, turning and turning on the bubbling current, they'd gone.

Some minutes later, once he trusted himself to conduct a conversation, he tried to make contact with Padraig. Before returning to the cottage he'd picked another bunch of scabious, and they were still in his hand. The number rang and rang but no one answered. Finally, emotional again, he left a message.

'Done,' he said.

10

SATURDAY, 30 JUNE 2012

The Exe Vale Hotel lies among a range of hills to the west of the River Exe. The hotel pitches to a broad clientele from Americans touring the South West of England to punters heading for a couple of days at the nearby racecourse. The management offers hiking, cycling and horseriding on a variety of local trails for the livelier guests and has made a sizeable investment in the hotel grounds. Views from the bedrooms are framed by mature oaks and elms. Responsibility for maintaining these trophy trees lies with a one-man outfit trading under the man's own name: Adrian Saunders.

The hotel manager contacted Adie Saunders at the beginning of the week. A guest who knew a thing or two about trees had spotted a weakness in a couple of the upper branches of one of the bigger oaks. Given the general dreadfulness of the summer weather and the hotel's liability in the event of an accident, the manager wanted Adie to drive over asap for a look. Adie had a crowded diary. Bookings were going mental. The best he could do was six in the morning on the Saturday.

Adie arrived on time. He knew the tree well. He studied the rogue branches through a pair of binoculars and decided that the guest had been right. Returning to his van, he gathered the climbing equipment he'd need, plus a chainsaw. Rain had returned overnight and getting himself to the required height wasn't easy. Finding a perch at the root of an adjoining bough, he adjusted his harness and fired up the chainsaw. A guest at the window of one of the rear bedrooms, seconds later, saw him go limp in the harness, dropping the chainsaw as he did so. The saw swung beneath him on its leash, still roaring, the automatic cut-off failing to work.

The guest rang reception. Apart from the chainsaw, he'd heard nothing. Staff ran towards the tree. A cleaner was first on the scene. She'd been outside for an early fag and had seen the figure in the tree go limp. Adie Saunders, a favourite of hers, was still dangling in his harness. Blood was dripping from a huge head wound. She couldn't be certain, but she wasn't sure Adie had a face any more. Interviewed later in the day, she recalled seeing blobby grey bits in the wet grass beneath Adie's body. By now the on-call pathologist had identified these remains as brain tissue.

★　★　★

Jimmy Suttle, in bed with a stuffed panda bear, took the call at seven fifteen. Houghton sounded less than pleased. Suttle dragged a razor over his face, threw on a suit and ran to the car. Houghton, he knew, was right. Losing two bodies to a serial killer — or killers — was deeply

271

unfortunate. A third within a week was taking the piss.

Det-Supt Nandy was already in Houghton's office. The news that Major Crime was now dealing with three investigations had stretched his patience to the limit. The Saunders killing had just become Operation *Bellwether*. At this rate, Nandy growled, he was going to run out of bloody code names.

Houghton, normally unflappable, was struggling to retain some clarity. The data from the military had yet to arrive. Until it did she wanted to focus on the obvious. According to reports from the Crime Scene Manager out at the hotel, Saunders had been shot in the head, presumably from a distance. The exit wound had removed most of his face. Retrieving the single bullet, given the uncertainty about the precise line of fire, would once again be a huge forensic ask. The MO, in short, was identical to the other two killings.

'So where are we, boss?' This from Suttle.

Houghton was grateful for the question. Nandy, firing on all cylinders, was practically epileptic. Get a helicopter up. Put a trillion POLSA searchers into the surrounding country-side. Call the Royal Marine ATOs. Fend off the press. And take no calls from dickhead MPs.

Houghton ignored him for once. 'Intel, Jimmy. That's where it begins and ends. We need to know about this man. He had an admirer, a local girl who works as a cleaner at the hotel. Gently gently, yeah?'

'She's got a name, this girl?'

'Leanne Carter.'

'And where's Luke?'

'Outside in the car. Waiting for you.'

* * *

Suttle and Golding were at the hotel by twenty past nine. Scenes of Crime had arrived in force and Suttle counted five Transit vans parked among the guests' cars. These could only have contained the small army of uniformed officers Nandy had been demanding for the POLSA search. For a force spatchcocked by cuts, this was deeply impressive. Panic was clearly spreading among the Chief Officer Group at Middlemoor HQ.

Suttle wanted to check in with the Crime Scene Manager to find out what forensics had turned up, but Golding talked him out of it. Houghton, he said, had been extremely clear in her instructions. Focus on the girl. Dig deep. Find out about Adie Saunders. And go wherever her account takes you.

Leanne Carter was resting in one of the empty guest rooms. Suttle and Golding found her stretched on the bed, the curtains pulled tight, sobbing her heart out. She was small and startlingly pretty in a slightly doll-like way. Suttle judged her age at around eighteen, certainly no more.

'I need water,' she wailed. 'Something to drink.'

Golding filled a glass from the bathroom. A lipstick lay on the glass shelf below the mirror.

Maybe young Leanne had been readying herself for the inevitable TV crews. Suttle had persuaded her to sit up. When he opened the curtains the room was flooded with sunshine. Golding had been right about the lipstick. A slightly labial mauve, already smudged.

Suttle wanted to know about Adie. How long had she known him? What could she tell them?

'He was a lovely guy. A lovely lovely guy. This is, like, a fucking nightmare. Why? Why would anyone want to do a thing like that?'

'We don't know, Leanne. That's why we need your help.'

'What do you want to know?'

'Everything. Anything. Listen — ' Suttle's mobile rang. He checked caller ID and motioned Golding to take over. It was Houghton. A D/C in the MIR had just come up with a business address for Saunders. The address turned out to be a rented new-build in the village of Whimple, to the east of Exeter. The D/C had talked to the landlord, who'd confirmed Saunders' name on the tenancy agreement. To the landlord's certain knowledge, there was someone else living at the address as well, a woman called Kirsten. He'd no idea whether these two had any kind of relationship but thought it worth a mention.

Suttle made a note of the name and address and hung up. Leanne was clearly warming to Luke Golding.

He asked her whether she and Adie had been friends.

'Yeah.' She nodded. 'That's why this whole

274

thing's so devastating. We were . . . you know
. . . close.'

'Really close?'

'Yeah. *Really* close.'

'How does that work?'

'I dunno what you mean.'

'Did you see him outside hours? Outside work?'

'Yeah, of course.'

'Where?'

'We'd meet in a pub. There's a lovely place
down in Dunchideock. He'd buy me a meal. He
was a laugh, Adie. I really liked him.'

'Was he married?'

'No. Had been once but not any more.'

'Partnered?'

'No.' She shook her head again. 'He said he'd
had enough of all that.'

'All what? What did he mean?'

'Relationships. All that stuff. He said certain
kinds of women were more trouble than they
were worth. I think he meant older women.'

'Not you.'

'No, not me.'

'So what happened?'

'What do you mean?'

'With you and Adie.' Golding's gesture
bridged the gap between them.

Leanne stared at him a moment. Lovely eyes.

'Did we screw, do you mean? Is that what
you're asking?'

'Yes.'

'Of course we did. He had a mattress in the
back of his van. It's easy round here. There are
loads of places.'

'This happened often?'

'I can't remember. I wasn't counting.'

'But more than once?'

'Of course. Whenever we could manage it.'

Golding nodded, scribbled himself a note. The sight of his racing biro put a frown on Leanne's face.

'Why do you want to know this stuff? What's that got to do with anything?'

Suttle took over. Leanne had been close to Adie. That was obvious. Had he ever talked about making enemies? Some competitor at work? Someone in his private life?

'Never. He was cool that way, Adie. Nothing ever bothered him.'

'You were never aware of being followed? When you were with him?'

'No way. You'd notice, wouldn't you?'

'What about his mobile? Did he ever get calls that seemed, you know, a bit odd?'

'Never.' She began to sniff again. 'He was just a lovely guy, a lovely lovely guy. You know what I mean?'

★　★　★

Lizzie picked up the first news reports of the Saunders shooting as she and Rob Merrilees were driving to Hasler Company. A police spokesman, interviewed on local radio, said it was too early to confirm a link between this latest incident and two earlier deaths but admitted there might be similarities. Lizzie slowed for a tractor and threw Rob an enquiring glance. In Pompey she'd picked up media chatter about some guy shot dead in a Devon holiday camp but had been too busy to enquire further. Now she wanted to know more.

Rob said he couldn't help her. Maybe she should call her husband? Surely he'd be in the loop?

For a second or two Lizzie was tempted. Then she shook her head. She knew too much about the kind of pressure Jimmy would be under. Trying to bottom out a single homicide was a real stretch: mad hours, little sleep, snatched meals, plus all the other aggravations. Coping with three, with the possibility of a serial killer at large, would be crazy.

'I'll leave him to it,' she said. 'The last thing he needs is me on the phone.'

Hasler Company lay within the walls of HMS *Drake*, the Navy's huge shore establishment in Devonport. Rob had warned her about the security guys on the gate and he wasn't wrong. She was photographed, interviewed and sat down in front of a health and safety lecture. Nearly an hour later she finally made it to the grey, three-storey block which housed the rehab facilities.

By now, thanks to Rob, she fancied she knew a great deal about the realities of front-line service in Afghan. He had the gift of making Helmand come alive for her — the heat, the dust, the language, the sheer strangeness of the place. He'd rewarded her curiosity with a candour that she'd never found in any other serving soldier, and it was impossible not to be moved by the

277

thick residue of anger and disgust he'd brought back from theatre. The commitment to Afghanistan — overhasty and poorly thought out — was sucking the military dry, and the real price was still being paid by the guys at the sharp end. IEDs. Sniper attacks. Suicide bombers. And now, grotesquely, the prospect of being shot by Afghani police or soldiers, the very guys we were there to train and protect. All this had taken Rob to a very dark place, and in the shape of Hasler Company, last refuge for the guys the war had maimed, Lizzie expected to find the living proof that he'd got it right.

Yet it wasn't like that at all. The moment she stepped inside the building, Lizzie could sense a buzz in the air. A shouted one-liner echoing down a nearby stairwell. A bark of answering laughter from somewhere closer still. Two amputees high-fiving as their wheelchairs met along the corridor. And the warmest of handshakes from the burly Warrant Officer tasked to show her round.

In one of the interview sessions on Whale Island, the day Lizzie had first met Rob Merrilees, he'd talked about the Commando Spirit. He'd described it as something akin to a drug. It came with one of the toughest training regimes ever devised and lasted a lifetime. Being a marine, he'd said, is the longest job interview in the world. Why? Because it never ends. At the time this had made her smile, but now, catching the frankness of the appraising grin on the face of yet another amputee as he wheeled past, she began to understand what Rob had meant. Man up and crack on, she thought. Too right.

The Warrant Officer, with Rob in tow, sat her down in an office and organised coffee. The place had been going a couple of years, he said. Just now they had more than ninety guys on the books. The programme was open-ended. A man stayed as long as he needed to stay, as long as it took to chart his journey forward. A handful might return to their units. Most stepped out into civvyland. Whether they had legs or not was immaterial.

'What matters is what's in here.'

The Warrant Officer leaned across the table and touched her head. The frankness of the gesture, its intimacy, took Lizzie by surprise.

'You're telling me everyone reacts this way?'

'Of course not. Everyone's different. We know that. That's why everything we do is bespoke. We tailor programmes individually. Some lads may take a while. One or two will always be casualties. But remember this: we're a family, we respect each other. Getting the beret doesn't happen by accident. It's something you earn, *really* earn. And that means you'll never be alone.' He nodded. 'Ever.'

She went on the tour. She saw the library and the education centre. She talked to an earnest young marine in the computer learning facility. She viewed the plans for a brand new £10 million facility taking shape nearby. She spent time in the gym, watching a guy called Dave pumping iron with his one remaining limb, and when he stopped for a breather she had a brief chat.

He'd been blown up by an IED on a canal side patrol outside Sangin. The last thing he remembered, he said, was the uppercut of scorching air that lifted him off his feet, but the thing that really pissed him off afterwards was the tatt he'd lost on his right arm. He'd had it done in a tattoo parlour off Union Street, a birthday present from his ex-girlfriend, and he knew for a fact that the guy who'd done it, a real artist, had gone on the vodka since and disappeared.

'I had the other one done, yeah?' He nodded down at his bulging bicep. 'But it ain't the same.'

The tour ended in one of the Marines' rooms on the ground floor. Lizzie was sure that the guy who lived in this cosy little space had been hand-picked for nosy journalists like her, but by now it didn't seem to matter. She'd seen dozens of faces, heard accounts of hideous injuries and their aftermath that had deeply impressed her. Not because they were shocking — they were — but because the survivors were so matter-of-fact, so fucking *cheerful*. Shit happens, they seemed to be saying.

This Marine had his heart set on becoming a helicopter pilot. The learning curve was brutal, he said, and there were funding implications that made his eyes water, but having something to aim for was definitely the best route forward. One day he wanted to be in charge of his life again. And flying a chopper might just do it.

Lizzie nodded. She understood. She really did. But her eyes kept straying to the corkboard on the wall. The board was covered in souvenir snaps: a column of amputees struggling up a mountain path in thick snow, a bunch of one-legged guys in wetsuits on a surfing beach, a triple amputee dangling from an abseil harness on a sheer cliff face.

'That guy's really special.' The Marine had noticed her interest in the abseiler. 'Next year he's down for an Iron Man. No way he won't do it.'

Lizzie nodded. She had no idea what an Iron Man was but she guessed it involved serious pain. Hadn't these guys, already monstered by Afghan, had enough of pain?

She voiced the thought aloud. The guy laughed.

'You know what they tell us here? They tell us that we're no different to what we were before. They tell us that pain's an opinion. That's what they always told us in training. And you know what? They're right.'

The Warrant Officer brought the tour to an end. Lizzie had spent most of the last two hours in the company of this man. His bulk and sheer presence gave him a natural authority, and it wasn't hard to picture him on a parade ground or an assault course. You'd listen to someone like this, and you'd doubtless do his bidding. But he was clever too, and artful in ways she recognised only too well.

He took her hand in his. They were standing on the steps outside the main entrance. The sun was out and there were seagulls wheeling over the huge gantry cranes in the nearby dockyard.

'You know why they call this place Hasler Company?'

She shook her head. This felt like an exam question. And she'd just flunked it.

'No,' she said. 'Tell me.'

'It's named after a guy called Hasler. Blondie Hasler. He was one of the Cockleshell Heroes. This is Second World War stuff. It won't mean anything to you, but he was one of the guys who canoed into Bordeaux and blew a couple of ships up. Two of the blokes made it back. One of them was Blondie.'

'Great.'

'Yeah. But here's the important bit. After the war he took up yachting, did lots of solo Atlantic crossings, all that stuff. But he was an inventor too. Self-steering gear? That was down to Blondie Hasler. So this is the guy who revolutionised ocean sailing. The guy who made solo journeys in shit weather a real possibility.' He gestured at the empty wheelchair parked beside the door. 'Solo journeys? Shit weather? You want to write that down?' He laughed. 'All the other journos do.'

⋆ ⋆ ⋆

Suttle and Golding were in Whimple by late morning. The news from Carole Houghton, as expected, was bad. Johnny Hamilton had conferenced with his London lawyer. Apart from confirming his name and address he'd blanked every question with a cheerful No Comment. The interviewing team was doing its best to

282

emphasise the gravity of his situation in the hope that he might be tempted to shed a little light on the tall stranger with the white van, but to date they'd learned nothing. Hard-disk analysis, in the meantime, was still a promise waiting to happen. As was the sniper list from Southwick Park.

Worse still, the force chopper had been airborne over Exeter for a couple of hours without a sighting of the van. From the air, emblazoned with a Union Jack, it should have been an easy spot, but so far the crew had drawn a blank. The pilot had only just joined the force, but the observer thought he'd seen it a couple of times a while back. 'A while back' turned out to be around Easter, when Seydou had clocked the mystery visitor leaving McGrath's place. Hence Houghton's growing exasperation: what on earth had happened to it since?

The address for Adie Saunders took Suttle and Golding to a cul-de-sac of newbuilds on the edge of the village. The tiny houses were a favourite of young police officers looking to buy their first properties, and the netherlands of Exeter were also full of them. Golding himself had bought one. It took him five minutes to walk to work and there was just room for his car on the hard standing out front, but if you fancied throwing a party in the tiny lounge-diner, you were struggling. In Golding's view they were built for midgets with a taste for living alone.

Saunders occupied number 5. A knock on the door produced no response. Suttle peered in through the front window. There were packets of cereal and a couple of bowls on the breakfast bar, copies of *Hello!* and *Living Today* on the carpet beside the black leather recliner. Golding had gone round the back. When he returned, he shook his head. The door was locked.

A twitch of curtain from across the street caught Suttle's attention. He went over and was about to push through the gate when the front door opened. The woman was in her sixties. She was thin with grey permed hair. She wore an apron over a white blouse and patterned trousers and her eyes glittered behind scary glasses.

'Who are you?' she asked.

Suttle produced his warrant card. She barely spared it a glance.

'You'd better come in,' she said.

The house was a clone of the property across the road. The volume on the TV in the living room was deafening. Half-watching the cricket was a huge man, also in his sixties. His bulk overlapped the armchair and there was a vagueness in his eyes that told Suttle he wasn't well.

'Dennis?' The woman was shouting. She gave him a shake. 'It's the police.'

The man didn't appear to hear. Instead, very slowly, he tried to move her out of the way of the TV.

Suttle asked her to turn the sound down. Otherwise they'd have to talk outside. She shot him a look and seized the remote. The man in the armchair, childlike, protested. She ignored him. Turning back to Suttle, she wanted to know whether he'd had any experience with stroke

284

victims. Suttle shook his head.

'Just as well,' she said briskly. 'I don't recommend it.'

Dennis turned out to be her husband. He was flailing around now, genuinely distressed by the sudden absence of noise. Unable to speak, he made strange gurgling noises, lifting a finger in the direction of the telly. Make it talk to me again, he appeared to be saying. Give me back my friend.

Golding suggested they go out to the car. The woman wouldn't hear of it. She couldn't leave Dennis by himself. God knows what he might do.

Suttle took the woman into the hall, leaving Golding to keep an eye on her husband. She could see them both through the open door. Suttle wanted to know about the house across the road.

'Number 5, you mean?'

'Yes. Who lives there?'

'A man called Saunders. He's got a van. The name's on the side. Adrian Saunders. I believe he does something in the tree line.'

'Has he been across the road long?'

'A year at least. No one knows anyone any more.'

'Does he live alone?'

'He used to. Now there's — ' She broke off. Her husband had slumped in the chair.

Golding was looking alarmed. 'Something I said?' He was bent over the armchair, staring down at the huge grey face.

The woman fetched a flannel from the

kitchen. It dripped on the carpet as she hurried back. She knelt beside her husband, bathing his face, whispering in his ear. She's done this before, Suttle thought. Probably often.

The man was stirring. His eyes opened. He looked totally blank, as if revived after a long sleep.

'More cricket — ' she nodded at the TV ' — if you're good.'

She looked up at Suttle. There was a woman living in the house across the road, she said. She didn't know her name but she knew she worked at the Met Office in Exeter because she'd talked to her once, on the station, waiting for the train, before the stroke happened and everything changed. She must have been living somewhere else in the village. That's all she knew.

'This man Saunders. Have you ever talked to him?'

'Once or twice, yes. He was nice enough if you like that kind of thing.'

'What kind of thing?'

'He's a smoothie. You know what I mean? All charm. All smiles. Not like my Dennis, poor dear.' She stroked her husband's cheek. He tried to catch her hand but missed. She gave him a little pinch, almost playful, then looked up at Suttle.

'Have you finished with me, young man?' She nodded at her husband. 'Only it's nearly feeding time.'

★ ★ ★

Suttle phoned Houghton from the car. When she asked about progress at Whimple, he confirmed that Saunders lived at the address. There was a woman in the house too, who appeared to work at the Met Office.

'Kirsten Kilpatrick,' Houghton said at once. 'Scenes of Crime recovered a Met Office card from Saunders' wallet. She's in the IT department.'

'Anyone contacted her?'

'We tried. She's at a conference in Manchester. Due back in the office first thing this afternoon.'

'She's not answering her mobile?'

'No.' For once Houghton was laughing. 'Her card was one of half a dozen. Saunders must have been a busy boy.'

★　★　★

Lizzie drove back to Bere Ferrers alone. Rob had a lunchtime conference at 3 Commando Brigade HQ in Devonport, followed by a series of meetings in the early afternoon. Planning for the next Afghan rotation was no respecter of weekends, and given his posting in Cyprus he had to keep in the loop. He suggested a late-afternoon rendezvous at a café in the new shopping centre but Lizzie said no. If it was OK with him, she preferred to go back to the cottage and get her thoughts in order.

'No problem.' He'd tossed her the keys. 'Was Hasler OK?'

'Hasler was perfect.' She'd kissed him. 'Better

287

than I'd ever expected.'

In a way it was true. Something had been nagging at her for days and now she knew what it was. The whole thrust of the *News* supplement had been getting darker and darker. This undoubtedly matched the facts as she understood them from Rob and from the young academic Gill had unearthed from Chatham House, but she knew as well that the whole Help for Heroes thing carried enormous clout among their readership.

People got emotional about soldiers putting themselves in harm's way. These were our boys. This was our blood. Proving beyond reasonable doubt that much of that blood had been spilled in vain might well end up antagonising the very people she was trying to reach. There had to be an upside, a glimpse of light at the end of the Afghan tunnel, and in the shape of Hasler Company she'd found just that. She'd big the place up, stress that this was cutting-edge care, probably unmatched anywhere else on the planet, partly because it restored a kind of balance, but largely because she suspected it was true. The Army was taking note of what the Navy had achieved. The Hasler model was spreading nationwide.

Bere Ferrers was as empty as ever. She let herself into the house, put the kettle on and cleared a space for herself on the kitchen table. She'd used a mini-recorder at Hasler Company and she wanted to review her morning's work, filleting each interview for quotes that would find their way into the finished piece.

She was midway through the first interview — with the Warrant Officer — when she noticed the power warning light flicker. *Shit*, she thought, *have I brought spare batteries?* The answer was no. She went upstairs and rummaged through her bag. Nothing. She went back to the kitchen and went through likely drawers in case Rob had a spare set. Again zilch. Finally she thought of phoning him and asking where else she might look, but then she thought of all the stuff he had on his plate and decided against it. The last thing he needed was an interruption from some ditzy journalist who hadn't remembered to bring the right gear.

Ignoring the red light, she laboured on. The interview had reached a critical point when the power failed completely. The Warrant Officer had been making the very reasonable point that no Marine ever went to war with the intention of coming back in a box. Kids that age were only hungry for one thing: combat. When the shooting started in earnest, they regarded themselves as immortal. It went with the territory, with the tidal wave of hormones that the months of intense training had been so careful to surf. Only later, on the second or third tour, would the older guys wise up. Experience was a great teacher. Experience taught you the harder lessons about the odds you faced but these careful calculations were lost on the younger guys.

She stared at the recorder, hating it, trying to will it back to life by the sheer force of her anger. Finally she thought about another cup of tea, or maybe a glass of Sancerre from the remains of last night's bottle. Then she had another thought. Maybe Rob kept his batteries upstairs. Maybe she should look in his bedroom.

She went upstairs. A cursory search revealed nothing but a neat pile of dirty laundry. A chest of drawers stood against the wall beside the door. Maybe this was where Rob stored his odds and ends. The top drawer was full of underwear, mainly socks and singlets and a neat pile of boxers. She pulled out the drawers beneath, finding more clothes. Would he really store a set of batteries here? Among the carefully ironed sweatshirts he appeared to have collected from various corners of the planet? She thought not. Finally, on her knees now, she pulled out the bottom drawer.

At first, in the dim light, she saw nothing but more clothes. Only when she began a proper rummage did she find the little bundle of letters and postcards secured with a rubber band. She took them out, curious and slightly guilty. Was it really her job to poke around in this lovely man's private life? Help herself to his correspondence? Try and get a fix on who else might once have won his heart? The answer was no, but the temptation to find out more was overpowering.

She checked her watch and then sat on the bed, the small pile of correspondence on her lap. On top was a postcard. Pink cherry blossoms framed the White House. She turned the postcard over. The handwriting was tiny, the work of someone with a great deal to say. She reached for the bedside light, turned it on.

You can't believe how frustrating this is. Two weeks to go and no way your sweet Mivi can figure out making that wait shorter. Are you thinking what I'm thinking? Two weeks with nothing to think about but each other, nothing to touch but each other, and the whole thing impossibly legal? You'll be glad to know that life here is as complicated and boring as ever. I once thought this job was worth the wait. But nothing is. Except you. Hasta viernes. YSM

The message was sealed with a single kiss. Lizzie's eyes went to the postmark. It was badly smudged but just legible. She held the postcard under the light, praying that she'd got this thing wrong. She hadn't. Saturday, 23 June. Exactly a week ago.

11

SATURDAY, 30 JUNE 2012

Suttle and Golding were in the atrium at the Met Office, waiting for a woman from Human Resources to sign them in. Kirsten Kilpatrick had been in the building for just fifteen minutes. A room had been made available for the two officers to interview her. Over the phone, when the HR lady had enquired about the reason for their visit, Suttle had simply told her they were on a major crime enquiry. She hadn't asked the obvious question but given the sheer weight of media coverage, she didn't have to.

Golding was watching a *News* 24 feed on the plasma screen on the other side of the reception area. Uniforms were still blitzing the rolling hills around the hotel, hunting for some tiny scrap of evidence that might take *Bellwether* in a new direction. Then came a shot of Saunders' Bedford van.

'Fanny rat?' Golding murmured.

'Has to be.' Suttle nodded. 'The girl Leanne? A wallet full of other women's details? All that stuff from the woman across the road? Mr Charming? Mr Smoothie? This guy had women forming an orderly queue. Lucky old him.'

'You're kidding.'

'I am.'

Suttle got to his feet. For some reason female

292

HR executives always wore black two-piece suits, conservatively cut. She glanced at Suttle's warrant card and then led them into the building. Nice legs.

The office they were to be using was on the third floor. The chair behind the desk was already occupied.

'Ms Kilpatrick?'

The woman nodded. She too was wearing a two-piece suit, a light cream this time. Saunders had been forty-one when he died; Kilpatrick looked a year or so younger. She watched the HR lady leave the room then turned to Suttle.

'I know already, if you're wondering,' she said. 'Just to spare you breaking the news.'

'How did you find out?'

'I heard it on the radio driving down. I was talking to Adie first thing on the phone. He was on his way out to the hotel. It had to be him. No one else worked on those trees.'

'I'm sorry.'

'So am I. As you might imagine.'

Under the circumstances, thought Suttle, she was holding it together remarkably well. The long blonde hair and the gym-honed figure would turn most heads, but there was something in her face that suggested a deep unhappiness.

Suttle asked about the relationship with Saunders.

'We were together,' she said. 'Had been for a while.'

'Since when?'

'Since the year before last.' She paused, fidgeting with a ring on the second finger of her right hand. 'I might as well tell you the whole story. You'll find out anyway.'

'Is this something you prefer not to talk about?'

'What do you mean?'

'Would you like a lawyer present? Should we make this official? Take you down to the police station?'

'Christ no, why would I want to do that?'

'I'm just thinking of your interests, Ms Kilpatrick. If there's something germane to the enquiry, then we'll need to statement you, do the thing properly. Otherwise . . . ' he glanced at his watch ' . . . we just press on.'

She nodded, said nothing. Then she leaned forward over the table, addressing herself exclusively to Suttle. She'd first met Adie, she said, at a quiz night in the local pub. He'd been guesting for the team on a neighbouring table. They'd won, and after standing the runners-up a round of drinks with his winnings, Adie had taken her aside. They'd talked for maybe an hour. They'd really got on. The following week he'd joined her own pub quiz team and within a month they'd found themselves in a relationship.

'Were you alone at the time?'

'No, I was married. Still am as a matter of fact.'

'I'll need your husband's details.'

'Really?'

'Yes.'

'Why?'

'Because this is a murder enquiry, Ms Kilpatrick. A man has died. A man you were

294

living with. We start in the middle and work slowly out. You, I'm afraid, are the middle.'

'Thank you.'

'My pleasure.'

She held his gaze for a moment, then gave him the information he wanted. Michael Pleasant. Kissing Well Cottage, Rockbeare. 07967 385911.

'You're still in touch?'

'What makes you think that?'

'You seem to know his mobile number.'

'You're right. How come we always remember the bad things?'

'You're telling me you're *not* in touch?'

'Not at all. I'm telling you I have a memory for figures. Maybe it comes with the territory.'

'You mean separation? Trauma? Stress?'

'IT. It's what I do for a living.'

'I see.'

Suttle was uncomfortably aware that this exchange was developing into a fencing match. And that Kilpatrick was scoring the important hits.

'You left your husband? After meeting Adie?'

'Yes.'

'How did your husband react?'

'Not well. The thing hadn't been working for a while but I don't think he expected me to move out.'

'So he was upset?'

'Yes.'

'Very upset?'

'Yes.'

'And now?'

'Now we don't talk, don't email, don't see

295

each other at all. I told him it was better that way. For all of us.'

'Do you have children?'

'Only Michael.' She offered a cold smile. 'That's a joke by the way.'

'Sure. What about divorce proceedings?'

'I went to my solicitor a couple of weeks ago. Adie and I wanted to get married.'

'His idea or yours?'

'Ours.'

'And Michael?'

'I've no idea. My solicitor said he'd be getting in touch. I don't know whether that's happened.'

'But you think it might have?'

'I don't know. Maybe you should phone him. Find out for yourself.'

She gave him the details of her solicitor. Golding wrote them down. Suttle was watching her carefully.

'Forgive me, Ms Kilpatrick, but you don't seem very bothered.'

'Really? The man in my life has just been killed. That bothers me a great deal. Am I allowed to say that?' She nodded at Golding's racing pen. 'Do you want to write it down?'

'That wasn't what I meant. I start on the assumption that we share the same objective.'

'Which is?'

'To find out who might have done this. It would help if you were less . . . ah . . . '

'Upset?'

'Antagonistic.'

'Right.' She was picking at a nail. 'Right.'

'So let's start with anyone Adie might have

crossed. Do any names spring to mind?'

'I'm not with you.'

'Professionally? People who might have some kind of grudge against him?'

'Christ, no. He was the laziest self-employed businessman I've ever met. He'd never beat anyone to a contract because he couldn't be arsed. That was his charm, in a way. He'd figured out what mattered in life and turned his back on the rest. That's rare in case you were wondering.'

'So what mattered? To Adie?'

'Me? Can I say that?' Her eyes were suddenly glassy. Golding had stopped writing. Suttle didn't move.

'What about his private life?' Suttle said at last.

'I was his private life.'

'You're sure about that?'

'Yes. Unless you're telling me different.' She'd found a tissue. She ducked her head and blew her nose. Then she was back with Suttle. 'Are you telling me different?'

'We have reasons to believe that Adie spread himself around a bit,' Suttle said woodenly. 'And that may be an understatement.'

'You're talking about that little tart at the hotel? Leanne?'

'You know about her?'

'Of course I do. The point about people like Adie is they can never keep a secret. Why? Because they're too stupid.'

'You found something?'

'Saved texts. On his bloody mobile. When I challenged him he admitted it straight away. The girl put out for him. She was pretty. She was available. What kind of man would say no?'

'You forgave him?'

'Yes.'

'Because?'

'I don't know . . . ' She tipped her head back, defiant. 'Just because.'

'So what if there were other women?'

'There weren't.'

'How do you know?'

'He told me. I asked him, and he swore to God he'd never touch another woman in his life.'

'You believed him?'

'I had to. I had no choice.'

'You had every choice. You could have gone back to your husband.'

'No way. I'd have died with that man. He was killing me.'

'He was violent?'

'Quite the reverse. Pleasant by name, pleasant by nature. Try living with a blancmange. Give me Adie any day.'

She started to cry properly this time, tears pouring down her face. Suttle left the mopping-up to Golding and abandoned the office to call Houghton from the corridor.

'I'm looking at the data set from Southwick Park,' she said at once. 'It came in half an hour ago.'

'And?'

'Three hundred and three names — but that's nationwide.'

'These are snipers, yeah?'

'Ex-snipers, most of them. But yes, these are

298

the guys with the knowledge. We're sorting out a matrix. Mr Nandy thinks we're on the move at last.'

'Excellent.'

Suttle briefed her quickly about Kilpatrick. In his opinion it would be a huge stretch to put her in the frame for anything but gullibility. She seemed to have loved the guy to death, no matter who else he was fucking.

'Unfortunate choice of words, James.'

'Fucking?'

'Death.'

Suttle grinned. Houghton only used his correct Christian name to signify disapproval. In a way he rather liked it, largely because it reminded him of his mum.

'The woman's in bits, boss. There's not a lot we can do with her now. The way I see it, we need to start working the other women he was into. Plus Kilpatrick's husband.'

Houghton agreed.

'Do it,' she said.

'*All* of them?'

'The husband. We'll take care of the rest. By the way . . . ' She paused for a moment. 'We've got a confirmed sighting on the white van. The standby observer remembers it parked on an Exeter estate back in March when he was tracking a couple of kids in a twocked car. He thinks he might even have it on camera. He's checking for the footage as we speak.'

'Shit.'

'Exactly . . . James.'

Lizzie was sitting in the garden when Rob Merrilees finally got back, her face tilted up towards the sun. She heard the slam of the front door and then his footsteps as he made his way through the kitchen. She'd spent the last couple of hours trying to work out how she'd play the next few minutes but was no closer to any sane conclusion. The obvious had been staring her in the face and she'd totally missed it. Even Gill would have scented the trouble she was in.

She felt his presence behind the deckchair. When he cupped her face in his big hands, she did her best to smile.

'I bought you a present,' he said. 'I thought we might celebrate.'

Lizzie found herself looking at a bottle of Krug. His departure for Cyprus, he said, had been delayed until Tuesday. Might she stay one more night?

'You'd like that?'

'I would. Very much.'

She nodded. Whoever had sent the postcard wasn't due back until the end of the week. Lizzie's Spanish was sketchy but she was sure that *viernes* meant Friday. Enough time to delete Lizzie Hodson from his life and pick up where he'd doubtless left off. Clever.

Rob had found another deckchair.

'Shall I get some glasses?' He was back beside her.

'Why not?'

'Something the matter?'

'No.'

'Now, then? We'll have the champers now?'

'Yeah.'

He'd sussed her. She knew he had. He'd sensed that something had happened. It went with the person he was, with the person she'd trusted, with the openness of his smile and the way he could be so instinctive.

She heard the clink of glasses from the kitchen. He came out with an occasional table from the living room, disappeared again and returned with the fizz. Normally she'd love the combination — a hundred-quid bottle of champagne on a battered old tin tray — but her sense of humour had deserted her. Inside, where it mattered, she felt nothing but a small, hard anger.

Rob uncorked the bottle and poured two glasses. His face was very close.

'To us,' he said.

'To us.' She sipped at the champagne. It tasted of nothing. 'Tell me something,' she said at last.

'Anything.' He was grinning at her. 'Try me.'

'Who's YSM?'

Rob gazed at her for a moment, and Lizzie knew she'd been wrong about sussing her. The last question he'd expected was this.

'I was looking for batteries for my recorder,' she said. 'I found some letters and stuff in your chest of drawers. Unforgivable on my part, but there you are.'

He nodded, looked away.

'You read them?' he asked at last.

'I read the postcard from Washington. That was enough.'

'And what do you think?'

'I think you're a devious, lying bastard. There's no way you're going to Cyprus on Tuesday. Absolutely none. It's a lie, a fiction, like everything else you fucking made up.' She turned to face him. 'Or have I got this wrong?'

'Not at all.'

'So who's YSM? Am I allowed to know?'

'Of course. Her name's Nina. She's a major in the Intelligence Corps.'

'And she's coming back on Friday? Am I right?'

'She is. And you want to know why?'

'Surprise me.'

'Because we're due to get married. On Saturday.'

12

SATURDAY, 30 JUNE 2012

Michael Pleasant lived on the northern edge of Rockbeare. The straggly village would win no awards for chocolate-box looks, nor was Kissing Well Cottage a strictly accurate description of the spiritless 60s bungalow at the end of a cul-de-sac that this man appeared to call home. The property was within sight of the sturdy church, and the evening wind carried the roar of jet thrust from the neighbouring airport.

There was no answer to Suttle's knock. The rusting Mondeo parked on the hard standing suggested someone was at home. Suttle tried again. No response. A path led round the side of the bungalow, the view curtained by a tall fence that smelled of creosote. At the back of the property was a neat little garden: carefully tended rows of lettuces and spring onions backed by a long stand of runner beans. Birdfeeders hung from the branches of an apple tree and sparrows scattered at Golding's approach.

'There. Look.'

Suttle followed Golding's pointing finger. At the bottom of the garden, almost hidden by the runner beans, was a wooden shed. It was a decent size and looked too new to be in keeping with everything else. The door was flanked by two windows, both of them screened by white venetian blinds.

Golding was first to the door. He knocked a couple of times, then stepped back. Suttle saw a hand spread the slats inside the window on the left, then a glimpse of a face peering out. Golding was holding up his warrant card. Moments later the door opened.

'Michael Pleasant?'

'That's me. What's this about?'

'May we come in?'

'Of course.'

Suttle found himself in an artist's studio. Finished paintings, as yet unframed, hung from clips around the walls. A curling watercolour, half-complete, lay on a table beneath the other window. In the middle of the room, among a rich clutter of paintbrushes and half-used chalks, stood an easel.

Golding was already inspecting the work in progress. From a wash of greens and browns, the shoulder of a valley was beginning to appear. The hint of grey/blue snaking down the middle of the picture might have been a river.

'The Exe near Dulverton. Do you know it at all?'

Pleasant was tall and thin. He wore a cotton smock over a pair of faded jeans and moved with an awkwardness, a lack of coordination, that was probably lifelong. This is the class geek, Suttle thought. The guy who never quite made it in the playground or on the sports field but compensated in more interesting ways. His hands and face were deeply tanned. A wispy beard, greying at the edges, hid a receding chin. One earlobe sported a tiny jewel, the deepest red.

Golding, it turned out, had kayaked on this stretch of the river. He and a couple of mates had camped illegally on the riverbank near Exebridge and spent most of the night fending off the water bailiff.

Pleasant laughed. He knew the bailiff well. Guy called Darren. Ex-copper.

Golding nodded. Something had caught his eye, and he stepped over to a pile of what looked like photos on a shelf at the back of the hut. Suttle, meanwhile, was suggesting they might all talk in the house.

'About what exactly?'

'About a man called Adie Saunders. I understand you know him.'

'Of course I know him. I could hardly not.'

'Right.' Suttle was still watching Golding. 'So do you know what's happened to him?'

'No idea. Should I?'

'Only if you listen to the radio, or watch TV, or buy a paper.'

'None of the above, I'm afraid. Nothing serious, I hope?'

Suttle tried to mask his smile. It was impossible not to miss the irony. He rather liked this man and what he seemed to have made of his life.

Pleasant was still waiting for news of the trespasser who'd barged in and stolen his wife. What on earth had happened?

'Someone killed him, Mr Pleasant. Which is why we ought to talk.'

The news seemed to make little impact. Pleasant arched an eyebrow, then agreed they should abandon the studio for somewhere a little more spacious.

The bungalow, like the studio, was awash with the debris of a bachelor's life. Pleasant cleared a pile of assorted magazines from the sagging sofa, retrieved a plate on which he'd probably had his lunch and went next door to fetch another chair. There was no sign of a TV, and the copy of the *Guardian* beneath the cat's bowl was more than a month old. The walls were jigsawed with photos, many of them black and white, all featuring bits of what Suttle assumed was Devon: sunken lanes brimming with drifts of spindle and dog rose, a stand of cattle against the flare of a dying sun, the humpy whalebacks of Dartmoor, granite-black beneath towering summer thunderheads.

'These are yours?' Golding again.

'I'm afraid so.'

'They're great.'

'Thank you.'

Suttle explained about Saunders. He understood the dead man had been living with Pleasant's wife.

'You've talked to Kirsten?'

'Yes.'

'Then you'll know already. She went off with him a couple of years ago. To be frank, there wasn't much I could do about it.'

Suttle nodded. He wanted Pleasant to account for his movements last night.

'You think I might have done it? Killed him?'

He sounded amused.

'It's a question I have to ask, Mr Pleasant.'

'Then the answer's no.'

'So where were you? Last night?'

'I was giving a talk. Over in Honiton. The people who organised it were nice enough to buy me a meal afterwards. Then I came home.'

'And first thing this morning?'

'I was still here.'

'Alone?'

'I'm always alone. In many ways it's a bit of a blessing.'

'After Kirsten, you mean?'

'Of course. Investing a lot in a single relationship isn't something I'd recommend. Not any more. To be frank, a couple of cats are a safer proposition. Animals repay attention. That's something my wife never quite mastered.'

'She'd cheated on you before?'

'She might have done. I don't know. But boredom was the real killer. If you want the truth, we just weren't suited. Different people, different interests. Saunders or someone like him was bound to happen in the end.'

'Kirsten thinks you were upset when she left.'

'She's right. I was. She broke my heart, that woman.'

'And now?'

'It's over. You learn the lesson. You grow the shell. Never again, you tell yourself. Not after something like that.'

They'd been colleagues at the Met Office, he said. He'd been running a team of forecasters. He'd never kidded himself it was anything but a management chore and after a while, after the move down from Bracknell, he began to yearn for a job in the open air. All his life he'd been passionate about other people's art. An evening class he'd taken in watercolours convinced him he might have talents of his own. At this point he started spending every spare moment out in the field, sketching and painting *en plein air*.

'And Kirsten?'

'We weren't together then, not properly, not man and wife. She knew what she was getting into, what she was taking on, and at the time I think she thought I was a bit different, a bit special. That's not true, of course. Artists of any kind are deeply selfish. I suspect that was something she never realised. Not until it was too late.'

'She resented the painting?'

'Not resented. Not exactly. She always said the right things about the final product. But it was the doing of it that flummoxed her.'

Suttle caught Golding's eye. Flummoxed was a wonderful word.

'She never came with you? On these painting expeditions?'

'At first, yes. But she got bored. It wasn't her thing. And neither, as it turned out, was I. The rest you know about.'

Golding asked how the painting worked for him now. Did he make a living from his pictures? Or was he still at the Met Office?

'No to both, I'm afraid. I left the Met Office after Kirsten went. I just couldn't be there any more, seeing her every day, knowing she'd started a new life. As for the pictures, you've got to be very very special to make any kind of living.'

'So how do you get by?'

'My mother died. I was the only son. They had a nice house, my parents, and no mortgage, so I inherited the lot. I also do a bit of teaching now, in one of the FE colleges, and there's a scrap of a pension from the Met Office. I was there for twenty-three years. It all adds up. It's not a fortune but it's enough.'

Golding nodded. He wanted to know about the picture on the easel.

'I told you. It's that stretch of the Exe near Dulverton. I'm doing a whole series of pictures there. I've teamed up with a poet from Cullumpton. He's good, really good. The plan is to get something together in book form for Christmas. My pictures, his words. You can self-publish these days, no problem, and we might sell a few.'

'So where does the dog come in?'

'The dog?'

'That little photo taped to the shelf? Where you keep your brushes?'

'Ah ... ' Pleasant was smiling now. 'That's another project. A present, really, for a friend. He lost his dog and it's my job to bring the little mutt back to life. That should be ready by Christmas too, fingers crossed.' His eyes strayed to the window. 'Is that all, gentlemen? Only I need to get the first wash finished before the light goes.'

Minutes later, back in the car, Suttle wanted

to know more about the dog. Golding was looking at the bungalow.

'I dunno,' he said. 'Except I've seen that dog before.'

'Where?'

'That's the problem.' He settled in the seat, checked his watch. 'I can't bloody remember.'

★　★　★

Lizzie spent the best part of an hour and a half trying to get to the bottom of why Rob Merrilees had strung her along, of what exactly he'd been after, of how on earth he'd reconcile the time they'd spent together with the fact that he was about to get married.

Was he greedy? Was it a straightforward trophy thing? Did he get the usual male kick out of putting another notch on his belt? Of taking another scalp? Or was it something more complex and maybe more sinister, something that only Rob himself could possibly own up to?

They were still in the garden, the rest of the champagne untouched.

'Neither,' he said. 'You and I met. We talked. We fancied each other. And after that I'm afraid it rather ran away with me.'

'But you knew. You knew all the time.'

'Knew what?'

'That she was coming back. That you loved her. That you were going to get fucking *married*, for Christ's sake. Last night was real. Just nod. That's all you have to do. Last night mattered. Last night was something pretty special,

310

something fucking rare. How could you do that, how could you be there, be that person, be that close, do that stuff, say those things, and know that a couple of days later you were going to be looking her in the eye, pledging your undying fucking loyalty, slipping the ring on her finger? Just give me a clue. Just tell me how that can ever be fucking possible.'

'I don't know.'

'That's pathetic, if you don't mind me saying so. You have to know. Because otherwise I'm going to think the worst.'

'Which is?'

'That you did it on purpose. That you knew exactly what you were doing. That you took what you could when the going was good and then you'd pretend to fuck off to Cyprus. After which little me would be history.'

'That's not what I intended.'

'Fine. So the marriage is off. Yippee. Let's go for another bottle. Let's celebrate properly this time. Do we have a deal?'

'Of course we don't.'

'So why not? Tell me. Tell me the truth. Why not?'

'Because . . . ' He shrugged. 'It's going to happen.'

'And you can't stop it? You can't do the commando thing? Be brave? Man up? Crack on? Tell the little lady it's crashed and burned? Explain to her you've met this hot little chick who gave you the blow job of your dreams? This hot little chick who sees life exactly the way you see it? This hot little chick who's dreaming of a new life in the Tamar fucking Valley? That's an ask too far? Too difficult? Too tricky? Too fucking *off-piste?*'

'This doesn't help, Lizzie. You're being emotional.'

'Too fucking right. And I wonder why that might be? You can blame me for a lot of things. You can blame me for believing you. You can blame me for taking you at face value. You can blame me for getting within touching distance, for trying to turn what we had into some kind of future. But you can't blame me for getting a bit upset. Why? Because there never was a future. Never. Because you had the script. Because you'd already written the fucking thing. Because you knew the way all this was going to end.'

'What makes you think that?'

'What?'

'That it was going to end?'

Lizzie stared at him, not believing what she'd just heard.

'Ah . . . ' she said at last. 'I get it. When it suited you, you were going to get back in touch. Months later, maybe even a year later, I'd get a call. You've somehow got married. You may even have a baby. But you'd like to meet again, pick up where we left off, crack a bottle or two, roll around in some hotel bedroom, gaze into each other's eyes, then home to wifey. Is that what you mean? Is that what's on offer?'

'No. Of course not.'

'Then what are you saying? Apart from sorry?'

'I want us to be friends. I want us to be the people we are.'

'Great. And you know what? That's exactly the story of the last few days. We *are* the people we are. That's the whole point. That's why it worked so brilliantly. You. Me. The people we are. No pretending. No lying. Just us. Just naturally us. Being ourselves. Except that now it turns out you had other plans.'

He nodded. He'd been crazy. He'd been out of his mind.

'You're telling me you regret it?'

'Of course not. How could I regret it?'

'Is that a serious question?'

'Yes.'

'Then let me tell you. Unless I've got this wrong, you're going to have a very big problem. And that very big problem isn't me, it's us. Why? Because I'm giving you the benefit of the doubt. I'm assuming the person I've got to know is the real you. And I'm also assuming you've been feeling what I've been feeling. And if that's true then poor little Nina and poor little you are in for a rough time. You can't pick up the phone because I won't be there. There's no point trying to get in touch any other way because I'll ignore you. Unless, of course, you bin the marriage. And even then I'm not sure I'll ever trust you again.'

'Thanks.'

'My pleasure.'

At this point she kissed him, more out of sorrow than anger. He stared at her for a moment, then put his arms round her, wanting to hold her again, wanting to be close, wanting to taste what they'd had, but she pushed him away.

There was something else she needed to get straight, she said.

'What?'

'All the stuff you've told me about Afghan.'

'What about it?'

'I want to build it into a big feature piece. I want to share it. I want people to know what's really going on out there. You must have sussed that. I can't believe you haven't.'

'You're joking.' He looked horrified. 'No way.'

'You're telling me I can't use it?'

'Of course not. That was private. You and me. That's how much I trusted you.'

'*Trusted* me?' Lizzie was close to tears. None of this made sense. Not a single fragment of what little there was left. 'How can you talk about trust when you were letting me fall in love with a guy about to get married? How does that compute?'

'It doesn't.'

'Exactly. So maybe you owe me.'

'That sounds like a threat.'

'Not at all. I can put you on the front page of every newspaper in the land. I can get you on prime-time TV. If Afghan's really such a piss-off maybe that might sound like a good career move.'

'I couldn't do it.'

'Do what?'

'Shit on the Corps. It's everything. It's my life.'

'Great. Is this you I'm hearing, or wifey?'

'Nina feels the way I feel.'

'About Afghan?'

314

'Yeah. And that's because she's got the bigger picture. She works in intel. She knows we've been fighting the wrong war.'

'So what's she going to do about it?'

'Nothing. Because that's how it is in our business.'

'Man up and crack on?'

'Exactly.'

'Spill more blood? Waste more treasure?'

'Sure. If that's the way it has to be.'

'But it doesn't, my love. It doesn't have to be that way. It might have escaped your attention but we live in a democracy. If we really want to, we can change things.'

'You're wrong. You can. But not me.'

'Bollocks. Believe me, we can do this thing. We really can.'

'No, in our position it's impossible. We can't.'

At this point, Lizzie lost it completely. She wanted to hit him. She wanted to batter him with every Afghan memory he'd shared with her. She wanted to take him by the throat and make him face the real-life consequences of the pictures he'd painted. Then, as he tried to calm her down, she was struck by another thought.

'I'll do it anyway,' she said. 'Publish and be damned.'

'No way.'

'Try me. Keep checking the websites.'

'I'll deny it.'

'Great. What will Nina say?'

'Nina? You wouldn't.'

'Wouldn't I?'

At this point, exhausted, she fled upstairs and

packed her bag. She could hear him prowling around the kitchen, then the living room. She thought she heard him make a call but couldn't be sure. When she got downstairs again, he was in the hall. She suspected he might have been crying. She knew he couldn't wait for her to go.

She went to the front door. It was still warm outside, the street bathed in sunshine. She began to say goodbye but he was already turning away. He wanted to shut the door. He wanted her out of his life.

'Just tell me one thing,' she said. 'Just tell me it mattered.'

He looked at her for a long moment. Then he nodded.

'It did,' he said. 'And it still does.'

★ ★ ★

Walking into the Major Incident Room at Middlemoor, Suttle noticed the change in atmosphere at once. This morning, first thing, the place had been a morgue. A week of frantic activity had produced very little in terms of the kind of hard evidence that would matter. Thousands of actions had taken all three enquiries nowhere. The small army of detectives was becoming disenchanted. You expected quality jobs like these to be a challenge, but even the most experienced officers had a struggle recalling so much effort expended for so little return.

Now there was a real buzz in the air. The civvy inputters, bent over their terminals, were trying to cope with a mountain of written statements. A small queue of detectives was waiting for the ear of the D/S in charge of the General Enquiry Team. Both whiteboards were a maze of interlinked Pentel scribbles, one scarlet arrow leading hopefully to another.

Suttle checked in with the Statement Reader, promising the yield from his day's work as soon as, then took the stairs to the office that Houghton was using. He found her staring at a PC monitor.

'We've got it down to forty-six names,' she said. 'You want a look?'

She angled the screen towards him and leaned back in her chair. She looked exhausted but there was a gleam in her eyes that Houghton hadn't seen for days. Someone had stolen into *Bellwether* and switched the lights on.

Suttle was looking at a grid of names. Each was prefixed with a rank — Marine, L/Cpl, Cpl, Sgt — and accompanying contact details. Most of the addresses were local.

'What are these tags?' Suttle indicated the names highlighted in yellow. No more than a dozen.

'Guys we've already eliminated.' She began to go down the list. 'This one's on maritime protection. He spent the whole week on a container ship in the Bay of Bengal. This one's on the same gig with a different company. This one's moved to France. According to people who should know, he's doing head jobs for Gulf Arabs.' She looked up. She was smiling. 'Ten grand a hit, if you're interested. These people fly you out, supply the weapon, give you a couple of days for a decent recce, then — bang — you do the job, return the weapon and head back to the airport. Offshore account of your choice. Money for nothing.'

'This is kosher?' Suttle was astonished.

'So I'm told. It's supply and demand, Jimmy. These guys have the skills, the Arabs have the money, the rest is conversation. This particular guy spent most of last week in Dubai. We checked.'

She went on down the list. Ex-snipers who had become game-keepers on the big estates in Scotland, a couple of bootnecks running a paintball centre on a brownfield site in Liverpool, three more who were working for an insurance company, retrieving nicked high-end vehicles from addresses across Eastern Europe, plus one Troop Sergeant who'd binned Afghan to start a contract-cleaning business in Devon, specialising in restaurant ovens.

'The guy works nights. Five hundred quid a pop. No overheads. No one to piss him off. He never sees the missus because she works days, but neither of them think that's a problem. Sweet, eh?'

Suttle was counting the remaining names. There were fifteen.

'These are all Marines?'

'All but two. And they've all left the service. The people we've been talking to are in management positions. They run the Corps and they seem to have a problem: Afghan's losing its charms.' She nodded at the screen. 'Most of

318

these guys have doubled their money. They get decent leave and no one's trying to blow them up. Sounds like a no-brainer to me.'

The Navy, she said, had put a serving Royal Marine Major at their disposal. Nandy had found him an office down the corridor and he was due to start work first thing tomorrow morning. His name was Toby Watkins. He'd have access to service personnel records and would be riding shotgun on the rest of the list.

'And what if they all turn out to be blanks?'

'We widen the search parameters. Start all over again.'

'What about the white van?'

'We're still waiting on the observer from the chopper. There's some kind of glitch on the video he's trying to access.'

'Right.' Suttle checked his watch. It was already half seven and he'd yet to write up his notes. 'Anything else, boss?'

'Yes.' Houghton bent to her keyboard. A couple of keystrokes took her onto the Internet. 'Take a look at this.'

Suttle gazed at the screen. The website was a mess of greens and reds.

'What's Deffo?' he asked.

'It's an employment agency run by a couple of guys here in Exeter. They're both ex-bootnecks. The way I understand it they're trying to build a bridge into civvy life for lads about to leave. You register on their database, list what you're good at, and they spread the word.'

'And Deffo? The word itself?'

'Slang. I gather it means for sure, for certain.

319

All the world loves a soldier. A job within a month guaranteed or you get your money back.'

'Great.' Suttle saw the logic at once. 'So what's in it for us?'

'We got a call just now from the guys doing hard-disk analysis on Hamilton's laptop.' The smile was back on Houghton's face. 'First he did a Google search on Deffo. Then he fired off a couple of emails. This was back in April. Then he deleted the lot.'

'When?'

'Yesterday. After you and Luke left.'

★ ★ ★

Lizzie was back at Chantry Cottage by ten o'clock. Briefly, climbing out of the gathering darkness of the Tamar Valley, she'd toyed with driving straight back to Pompey but knew it was out of the question. For one thing, three long hours on the road were beyond her. For another, she couldn't face the prospect of sharing tomorrow's breakfast with her mother. Even Chantry Cottage, with all its nightmare memories, was preferable to getting beaten up again.

The key to the back door, as Lizzie had expected, was still under the water barrel behind the shed. She let herself into the kitchen and turned on the light, wondering about Jimmy's lodger. All she knew about this man was that he worked shifts at A&E in Exeter. She supposed he was some kind of doctor, or maybe a nurse. Was he at the hospital tonight? Coping with the usual flood of weekend casualties? Or was he out partying? She had no idea.

She'd bought a bottle of decent Macon at an offie in the outskirts of Exeter. She was going to wait for Jimmy to come back before treating herself to a drink but the moment she walked through to the living room she knew she couldn't wait. She couldn't remember feeling so empty, so bewildered, so shafted, so fucking angry. The very least she owed herself was a large glass of wine.

Lizzie returned to the kitchen and found the corkscrew in the usual place. For the first time she noticed the flowers on the little shelf beside the fridge. They were tucked untidily into a cracked glass vase but they were beautiful, a soft explosion of cornflower blues that added a brightness and warmth to the room. She gazed at them, still levering the cork out, wondering whether this might be a woman's work. Jimmy had never had the slightest interest in flowers. He might buy her a duty bunch on special occasions but that was about it. What if he came back with company? What if there was someone else in his life?

She poured herself a brimming glass of the Macon, letting her thoughts race. She might be a fellow detective, some officer on Major Crime. She might be someone the lodger knew, a nurse maybe. God knows, the lodger might be a woman. She glanced at her watch, uncomfortable now, wondering if being back in the cottage, waiting for Jimmy, was really such a great idea, but then she knew she didn't have a choice. The thought of some hotel room, drinking alone to numb herself to sleep, was hideous. For better or worse, she needed company and maybe a listening ear.

The first glass of wine was empty within minutes. She poured herself another and then decided to go upstairs. A precautionary peek into the spare bedroom told her that her fears about a female lodger were groundless. Only a man would leave a pile of assorted boxers on the carpet. She closed the door and stepped across to the other bedroom. She'd spent nearly a year in the chill and the dampness of this room, and she'd hated it, but the sight of Grace's panda propped against a pillow brought a smile to her face. She took another gulp of wine and crossed to the window.

It was dark now, the field across the lane silver in the moonlight. She could hear the stir of wind in the trees at the back of the cottage and seconds later came the distant hoot of an owl from up the valley. Was this the same owl she remembered from last year? Did owls fall in love with this place, the way her husband had done? Did they never move on? Find the nearest city? Get themselves a proper life?

She drained the glass, then got undressed and slipped under the duvet. The bear, to her quiet delight, smelled of Jimmy. She held it a little tighter, gave it a kiss. Sleep came seconds later.

★　★　★

Suttle didn't make it back to Colaton Raleigh until nearly midnight. His completed notes had gone to one of the civvy inputters and he'd had a brief chat to the D/S driving the General Enquiry Team, who'd confirmed that they were throwing bodies at the sniper list and that the possibles without cast-iron alibis were now down to single figures.

Leaving Middlemoor, Suttle had met Houghton in the car park. When he enquired about the Deffo lead, she said the High-Tech Crime Unit still had it under development. One of the two guys who ran the agency was an ex-sniper. The other was also a Marine, recently discharged after a run-in with an IED. His wife, it seemed, did the bulk of the heavy lifting on the IT side. By tomorrow, thanks to Toby Watkins, they should have full details on both men. In the meantime Nandy had ordered twenty-four-hour surveillance on the registered address.

As he turned into the lane that led to Chantry Cottage, Suttle was wondering why Nandy and Houghton hadn't gone for an immediate arrest. These guys' backgrounds put them squarely in the frame. The deleted emails on Hamilton's laptop rang a very loud alarm bell. Three men might already have died at their hands; why not cut to the chase and scoop them up?

The answer was all too obvious. Nothing in the recent history of the Devon and Cornwall force had attracted so much media attention. An over-hasty arrest would be reported nationwide. Without quality evidence, there'd be no guarantee of a result. And the last thing Major Crime needed was a release without charge and yet more phone calls from irate MPs. That would be amateur time. And Nandy, for one, wanted no such thing.

Suttle rounded the last bend. The throw of the headlights settled briefly on a white Toyota before he made the turn onto the gravel outside the cottage. *Lizzie's car. Had to be.* She'd dropped by to wish him a happy birthday. He could cope with that.

He parked up and locked the car. The kitchen light was still on. He shut the door behind him, gazing at what was left of the bottle of Macon on the table. What kind of present was that? He went through to the sitting room, surprised not to find her. Bed, he thought. She must have gone to bed. His spirits lifting, he headed for the stairs. Halfway up, he could hear her snoring. He pushed softly at the bedroom door. She was cheek to cheek with the panda bear, the duvet heaped around them both. For a moment he was tempted to take a shot on his mobile. He could mail it to Grace. He knew she'd love it. Mummy in Daddy's bed. Result.

Lizzie stirred, yawned, half-turned under the duvet, then began to snore again. Suttle got undressed and slipped in beside her. The slow rhythm of her breathing changed. She opened one eye and smiled.

'Later,' she mumbled. 'I owe you.'

13

SUNDAY, I JULY 2012

A beautiful morning. The cawing of distant
crows from a stand of trees up the valley. Apart
from that, nothing.

'No one works on Sunday.'

'You have to be kidding.'

'Come back to bed.'

'I can't.'

'You can. What time is it?'

'Half six. I have to be out by seven.'

'So what's the problem?' She threw back the
duvet. The bear rolled onto the floor. Naked, she
looked up at him. 'Your call,' she said, 'birthday
boy.'

Afterwards, she followed him downstairs.
Sunshine had already warmed the kitchen. She
felt infinitely better.

'So what have you been up to?' Suttle asked.
'Why the trip?'

'I had a thing to do in Plymouth.'

'This is work?'

'Yeah. For the rag.'

'And was it good?'

'It was excellent.'

'You want to tell me more?'

'Not really.'

Jimmy was spooning coffee into the cafetière.
He should have been gone ten minutes ago.

'Stay,' he said.

'I'd love to.'

'We need to talk. There's stuff we need to sort out.'

'Yeah? You want to tell me more?'

He looked at her a moment. Then he poured hot water into the cafetière and reached for his jacket. 'Not really,' he said, heading for the door.

She followed him out into the sunshine. A tractor was bumping down the lane. Suttle already had the car door open.

'What about your lodger?' she called. 'Should I wake him up?'

'No need.' He waited for the tractor to pass. 'He died on Monday night.'

★ ★ ★

Houghton and Nandy were in the Major Incident Room when Suttle finally made it to Middlemoor. With them was a fit-looking man in his late forties with thinning hair and a ruddy complexion. His camouflage jacket badged him at first glance. This had to be Toby Watkins, the Marine liaison officer. He was obviously getting the induction tour. Nandy, talking him through the evidential chain that ended with the Statement Reader, had nearly finished. He wanted Suttle in Houghton's office in five. Major Watkins, it seemed, would be briefing them on the guys behind Deffo.net.

Suttle had time to put a call through to Chantry Cottage. At first, when there was no answer, he assumed Lizzie had packed up and

326

had already hit the road back to Portsmouth. Then she was suddenly on the phone. She'd been down to the little stream at the bottom of the garden, picked some more of those lovely scabious.

Suttle wanted to tell her about the immersion heater.

'It's fucked,' he said. 'The element's gone. There's no hot water.'

'I know. I just tried to have a shower. Nothing changes round here, does it?'

'I've got the guy coming first thing tomorrow. It's not a huge job.'

'You think I can hang on that long? I'm a working girl.'

She sounded amused. Suttle stared at the phone. This was definitely something new.

'Boil a kettle,' he said. 'I'll phone later.'

★　★　★

Nandy and Watkins were already in Houghton's office by the time Suttle joined them. Nandy had no time to waste. He nodded in Watkins' direction. Fifteen minutes max, he said. Then he and Carole had to prepare for a squad meet.

Watkins had a strong Yorkshire accent. He'd try and keep this as brief as he could but he didn't want to short-change them. Some of this stuff, he seemed to be implying, was more complex than you might expect.

'As you see it, Major.' Nandy gestured for him to carry on.

Watkins extracted a couple of files from his

327

briefcase. The men in question, he said, had both served in 40 Commando. One of them, Marine Oli Jenner, had done the specialist sniper course at the Commando Training Camp at Lympstone in 2005 and served as a sniper ever since. Watkins had accessed his combat records, read every available assessment and talked to a couple of the guys who'd been in theatre with him.

One of them, a Captain who was still with 40 Commando, had described him as a loner. The bloke was hard to reach, he said, but utterly dependable. He'd never let the troop or any of his fellow Marines down. He didn't have too many mates and tended to avoid the noisier runs ashore, but the sniper badge had earned him automatic respect and no one had a bad thing to say about him. He'd left the service just under a year ago under circumstances that might bear further exploration. More of that in a moment or two.

'And the other guy?' Nandy, unusually, was making notes.

'Sean O'Neill. This lad is really interesting. He's half-Caribbean, half-Irish. His dad came from the Windward Islands, which is why the blokes called him Fyffie. He did really well in training, popular lad, took everything on the chin, great sense of humour, hoofing bloke. In theatre he couldn't get enough of the rough stuff, volunteered for everything going, couldn't wait to slot the bad guys. He did a tour on *Herrick8* — that was in 2008 — and was back out again two years later for *Herrick12*. That's when he got blown up.'

'What happened?'

'He was riding top cover in a Mastiff. That's an armoured vehicle. The Taliban triggered a roadside IED. The blast took him out of the vehicle and dumped him on the road. The first guy to get to him was a Marine from the vehicle behind. Stuff from the IED had sliced into O'Neill's carotid artery, just here . . . ' Watkins drew a finger over the side of his neck. 'Apparently the wound was huge, the inside of his neck exposed, blood pumping everywhere. The bloke from the second vehicle got his hand in there and used his elbow to shut the artery down. O'Neill was bloody lucky. In theory he should have been dead.'

'They got him out?'

'Yeah. The Man Down serial is impressive. There was already a Chinook airborne. O'Neill was in Bastion, under the knife, in less than forty minutes. By then he was going to pull through.'

'But this other guy saved his life. Is that what you're telling us?' This from Houghton.

'Exactly. He did. It wasn't a perfect job, but under the circumstances he did remarkably well. Top marks for initiative. Brave too. The Talib were still around.'

'Perfect job?' Nandy wanted to know more.

'The carotid artery supplies blood to the brain. It didn't get quite enough.'

'Meaning?'

'O'Neill isn't the man he was.'

'Still alive though? And kicking?'

'Absolutely.'

'So who saved his life?'

'Guess.'

Nandy and Houghton exchanged glances, but it was Suttle who voiced the obvious.

'Oli Jenner,' he said. 'Has to be.'

* * *

Lizzie got the first call from Rob Merrilees in mid-morning. She'd found a deckchair in the outhouse and was relaxing on the patio at the back of the cottage, enjoying the sun. When she recognised Rob's number from caller ID she put the mobile to one side.

Minutes later a text arrived. 'Lizzie, we have to talk. You're right, I'm a twat, but nothing is forever. Think positive. This thing may not be quite the way you think it is. Please phone me. Rob.'

Lizzie read the text twice, then deleted it. *Nothing is forever?* Too fucking right.

She made herself another cup of coffee, instant this time. Waiting for the kettle to boil, she went upstairs and took a closer look at the spare room. Nothing seemed to have been tidied since the man's death. In a wallet beside his bed she found a driving licence among a sheaf of credit cards. Dr Eamonn Lenahan had a grinning pixie face and gorgeous eyes. She frowned a moment, then looked at the licence a second time, realising that she knew this man. He'd been the guy who'd coxed Kinsey's racing quad last year, the guy who'd saved her life after she'd been swept overboard off Exmouth dock through no one's fault but her own. He'd clambered into the safety boat after she'd been hauled out of the water, getting to her just in time to start the resuscitation drills. The fact that her lungs had been emptied of froth and gallons of seawater was down to him. And now he was dead.

Shit, she thought. She hadn't known him well, but that morning, teaching her the elements of a racing start, he'd been warm, and funny, and endlessly patient. The fact that she hadn't let the rest of the crew down was wholly his doing, and later, once she'd been discharged from hospital, she'd dropped him a note of thanks.

Within a week she'd stepped out of her marriage and taken Grace back home to her mum, but Lenahan's answering postcard had somehow found her. The card had featured a long line of women schlepping down some African road in the middle of nowhere. Each carried a sack of food or a gourd of water on her head. But it was the brightness of the wraps they wore that had caught Lizzie's eye. The reds and vibrant yellows told you that these were proud women. She'd kept the postcard and through the darker days it had helped sustain her. Not just the women but Lenahan's scribbled message on the reverse side. '*Back from the dead?*' he'd written. '*Make the most of it.*'

Now she heard her phone ring again. Instinctively she knew it was Merrilees and when she made it downstairs it turned out she was right. Another text, more desperate this time. 'Sorry's too small a word. I've been in touch with Nina. She knows. Rob.' Lizzie stared at the message until the words began to dance in front of her eyes. The temptation was to phone him, to find out more, to understand what he really meant, to ask whether or not he still intended to get married, but then she realised all this melodrama told its own story. Had she not looked for the spare batteries, had she not read the postcard, she'd already have been out of his life. Rob Merrilees, her dream fuck, had dug a very big hole for himself and it wasn't her job to get him out.

'Good luck on Saturday,' she texted back. 'I won't be thinking of you.'

*   *   *

The squad meet over, D/I Houghton convened another get-together, this time at Suttle's request. He and Golding had been reviewing their own little corner of the three enquiries, and Golding had some thoughts he'd like to share.

Houghton was alone in the office. Nandy, she said, was closeted once again with the Chief Constable, ahead of a specially convened press conference at noon. Deffo's registered address turned out to be an ex-council house on an estate to the north of Exeter. This was where O'Neill and his wife lived. Surveillance had been in place for a couple of hours. According to the obs guys, O'Neill and his missus had two kids who played in the garden a lot. So far this morning there'd been no sign of either parent. Jenner, meanwhile, was proving harder to find. Toby Watkins had provided an address, but according to neighbours he'd moved a couple of months ago.

'The Chief will be announcing a breakthrough,' Houghton said. 'In Plymouth. No more details at this time but stay tuned.'

Suttle was frowning. Golding got it at once.

'Clever,' he said. 'Disinformation.'

'Exactly.' Houghton threw him a look. 'Black propaganda. If we're on the money with O'Neill, then he'll be checking every corner of the media. The moment he susses we're developing some line of enquiry in the wrong city is the moment he might think he's home free.'

'And then?' Suttle wasn't convinced.

'Who knows, Jimmy? That's when people make mistakes. Fingers crossed, eh?' She looked at Golding. 'So what do you have for me, young man?'

Golding took his time. He and Jimmy had been having a think, looking for patterns, squeezing what little evidence they had to try and figure out what motive might link these three killings.

'And?'

'The last two are the clue, boss. McGrath was an arsehole. So, in a different way, was Saunders.'

'Meaning?'

'Meaning these Deffo guys might be into waste disposal. McGrath is pretty straightforward. There's a long list of blokes he seriously pissed off but the one who matters is still downstairs.'

'And still going No Comment. We're going to have to bail Hamilton soon. Unless you can come up with something.'

'Right. But let's assume he got in touch with Deffo. Let's assume these guys — certainly Jenner — have the necessary skills. What more does it take? Apart from money?'

'Nerve,' Houghton said at once, 'and you'd need to be just a bit psychotic too.'

'Really, boss?' Suttle this time. 'These guys are highly trained. Killing is what they do. At long range it's anything but messy. You do the recce. You find somewhere nice and comfy. You adjust the scope. And then you do three things. Number one, you line up the target to make sure we're never going to find the spent round. Number two — bang — you take the shot. And then, number three, you fuck off.'

Houghton nodded. She wanted more. She was still looking at Golding.

'So how does that play with Saunders?'

'I don't know. The obvious guy is Pleasant, the husband Saunders fucked over, but to be honest I don't see it. Maybe there's someone else he's seriously pissed off, someone we haven't found yet.'

'Sure. And Corrigan? You're telling me he was an arsehole too?'

'No. That's a problem. He doesn't fit at all.'

'But his partner? Bella whatever? The writer woman? She went to Deffo too? Is that what you're telling me?'

'It's possible.'

'We can prove it?'

'Not yet. Not until we turn O'Neill and Jenner over.'

'That's not going to happen. Not yet. Not until we've got something really solid to throw at them.' Houghton paused. 'I had Toby Watkins back in here just now. He's managed to trace the bloke who partnered Jenner in the troop sniper team. He's out of the Corps now, just like Jenner, and he's happy to talk.'

'Is he local, boss?' Suttle was checking his watch.

'Exmouth. His wife says he's windsurfing this morning. Get down there sharpish and he'll meet you on the beach.'

She scribbled a mobile number and passed it across. Suttle got to his feet and shot Golding a look. Golding hadn't moved.

'There's one other thing,' he said.

'This is important?'

'It might be. Try writing Deffo backwards. See what you get.'

Houghton frowned, then reached for her notepad. Suttle was watching her with interest.

'Offed.' She looked up. 'Have I got that right?'

'Yeah. Street talk for a killing. You off someone? You kill them.'

'You have to be joking.' Houghton's eyes went back to the pad. 'They're taking the piss, aren't they?'

*　*　*

It was early afternoon when Suttle and Golding made it down to Exmouth. The wind had backed with the falling tide and half a dozen windsurfers were stitching back and forth between the long curve of beach and the gleaming brown hump of an offshore sandbank.

Suttle had phoned Jenner's mate from the car on the way down. His name was Gary Middleton and he was waiting for them on a patch of grass opposite a new-looking building on the seafront. He'd already dismantled his rig and strapped the board to the roof rack of his Transit van. According to the side of the van, he now made his living as an electrical contractor.

Middleton had a flask with him. He'd changed into shorts and a North Face top and spread a blanket on the warm grass.

'Help yourself.' He nodded at the blanket. 'No sugar in the coffee, I'm afraid, but you're more than welcome.'

Both Suttle and Golding declined. It was rare to conduct what might be a key interview in circumstances like these, but Suttle had already decided they had no choice. Middleton looked the kind of guy you could do business with — shaved skull, blue eyes, huge hands, an evil-looking dagger tatt down his right leg — and Suttle sensed it wouldn't be the longest chat in the world.

'This is about Oli Jenner,' he said.

'I know. That boss of yours told me. Nice lady.'

'So how well did you know him?'

'Really well. We went through two tours together. Plus all the training bollocks before and afterwards. I had the most experience, so most of the time I was eyes on.'

336

'And Oli?'

'Oli pulled the trigger.'

Sniper teams, he explained, always worked in pairs. One would spot while the other had the rifle. The key to a successful snipe was preparation. Prepping the KZ could take hours, especially with multi-targets. You had to sieve the high-value targets from the rubbish. Otherwise you were wasting your time.

'You normally get one shot,' he said. 'That's the way it works.'

'KZ?'

'Killing zone.' Middleton's eyes had strayed to a couple of windsurfers slicing out through the ebbing tide. The wind was strengthening by the minute. Under different circumstances, thought Suttle, this guy would be back out there with them.

Golding asked him about killing at long distance. Did snipers ever have qualms about what they were doing?

'I'm sorry?'

'Qualms. A conscience. You're killing some-one. Does that ever bother you?'

'Never.' He shook his head, reached for the coffee. 'We do everything in code. When we prep a target, an Alpha is a house or building. A Bravo is a male. An Echo is a woman. Mobile means moving by vehicle. So when you slot someone it's not a bloke at all, it's a Bravo. End of.'

'As simple as that?'

'Absolutely. Otherwise you'd lose it. And that wouldn't be helpful.'

'Sure. And that's something you take with you

afterwards? After you've left? After you step back into real life?'

'Real life' put a smile on Middleton's face.

'You're asking me about Oli, aren't you? You're asking me whether killing those people — if he's the one who did it — would upset him. Have I got that right?'

'Yeah.'

'Then the answer's no. If the circumstances are right, if he's got the thing tactically sound, if he thinks the bloke deserves it, there wouldn't be a problem.'

Suttle was watching him carefully.

'You think he might have done it? You think he might have been capable?'

'Capable? Of course he's capable. Did he actually do these blokes? I haven't a clue. That's your call. That's for you lot. That's your job, not mine.' He frowned, eyeing each of them in turn. 'You need to understand something about Oli. I'm not sure I should be telling you this, but you're bound to find out anyway so maybe it's best coming from me. You OK with that?'

'Go on.'

'Oli had a bit of a crisis on that last tour. In fact he had two things happen that really got to him. One was about his missus. He got a bluey from her halfway through the draft. Turned out she'd been shagging a Troop Sergeant for the last year and a half and Oli had never noticed. The thing had got out of hand and she was binning the marriage for matey down the road.'

'Oli knew this guy?'

'Yeah, he did. Not well, but yeah . . . '

338

'Kids?'

'Two nippers. Both boys. And they meant the world to Oli. They went with the mum, of course, because that's the way it always works. Broke Oli's heart. I was there in Helmand when it kicked off. He couldn't get over it. He was never the most talkative guy in the world but he just clammed up completely. It was horrible to watch. It was all churning around inside him and he had nowhere to turn. That man was fucked. Totally shafted.'

'Why didn't he do something about the Troop Sergeant?'

'That's what I asked him. He wouldn't say, not at first, but weeks later he told me he couldn't.'

'Why not?'

'Because it would be unfair on the kids. Whatever the rights and wrongs, the new bloke was their dad now and tearing his head off would only make things worse. He may have been right, but it didn't help him in here.' Middleton tapped his temple. 'Know what I mean?'

'You're telling me he lost it?'

'Yeah. Definitely. Then something else happened.'

'Like what?'

'Oli adopted a dog, a local stray, a little terrier thing that appeared in the FOB one evening. Oli loved animals. I think he trusted them more than people and he was probably right. Anyway, he fed this little thing and made a fuss of it, and of course it wouldn't leave us alone. There was no way me and Oli could have it around when we were tactical, but it started going out with the rest of the blokes on patrol. One of them didn't like the bloody animal at all. So one day he got rid of it.'

'Killed it?'

'Yeah. Shot the little bugger. Oli was mortified. You can imagine. First his kids, now the fucking dog. How much grief can a bloke stand? How much does he *deserve?*'

Suttle and Golding exchanged glances. Michael Pleasant, Suttle thought. Equally shafted. Equally broken-hearted. The artist with a dog to paint for one of his few friends.

Suttle turned back to Middleton.

'You'd recognise this dog? If we showed you a photo?'

'Of course.'

'Right.' Suttle checked his watch. 'So what's Oli up to now?'

'I dunno. Last time I checked, he was living in some doss in Heavitree. Real scran-bag. Fucking sad in my book.'

'Scran-bag?'

'Scruffy as you like. Wasn't taking care of himself. Like I say, the guy had lost it.'

Suttle got to his feet. Golding was making a note. Middleton asked again about coffee.

'No, thanks,' Suttle said. 'We'll need your address.'

'What for?'

'To show you the photo.'

'Of the dog, you mean?'

'Yeah.'

'No problem.' He gave Golding an Exmouth address and told him to phone first to make sure he was in. Then he was looking at Suttle again. 'When's this likely to happen?'

'A couple of hours. If we're lucky.'

'Fuck, really?' He looked surprised, then pleased. Up on his feet, he extended a hand. 'It's been a pleasure,' he said. 'Just one more thing.'

'What's that?'

'There's an old saying in our business. Don't tell me you've never heard it.'

'Go on.'

'Never run from a sniper.' He grinned. 'You'll only die tired.'

* * *

Michael Pleasant was in his garden when Suttle and Golding returned to Rockbeare. On his knees among the spring onions, he peered up at the two figures silhouetted against the sun.

'You again.' He struggled to his feet. 'What have I forgotten to tell you?'

At Golding's suggestion, they talked in the hut at the bottom of the garden. Pleasant had been working on his current picture since they left last night, and Suttle could make out a lone figure in waders, casting a fly onto the golden water. On the riverbank behind him stood a small dog, a perfect replica of the mutt Golding had seen in the photo last night.

The photo had gone. Golding wanted to know what he'd done with it.

'It's in here.' Pleasant retrieved a box file from the floor.

Golding opened it. The picture Pleasant had

used for reference was on top of a pile of other shots. He sorted quickly through them. They all featured the same dog. Then, at the very bottom of the pile, came another photo, bigger than the rest. He lifted it out. The summer heat inside the tiny studio had curled the edges and Golding flattened it on top of a chest of drawers Pleasant used for storage. The shot was striking. A bunch of soldiers in full combat gear were posing for the camera, some kneeling, others joshing in an untidy line behind them. The beaten red earth of the compound and the rough mud walls suggested Helmand. In front of the soldiers, up on his thin little hind legs, was the dog.

Suttle was looking at Golding. 'Afghanistan, right? Has to be.'

'Sure. And look at this.'

Suttle followed his pointing finger. At the bottom right-hand corner of the shot the photographer had scrawled a message. '*For Oli,*' it said. '*All the best. Hans.*'

'Oli is your friend?' Golding was looking up at Pleasant.

'Yes. He's on the river most days. We talk and talk.'

'And this is Oli Jenner?' Suttle nodded at the fisherman in the picture on the easel.

'Yes.'

'And you say you chat a lot? On the riverbank?'

'Yes.'

'About?'

'Everything.'

Suttle nodded, his eyes returning to the photo.

342

'Everything' might well include the fact that Adie Saunders stole this man's wife, a debt of blood just begging to be settled.

When Suttle asked to borrow a shot of the dog to show Terry Middleton, Pleasant said no problem.

'So who's Hans?' Suttle asked.

Pleasant shrugged. He said he didn't know. Some guy Oli had met in Afghanistan? He'd no idea.

Suttle took the photograph and headed for the door. Outside in the garden he glanced at Golding. Golding had a smile on his face.

'I've seen that dog before.' He nodded at the photo. 'I told you last night.'

'Where?'

'At Erika's place. You remember? The German woman? Out on Dartmoor? That bloody Great Dane of hers? She's partnered to a combat photographer. She showed me some of his work. That's him. That's the guy. Hans.'

* * *

En route to Dartmoor, Suttle phoned Carole Houghton. After he'd briefed her on the news from the meet with Gary Middleton, she updated him on another development. The observer on the chopper team had finally come up with the video sequence that nailed the white van.

'Where was it?'

'Parked on the same estate as O'Neill's place. Couple of streets further south.'

343

'You got someone round there?'

'Of course.'

'And?'

'The van belonged to a serving Marine.'

'He was there?'

'No. He got blown up in Afghan six weeks ago. Died at Bastion.'

'Shit.'

'Wait, Jimmy. His wife said he used to lend the van out sometimes. Just to blokes he knew. She's got rid of the van now, sold it to some guy up in Bristol, but that's not the point. Round Easter her husband lent it to guess who.'

'O'Neill?'

'Wrong. Oli Jenner. He was looking to move.'

'And he borrowed the van?'

'He did. For about a week, she thinks.'

'Did she have his new address?'

'Sadly not.'

Suttle nodded, letting the news sink in. Then he asked about O'Neill and Jenner. Where were they now?

'O'Neill left the family house just after midday with a couple of bags. He drove down to a place in Heavitree. We checked it out. Three flats. According to the landlord, Jenner's been living in the bottom one for a couple of months.'

'So how come our Marine Liaison Officer didn't know?'

'Pass. My guess is Jenner kept it to himself.'

'What's it like, this place?'

'Looks like a doss, according to the obs guys. They're sitting on it now.'

344

Suttle nodded, remembering Terry Middleton's phrase, just a couple of hours earlier. *Real scran-bag. Fucking sad in my book.* No wonder Jenner wasn't keen on sharing his new address.

'So where are we, boss?' Suttle bent to the phone again.

Houghton explained that Nandy had established a command team in an office adjoining the Major Incident Room. They had secure comms to the guys on obs, and the Firearms Unit was on immediate standby. The current thinking, given the gathering weight of evidence against them, was that O'Neill and Jenner might have another hit in mind. If so, Nandy would let it run until *Bellwether* was in a position to go for hard arrest once the job was underway. No jury would acquit a couple of ex-Marines in possession of a sniper rifle and whatever else they might need for a fourth head job.

'Top plan, boss.' Suttle was grinning. 'As long as we don't lose them.'

* * *

Suttle and Golding were out on the edges of Dartmoor by late afternoon. White cumulus clouds were boiling over a distant tor and Suttle caught a glimpse of a buzzard catching a lazy ride on a summer thermal. Barely a week ago, he thought, he'd been watching another buzzard, just a couple of miles away, seconds before he got the heads-up from Houghton about a body in a black VW. Since when, the world of Major Crime had been turned upside down.

Suttle pulled off the lane and bumped towards the farmhouse. Golding sat beside him, stressing about the Great Dane.

'Why don't you go in first?' he said. 'Get her to lock the fucking thing up?'

Suttle got out of the car. When she finally came to the front door, Erika Maier was wearing a silk dressing gown that was several sizes too big for her. The dressing gown was loosely tied at the waist and she hadn't got much on underneath.

Suttle apologised for the interruption. She shrugged. It wasn't a problem. She said she'd been sunbathing in the yard at the back of the farmhouse. How could she help?

'It's about your partner,' Suttle said. 'It might be better to do this inside.'

The farmhouse was cool after the afternoon heat. Erika took him into the kitchen. A bottle of suntan lotion stood beside a pile of Sunday papers. There was no sign of the dog but Suttle had decided to leave Golding in the car anyway.

'We understand your partner's done some work in Afghanistan,' Suttle began.

'Hans? Of course. He goes where the wars go, where the violence goes. He's worked many times there. With the Americans, with the Dutch, with the Germans one time. Why not?'

'And the Brits? He's worked with the Brits in Helmand?'

'Of course,' she said again. 'Often.'

'Does he talk to you about these assignments at all?'

'When we see each other, when he has time,

346

yes. Hans is not here most of the time. You should know that.'

'And has he made friends at all, among the soldiers, the guys he photographs?'

'All the time. You want to give me a name?'

'Jenner?'

'You mean Oli?' She laughed. 'Tall guy? Very quiet? Sure. You want to know about this man? You should talk to me, not Hans.'

Oli Jenner, she said, had become a friend. A friend of Hans and a friend of hers. He wasn't a soldier anymore and sometimes he came out to the farmhouse. He liked being with the animals. She had kennels at the back. She looked after other people's dogs. He'd take some of them for a walk. A nice man, she said.

'Does he always come by himself?'

'Now, yes.'

'And before?'

'Before, no.' She looked down and picked at a nail. This wasn't a woman who embarrassed easily, Suttle thought, wondering why she'd suddenly gone quiet.

'He had a friend? Oli Jenner?'

'Yes.'

'And?'

'And what?' Her head came up. Amazing eyes, a shade of blue that defied description. 'What do you want to know?'

'I'm curious. I'm just asking who this friend was.'

'You want his name?'

'Yes, please.'

'It's important?'

347

'It might be, yes.'

'Should I ask why?'

'No.' Suttle shook his head. 'You shouldn't. Not now. Not just yet.'

'OK.' She shrugged. 'His name's Sean. He's a friend of Oli's. They have something going together, some work thing.' She frowned. 'Feddo?'

'Deffo.'

'You know about this already?'

'Yes.'

'So why the questions?'

'I want to know about Sean. I want to know why he doesn't come here any more.'

'That's simple. This guy isn't . . . you know . . . very well. Sometimes he can be a little bit crazy, do crazy things, think crazy thoughts.'

'About what?'

'Me.'

'I don't understand.'

She was looking uncomfortable now. She crossed her legs and tightened the belt on the dressing gown.

'He thinks, you know, we should be together. Like I said, a little bit crazy.'

'He fell in love with you?'

'Yes.'

'And told you?'

'Many times. Here, in this kitchen. Sometimes on the phone. Often on the email. He's married, this man. He shouldn't be giving me all this shit.'

It was impossible not to miss the venom in her voice.

'It's still happening?'

'Yes.' She nodded. 'He doesn't come here any more because I made Oli promise he wouldn't, but I still get the phone calls and the other stuff, the emails.'

'What does he say?'

'He says he wants to live here, with me. He says he knows I have other men. He says he wants to leave his wife. He tells me how happy we'll be together. And there's other stuff too, sexual stuff. This is a man not right in the head.'

'Change your email.'

'I will.'

'And your phone number.'

'Of course.'

Suttle studied her for a long moment. At length he decided there was no point not asking the obvious question.

'So is it true?'

'What?'

'About other men in your life?'

She shook her head. Suttle sensed it wasn't a denial, but simply a refusal to answer the question. He went at it another way.

'Was Corrigan one of those men?'

'Michael?' She shook her head. 'No. I liked Michael. I loved the baby. But no.'

'What about Sean O'Neill? Did he think you were with Michael?'

Her head was back now, her eyes narrowed, and the expression on her face told Suttle she was impressed. He was right.

'You're a clever man, Mr Detective,' she said. 'That's exactly what Sean thought. He said he

349

knew I was fucking Michael. He said it was obvious.'

'So what did you say?'

'I said he was talking shit. I told him it wasn't true.'

'And?'

'He was upset. He said it was unfair.'

'*Unfair?*'

'That's the word he used.'

'What did he mean?'

'I don't know. I've no idea. He began to spook me, frighten me a little, you know? That's when I told Oli. I haven't seen Sean since.'

'This was before Michael was shot? Before last Sunday?'

'Yes.'

Suttle nodded. For a split second he thought he heard a door close upstairs. Erika didn't move.

'Is that all?' she said. 'Have you finished?'

Suttle nodded. He said he was grateful for her time. She was deeply tanned already but he guessed she couldn't resist a top-up. Maybe she should get back outside, while it was still sunny.

'I'm sorry to have bothered you.' He got up to leave, then paused. 'Just one more thing. Do you have Oli's mobile number? And maybe one for Sean?'

'You're going to talk to them?' She was looking alarmed.

'No. Not yet.'

She hesitated, then shrugged and got off the stool. Her mobile was on the kitchen table. Suttle made a note of both numbers.

'Thanks,' he said. 'Enjoy the rest of your day.'

Back in front of the farmhouse Golding had the car door open. He was talking to someone on the phone. By the time Suttle was back behind the wheel, the conversation was over.

Suttle was reaching for the key. Golding stopped him.

'I took a walk round the back,' he said. 'There's a camper van parked up. Plus a couple of sunbeds.'

'She's got a camper van?'

'No.' He nodded at the mobile on his lap. 'I just checked out the number. It's the one Goodyer bought.' His gaze strayed to the farmhouse. 'Interesting or what?'

★   ★   ★

Suttle pulled into a lay-by on the A38 and phoned Lizzie on the way back to the Major Incident Room. She answered on the first ring.

'You OK?'

'I'm knackered.'

'Why?'

'I've been having a go at the garden.'

'Which bit?'

'The worst bit.'

'That means nothing. That could be any-where.'

Suttle could hear her laughing.

'A bath would be really nice,' she said.

'You're staying?'

'Only if you want me to.'

'I do,' he said. 'Very much.'

351

★ ★ ★

It was half five when Suttle and Golding got back to the Major Crime complex at Middlemoor. Houghton and Nandy had ducked out of the Incident Room to conference in the relative peace of Houghton's permanent office. In Nandy's phrase, the time had come to take a breath or two: to review the investigative options, to take a hard look at synergies thrown up by the three separate enquiries and to plot a sensible and effective pathway through the coming hours.

Suttle's head round the door appeared to come as something of a relief. Houghton gestured for him to join them, and the moment he stepped into the office, he sensed the discussion had stalled. Houghton had found a fan from somewhere but it didn't seem to make much difference. The air tasted stale. It was still far too hot. Both Houghton and Nandy looked knackered. Suttle wanted to throw open the windows, table an idea or two, maybe point the investigation in a different direction.

He briefed them on the day's progress. Gary Middleton, the windsurfing ex-Marine, had painted a sombre picture of Oli Jenner. His broken marriage had taken him to a very dark place. The war had robbed him of his precious dog. This was a guy who'd burned himself to a frazzle on re-entry from Afghan, ending up in some shit-hole flat in the badlands of Heavitree. No family. No kids. No one to be close to except the guy whose life he'd saved.

'This has to be O'Neill.' Nandy was looking brighter.

'Yes, sir. But O'Neill's got a problem too. He survived the IED but according to Middleton was never the same afterwards.'

'That's right.' Houghton slipped a report from the mountain of files on her desk. It had come, she said, from Toby Watkins. Suttle found himself looking at O'Neill's medical records. There were pages of detail on the damage he'd taken from the IED and the treatment he'd received afterwards, but it was a sentence at the end, highlighted in yellow, that caught his eye: 'O'Neill suffered significant neural brain damage as a result of reduced blood flow through the carotid artery in the crucial minutes after the explosion.' Suttle looked up. Jenner had saved his life, he suggested, but not all of it.

'Spot-on, Jimmy.' Houghton nodded. 'That's the way we're reading it. According to Toby, that's the reason he was discharged from the Corps.'

'Which would have affected him?'

'Undoubtedly. By all accounts he was a fine soldier. To these guys the Corps becomes the real family. The last thing they need is getting dumped on their arse in civvy street. That's Toby's take on it, by the way, not mine.'

Suttle was looking at the medical report again.

'No other physical injuries? He didn't lose a leg or anything?'

'No.' Nandy this time. 'The medics did a brilliant job, sewed him up a treat. Otherwise he'd have been in rehab for months.'

353

'What about counselling?'

'Apparently he wouldn't hear of it. The guy just wanted to crack on, but that didn't happen.'

'Why not?'

Neither Nandy nor Houghton knew. Orphaned by the war, O'Neill appeared to have ghosted himself back to the bosom of his family, shut his door on the world and brooded. The High-Tech Crime Unit had spent the best part of a day and a half exploring Deffo.net. The Web-based business had only been active for the past couple of months. For more than a year O'Neill had probably done fuck all.

'But what about the Corps?' Suttle said. 'Don't they keep tabs on these people?'

'They do. They have specialised welfare officers. These guys are worked off their feet. They have huge caseloads. They're often with the families for years on end. But like Toby said, O'Neill didn't want to know about any of that stuff.'

'So how did he live? How did he keep himself going? This is a guy with kids, right?'

Nandy glanced across at Houghton.

'He's got a couple of kids,' Houghton said. 'His wife was working as an agency nurse but jacked it in once O'Neill came home.'

'So what did they do for money?' Suttle asked again.

'That wouldn't have been a huge problem. O'Neill would qualify for a decent pension plus a lump sum. Toby described it as a severance payment. Interesting phrase if you've lost a limb.'

'But he hadn't?'

'No. In every physical respect this guy is normal.'

'Except he isn't.'

'Exactly. Toby talked to a shrink. Ran the brain stuff past him. Apparently you'd expect depression, mood swings, extreme volatility. Plus the guy would probably have all kinds of grudges.'

'Against?'

'You name it.' Nandy again. 'The Taliban first. For killing his mates. And for fucking him up. Then a long list of other targets.'

'Targets?'

'These guys are highly trained. They have a mindset. You don't shake that off in an afternoon. Most of them don't have a problem with the transition to civvy life but if the wiring's dodgy then you're looking at a different story.'

Suttle nodded. This was beginning to make perfect sense, he thought. A brain-damaged Marine with debts to settle, buddied up with an ex-sniper fighting demons of his own. Under different circumstances, he thought, this might have the makings of a therapeutic exercise. Three men may have died, but the real victims were the guys who'd killed them. He was tempted to voice the thought but knew that Nandy would flatten him. Twenty years of Major Crime had given him a very black and white view of the world. He had no time for bleeding-heart, wishy-washy hand-wringing. Find whoever did it. And lock the fuckers up.

Suttle described the visit to Michael Pleasant. The link between the landscape painter and

Jenner was rock solid. Jenner went fishing a lot. Pleasant had met him on the riverbank. It turned out they had a lot in common: a love of the outdoors, a need for peace and quiet, and marriages that had ended in disaster. Gary Middleton had also ID'd the dog when they'd showed him the photo.

'You think they compared notes?' Houghton asked. 'Jenner and Pleasant?'

'Must have done.'

'So Jenner would have known about Saunders? The guy who nicked Pleasant's wife?'

'Yeah.'

'And Pleasant paid him to knock the guy off?'

'I doubt it. Pleasant's a tree-hugger. The way I read it there isn't an ounce of aggression in the guy. He's practically a Buddhist when it comes to violence.'

'Hang on.' Nandy was frowning. 'You're telling me Jenner's a fisherman?'

'Yes.'

'Where?'

'On the Exe. Between Dulverton and Exebridge.'

'That costs a fortune. Where does he get the money?'

'I've no idea, sir.'

'Maybe his new mate? Maybe Pleasant?'

'No, sir. That doesn't work. He'd been fishing long before he met Pleasant.'

'So Pleasant never bunged him? Is that what you're saying? You're telling me Pleasant was on a freebie?'

'Yes, sir.'

'Really? So how does that work?'

Suttle was aware that he was starting to go dangerously off-piste but he didn't care. The longer he thought about these two men, the more he sensed that they'd backed themselves up a very dark cul-de-sac.

'Jenner has a grudge too,' he said. 'Against the guy who nicked his wife. He never did anything about it because in the end it would damage his kids, but when he starts talking to Pleasant he finds himself looking at exactly the same situation. More to the point, there's something he can do here. He knows the bloke's name and where he lives — Pleasant would have told him. He knows what he does for a living. He knows he spends half his life way up some tree dangling from a harness. Given his MO, Saunders is the perfect target. Number one, the guy's an arsehole. Number two, no way are we ever going to find the bullet. At that point Saunders is a dead man. Job done.'

'As simple as that?'

'Yeah. And as complicated too.'

Houghton wanted to know where this left Johnny Hamilton. She'd managed a PACE custody extension of twenty-four hours, but keeping him longer had required an application to a magistrate's court. Such an extension demanded the likelihood of fresh evidence and Houghton had entered a successful plea on the basis of the three on-going enquiries, but time was running out again and Hamilton was still refusing to cooperate.

'Was that a favour too?' Nandy asked. 'Are

357

these guys playing the vigilante card? Upholding truth and justice?'

'My guess is Hamilton paid,' Suttle said.

'Sure. But we can't prove it, can we?'

'We will, sir.' Houghton was looking weary again. 'Come the finish.'

Nandy shot her a look. Then he was back in Suttle's face, forcing him to justify himself, testing all this wank psychology to the limit.

'So what about Corrigan? Out on the moor? The little nipper in the car? How does that fit in?'

'It doesn't, sir. Not obviously. But you're right. McGrath and Saunders were bad guys. In my view there'd have been money in it from Hamilton, but it can't be that tough pulling the trigger if you think you're doing the world a big favour. Corrigan's different. He wasn't an arsehole. So there has to be another explanation.'

'Excellent. I agree. So what might that be?'

Suttle described the conversation with Erika. O'Neill had become obsessed with her. He was bothering her day and night. He wanted to move in. He wanted the whole deal, but no way would that ever happen.

'Why not?'

'Because she wasn't interested. But that didn't cut it for O'Neill. Her partner was away most of the time and O'Neill was convinced she was kipping with someone else.'

'Who?'

'Corrigan.'

'And was she?'

'She says not.'

'Do we believe her?'

'Yes, I think we do.'

'Why?'

'Because she's kipping with someone else.'

'Who?'

'Goodyer,' Houghton said softly. 'Has to be.'

Suttle was impressed. Nandy wanted to know more. Houghton pointed out that Goodyer had every reason to screw his ex-mate any way he could. Corrigan may have fancied Erika. He certainly trusted her enough to let her look after his infant son. What if O'Neill wanted Corrigan off the plot? And what if Goodyer helped make that happen?

Suttle blinked. Try as he might, he couldn't fit Jenner into the Corrigan hit. This appeared to be a guy with a conscience. Slotting McGrath and Saunders wouldn't be a problem. But Corrigan was different. Because Corrigan, by all accounts, was a good guy.

'So what happened, boss? How does that work?'

'I don't know,' she said. 'But what if O'Neill pulled the trigger? What if he borrowed the sniper rifle? What if Jenner wasn't even there?'

'But he'd need an accomplice. Someone down on the road to stop the car.'

'Of course.' She smiled. 'And that someone would be Goodyer. Think about it. He's got the motivation. Plus he's the one who would have taken Corrigan's phone and raised the alarm. Why? Because the kid's in the back.'

Suttle nodded. Clever, he thought.

'So how did he get out there? Out to the moor?'

'Maybe O'Neill picked him up.'

'Corrigan would have known. He was up early too.'

'Then maybe he didn't spend the night there at all. Nicky, the girl, was in London. Corrigan could have been in the house alone. With the guy dead, Goodyer's home free. No one else would know he'd kipped somewhere else.'

'With the woman? Erika?'

'Maybe.'

There was a brief silence. Houghton was staring at Suttle.

'O'Neill's got a van,' she said. 'It's in the surveillance logs. Goodyer could have kipped in the back.'

'Then we need to bosh it.' Nandy was on his feet. Time was moving on. 'We should be framing an arrest strategy. This thing is dragging out. We need to scoop these guys up, cut to the chase.'

'Great.' Houghton was looking up at him. 'So what do we do for evidence? We're still waiting for bank statements. There's a delay on some of the mobile billings. We need this stuff in place before we move.'

'Makes no difference. What if they slot someone else? The Chief will hang us out to dry. And for my money he'd probably be right.'

Houghton shook her head. She was never slow in fighting her corner but she also knew that Nandy was under the cosh. She was pointing out that both men were still under surveillance, making a fourth hit unlikely, when Suttle cleared his throat.

'There might be another way, sir.'

Nandy had turned to leave. 'Like what?'

'Like we set up a TP.'

'Test Purchase?' Nandy was frowning. 'How would that work?'

'We put someone in to play the punter. Someone with a problem. Someone who offers them a really juicy target. Another McGrath. Another Saunders. Total arsehole. We set O'Neill and Jenner up. The way I read it, these guys are off the planet. We let them run, and then we catch them in the act. Video. Stills. Hard evidence. Sniper rifle. Target plotted up. The whole deal. Stone-bonker verdict. Plus publicity to die for.'

It was mention of publicity that drew Nandy back towards the desk. He'd always had a soft spot for bold moves and this, Suttle knew, was one of the boldest.

'So who might be the target?'

Suttle held Nandy's gaze.

'The target doesn't matter, sir,' he said. 'The target will be fictitious.'

'And the punter?'

'Me.'

★ ★ ★

Suttle was home by eight. To his relief Lizzie's car was still there. He found her in the kitchen, the door to the garden wide open, opera blasting out from Lenahan's portable CD player. *Tosca*,

361

Suttle thought. Act two.

'I found it in his bedroom.' Lizzie was making a huge salad. 'I don't know much about opera but I thought it might be fitting.'

Suttle was looking at the rest of the meal. Two decent-sized fillets of what looked like haddock lay in a glass dish. New potatoes were bubbling on the stove. Lizzie had prepared a pile of runner beans and Suttle caught the tang of freshly chopped garlic from the board on the table. This could have been a vintage Lenahan night, he thought. All it needed was a bottle or two of white.

He reached for his keys again.

'I'll go down to the shop,' he said. 'They've got a Sancerre on offer.'

'Done.' Lizzie opened the fridge. Two bottles of Chablis plus one of champagne. 'I went down to Exmouth for the sea bass and the wine. The rest is home grown. Since when did you become a gardener?'

'I didn't. That was down to Eamonn. He was out there all hours. And the guy cooked like an angel.'

Lizzie had taken the champagne out of the fridge. She gave him the bottle and asked about glasses. Suttle was still marvelling at what was to come.

'So what brought this on?' he said.

'You.'

She reached up for him, lingering over the kiss. Suttle could smell a perfume he couldn't place. Another surprise.

'You miss him, don't you? Eamonn?'

'I do.'

'So what happened?'

Suttle tried to explain. It took a while. The big mistake, he said finally, was believing that doctors knew best.

'But that wasn't your fault. You didn't kill him.'

'I did. That's exactly what I did.'

'You didn't, Jimmy. You respected his decision, his judgement.'

'Yeah? But there's a difference, isn't there? I think his judgement was spot-on. I think he knew what had happened to him. The decision he took was to busk it. Or maybe worse. By taking him to hospital, I might have saved his life. That's not easy to live with.'

He told Lizzie about the results of the post-mortem. The news that Lenahan was carrying the Aids virus first astonished then alarmed her.

'Have you had a check?'

'No.'

'Why not?'

'No time.'

'No *time?* Jesus.' She was trying to work out whether an early-morning fuck had been such a great idea. Suttle could see it in her face.

'Would it have made any difference?' he asked at last.

She looked at him for a long moment, then held her arms out.

'No way,' she said. 'Happy birthday.'

★ ★ ★

363

They had dinner on the patio. It was still warm, not a whisper of wind, and Suttle couldn't believe what Lizzie had done to the garden. She'd taken a scythe to the nettles and long grass, raking them into a neat pile down by the stream. She'd tidied up the scatter of flowerpots and made a start on weeding the scruffy patch of turned earth Lenahan had been reserving for next year's daffs. She'd even attacked the wild hedge that bordered the outhouse. If anything, he told her, it looked worse than before.

'I know.' She was busy filleting her fish. 'Think punk.'

'So how come you found time to go to Exmouth?'

'Easy. Straight in, straight out, no messing. The supermarket's at the top of the hill. I was back within the hour.'

'Not tempted to look further? The seafront? The rowing club? Old times?'

Lizzie looked up. Not once over the past year had they been brave enough to tear the plasters off old wounds. What happened in Exmouth had shattered the marriage. Best not to go there.

'I thought about it,' she said. 'If you want the truth.'

'And?'

'There wasn't any point. It's gone. It's over. I'd say sorry but you'd never believe me.'

'Why don't you try?'

'Then I'm sorry. Sometimes I get things wrong. More wrong than you'd ever believe. What I need is a change of career. Something more hands-on. Something that would sort me out. Gardening might just cut it.'

'You're joking.'

'I am.'

Suttle realised she was drunker than he'd thought. He reached for the bottle and refilled her glass.

'Why would you need sorting out?' he murmured.

'Don't ask.'

'I'd like to know.'

'Why?'

'Because you're my daughter's mum. And because we're still married.'

'Does that give you rights?'

'Yes. Since you ask.'

She ducked her head, ran her finger around the top of her glass. Then she asked him about his own love life.

'There isn't one,' he said.

'I don't believe you.'

'It's true. Eamonn moved in a while back. We got on really well. He made a difference.'

'After moody old me?'

'That's not what I said. After you went there was nothing. If you want the truth I was going bonkers.'

'Here? Alone?'

'Yes.'

'Welcome to the club.'

'Thanks. You're right. This is no place without company. Eamonn was an amazing bloke. I owe him everything.'

'Like Aids?'

'That's cheap. He had spirit, that man. He just *knew* so much. He'd been so many places. He made me laugh. He was like the central heating system that never lets you down.'

'The *what?*'

'The central heating system. I told him once. You warm the place up, I said. And it doesn't cost me a penny.'

'I bet that pleased him.'

'It did.'

Lizzie studied him a moment then looked down.

'He was gay, wasn't he.' A statement, not a question.

'Yeah. How did you guess?'

'Because he sounds far too interesting to be straight.'

'Thanks.'

'Not at all. Did he come on to you?'

'Sometimes.'

'And?'

'Nothing ever happened.'

'Did that matter?'

'Not to me, no.'

'To him?'

'Yes, I think in the end it did. He was making noises about leaving, about going back to Africa.'

'That would have been terrible.'

'It would. You're right.'

'So would you have slept with him? Seen it his way? Given him what he was after?'

The bluntness of the question brought Suttle to a halt. He pushed his plate to one side and

366

looked away a moment. The cottage was beginning to blur. Then he felt Lizzie's hand on his.

'I'm sorry,' she said softly. 'Put it down to the wine. I'm a bit pissed.'

'Yeah?'

'Yeah. Once a journo . . . You know how it goes.' Suttle nodded. Lizzie gave his hand a squeeze. 'And it doesn't matter if you'd have said yes. Just for the record.'

'To kipping with him?'

'Yes.'

'It wouldn't?'

'No. Not if you'd meant it. Not if you'd loved him.' She paused. '*Did* you love him?'

'Yes. In a way I did.'

'Then I'm even sorrier.'

Suttle was fighting for control now, determined not to break down completely. Lenahan had mattered. Lizzie was right. But quite how much had come as a huge surprise.

'It gets worse,' he said. 'Thank Christ I'm busy.'

Lizzie was kneeling beside him now, her arm around his heaving shoulders. He opened his eyes and turned his face away, ashamed of himself, not wanting her to see him this way. *Change the subject*, he told himself. Get to the real business.

'We need to talk,' he said.

'You're right.'

'No, about something else.'

'Yeah?' She kissed the wetness on his cheek. 'So tell me.'

'This is Job talk,' he warned her. 'You're not going to like it.'

'Try me.'

Suttle told her about the three killings, about the links between them, about the investigative net closing around a couple of ex-Marines. These were damaged people, he said. One of them had been blown up in Afghanistan. The other had saved his life. Neither of these guys would ever be the same again.

'Tell me about it.'

'What does that mean?'

'It doesn't matter.' She kissed him again. 'So what happens next?'

'We're going to flush them out. Strictly speaking it's entrapment, but you won't believe the pressures we're under.'

'Entrapment?'

'I don't want to go into it but . . . '

'But what?' She sounded alarmed.

'It could be dodgy.'

'How? For who?'

'Me.'

'How dodgy?'

'I don't know. No one knows. We take precautions. Nothing moves in the Job these days without everything being risk-assessed to death.'

'You mean that?'

'About risk assessments?'

'About death.'

Suttle laughed softly in the gathering darkness. In truth he didn't know. He'd do his best not to get himself killed, he said, and given the resources his bosses would be putting in place, that was highly unlikely. But nothing was certain in this life, he said, and if something horrible did happen he wanted her to know that she still mattered to him.

Lizzie didn't know what to do, what to say. A birthday celebration seemed to have turned into a wake.

'Bin it,' she said quietly. 'Say no. Un-volunteer yourself. Whatever this thing is, turn it down.'

'I can't. It was my idea.'

'And if it kills you?'

'Then maybe I deserve it.'

'Because of Eamonn? Because of what happened?'

'Yes.'

'And what about us? Me? Grace? Where do we figure in all this?'

Suttle blinked. He could sense her anger. It was there in her voice, in the way she'd physically stiffened. He tried to force a smile. The last thing he wanted was a ruck.

'Good question.' His hand reached for hers. 'Let's talk about something else.'

★   ★   ★

They finished the bottle and went to bed, drunk now, not caring any more. Lizzie had gone beyond bemusement, beyond disbelief, beyond anger. She seemed to have reconnected with this husband of hers in the worst possible circumstances. He was more lost, more vulnerable, than she could ever remember, but whatever tomorrow held for him was beyond negotiation. She

369

knew there was nothing she could say to him that would have the slightest impact on what was going to happen. He'd made some private pact with himself, and whatever decision he'd come to was utterly beyond her control. If it went well, she sensed it might bring some kind of redemption. And if it didn't, she preferred not to think about the possible consequences.

She woke in the middle of the night. For a long moment she had no idea where she was, but then the window overlooking the lane outside resolved itself, and she rolled over to reach for him, finding nothing but the emptiness of the bed. She got up on her elbows, rubbing her eyes, aware of a hint of music from downstairs. She got out of bed and crept onto the landing. From the top of the stairs, in the spill of light from the kitchen, she could see Jimmy sitting on the sofa, his head in his hands. A woman's voice from the CD player at his feet, the volume turned down. 'O mio babbino caro,' she sang. 'Mi piace, è bello, bello . . .'

14

MONDAY, 2 JULY 2012

Lizzie was barely awake when Suttle left. She was aware of him bending over the bed with a cup of tea. He was wearing jeans and a T-shirt she'd bought him years ago at an AC/DC concert. His hair was wet. He carried the scent of shower gel. She peered up at the window. A beautiful day. Then her gaze found Suttle again.

'You mended it?'

'No way. I had a cold one.'

'Fuck.' She blinked. 'What time is it?'

'Nearly seven. I have to go.'

'Why?'

'Because.' He bent to kiss her. 'Will you be here when I get back?'

She stared at him, alert now and remembering.

'Silly question,' she said.

★　★　★

Suttle was at Middlemoor by eight, noting the thicket of media vans and outside-broadcast vehicles in the pub car park across the road from police headquarters. An enterprising guy with a van was already doing a brisk trade in bacon rolls and jumbo mugs of coffee, and if Suttle needed proof that a couple of the nation's heroes had given serial killing a new twist, then here it surely was. As he turned the Impreza across the oncoming traffic stream and headed for the barrier, he tried to picture the headlines if Oli Jenner turned out to be down for the three murders. MARINE SNIPER GOES ROGUE would do the past eight days less than justice.

Suttle parked and headed for the Major Crime complex. Houghton and Nandy were conferring upstairs in Houghton's office. Nandy, it seemed, had spent half the night reviewing Suttle's Test Purchase suggestion, trying to turn the boldness of the idea into an operation that would survive the rigours of the risk-assessment process. First he needed to be sure that Suttle had done undercover work before.

'I have, sir. I told you last night.'

'I know you did, son. When? Where?'

'In Pompey four or five years ago. We mounted a sting against an Iraqi businessman funding cocaine imports. Guy called Hassan. You're talking a seven-figure deal.'

'And your role?'

'I wanted part of the action. I was young, ambitious, and I needed to get in his face.'

'It worked?'

'Sadly not. The guy got taken out by a local player. Ended up with broken legs and a torched Beamer.'

'These were drug debts?' Nandy was intrigued.

'No, sir. They both played for pub sides. Dockyard League. It was a ruck about an offside decision.'

To Suttle's relief, even Houghton laughed. The story was fiction, just like every u/c legend, but Nandy seemed to buy it.

'OK,' he said. 'These are the parameters. We go with the plan but it has to be somewhere public. I'm suggesting a pub with a big car park. There's a Beefeater place out on the Topsham Road. The Countess Wear. I drove in that way this morning. It's not perfect but it'll do. We'll need to plot it up. I'm thinking a couple of guys inside plus a MAST unit in the car park and maybe an ARV in the vicinity as well.'

Suttle nodded. MAST was cop-speak for a Mobile Armed Surveillance Team. These guys were trained to sit on a target and intervene if necessary. Armed Response Vehicles were BMW estates. Two officers plus a box of guns in the back. Escalating the operation this way needed the authority of an Assistant Chief Constable.

'You've talked to the ACC, sir?'

'I'm going over there now. I belled him first thing. This legend of yours, run it past me again.'

Suttle explained the pitch he'd be making to Jenner and O'Neill. A long-standing relationship had crashed and burned. His ex had moved in with another bloke. Word had got back that the new man in her life was fucking his twelve-year-old daughter. The girl had virtually confirmed it, as good as. Worse still, she appeared to be in love with the man. Suttle had confronted the guy but he'd denied everything.

'So how can you be sure he's at it?' Houghton wasn't convinced.

'My daughter's got a best friend. She's telling

373

her everything. The best friend's got a mum. Someone I know. Someone I trust. And this woman has been on to me. I have to do something about this arsehole, boss. She's still my daughter, for Christ's sake.'

Suttle had slipped into character. There was a hint of approval in Houghton's smile. Both Jenner and O'Neill had young kids. Nice storyline.

'So how long do we let this run?' She was looking at Nandy.

'As long as it takes. We're after some form of admission, Carole. All these people have to do is offer their services. Then they're on a nicking.'

'Does Jimmy need some shots of this guy? Something to show them?'

'Sorted, boss.' Suttle produced a couple of photos. Both showed a man in his early thirties. He was on a beach, stripped to the waist, a football at his feet.

'Who's this?' Houghton wanted to know.

'My best man, boss. A while back.'

'Pompey?'

'Yeah.'

Nandy glanced at the photos. He wanted to know how Suttle was going to make contact with these people. In their place that would be his first question. Why come to us?

Suttle nodded. He'd spent most of the night trying to figure out a plausible story. Only on the drive in had he remembered something Lenahan had told him, an incident he'd brought back from a shift on A&E.

'I'm working on it, sir. I have to make a couple

of calls, maybe go over to Heavitree. What's the time frame here?'

'I'm thinking you set the meet for lunchtime. Assuming these people agree to turn up.'

'Fine.' Suttle checked his watch. 'I need to get moving.'

Nandy was already on his feet. The ACC would be at his desk by now, expecting him to make his case for armed back-up. Nandy left the office and Suttle heard the clatter of his footsteps on the stairs.

Houghton had reached for the photos of Suttle's best man. She studied them a moment and then looked up.

'How's Lizzie?'

'She's at home.'

'In Portsmouth?'

'At the cottage.'

'Really?' Houghton looked surprised. 'You mean she's back?'

'I've no idea, boss. That's something else I've got to sort.'

★   ★   ★

Lizzie drifted downstairs to make the call. A couple of ibuprofen from the bathroom cabinet had stilled the thunder in her head and a second cup of tea had steadied her stomach.

'Gill? It's Lizzie.'

Gill Reynolds, it turned out, was stalled in traffic en route to work. She wanted to know about Merrilees, about how it had gone, about when she could expect first sight of the Afghan

375

piece that would anchor the special supplement.

'Bit of a fuck-up, Gill. I can't go into it now.'

'He didn't come across?'

'He came across in spades.'

'Are we talking copy?'

'Sadly not.'

'What then? What happened? Just tell me, Lou. Stop pissing around.'

Her voice had hardened. There was a lot riding on Rob Merrilees for both of them, and Gill had limited patience when it came to excuses. She asked again about the weekend.

'You're telling me you never got out of fucking bed? Is that it?'

'No.'

'You never got *into* fucking bed?'

'That wasn't a problem.'

'Glad to hear it. So why aren't you pinging me pages of stuff I can show Boulton? You used to be good at all this, Lou.'

Lizzie said nothing. She was standing at the kitchen sink, staring out at the drift of blue scabious at the bottom of the garden. Gill was right, she thought. *I used to be good at all this.*

'I'm not too bright, Gill. I'm staying down for a couple of days.'

'With the Marine guy?'

'With Jimmy.'

Gill protested. She needed, at the very least, a summary of what Boulton could expect from his star reporter's weekend. By lunchtime. Via email.

Lizzie shook her head. The sight of the pile of dirty plates turned her stomach.

376

'It's not going to happen, Gill,' she said. And ended the call.

★ ★ ★

Suttle met the duty Inspector at Heavitree police station shortly after nine o'clock. He'd phoned ahead, asking him to access the operational log for Sunday, 24 June. Now they were together in the Inspector's office. He was a thickset man in his late forties, slightly ponderous. The sight of a Major Crime detective in jeans and a T-shirt appeared to upset him.

'What exactly are you after, young man?'

Suttle explained about a drunk found unconscious at the bottom of a trench dug by one of the utility companies. The trench, as far as he could remember, had been in Heavitree.

'And our involvement?'

'The guy appeared to have been assaulted. The staff at A&E phoned you on the Sunday, and my guess is that you probably sent a couple of officers up there.'

The Inspector's eyes returned to the log. Suttle's account appeared to have triggered a memory. One fat finger found an entry towards the bottom of the PC screen.

'You're right. 10.39. Duty shift. Two blokes.'

A couple of keystrokes took him to their report. The guy brought in unconscious was a well known local pisshead. He couldn't remember anything about getting battered and the bedside interview had been evidentially useless, but enquiries the next day had taken the same

377

officers to a Sikh-run corner shop close to the roadworks.

The Inspector was squinting at the screen. It seemed the owner knew the pisshead well. He was always hassling them for cut-price booze. He had also caused trouble in a laundrette along the street, pestering some of the young mums who went in there. The Sikh bore the drunk no malice but thought he'd been sorted out by a guy who also used the laundrette.

Suttle wanted to know more about this man.

'Did the Sikh offer any description?'

'No. He just said he was tall. And fit. That was about it.'

'So what did your guys do?'

The Inspector abandoned the screen. At last he'd recalled the incident in full. His officers, he said, had paid a visit to the laundrette later that day. Two women were in there and they both knew the guy who'd taken a beating. Neither was prepared to get involved in any speculation about who may have done it, but the officers suspected they both knew. Given the state of the guy who'd been beaten up and the fact that he wasn't pressing for any kind of redress, the matter was allowed to rest on the file.

'No further action?'

'You're right. As if we hadn't got better things to do.'

Suttle nodded. From the surveillance log he knew that Jenner's flat was very close to the laundrette. If he didn't have access to a washing machine, it was more than likely he used the laundrette. This was a guy who might well have killed two blokes for crossing some private line. The neighbourhood drunk, under the circumstances, had probably got off lightly.

'I'm grateful.' Suttle got to his feet. 'I'll bell you if I need anything more.'

★   ★   ★

The laundrette was a two-minute drive from the police station. Suttle ducked into a charity shop on the way and bought a handful of clothes. The woman manning the counter found him a black sack from the storeroom and Suttle emerged from the shop moments later with the clothes in the sack. The laundrette was empty except for two youngish women sharing a copy of *Hello!* magazine. One of them had a baby in a buggy. Suttle headed for a machine then paused, patted his jeans, produced a note, and asked one of the women for change. Between them they mustered five pound coins. Suttle loaded the empty machine and settled down to wait.

Getting into conversation with the women was easier than he'd anticipated. After a joke or two about David Beckham's love life, he casually asked about an incident last weekend. He'd heard about some guy found spark-out in the bottom of the trench outside. True or false? One of the women nodded. The guy deserved it, she said. Total nightmare. Always in here. Always getting in your face. Always pissed out of his head. Always giving the girls a hard time. Always on the scam for money. Thank God someone had the bottle to sort him out.

'So who did that?'

The woman blinked. The question, Suttle knew, was far too blunt, but he was running out of time. She wanted to know who he was, why he was interested. A conversation about overpaid superstars had rapidly become something else.

'It's just I've got a problem of my own,' Suttle said.

'Yeah?'

'Yeah. I just need a word with someone. Know what I mean?'

The two women exchanged glances. The baby had started to struggle in the buggy. The mother dug in her bag and found a bottle of milk. The other woman was still looking at Suttle, trying to make up her mind.

'You could Google a site called Deffo,' she said at last. 'See where it takes you.'

Suttle went through the motions of checking out the site on his smartphone. He showed the woman the contact number.

'That's who I bell, right?'

The woman shrugged. She'd finished with this conversation.

Suttle made the call from his car. A woman's voice was on the line within seconds. She had a northern accent. Suttle asked to speak to Sean O'Neill.

'This is business? This is about Deffo?'

'Yes.'

'He's not here, love. You want a number?'

'Please.'

Suttle made a note of the mobile number, aware of the women watching him from the

380

laundrette. He'd call O'Neill from Middlemoor, he thought, once he knew Nandy had the ACC's backing for what might follow. He pocketed his mobile and reached for the ignition key, giving the women a little wave as he drove away. Only at the end of the street, nosing into the last of the rush-hour traffic, did he remember the clothes from the charity shop, still whirling away.

★   ★   ★

Nandy had returned from his session with the Assistant Chief Constable. To his relief, the pitch for armed back-up had been an easy sell. Matt Kilfoyle was a trophy acquisition from a force further along the coast. His rise through the ranks had been dizzying, but he'd packed a great deal of experience into his nineteen years' service. He was also extremely media-savvy, just one of the talents that had landed him the job with Devon and Cornwall, and he was only too aware of the enormous pressure on the top corridor to bring last week's string of killings to an end. If a detective of Nandy's standing saw serious evidential value in putting Jimmy Suttle into play, then he wasn't going to argue.

'Go for it, Malcolm,' he'd said. 'We'll talk again when I've made the calls.'

Now back in Houghton's office, Nandy was beaming. For the time being, responsibility for what happened next belonged to someone else. Firearms operations were driven from the very top. It would be Matt Kilfoyle's job to keep the show on the road.

'Down to you then, son.' Nandy was looking at Suttle. 'I suggest you bell Mr O'Neill and invite him to lunch.'

★ ★ ★

Suttle made the call from the squad office downstairs. The office was empty, the D/Cs still out on actions, still working *Graduate* or *Scorpion* or *Bellwether* or — in some cases — all three. Suttle keyed O'Neill's number into his mobile and waited at his desk. He'd never met either O'Neill or Jenner. He had no idea what two ex-Marines with a taste for long-distance killing might look like. All he sensed was that both of them, maybe to varying degrees, were seriously damaged.

The number answered. A strange voice — light, almost falsetto.

'Yeah?'

'My name's Glendenning. Ross Glendenning. Am I speaking to Sean O'Neill?'

'Yeah.'

'I got your number through the Deffo site. I talked to a woman there.'

'Yeah?'

'Yeah. I've got a job you might be interested in. I'm wondering whether we could meet.'

'What sort of job?'

'I'd prefer to explain face to face. Do you mind?'

'Depends, bud. Are we talking today?'

'Yeah. If that's possible.'

'Anything's possible. Your name again?'

'Ross.'

'Ross who?'

'Ross Glendenning.'

For a moment Suttle thought he'd lost the man. He could hear another voice in the room. Then O'Neill was back again.

'Where?'

'I beg your pardon?'

'Where do you wanna meet?'

'I thought a pub. You know the Countess Wear?'

'Of course I know the Countess Wear.' A cackle of laughter. 'Is that where you live then? On the estate? You one of them Countess Weirdos?'

Suttle wanted to bring the conversation to an end. One o'clock, he said. I'll sort a table for two. Jeans and an AC/DC T-shirt.

'I get lunch?'

'Yeah.'

'On you, bud?'

'Of course.'

'Make that two. I'll bring my oppo.'

★   ★   ★

Lizzie forced herself to go down the lane to the shop in the village. It was a beautiful day and the sunshine lifted her spirits. She was still thinking about the phone call to Gill Reynolds and what it might mean for her prospects on the *News* when she heard someone calling her name.

It was an elderly man from one of the nest of bungalows that signalled the start of the village.

A retired carpenter, he'd helped Lizzie out with a couple of minor jobs on the cottage last year. He'd been very fond of Grace, and his wife, equally smitten, had baked cakes for the little treasure.

The carpenter's name was Joe. 'Lovely to see you,' he said. 'How's Madam?'

'Madam' had always been his code for Grace. Lizzie told him that Madam was fine.

'Is she with you? Can you bring her down for tea?'

'I'm afraid not. She's back in Portsmouth. With my mum.'

'Ah . . . ' He nodded, disappointed. Lizzie knew exactly what was coming next, and she wasn't wrong. Her year-long absence had probably been the talk of the village. Here was a chance to catch up on the latest. 'You coming back then? Only that would be nice.'

Lizzie looked away. The sun was hot on her face. It hadn't rained for a while. And she was worried sick about Jimmy. Three good reasons for reviewing her sainted life plan.

'I might,' she said. 'Who knows?'

'That's good. Really good.' Joe shuffled closer. 'And how's that husband of yours?'

'Busy.' Lizzie managed a smile. 'As ever.'

⋆   ⋆   ⋆

The Countess Wear lay beside a big roundabout on Exeter's inner ring road. Traffic was backing up on the road south from the city centre when Suttle joined the queue. He found himself behind a bus, his view of the pub blocked until he was practically on top of the car park. He was listening to a chat show on local radio, and a series of callers were having a shout about the shortcomings of the men in blue. After a tirade about all the money going on layer after layer of management, one man suggested that this left the community woefully unprotected. 'People are getting shot every day,' he roared, 'and the police do nothing about it.'

Suttle made the turn into the car park, trying to spot the surveillance team. The fact that they weren't immediately obvious was, he supposed, a crumb of comfort. Locking the car, he checked briefly through the pub door and then went in. An earlier nervousness, an uncomfortable knowledge of just how much could go wrong, had given way to something else. Given the circumstances and the time frame, the plan was as sound as it could be. He felt suddenly confident and intensely alive. He could nail these people. He really could.

The place was cavernous. Most of the tables were occupied by elderly couples. Monday lunchtime was evidently cut-price for OAPs.

A guy at a table near the window lifted a hand. Beside him was someone thinner, taller. Barely half an hour ago, in the Major Incident Room, Suttle had been shown the latest surveillance pix of both these men. O'Neill and Jenner. He picked his way through the diners. O'Neill ignored his offered handshake.

'You're late,' he said.

O'Neill was small and broad. Mixed blood

had given him the strangest face, dark, slightly lopsided and cratered by a savage attack of acne. A dagger tatt punctured the livid scar on the side of his neck, and it wasn't hard to see something deeply disturbing in the blackness of his eyes.

'This is Oli. Smile, Oli. The man's buying.'

Jenner didn't move. He was wearing jeans and a dark green T-shirt. He was very tall, his body folded into the chair. He had big ears and a face that wasn't made for smiling. He hadn't shaved for several days and he badly needed a shower.

'Mine's a Stella.' He nodded at his empty glass. 'In case you're wondering.'

Thin voice. Geordie accent. Suttle collected the glass. O'Neill wanted fruit juice. Suttle went to the bar, ordered a shandy for himself and returned with the drinks, wondering whether the surveillance guys had the interior plotted up. Did obs have OAP cops in reserve for special occasions? Or was he really the youngest man in the room?

The moment Suttle got back to the table, O'Neill wanted to know more about how Mr Ross Glendenning had found them. He'd checked with his missus about the morning call. That was definitely kosher. But how come he'd known about Deffo?

Suttle wasn't sure whether this was market research or something more sinister.

'I use a laundrette over in Heavitree.' He distributed the drinks and sat down. 'There was a bit of an incident last weekend.'

O'Neill shot a look at Jenner. He couldn't disguise his delight.

'*Incident?* Fuck me. Show the man, Oli. Go on, don't be shy, show him.'

At first Jenner didn't move. Then he slowly extended his right hand, bunching the knuckles. The worst of the swelling had gone but the bruises were still livid, purples and yellows. The pisshead at the bottom of the utilities trench, Suttle thought. Nice.

Mention of the laundrette had sparked Jenner into life. He wanted to know more about it. Had their new client been chatting up one of the girls? Suttle nodded.

'Describe them.'

Suttle did his best. Knackered baby buggy. Both wearing low-cut tops. One fat, one tasty. One a bit hyper, the other not.

'Hair colour?'

'One nicotine-blonde. The other mauve.'

'Trish,' he said at once. 'Lovely girl.'

Evidently satisfied, he caught O'Neill's eye and nodded.

O'Neill turned back to Suttle. 'So what do you want?'

Suttle went through his story. The thought of his twelve-year-old daughter getting shagged by some tosser who'd already gone off with his ex was a bit hard to bear.

'Too fucking right.' O'Neill offered a vigorous nod. '*How* old?'

'Twelve.'

'That's totally out of order.'

'I agree. So what kind of options do I have?'

'Options?'

'What can you guys do for me?'

'Right.' O'Neill hadn't touched his fruit juice yet. 'What do you think, Oli?'

'I think what you think. I think it's disgusting.'

'Yeah, but what do we *do* about it?'

Jenner shrugged. It wasn't his decision, he said. He left all that to O'Neill. Unless it was something personal, he'd do what he was told, what had to be done. O'Neill knew that. His call.

'*Personal*, Oli? You don't think this is personal? To this poor guy? You don't think this paedo deserves sorting out? You don't think we should do something? Get him out of her life? Give that young girl a fighting chance? You don't think that's personal?' Without waiting for an answer, he turned back to Suttle. 'Where is he, bud? Where do we find him?'

Suttle didn't see the door open across the room. Neither did he clock the thin figure making his way towards their table. The first he sensed of the presence behind him was the lightest touch of a hand on his shoulder. He glanced up, knowing instinctively that something had gone terribly wrong. O'Neill knew it too. He'd clocked a nod from the guy behind Suttle and his hand had gone round the back of his jeans. As he withdrew it, Suttle glimpsed the dull sheen of a Glock automatic.

Suttle at last looked up. Ian Goodyer. Corrigan's ex-mate from the Paignton house. The guy who — in all probability — had helped kill him.

'I wouldn't move if I were you.' Goodyer was enjoying every second of this. 'Else Sean here might shoot you.'

388

15

ACC Matt Kilfoyle was running the firearms operation from his first-floor office at Middlemoor. Det-Supt Nandy was with him. Kilfoyle had a secure comms link to the armed surveillance teams in the pub car park and had plugged the line into his speakerphone. So far, nothing.

Kilfoyle and Nandy were discussing the implications of the forthcoming elections for Police and Crime Commissioners when the speakerphone came to life. The subjects plus one plus D/S Suttle were leaving the pub. The subjects' battered old Discovery, in which they'd arrived, was a couple of metres away. Body language suggested that the smaller of the subjects, immediately behind Suttle, had a weapon.

'How close is he?' This from Nandy.

'Touching distance.'

'You can see a weapon?'

'Negative.'

Nandy was looking at Kilfoyle. This was a hostage situation. Couldn't be anything else. Whatever Suttle did next, he mustn't get into the vehicle.

'What's happening?' Kilfoyle wanted to know.

'He's getting into the vehicle.'

389

'Shit.' Nandy was shaking his head. 'He's definitely got a weapon.' He turned to Kilfoyle.

'Hard arrest, sir?'

'No way.'

Kilfoyle was already on another phone. He wanted the Gold Control Room fired up and ready for immediate occupation. He wanted a Loggist and a Chief of Staff to run the facility. Another call took him to a uniformed Chief Supt already standing by as Silver Command.

'We have a hostage situation, Les. Talk to Bronze. Tell him to keep his cool. Play it long. We have to let this thing develop.'

Bronze would be the commander closest to the action. He was a uniformed Sergeant and his name was Dave Bennett. Just now he was on standby, awaiting a call in case everything went tits up.

By now, according to the surveillance guys in the car park, the Discovery was nosing into heavy traffic on the Countess Wear roundabout. Aside from the obs guys, there was also an Armed Response Vehicle, an unmarked double-crewed BMW, lying in wait outside the pub.

'That's a follow,' Kilfoyle snapped. 'Repeat, a follow.'

★   ★   ★

Suttle was sitting in the back of the Discovery, Goodyer beside him. Jenner was driving. O'Neill, kneeling on the front passenger seat, was facing back, the Glock levelled at Suttle's head. Suttle, for some reason, was thinking of

390

Lenahan. *What now, Hawkeye?*

Goodyer wanted to know exactly how much fuel Jenner had on board. Suttle sensed he'd taken charge. How long had he known these guys? And how come he'd appeared in the pub?

Jenner said the tank was nearly full. They could drive for hours. They could go anywhere. Goodyer nodded. They were approaching the big roundabout at Sandygate that offered access to the motorway. The M5 ran north to Bristol and Birmingham, west to Plymouth.

'Go north,' Goodyer said.

Jenner gunned the Discovery up the ramp and onto the motorway. Traffic at this time of day was light. Jenner didn't take his eyes off the rear-view mirror and Goodyer kept looking back.

'You're Filth,' he said to Suttle. 'You'd fucking know.'

'Know what?'

'Like how many cars we can expect. Proper convoy, is it? Shit company for the next trillion miles?'

Suttle didn't answer. He was looking at O'Neill. His eyes were ablaze with excitement and it dawned on Suttle that taking a hostage had fired him up. This must be like war, Suttle thought. This is Afghanistan all over again, a sudden revving up of life after all the waiting around. He's buzzing fit to bust. However briefly, he's in the driving seat, and he's determined to enjoy every last second.

'They'll have you plotted up,' Suttle said at last. 'There's no way this won't end in tears.'

'Too right, bud.'

'So why not jack it in now? Before someone gets hurt?'

'Like who?' He leaned over the back of the seat, his pitted face inches from Suttle's. 'Leading us on, weren't you? Back there in the pub? Thought we were stupid. Thought we were there for the taking. Dream on, bud. It's us in control now and there's fuck all you lot can do about it.'

Suttle shrugged. He was beyond intimidation, beyond fear. He thought of Lenahan again, and the stories he'd be able to tell if he ever got through this thing alive. The wee man would have loved them. If only he'd survived.

'Known these guys long?' Suttle was looking at Goodyer.

'Yeah.'

'How long?'

'Long enough.'

'That's not an answer. Tell me about Corrigan. Tell me why it was so important to have him killed.'

'You think I did that?'

'I think you helped.'

Goodyer smiled and looked away.

Minutes passed. Then Suttle tried again. 'Mind if I ask you another question?'

'Depends what it is.'

'Why did these guys do it?'

'Do what?'

'Kill three people. In cold blood.'

Goodyer laughed this time, but there was a hint of admiration in the tiny lift of an eyebrow. Hostages in Suttle's position were supposed to be shitting themselves. This one wasn't. He turned to look at O'Neill.

'Sean? Filth wants to know why you slotted those guys.'

'Had to.' O'Neill was looking slightly pained. 'No choice.'

'But why? He's asking why.'

'Because they'd earned it.' He eased his position on the seat. 'Think of it as waste disposal.'

'Just like that?'

'Just like that. Single shot. We're in the judgement game, me and Oli. A decent sniper gets to play God.' He cackled and briefly disappeared behind the seat. When he emerged again he was offering Suttle half a bar of chocolate

Suttle shook his head.

'Mad,' he said softly.

'You're right.' Goodyer again, side of his mouth. 'The guy's off the planet.'

'And Jenner?'

'Jenner's different. Jenner's the way I used to be.'

'And what's that?'

'The man's all over the place. You're in this kind of death spiral. You're going down and down and pretty soon you don't give a shit what happens. That's where Sean comes in. Sean here cares a shit about everything, bless him.' He smiled, raising his voice. 'Sean is going to clean the world up if it's the last thing he does. Isn't that right, bud?'

O'Neill nodded, said nothing. His eyes hadn't left Suttle's face.

'So Oli takes his orders from Sean?' Suttle said. 'Is that what you're telling me?'

'No. Sean is the guy who puts some order into Oli's life. Sean is why Oli gets up in the morning. Man with a mission, Sean.'

'Sweet.'

'You think so?'

'I do.' Suttle nodded. 'In my game you get to thinking why people do stuff. Killing people is pretty extreme. But there has to be a reason.'

'Wrong. These are guys who've been doing it for a living. Slotting people? That's all they know. I've never seen Oli in the field but Sean says he's awesome. A single shot at a thousand metres?' He crooked his index finger. 'Bam. Job done. Sorted.'

Suttle found himself agreeing. It made a kind of sense. Against the odds he was beginning to feel comfortable with Goodyer. The man seemed completely at ease with the situation as if, at some deep level, he'd been expecting it. He was thoughtful too, and cogent, which was seriously cool with a trillion tooled-up cops on your case.

'So where do you figure?' he asked Goodyer. 'What's in it for you?'

'A woman. As always.'

'Does she have a name?'

'Everyone has a name.'

'I'm serious.'

'I know you are. It used to be a black lady called Nicinha. Now it's a German lady called Erika. Has it been worth it? Yes. Will it all end in tears? Undoubtedly. Do I care? No fucking way.' He nodded at O'Neill's automatic. 'Might have been a bad move, eh?'

'What?'

'Becoming a cop.'

The exit to Cullumpton was approaching. Goodyer leaned forward, telling Oli to signal left, do three circuits of the roundabout and then head back towards Exeter. Jenner hit the indicator and Goodyer twisted round to watch the road behind them. By the time they were on the opposite carriageway, accelerating south again, he'd done the vehicle count.

'You want the good news or the bad?' His question was addressed to Suttle.

'There isn't any good news,' Suttle said. 'But let's pretend if it makes you feel better.'

'Fine. We've got two of your guys up our arse, one a Skoda, one a BMW estate, both unmarked.'

'And the bad news?'

'There's an ambulance as well.'

* * *

The Gold Control Room was in the new extension of the Middlemoor block which also housed the Chief Officer Group. The windowless space was dominated by a star of six work stations plus some extra desks around the edges of the room. Empty most of the time, Matt Kilfoyle had it manned and operational within fifteen minutes of Suttle departing in the Discovery.

Nandy declined the offer of a desk, preferring to prowl the room as the situation developed.

For once, despite being a dedicated non-smoker, he understood the crushing need for a nicotine hit. This is shit, he kept telling himself. This should never have happened.

Matt Kilfoyle was still organising the resources he'd need to somehow restore a sense of control. The Bronze Commander, Dave Bennett, was currently monitoring the progress of the Discovery plus the modest follow-convoy from a lay-by at the big Sowton motorway interchange. Bennett would be the closest Kilfoyle got to the action. Parked behind Bennett's badged BMW was a silver Galaxy, with Silver Commander Les McDermott sitting beside the driver. Never more than 500 metres from the target vehicle, it was his job to turn Kilfoyle's strategic thinking into the web of actions that would, God willing, resolve the crisis.

At Carole Houghton's insistence, a Family Liaison Officer had already been dispatched to Chantry Cottage. The force helicopter, Oscar 99, was being refuelled after a long flight up from the Isles of Scilly and would shortly be scrambled. The force's top hostage negotiator, a talented Det-Supt famed for his coolness under fire, was on standby pending the next phase of the operation. And a call had gone out for the force's Head of Media, an ex-Whitehall political adviser who knew exactly how to rein in the inevitable press and television clusterfuck.

Already rumours were surfacing on the Internet after no less than three drivers had reported sightings of a handgun in a Discovery on the M5. Soon Sky News would have its chopper up. After that, in Nandy's terse description, they could expect bedlam.

Nandy was standing at Matt Kilfoyle's elbow, waiting for the ACC to come off the phone. One of the Gold Commander's top priorities was to keep a running log of the decisions he made and the actions he authorised. The ring-bound file lay on the desk in front of him. Already he'd made a start on page 7 — *Threat and Risk*. The first line belonged to D/S Jimmy Suttle. Of the four categories available — *High, Medium, Low, Unknown* — Kilfoyle had ringed the first. The person in the world he'd least want to be just now was D/S Jimmy Suttle.

Reaching for the log, Kilfoyle ended the call. Nandy wanted to know whether he was minded to authorise the use of stingers laid across the motorway to puncture the Discovery's tyres and bring the vehicle to a halt.

Kilfoyle shook his head. Traffic was heavy. 'We let it run,' he said. 'Just now we have no choice.'

★　★　★

The Discovery was west of Exeter, heading towards Okehampton on the A30, when Goodyer demanded Suttle's wallet. Suttle dug in his jeans pocket and produced it. Under the circumstances, getting robbed was the least of his problems.

Goodyer opened the wallet and went through it. Suttle had earlier removed his credit cards and driving licence, an obvious precaution in case he'd been searched. He watched Goodyer leaf through the thin wad of ten-pound notes. Among them was a folded white postcard. Curious, Goodyer spread it on his lap. Suttle closed his eyes, lay back against the seat, shook his head. *Shit*, he thought. *Shit, shit, shit*. The card had been left at the cottage by a postman unable to deliver a parcel. Suttle had been meaning to collect it all week.

'Mr J. Suttle,' Goodyer read, 'Chantry Cottage, Hawkerland Lane, EX5 1EX.' He looked over at Suttle. 'Is this where you live?'

Suttle wouldn't answer. For the first time he could taste fear. Goodyer was leaning forward. Jenner had a TomTom. Goodyer repeated the postcode. Jenner entered the details. A green exit board lay ahead. The A382 exit to Moretonhampstead.

'Go left,' Goodyer told Jenner. 'And then head back towards Exeter. Chantry Cottage should do us nicely.'

★   ★   ★

Lizzie was startled by the knock at the door. The afternoon had clouded over and she'd been asleep in the armchair in the living room. She got to her feet, rubbing her eyes, and checked through the window. A woman she'd never seen before was standing on the patio, a briefcase tucked under her arm. She was about to knock again when Lizzie opened the door.

'D/C Atkins.' The woman showed her a warrant card and then extended a hand. 'Most people call me Wendy. May I come in?'

Lizzie didn't move. What had gone wrong? What was this woman doing here?

'Is it Jimmy?' she said.

Atkins nodded. Lizzie stepped to one side, letting her in.

'What is it? What's happened?'

Atkins suggested they sit down. Lizzie shook her head. She didn't want to be treated like a child. Or a widow. She repeated the question: 'What's this all about?'

Atkins explained about the incident at lunchtime. Jimmy had gone in as a u/c with a couple of persons of interest but the plan had misfired.

'Persons of interest?' The phrase sounded innocuous enough. 'We're talking suspects in last week's killings, am I right?'

'Yes.' Atkins looked surprised. 'Jimmy told you?'

'He warned me. Last night. It happened to be his birthday. *Persons of interest?* Are you kidding?'

'We have the situation under control, Mrs Suttle.'

'You have? You're telling me he's still alive?'

'Very much so.'

'So where is he?'

'In a vehicle on the M5.'

'With these persons of interest?'

'Yes. To the best of my knowledge.'

'The best of your knowledge? So you don't know. Is that it?'

'These incidents can be very dynamic. Things change all the time.'

'I'm sure they do.'

'Often for the better. It may have been resolved by now.'

'But they'd tell you, surely, knowing you're out here.'

'That I don't know. I'm sorry. I'm really sorry.'

The apology was obviously genuine. Lizzie sensed this woman had at last departed from whatever script she'd learned, realising that no amount of official reassurance was going to make Lizzie feel any less alarmed. Better for both of them that they start behaving like human beings.

'Would you like some tea, Wendy?' she said. 'Or maybe something a bit stronger?'

★ ★ ★

The Discovery left the motorway via the last of the Exeter exits, heading east towards Sidmouth. The presence of a police helicopter, tracking the convoy from a thousand feet, had brought conversation to an end. O'Neill was still kneeling on the front passenger seat, still in Suttle's face, the handgun steady, his eyes as black as ever. Goodyer had rolled a couple of thin spliffs, passing one forward to Jenner, and the bittersweetness of the weed hung in the air but the real killer was the helicopter, off to their left, always watching, always there. If I ever get through this, thought Suttle, I'm going to buy those guys a very big drink. Whether they knew it or not, they'd become the avenging angel, the living proof that this endless chase was going nowhere.

The miles unrolled. This was Suttle's route home, the roads he took every working day of his life. At a roundabout on the edge of Newton Poppleford, checking the TomTom's tiny screen, Jenner hauled the Discovery onto the Exmouth exit. The convoy behind them had grown now, any attempt to stay covert long abandoned. An unmarked Skoda for the armed surveillance team. Two BMW estates, one with the Armed Response guys. A silver-grey Ford Galaxy which had joined the carnival about forty minutes ago. Plus an extra ambulance to help tidy up the mess afterwards.

Suttle was thinking hard. He'd been in similar situations back in Pompey, incidents that had kicked off with a badly planned smash and grab or a domestic that got out of hand. Escalation happened quicker than you'd ever believe, and within minutes you were looking at a hostage situation. Gold Command, Silver Command, Bronze Command, Suttle thought. A blizzard of decisions that cascaded down and ended with one of the guys behind him. He'd be Bronze. He'd be closest. And within minutes Suttle's life would probably be in his hands.

They were on the hill that plunged into Colaton Raleigh. The village was a straggle of houses along the main road, with more properties on either side. The lane that led to Chantry Cottage was coming up fast, a tight right-hander. It was suddenly tense in the Discovery. Even O'Neill had risked a glance over his shoulder as Jenner slowed for the turn.

A tractor towing a muck spreader was

approaching on the other side. The farmer was indicating left. As he began to turn, Jenner glanced in the rear-view mirror, then gunned the engine and wrenched the steering wheel to the right. The gap was narrowing by the second. The farmer was shouting. Suttle closed his eyes. *Why not die now?* he thought. *Why not here? Covered in pig shit from the farm down the road?*

The Discovery rocked on its springs, then steadied again, picking up speed. Suttle opened his eyes. They'd made it. More importantly, the tractor was now behind them, blocking the narrow lane. Suttle could hear the howl of sirens, could picture the frustration on the faces of the cops behind. The police chopper had dipped lower, holding station to the left, and for the first time Suttle realised there was another helicopter up there, on the other side. Sky News, he thought. Yippee.

Goodyer was looking at Jenner, a rare smile on his face.

'Nice one, Oli,' he said.

*　*　*

Lizzie and Wendy Atkins were on their second cup of tea. Atkins was talking about Suttle's first year on Major Crime, the impact he'd made, the jobs he'd helped clear up, how it had taken a while to realise how tough and organised he was behind the laid-back exterior.

'Laid-back?' Lizzie wanted to know more.

'Yeah. We got him wrong to begin with. He's the nicest fella. He's great company. An hour in the pub with him goes like that.' A click of her fingers. 'But the truth is he's different, isn't he? The guy's a loner. He's deep. He's watching all the time. He's listening, he's thinking. After a while you can spot it. That's not a turn-off, don't get me wrong, but your Jimmy's his own man.'

His own man.

Lizzie nodded. That's exactly who Jimmy was. Is. Will always be.

'You're telling me he's got no friends? No mates?'

'Not at all. He's very popular. But you realise he doesn't need people the way some others I could name do. He gets by. He's happy in his own company.'

'His own skin?'

'Exactly. Just now he's working with a younger guy, a guy called Luke. He's good too, very bright, knows his own mind, and they get on really well, you can see it. The A team. Definitely.'

Lizzie nodded. In the distance she'd caught the wail of a police siren. It seemed to be getting louder. She could hear the rumble of a tractor too. And then, much closer, came the rattle of a diesel engine.

Atkins was on her feet. The diesel engine had died. Doors were slamming. Footsteps. Shouts. Then a face at the window. Someone kicked the door open and Lizzie turned to see a tall guy with a rifle pointed at her head. Behind him a familiar face. Jimmy.

'Put the fucking thing down, Oli,' Suttle shouted. 'That's my wife.'

* * *

The video feed from the police chopper brought a moment of absolute silence to the Gold Control Room. Seconds before the Discovery made the turn into Hawkerland Road, Matt Kilfoyle, realising far too late that O'Neill and Jenner were heading for Chantry Cottage, had issued the order for hard arrest. Now the vehicle was slewed across the road outside the cottage and all four of the tiny figures were inside the property. The pursuit convoy, having finally made it past the tractor, was backed up down the road. And the Sky News chopper was beaming pictures to the wider world. This, as everyone knew, was as bad as it gets. It fell to Matt Kilfoyle to voice the obvious.

'It's gone static.' He was already reaching for his phone. 'Total nightmare.'

16

It was O'Neill who turned on the TV in the cottage. Jenner had Suttle roped in a chair in the corner of the room, the rifle levelled at his head. Goodyer was upstairs in the lavatory. Lizzie and Atkins had yet to make a move.

The TV came to life. Signing up for a Sky package had been one of Lenahan's ideas, a little gift to try and escape the otherwise shit TV. Now the breaking news from the remoteness of East Devon had suddenly become the must-watch event.

The studio anchors were voicing-over live pictures from the Sky chopper. Lizzie could hear the *whump-whump* of rotor blades overhead, but seen from above it took her a moment to recognise the green spread of the garden, the silver hump of the polytunnel, the boxy outline of the cottage itself. *We're under that roof*, she thought. Waiting for the guys outside to do something.

Goodyer had returned from upstairs. His eyes swept the room then settled on the TV. He was standing beside Lizzie. He seemed to be enjoying himself. 'Fame at fucking last,' he murmured.

Lizzie was still looking at the TV. They were back with the anchors in the Sky News studio. In a moment or two they were going to run a

405

package for viewers new to the story. How it had kicked off. Where the chase had led. And what the coming hours might bring. One of the anchors was grave. The other was breathless with excitement. There was the scent of blood in the air.

'Stiffietime,' she said.

★ ★ ★

In the Gold Control Room Matt Kilfoyle was conferencing with his Silver Commander on the phone. Known facts first. Two hostages.

'Three, sir.' This from Nandy.

'Who's the third?'

'Wendy Atkins. The FLO. She phoned before she went into the cottage. That was half an hour ago.'

'Shit. You're right.' Kilfoyle bent to the phone again. 'Make that three hostages. At least two weapons, the handgun and the sniper rifle.'

'We're sure about the sniper rifle?'

'We are. We're talking a mile-plus range.'

The conference developed, decision after decision tumbling down the command chain. Two more Armed Response Vehicles summoned from Barnstaple and Bodmin. Armed teams covering each quadrant of the cottage. An Emergency Entry Squad in full body armour. A Rifle Officer to sort out a firing position overlooking the property. At least twenty-five uniforms to secure the outer cordon. The hostage negotiator to get himself out to Colaton Raleigh, quick time. An R/V point for the inevitable media army. Assets from the Fire and Rescue people in case the targets decided to torch the cottage. Evacuation of nearby properties. Thoughts on a Community Impact Assessment for the wider village. A rotation schedule to relieve key officers. Liaison with the Independent Police Complaints Commission. Catering arrangements in case the incident stretched and stretched. And, God help us, more ambulances. No one in the room, thought Nandy, has any idea when or how this thing might end. In five brief minutes a chase had become a siege.

★ ★ ★

Attempts to start negotiations had begun at once. First a call on Suttle's phone. Then Wendy Atkins'. Goodyer had taken both mobiles, Lizzie's too. The only call he answered was the one on Wendy's phone. Refusing to identify himself to the negotiator, he'd confirmed that they were holding three hostages, that there were no injuries, and that they had enough weaponry to bring this thing to a very ugly end. Pressed to explain exactly what he meant, he'd simply handed the phone to Wendy.

'Tell them about the guns,' he'd said. 'Tell them what we've got.'

She tallied the weapons: a Glock automatic, plus what looked like a sniper rifle.

Jenner had interrupted at this point.

'It's an Accuracy International .338,' he said. 'Tell them that.'

She repeated the information, then looked across at him again.

'Ammunition?'

'Lapua Magnum. More than enough.'

Goodyer had stepped across and retrieved the phone.

'OK?' he'd said. And ended the call.

★   ★   ★

Now, more than an hour later, came a shout from somewhere at the back of the cottage. Suttle broke the silence. He'd recognised the voice, a uniformed Sergeant called Dave Bennett he'd worked with on a job in Ilfracombe.

'That'll be the Bronze Commander,' he told Jenner. 'I expect he wants a word or two.'

'Ignore him.' This from Goodyer. He'd been making tea in the kitchen while O'Neill and Jenner held everyone else at gunpoint. Now he was rolling another spliff.

Dave Bennett didn't give up. He wanted to bring this thing to some kind of conclusion. There was no way the guys inside would be allowed to leave. They had the scene totally contained. And if Sean and Oli didn't believe him, they could turn the telly on. Which he guessed they already had.

'Don't I get a mention?' Goodyer sounded disappointed.

Dave Bennett appeared to be taking a break. Nobody said a word. Even the choppers had backed off.

Lizzie was looking at Goodyer. 'You'll need a

408

negotiator in the end,' she said. 'You'll have to start talking to these people.'

'That's easy.' Goodyer lit his spliff. 'We phone them when we're ready.'

'That's not what I meant. They'll have their own guys outside. The clever thing is to nominate someone else. Someone who isn't on their payroll.'

'And who might that be?'

'There's a guy I know who'd be perfect.'

'How come?' Despite himself, Goodyer was intrigued. Lizzie could see it in his face. She'd sensed his need for control. Over O'Neill. Over Jenner. Over her. But with control came an eye for every passing opportunity. Including this one.

'His name's Rob Merrilees,' she said. 'He's a Captain in the Marines. Try the name on your guys. They may know him.'

O'Neill had never heard of him but Jenner most certainly had. They'd gone through training together, at Lympstone.

'This is basic training?'

'No.' Jenner shook his head. 'The sniper course.'

'Rob was a sniper?'

'Yeah. Top bloke too.'

'Perfect. You want to give him a ring? His number's in my directory.'

Lizzie's mobile was still with Goodyer. He turned it on, found the number. Then he looked up.

'So tell me what we get out of this.'

'You get someone the police will trust, someone they'll let into the loop. You'll also get someone who understands the Marine mindset, who will maybe see it these guys' way.'

'That won't get us off the hook.'

'Of course it won't. But nothing else will either. So maybe it's worth a shot . . . Yeah?'

Goodyer looked faintly disappointed.

Lizzie shook her head. Despite the guns, despite the tension, despite the fact that the next few minutes could be her last, there was something surreal about this situation. These guys were off the planet. They lived in a world of their own.

'You have something else in mind?' She was laughing now. 'Guaranteed passage out to the airport? A charter jet? Drinks on board? Breakfast in Acapulco?'

'I was thinking Croatia. Since you ask.'

'Dream on.' This from Suttle. 'It won't happen.'

'So what happens if we shoot you?'

'They'll kill you all.'

'And what happens if we don't?'

'They'll starve you out,' Suttle said. 'Else you'll get so tired you won't care any more.'

Goodyer nodded, said nothing. He was looking at the phone again. Finally he handed it to Lizzie.

'You make the call,' he said.

'What do I say?'

'Fuck knows.'

'But what do you want to happen?'

'I want him in here with us,' Goodyer said. 'We frisk him first. Any weapons and we shoot him.'

'Captain Merrilees?' Jenner was frowning. 'No fucking way.'

'It won't happen,' Suttle said. 'They'll never let him anywhere near you.'

Goodyer glanced from face to face. For the first time, Lizzie thought, he looked uncomfortable. Then he nodded at the phone. 'OK. Do it.'

She found Rob's number and pressed Call, aware of Suttle watching her. Rob picked up on the first ring.

'Lizzie? Is that you?'

'Yeah.'

'Where are you?'

'Out in the country.'

'You want a meet?'

'I do.'

'No problem. Give me an hour. Where exactly are you?'

Lizzie turned around, using her body to shield the call, only too aware of her husband's growing interest in this conversation. Merrilees was asking where she was again. He sounded confused. She wondered whether it was true he'd owned up to Nina. Given his eagerness to see her again, she rather suspected he had.

'You've got a pen?' she said. 'I'm going to give you a mobile number. It belongs to someone in the police. I've no idea who, but just say you've had a chat with one of the hostages.'

'One of the what?'

'Hostages.'

'I don't understand.'

Lizzie explained about the chase, and now the siege.

'Shit.'

'Exactly.'

She gestured for Goodyer to give her Wendy Atkins' phone. The last incoming call was logged. She read out the number. Merrilees' manner had changed. He was brisker now, more business-like.

'So what's my role in all this?'

'I'm looking at two ex-Marines, Rob. They've both got guns. We need a negotiator.'

'What are these guys' names?'

'Sean O'Neill and Oli Jenner.'

'I know Oli. He was in Forty. Good guy. One of the best.'

'That's what he said about you.'

'I'm flattered.'

'So will you do it? Please? Will you phone the number?'

'No problem.' The phone went dead.

For a moment there was absolute silence. Then Suttle stirred.

'So who's Rob Merrilees?' he asked quietly.

★ ★ ★

Merrilees' call to the Gold Control Room was logged at 18.32. He'd been given the number by the Bronze Commander at Colaton Raleigh. He was put straight through to Matt Kilfoyle and introduced himself as Captain Rob Merrilees of 42 Commando, currently attached to 3 Commando Brigade at Stonehouse. He explained he'd been phoned by Lizzie Hodson, a journalist on the Portsmouth *News*, with whom he'd had some dealings. Lizzie, as Mr Kilfoyle undoubtedly knew, was in a spot of bother. Nominated by the bad guys as a negotiator, he was only too willing to help in whatever way he could.

Kilfoyle sat back. This was a development he hadn't expected. On the other hand, Merrilees sounded solid enough, and building some kind of bridge to the targets was rapidly becoming the top priority. A Marine talking to fellow Marines, albeit retired? A guy who'd know their mindset? Who'd understand which buttons to press? Was that such a bad move?

He bent to the phone again. He needed to make a couple of calls. Then he'd come straight back. He rang off, then accessed a number from his personal mobile. The call went to the commanding officer of 42 Commando, whom he happened to know. Their kids played rugby together. In a modest way they'd started to socialise.

'Tankie? It's Matt.'

Kilfoyle quickly outlined the situation. A guy called Rob Merrilees had been nominated by the targets as a negotiator. He needed a steer.

'On Merrilees?'

'Yes.'

'He's excellent news. Done a couple of tours in Afghan. Sharp. Organised. Dependable. Fun to be with. Come back in ten years and we'll *all* be saluting.'

'That good?'

'That good.'

Kilfoyle thanked him and rang off. Back on the line to Merrilees he said he'd be grateful for his help. He needed to get himself to Middlemoor quick time, then a car would take him out to the crime scene. He was about to ring off when Merrilees asked for a brief on the two men. Kilfoyle frowned. Surely that could wait until he arrived?

Nandy was at Kilfoyle's side. He'd just summoned Toby Watkins, the Royal Marines Liaison Officer on *Bellwether*, from the Major Incident Room, anticipating exactly this conversation.

'What does he want, sir?' Nandy nodded at the phone.

'He needs a brief on O'Neill and Jenner.'

Nandy suggested he talk to Watkins. Kilfoyle handed the phone over. Watkins listened to Merrilees for a moment or two, then offered some thoughts on both men. This is family talk, thought Nandy. This is exactly the way the thing should work.

At length Watkins returned the phone to Kilfoyle.

'Well?'

'He's fine, sir. Just two requests. One, he wants ten minutes with O'Neill's wife. Two, he'd like a nosey around Jenner's flat.'

'This is before he goes out to the scene?'

'Yes, sir. I took the liberty of saying yes to both.'

Kilfoyle nodded. The phone on his desk had started to ring. Nandy needed no prompting.

'Leave it to me, sir,' he said. 'I'm on it.'

★ ★ ★

414

Rob Merrilees arrived at Middlemoor forty-five minutes later. Watkins and Nandy met him at the gatehouse. Merrilees, it turned out, had come straight from his office at 3 Commando Brigade in Plymouth. He was still in uniform — boots, cam trousers, ribbed green sweater, Captain's epaulettes — which, given the task assigned him, was probably perfect.

With Kilfoyle's blessing, Nandy wanted to take him to Jenner's flat first. An Entry Team had already put the door in, and Scenes of Crime had made a start on boshing the place. Merrilees wanted to know if this request of his would be a problem. Nandy shook his head. He might have to wear a forensic suit but they'd have treading plates in place.

'Help-yourself time,' he said.

The pavement outside Jenner's flat had been secured with no entry tape. One of the SOC vans was double-parked in the street outside. Nandy pulled up behind it. Merrilees got out, looking up at the terraced house that contained Jenner's ground-floor flat.

The place, as Nandy had warned him, was a wreck. Like the other properties along the street, it was tall and forbidding, constructed in a dark red brick that seemed to eat the daylight. Water dripped from a broken gutter and the drain beneath the crumbling bay window was choked with assorted rubbish. The tiny front garden was littered with half-crushed cans of Special Brew and pizza boxes softened by the recent rain.

The door was open. Nandy used his mobile to summon a SOCO. Treading plates disappeared into the semi-darkness of the hall.

'How much do you want to see?' Nandy turned to Merrilees.

'Just a peek, that's all. I'm getting the picture already.'

The CSI led the way down the darkened corridor. Merrilees and Nandy followed. The place reeked of cats' piss and old cooking fat. The door at the end was open. Once the SOCO stepped aside, Merrilees could see a camouflage jacket hanging on a hook behind the door. Tucked in a corner were a pair of fishing rods.

'More?' This from the SOCO.

'Please.'

Merrilees stepped into the living room. A single glance told him everything he needed to know: the threadbare carpet stained with God knows what, the litter of abandoned coffee mugs, the brimming rubbish bin, the empty litre bottle of White Lightning propped against a table leg. This place was a prison cell, he thought. This was somewhere that would find you out. If something had gone badly wrong in your life, ending up here would probably drive you insane.

'Enough?'

Merrilees nodded. He and Nandy walked back down the corridor to the street.

'Bloody shame,' he said, getting into the car.

*   *   *

They were back at Middlemoor within minutes. Hurrying to the Gold Control Room, Nandy met Luke Golding. Earlier, he'd tasked the

416

young D/C to pick up O'Neill's wife and bring her in.

'She's downstairs, sir. Waiting.'

'You've talked to her?'

'Of course.'

'And?'

'I think O'Neill's worn her out. This woman's running on empty. You can see it on her face.'

'But did she know what he's been up to?'

'She says not.'

'Do you believe her?'

'Yeah. I think I do.'

Nandy introduced Merrilees. He needed to listen to this as well.

O'Neill, Golding said, relied on medication to get him through most days. He'd been taking this stuff — three or four separate meds — since his discharge from hospital in Birmingham after his run-in with the IED. Then, to his wife's horror, he'd decided to bin the lot.

'Since then she says he's been a nightmare. This woman's a nurse. She understands about drugs. The stuff he was taking took the edge off the mood swings and the depression, but in the end O'Neill wasn't having it. He told her his head was bursting. Next day she found him trying to flush the meds down the loo.'

'When was this?'

'A fortnight ago. She tried her best with him but she said it was hopeless. He took to the bottle. She started worrying about their kiddie. Yesterday he moved out for good.'

'Has he been in touch since?'

'Yeah. He called a couple of times. She says he

was in a right state, but when she tried to suggest something he just put the phone down. Like I say, sir. She's in the office. Waiting.'

*　　*　　*

Darkness stole over East Devon. After hours without contact with the outside world, Lizzie had given up on the possibility of Rob turning up. Maybe he doesn't fancy it, she thought. Maybe he's had a bit of a think and decided that his private life would be better if I didn't exist any more.

For a while now silence had fallen on the cottage. Suttle, still roped in the chair, appeared to have gone to sleep. Lizzie had told him very little about Merrilees. This was the guy who took me round a place down in Plymouth, she'd said. Very helpful. And very well-connected. Suttle appeared to be satisfied with this, but she knew he'd be thinking, wondering, trying to suss how all the bits of this latest jigsaw really fitted together. Wendy Atkins had been shrewd. Jimmy was deep, she'd said. Jimmy was a loner. Jimmy was his own man. Too right.

Lizzie shook her head. This wasn't the time to make problems for herself. If Rob Merrilees could find a way of getting this thing resolved, then everyone, her husband included, would be more than grateful. But how on earth would that ever happen?

She glanced across at O'Neill. He was glued to the TV, coming alive when the news coverage returned to the siege in East Devon. Wendy

418

Atkins was watching it too, her face impassive, her hands folded in her lap. Oli Jenner was the only one who hadn't moved, his rifle in his lap, his finger curled round the trigger, the barrel pointing squarely at Suttle. No one was talking any more. Probably because there was nothing to say.

Lizzie found the change of atmosphere deeply unsettling. The chopper had gone more than half an hour ago, and the gathering silence left her alone with her thoughts. She'd always been thankful for a lively imagination. Once she'd made the step into feature journalism, the gift of putting herself into other people's heads had been a huge advantage. Now, though, that talent seemed to have deserted her.

O'Neill she sort of understood. The man had some kind of psychosis. His body language, the way he talked, the way he never quite got to the end of a sentence, spoke of a chemical disturbance deep in his brain. He couldn't concentrate. He couldn't look you in the eye. He was always on the move, like some kid gone way beyond hyper. All this, she recognised, had probably taken him close to madness — and Jenner too was anything but normal.

Quieter than O'Neill, he seemed to have given up on the world. There was a deadness in his eyes, a refusal to engage, a mutely passive acceptance that other people had nothing more to offer him. This numbness, in a way, made him as scary as O'Neill. But the real puzzle was Goodyer. Try as she might, Lizzie couldn't fathom him. Why was he here? Why was he part of this craziness? And what the fuck did he expect to happen next?

The sound of her mobile made her physically jump. It was still with Goodyer. He was checking caller ID. Distant at first, then louder and louder, came the clatter of the returning helicopter.

'Mr Merrilees,' Goodyer had the mobile to his ear. 'What a surprise.'

★   ★   ★

Merrilees was in the Galaxy with the Silver Commander and the Det-Supt who'd been appointed police negotiator. Another officer was acting as note taker. The video feed from the force chopper showed the back of the cottage.

Merrilees asked who he was talking to. A voice at the other end said that didn't matter; the guy he needed was over the other side of the room. The chopper was so loud, no one could hear themselves think. Couldn't they tell the fucking pilot to go and deafen someone else?

Merrilees passed on the request. There was no point trying to conduct a negotiation under these circumstances. The Silver Commander was in touch with the helicopter pilot. He muttered an order. Moments later, the helicopter lifted and sped off into the darkness. Then came another voice on Merrilees' mobile, a voice he dimly recognised. He smiled to himself. Lympstone, he thought. Plus weeks and weeks of specialised training up on Woodbury Common.

'Oli. Long time, eh?'

'Seven years, boss. Sniper course? CTC?'

'You got it. How was Afghan last time out?'

'OK. We did the business.'

'Miss it at all?'

'Sometimes, yeah. You?'

'Not really. Not if I'm honest. A war's a war. The quicker we're out of there, the better.' Merrilees laughed. 'You'll love this — I'm off to Bloodhound next.'

'Cyprus? The R&R place? Hoofing or what?'

Silver Commander Les McDermott was exchanging glances with his note taker. This wasn't negotiation, he thought. This was some kind of family reunion, old mates swapping war stories.

In the cottage Lizzie couldn't take her eyes off Jenner. The man was transformed. He was sitting upright in the chair, the mobile to his ear. The rifle was still trained on Suttle, the barrel motionless, but at last the guy had a smile on his face. O'Neill had noticed it too. He gave the handgun to Goodyer and demanded a go on the phone.

'Gimme, Oli. Let me have a word.'

Jenner surrendered the mobile. O'Neill was beaming.

'Sean O'Neill,' he said. 'Forty. Like Oli. Never had the pleasure, sir.'

'Rob Merrilees.'

'Mr Merrilees? I had an oppo serve with you in Helmand. *Herrick 12.*'

'Name?'

'Duffy. Crazy as fuck.'

'Jed Duffy? Eagle tatts? Big Millwall fan?'

'The very same. Major pisshead. Total respect.'

Duffy, he told Merrilees, had been on a run ashore one night when they were on exercise with the US Navy on Honolulu. He'd got so pissed the USMC guys had brought him back on a stretcher, dumping him at a bus stop outside the hotel they'd been using. A passer-by had called an ambulance, landing Duffy with an $800 bill for the subsequent stomach pump and overnight recovery.

'That's him. That's Duff. Mad as fuck and twice as fucking ugly.' O'Neill rocked back and forth at the memory, his arms crossing and uncrossing in front of his chest.

This is vaudeville, Lizzie thought. Somehow Rob, in the space of less than a minute, had unlocked these guys. They were different. They were back in a world they understood. This had to be good news. Only Goodyer, still nursing the handgun, seemed unimpressed.

'Talk later, yeah?' O'Neill passed the phone back to Jenner.

In the Galaxy Merrilees was digging in his pocket for his own smartphone. He accessed a video and laid the phone carefully on his lap. Then Jenner was back in his ear.

'I've just been round to your place, Oli.'

'In Heavitree?'

'Yes.'

'Shit.'

'Exactly. Need I spell this out?'

'No, boss. It's horrible. I know it is. My fault.

Should have made an effort. The state of the place, yeah?'

'Exactly. You know what I am, Oli? I'm fucking disappointed. That oppo of yours . . . '

'Sean?'

'Yes. Put him on again.'

Merrilees had the smartphone ready. With O'Neill back on the line, he played him the sound track from the video clip he'd readied.

'That's my missus,' O'Neill said at once. 'Where did you get that from?'

'I recorded it about an hour ago.'

'Where?'

'At the nick. She's worried sick about you, Sean, in case you're wondering.'

The Silver Commander, sitting in the Galaxy beside Merrilees, could see the smartphone. O'Neill's wife was talking straight to camera. She wanted Sean back home. She knew things had been difficult but she was sure they could work it out. This whole thing was horrible, unbelievably horrible, but the person Sean had become wasn't the person she'd lived with all these years, the person she loved, the person she and Tina and Casey were missing so much. With the right meds they could get him back. She knew they could. And then everything would be OK again.

'You believe me, Sean?' she asked before the tiny screen cut to black.

Merrilees was waiting for a reaction from O'Neill. Nothing.

'Are you there, Sean?'

'Yeah.' His voice was barely audible.

'Did you get all that?'

'I did, boss.'

'Who are Tina and Casey, Sean?'

'My kids.'

'You think your missus might be right?'

'Yeah. She is. I know she is. She's right. Dead right. Yeah. But it ain't gonna work, is it? Not after . . . not after . . . ' He seemed to be having trouble getting the words out. He swallowed hard, tried again. 'They're gonna put us away for a long time, yeah?'

'Not necessarily.'

'Not *necessarily*? Don't snow me, boss. Don't take me for a fool. I know what we done. I know why we done it too. Those people were horrible. We done the world a favour. Except no other fucker's gonna see it that way.'

'You're wrong, Sean.'

'Why? Why am I wrong?'

'Because you're ill. And that's not your fault.'

'Oh yeah? And how does that work?'

In the cottage Lizzie was still gazing at O'Neill. She couldn't hear Merrilees' end of the conversation but she didn't have to. This, she realised already, was a masterclass in negotiation, in getting into other people's heads, in making yourself comfortable and settling down.

In the Galaxy the note taker was scribbling furiously. This call was being recorded but even so there were points — headlines — he needed to get down.

'Tell me,' O'Neill said again. 'Tell me how it works.'

'We sent you to Afghan, Sean,' Merrilees was saying. 'We blew you up. And then we tried to

424

put you back together again.'

'You did, boss. That's true. You did. But it was me who went to Afghan. Because I *wanted* to go to Afghan. Because I couldn't fucking wait to slot those Taliban bastards. And that's what I did. Bang. Bang. Bang. Three of them. Different patrols, different operations, different fucking drafts. Then I got it wrong and they fucking blew me up. And it was Oli here who got me out of that shithole. But it was the ragheads who did it, boss. No one else.'

O'Neill was distressed now. He seemed to be blaming himself. *Wrong*, Lizzie thought. *Wrong. Wrong. Wrong.* Whatever Rob said was probably spot on. *Listen to the man.* We sent you. The politicians sent you. And now you're back with half a brain convinced you're the avenging bloody angel. Our fault. And, yes, the Taliban's too. But it takes two to start a war.

O'Neill had finished with Merrilees. Too distressed to carry on, he passed the phone to Jenner.

In the Galaxy, Merrilees indicated the change to the note taker. New conversation. Different tack.

'Where are you in this, Oli?' Merrilees asked. 'Be honest.'

There was a long silence. In the cottage Lizzie — for the first time — saw the rifle dip. Jenner swallowed hard, bracing himself for this conversation.

'I'm nowhere, boss. If you want the truth, I'm fucking nowhere. I've got kids I never see, a wife who doesn't want me and some slag of a Troop

425

Sergeant I should have battered long ago. I had a house once. I knew why I got up in the morning. That's history. Or it was until Deffo got going.'

'Deffo?'

Jenner explained about the website they'd got together, a kind of labour exchange for ex-bootnecks with nothing better to do.

'It worked, this thing?'

'In spades. Sean's missus did most of it. She's queen of the IT thing. She'd sign blokes up, collect the registration fee, match them with a whole pile of punters she had on the database, job done. Then blokes started coming to us for special jobs. Fuck knows why.'

'Special jobs?'

'Sorting people out. You've no idea how many people hate how many other people. I always said it was fucking crazy. I wanted nothing to do with it.'

'So what changed your mind?'

'Sean. In some moods that man can be beautiful.' His eyes strayed across the room to O'Neill. 'My life is shit. You've seen the flat. You know the way I live. How the fuck have I ended up like this?'

'You want to tell me about it?'

'I do, boss. I do.'

After months of turning down head jobs, Jenner said, a bloke came to them about a girl who ran a betting shop in Heavitree. He knew the shop and he knew the girl. He also knew the arsehole who was making her life a misery. The bloke who wanted the job done was offering them silly money. Ten grand was a fortune. Ten

426

grand, even at the prices they charged on his stretch of the Exe, would buy him years and years of fishing. And so he said yes.

'You killed him?'

'Yes. Just the way they taught us, boss. It was a class job. Not much wind, minimum deflection, eleven hundred metres, up-sun. You'd have been proud of me. Single shot and no trace of the expended round.'

'No regrets?'

'None. The guy was a Bravo. He was a fat bastard too. Fucking deserved it.'

'You got paid?'

'On the nail. Cash. Five grand each. Me and Sean. I was on the river the next day. Which is how I came to say thank you.'

'To who?'

'To this bloke I know. He's on the river too. He's a painter. Nice guy. Gentle. Bit soft in the head but gentle. And you know what? He'd been where I'd been. His missus went off with some cunt up the road and there was nothing he could do about it. This guy turned his life upside down, stole his missus. Something like that has consequences. Or should do.'

'So you killed him too?'

'Yep. Same deal. Dodgier job. Lots more wind. But yeah. Head job at seven hundred metres? The guy was up a tree. I left him hanging there, stone dead, and you know something, boss? I felt good about it. And you know why? Because I was doing what I was best at.'

'You're telling me it was our fault?'

'Fuck, no. It was me. My decision. I was the

one who pulled the trigger.'

'And now?'

'And now I'm fucked. But I was fucked before. So nothing's really changed.' He paused. 'You need to talk to Sean again.'

'Who says?'

'Sean.'

In the Galaxy Merrilees signalled another change of voice. Then O'Neill came on. He wanted to explain about the other killing. The first one. Corrigan.

'Go on.'

'That was nothing to do with Oli, Mr Merrilees. That was me.'

'You killed him?'

'Yeah.'

'Why?'

'Because he wanted my woman.'

'Your wife, you mean?'

'No.' O'Neill's voice was low now, as if he was sharing a confidence with a special friend. 'Someone else.'

'Who?'

O'Neill didn't answer. Merrilees asked the question again. Nothing. In the Galaxy, he glanced at the Silver Commander. Covering the mobile with his hand, he wanted the chopper back. As low as possible. As loud as possible. Blasting the cottage with full beam.

The Silver Commander nodded and passed on the request. Seconds later, in the distance, came the chatter of the returning helicopter. It grew louder and louder. Merrilees put the mobile to his ear, trying to raise O'Neill again.

428

'Sean?' he shouted. 'Talk to me.'

Inside the cottage came a blinding whiteness that seemed to fill the room. Goodyer still had the handgun. He got to his feet, edging towards the door, the automatic extended. The noise of the chopper drowned everything. It was hovering over the cottage, its bulk visible against the night sky.

Suttle shouted for everyone to stay calm. The chopper dipped even lower, almost touching distance, then abruptly swung away. Lizzie closed her eyes. Her hands were shaking and for the first time she realised she was truly frightened. This thing could get out of hand, she thought. Easily. She dreaded the return of the helicopter, so loud, so close, so physically intimidating. What if it pushed Goodyer and Jenner to the edge? What if they tried to shoot it down?

Jenner and O'Neill were exchanging glances. O'Neill still had the phone. As silence returned to the cottage, it was Jenner who took the initiative.

'Ask Mr Merrilees what he wants us to do,' he said.

O'Neill relayed the question.

'What do you think, boss?' he whispered. 'Be honest.'

In the Galaxy, Merrilees relaxed. Thanks to the chopper, he sensed some kind of breakthrough.

'I think you call it a day,' he said carefully. 'I think I stand up in court and do my best for you. I think you're twats for letting all this stuff get to you, but then I guess I'm bound to say that. Maybe you need a fucking good war. And maybe that's where it begins and ends.'

'So what do we do, boss?' O'Neill said again. 'Just tell us.'

'Wait one.'

Merrilees conferred with the Silver Commander. At least two of the guys had had enough. He didn't know about the other fella. How did McDermott want to play this?

'We need the weapons first. Tell them to chuck them out where we can see them. We need the chopper back. We need the lights.'

'Then what?'

'We need the hostages. All three. When we've secured them we'll pass the word to the subjects. They're last out.'

'I can't guarantee three, I'm afraid. My guys for sure. The other fella's a bit of a mystery.'

'Right.'

McDermott had an open line to Gold Control. He briefed them on the situation. Kilfoyle agreed the sequence of events. He would go with the release plan, but if the wheels came off he'd authorise emergency entry to save life. McDermott nodded and turned back to Merrilees.

'Weapons first,' he confirmed.

★ ★ ★

In the cottage it was O'Neill who took the order. He lifted the rifle from Jenner and headed for the door. Goodyer stopped him.

430

'What the fuck's going on?'

'We're out of here. I need your weapon.'

'No way.'

'Suit yourself.' O'Neill shot him a look.

Goodyer had the handgun trained on him. O'Neill brought the rifle up and for a moment Lizzie expected the worst. Then came the deafening *whump-whump* of the returning chopper and the garden outside was again flooded with light. Goodyer had lowered the handgun. He nodded towards the door, a gesture of contempt.

'Off you go,' he shouted. 'Make it easy for them.'

O'Neill held his gaze for a moment then turned away. With the door open the clatter of the helicopter swamped everything. O'Neill pitched the rifle into the bowl of light outside. He still had the mobile to his ear.

Merrilees was monitoring everything from the Galaxy.

'Where's the handgun?' Merrilees was shouting.

'Still here. Goodyer's not coming.'

Merrilees relayed the news to McDermott.

The Silver Commander was watching the video feed from the chopper. 'Hostages next,' he said.

Inside the cottage O'Neill motioned for Lizzie, Atkins and Suttle to leave. Jenner freed Suttle and tried to help him towards the door, but Suttle shook him off. All three of them stepped out of the cottage, heading for the darkness beyond the blinding light. Unseen hands led them to safety behind a brick wall.

'Now you two,' Merrilees told O'Neill. 'On your knees, guys. Hands behind your heads. And just keep going until we stop you.'

O'Neill and Jenner did what they were told. Merrilees was watching from the Galaxy. Slowly they shuffled across the lawn on their knees, heads down, as if the heavens had opened,

Finally they made it across the lawn and disappeared into the darkness.

McDermott was conferring on the phone with the Sergeant in charge of the Entry Team when a single shot from the cottage, barely audible above the noise of the helicopter, brought everything to a halt.

McDermott passed on the news to Kilfoyle at Gold Control. Accidental discharge? Suicide? Something more sinister? There was no way of knowing. He listened hard for a moment or two, shielding his other ear from the din outside, then nodded. Returning to the first phone, he told the Sergeant in charge of the Entry Team that he was on.

* * *

Eight minutes later Merrilees was watching the video feed when six officers in full body armour appeared from the shadows and began to approach the cottage. He recognised the familiar shape of the Heckler & Koch semi-automatics readied for action. According to McDermott, they also had tasers and stun grenades. The grenades went in first through the open door and

432

an adjacent window. Two explosions. Seconds later the officers followed, working in pairs. For a long moment there was nothing except the deafening chatter of the helicopter, still over-head, then came a second single shot, similar to the first. A moment later, two more shots, different weapon.

McDermott was monitoring everything on an Airwave frequency. The officers inside the house were in the same loop. For Merrilees' benefit, McDermott had turned the volume up.

'Man down,' a voice yelled. 'Repeat, man down.'

Seconds later two of the officers reappeared at the door. Hanging between them, his arms round their shoulders, was a colleague who seemed to have been shot.

In the Gold Control Room at Middlemoor Kilfoyle was on his feet. The video feed from the helicopter left no room for doubt. This was a disaster.

'Man down?' He was still in contact with Dave Bennett. The Bronze Commander was closest to the action.

'Wait one, sir.'

There was mayhem on the screen, officers running everywhere. Then Bennett was back with better news.

'Took a bullet on his chest plate, sir. Knocked him downstairs. Nothing serious.'

17

In the immediate aftermath of the siege Lizzie stayed close to Suttle. At the Silver Commander's insistence, they'd both been checked over by paramedics. Later would come the offer of counselling; for now, though, Suttle needed to find out exactly what had happened inside the cottage.

Dave Bennett had the story from the Sergeant in charge of the Entry Team. They'd cleared the downstairs, he said, and he'd sent two men up to the first floor. By now they were suspecting some kind of suicide in one of the bedrooms, but they'd been wrong. Goodyer had been waiting for the first guy up to the landing at the top. The moment he'd appeared, Goodyer had stepped out of the darkness and shot him at point-blank range. The bullet hadn't penetrated the guy's body armour, but the sheer force of the impact had thrown him back down the stairs. His oppo, gun raised, had shot Goodyer twice. End of.

Suttle nodded. A Scenes of Crime team was already in the cottage, securing the property prior to a full examination, and one of them had retrieved Goodyer's smartphone. Among the half-dozen texts he'd sent in the hours before his death was one to Erika Maier: 'No regrets. No apologies. See you in heaven. Or in hell. xxx'.

434

The other texts were similar in tone. Suttle read them all. This was Goodyer's farewell, he thought, a parting flutter of his hand before he lured the ninjas into range and tried to take one of them out. He must have known that it was a death sentence and Suttle felt a flicker of respect for the man. Goodyer, unlike O'Neill or Jenner, had known exactly what he was doing. He wasn't crazy. He hadn't given up on the world. He just wanted to land a punch or two before they blew him away.

⋆ ⋆ ⋆

Lizzie found Merrilees sitting in an unmarked car a hundred metres up the lane. She'd slipped away, leaving her husband still deep in conversation with one of the SOCOs.

'You were awesome,' Lizzie said. 'And I mean that.'

'You do what you do.' Merrilees shrugged. 'I know these lads. I know how they think. I know what matters to them. We understand each other. It was never going to be a problem.'

'You mean that?'

'I do.'

'You knew you could talk them round? You knew you could take them out of there?'

'Absolutely. And that's not a boast.'

Lizzie nodded. She believed him. The lane was a hive of activity: uniformed police, guys in body armour, paramedics, even the odd fireman. She gazed out at them all, still numbed by what had happened. *So close*, she thought. In the end we came so close to dying.

'So how about the wedding?' she murmured.

Merrilees looked at her. His face had that same openness, that same candour, that same richly physical glow she remembered from their first encounters. Except now she knew another Rob Merrilees.

'Well?' She was trying to hide her smile. 'Is it back on now?'

'Yes.'

'And was it ever off?'

He didn't answer her. A civvy at the window was offering a sandwich and a cup of tea from a tray. Lizzie shook her head.

'Party time,' Merrilees nodded down the lane towards the cottage. 'I'm glad you got your story in the end.'

'You're right. I have. Thanks to you.' She leaned across and kissed him. 'You owed me. You know that? And now we're quits.'

He nodded and began to murmur something but then had second thoughts. When he said goodbye he didn't look at her. Lizzie waited a moment, the door half-open, then got out.

'Bye.' She bent to the open window. 'And take good care of her, eh?'

★ ★ ★

Minutes later Lizzie was back with Suttle. She clung on to him this time, much to his surprise.

'Where've you been?' he asked.

'On the phone. Where do you think?'

'To who?'

'Gill. She'll be on to Boulton as we speak. He's my editor. You really think a girl goes through all this for nothing?'

'You'll have to make a statement,' he said stiffly. 'A lot of this stuff's sub judice.'

'I know. But one day it won't be. Not after those guys go down. And then I can do what I like. Does that make sense? Have I got that bit right?'

He nodded slowly. Lizzie could see by his eyes that he wasn't remotely convinced she'd been belling Gill, but she didn't care. She was still in one piece. Still married. And that, she'd begun to realise, mattered a great deal.

Suttle hadn't finished.

'Scenes of Crime have got your phone,' he said.

'I borrowed someone else's.'

'Like who?'

She looked at him a moment, then reached up and kissed him.

'Stop playing the detective,' she said. 'We made it through, didn't we?'

* * *

Later that night Nandy held an impromptu celebration for the *Graduate, Scorpion* and *Bellwether* teams back at Middlemoor. Dozens of detectives and other assorted staff had hung on all evening, absorbed by the developing drama out in East Devon, and now was the time to relax. A full debrief would shortly begin with Kilfoyle in the chair but first the Det-Supt wanted to say a word or two.

The Major Incident Room was packed. Bottles of Asti were circulating together with an endless supply of polystyrene cups. Nandy got up on a chair. He clapped his hands and called for order. He wouldn't detain them long, and he'd keep this little speech as brief as possible, but he wanted to mention a couple of names with regard to *Bellwether* and *Scorpion* and *Graduate* before any other bugger nipped in and stole the credit for himself. The line drew a roar of laughter from the assembled detectives. Even the Chief Constable, who'd dropped in to say his own thank yous, permitted himself a broad smile.

'So listen up, guys.' Nandy was enjoying himself. 'We all know these jobs are a team effort. We all know we've busted our arses over the last week to try and nail these people. Getting any kind of result with the media in our faces was never going to be easy, but you know how proud I am of the hours you all put in, of the sheer bloody drudgery of sorting out action after action knowing that most of them were going nowhere. But that's Major Crime. That's what we do. Lots of wheat. Lots of chaff. And hopefully something to show for it at the end.' He paused, looking around, hunting for a particular face. Finally, he found it. 'This isn't a beauty contest,' he said. 'Don't get me wrong. But there are two guys in the frame for a serious round of applause. Luke Golding, in my view, played a blinder. In cases like these you have to think outside the box. The lad did just that. Take a bow, son. It won't happen very often.'

Golding had coloured up. Someone thrust a cup into his hand. A bottle of Asti appeared at his elbow. The women in the room began to whoop. Young Luke, still single, had built up a sizeable fan club.

Nandy hadn't finished. Luke, he said, had partnered Jimmy Suttle. And Suttle too had played a major role in all three investigations. In jobs like these you looked for the key links, the connective tissue that bound one killing to the next. Jimmy had teased out these links and built the case until *Bellwether* was looking at just two names in the frame. Better still, he'd volunteered himself and his lovely wife for the final act, on which, mercifully, the curtain had just fallen. No greater love.

The applause was thunderous, Lizzie and Suttle swamped by grinning faces. Nandy fought his way through the mob, gave Lizzie a hug and apologised on behalf of her husband.

'You should never have got into that Discovery, son.' He was looking at Suttle. 'Never trust a stranger with a gun.'

'Is that right, sir?' Suttle felt Lizzie's hand tighten on his. 'Like I had some kind of choice?'

★ ★ ★

Denied access to Chantry Cottage, Suttle and Lizzie spent the night at a B&B in Topsham. The civvy in charge of fixing accommodation had first wanted to put them into the Exeter Premier Inn, where the force had an account, but after a

439

word from Nandy she changed her mind. The hotel was bang next door to the Countess Wear. What kind of thank you was that?

The Topsham B&B overlooked the river, and Suttle woke to the slap of halyards against metal masts. When he went to the window to check out the view, the tide was lapping at the mudflats beneath the window and a pair of swans were out in midstream paddling hard against the current. Lizzie was still asleep. Suttle watched the swans for a moment or two, wondering whether they really mated for life, then he smiled to himself and went back to bed.

★　★　★

Eamonn Lenahan's funeral took place nearly a week later. Lizzie had negotiated a fortnight's sick leave, blaming O'Neill and Jenner. To her mother's delight, she stayed down in Devon and did round after round of media interviews, both local and national, restricting her comments to the bare essentials: how she'd felt, how she'd reacted, how pleased she was to still be in one piece. A London literary agent made contact and asked her whether she'd be interested in penning a book-length account of the killings and the siege that had kept the nation spellbound. She said yes, for sure, and within two days — after a hectic auction — she found herself looking at a six-figure contract.

Jimmy Suttle spent three days at work before helping Lizzie with the last of the funeral arrangements. Both O'Neill and Jenner offered full accounts of how they'd killed first McGrath and then Saunders. Johnny Hamilton was re-arrested and charged with conspiracy to murder. Key to the killings had been an anonymous lock-up garage in the backstreets of Exmouth where Oli Jenner had kept his weapons. Jenner gave them the code to the garage and detectives, together with Scenes of Crime, opened it up. Among bits and pieces of furniture, all that was left of Jenner's married life, were ten boxes of ammunition for the sniper rifle. The CSI inspected one of the boxes. Looking at the nest of gleaming shells, Suttle wondered just how many hits O'Neill and Jenner had in mind. Given the sheer number of enquiries they claimed to have fielded, they'd never have been short of targets.

Both men had yet to be charged with the murders. Nandy, in designing the interview strategy, had deliberately left the killing of Michael Corrigan to last. Jenner had consistently denied any involvement. Yes, he'd lent the sniper rifle to O'Neill, but that was pretty much it. O'Neill, accused of shooting Corrigan, had confirmed once again that the hit was down to him. The guy had been shagging the woman he wanted to share his life with. Only Corrigan stood between him and the partnership of his dreams. He'd needed Goodyer's help to make it happen, but that had never been a problem. Goodyer had kipped in his Discovery on the Exeter estate and at first light they'd driven out to the moor. Goodyer had stopped Corrigan's car at a carefully pre-planned spot and O'Neill, from a range of fifty metres, from the field above the road, had done the business. End of. The thought that Goodyer himself might have had his eye on Erika had never occurred to him.

★ ★ ★

Eamonn Lenahan's funeral took place at the crematorium in Exeter. Lenahan, as a lapsed Catholic, had never expressed the slightest interest in asking God to take care of him. On the contrary, Suttle could remember two occasions when he'd explicitly asked for a cheerful consignment to oblivion when the need arose.

Lenahan's family, none the less, insisted on a service. His adoptive father came over from Ireland, together with half a dozen other relatives, and there was a decent turn-out of colleagues from A&E at the big hospital at Wonford.

After an afternoon of phone calls, Lizzie went down to the coast to muster a dozen or so members from the Exmouth Rowing Club, men and women who'd been with Lenahan on the water and had fond memories of him. Meeting these people again had been the strangest experience for Lizzie. After the events of last year, she'd dreaded a return to the club compound and the sight of the coastal quad that had nearly killed her, but in the event her fears were groundless. Catching up was a delight. People couldn't have been nicer. She even guested on a Tuesday row, returning to the beach to collect Jimmy before going to the pub. *I miss this*, she thought. *I really do.*

The funeral service was brisk. The priest, who'd never met Lenahan, talked of his ministrations to the sick and the poor in the Third World, and one of Lenahan's sisters, a small vivid woman with the same pixie smile, read Yeats' 'An Irish Airman Foresees His Death'.

Lenahan, thought Suttle, would have dismissed the poem out of hand. Too cheesy. Too laboured. Suttle had recommended '*O mio babbino caro*', only to have the suggestion ruled out by the family, but listening to the poem, Suttle realised Mairead had a point. A couple of lines in particular seemed to catch the essence of his dead friend:

'*A lonely impulse of delight*
Drove to this tumult in the clouds'.

'Impulse' was right. 'Delight' was spot-on. But 'tumult' was perfect.

Suttle sat with Lizzie behind Lenahan's family. Mairead returned from her reading, the priest intoned the Committal, and Suttle did his best to get through the long moment when the curtains slowly closed on the coffin.

Afterwards, the mourners gathered for a drink or two at a pub in Lympstone that Lenahan had often used. Lenahan's father put a hundred quid behind the bar and the wee man's medical colleagues got stuck in. After four pints Suttle was in no state to drive.

Lizzie took the wheel. It was raining. Suttle directed her through the maze of back lanes that climbed the long swell of Woodbury Common and then dropped down towards Colaton Raleigh. They were back in Chantry Cottage now, learning to live with the chemical aftermath of a full SOC bosh and the faintest scent of stun grenades. Lizzie pulled the Impreza off the lane and onto the gravel parking area. After the warmth and laughter of the pub, this was a homecoming she remembered only too well. Rain was sheeting off the roof. Weather for ducks, she thought. And full-time depressives.

Suttle was looking across at her.

'You've been great,' he said. 'I appreciate it.'

'I loved the man. He saved my life.'

'Me too. Funny that.'

They looked at each other for a moment, then Suttle told her to open the glove box. She found a wad of papers inside. They turned out to be details from estate agents.

'Why these?' she said.

'I've been doing the rounds. Seeing what's on offer.'

Lizzie began to go through the properties. They were all in Exmouth.

'Sea views,' Suttle said. 'Shops. Pubs. People. Plus trains to the real world. Interested?'

Lizzie was shaking her head. This was the last thing she'd expected.

'Kiss me.' She looked up. 'And tell me you mean it.'

Acknowledgements

This book came from conversations with a fellow sculler at Exmouth Rowing Club. His name is Billy Baxter, he's a big crime fiction fan, and has spent most of his working life in the Royal Marines.

Billy is still with the Corps, and once I'd developed the plot he offered lots of advice and opened countless doors. Those conversations, and the ones that followed, anchored and deepened my story in ways that encounters with real life can only make happen. So I owe another debt of gratitude to Jack Broughton, Tony Chattin, Ceri Lewis, Simon Richardson, Keith Stanton, Lindsay Stanton and Chris Stanton.

Pathologist Dr Debbie Cook, as ever, helped me through the grislier bits, while Maggie Sawkins, by winning the Portsmouth *News* Create-a-Character competition, kindly donated Layla Bird (or 'Birdy').

Steve Carey once again played a blinder when it came to the small print of Major Crime procedures, and ACC Paul Netherton — together with Steve — talked me through the way Devon and Cornwall Police would handle the incident which ends this book.

My wife, Lin, proved to know far more than I ever suspected about scabious, wised me up about what people really wear, and gave the first draft her usual shake. While my agent, Oli

Munson, helmed Jimmy Suttle's second outing through some pretty rough weather and headed it towards publication.

To you all, my sincere thanks.